The Lost Knight: Awakening

Written by Zachary M Watson

This is a work of fiction. Names, characters, places, and incidents either are the product of the author's imagination or are used fictitiously. Any resemblance to actual persons, living or dead, events, or locales is entirely coincidental.

Edited by Dana Morck, Jordan Perona,
Maria Kelly, John Watson,
& Chelsea Beyer

ISBN 978-1-7363099-0-2 (Kindle ebook)
ISBN 978-1-7363099-1-9 (Paperback)

For the friends and family who kept asking for more.

I – I

When I woke up, it was to pain.

That wasn't to say that I just had a headache. It felt like somebody had a rusty knife and was doing their best to drill into my brain. I groaned and started trying to get my blankets off, intending on digging up some medicine before taking a blistering hot shower.

I'd barely begun to move the sheets when a pair of hands slammed into my chest, pinning me to the bed. My eyes snapped open in shock, giving me a brief glimpse of white light, then one of the gloved hands shot up to cover my vision before I could see more than the vague outline of a figure.

"What the hell?"

Well, that was what I tried to say. It came out more of a loud mumble of random syllables than anything else.

"Wh... zhe he..!?"

"Calm down! I'm not going to hurt you!" A woman's voice; cold, crisp, and more than a little alarmed came from somewhere above me.

I wasn't really awake enough to fully process what she was saying, and truth be told, I was running on panicked reflex by that point. She grunted as I bucked up, my body sluggish as I tried to grab her wrists. After two tries I managed to get a hold of the arm pinning me down, and I immediately started shoving and twisting to try to get her the hell off of me.

I shouldn't have bothered.

Now, I wasn't the strongest guy in the world, but I wasn't the weakest either. Yet nothing I did so much as made her budge. Her arm was an iron bar keeping me locked in place, while the fingers of her other hand kept my head pinned and my eyes covered despite my increasingly frantic thrashing.

"I *said*," The stench of ozone suddenly filled my nostrils, and every hair on my body felt like it was standing on end, "*Calm. Down.*"

Even as she said the words it felt like a mattress made of air had been dropped onto my chest. It didn't hurt, but just because it wasn't causing me pain didn't mean it was comfortable. Both of my arms fell limply to my side, my muscles unable to fight the... whatever it was that was suddenly holding me down.

"Who... you?" Was all I could get out, doing my best to keep the very real fear and impending panic from my voice.

There was a soft, almost tired sigh as the hand on my chest vanished, though the one over my eyes remained. "That is a very complicated story, and one that you are unlikely to care for."

"In... my hotel... room?" It was getting easier to string words together, the pain in my head slowly receding to something merely awful. The cool glove over my eyes and forehead was starting to feel better, shifting from something I wanted off to something relieving against my aching skull. "How?'

There was a long pause before she spoke again, "You are not in a hotel room."

Huh? "Huh?"

Another gentle sigh came as her remaining hand pulled back, making my temples throb in protest at the loss of the cold leather. I left my eyes closed for a moment, then carefully opened them to slits. The pale lights definitely weren't the pallid yellow I was expecting to see, and the pristine white of the ceiling was another thing that was very wrong.

If nothing else it was obvious that she was telling the truth about me not being in my hotel room anymore.

Trying not to groan with the effort, I opened my eyes fully and turned to face my... captor?

She... wasn't Human.

She had the right build; two arms, two legs, and a head all in the spots they were supposed to be... but she was very much *not* Human.

The alien was settling into a chair beside the bed as I stared, regarding me with bright green eyes as it primly folded its hands in its lap. She... he...? It sounded like a she, with a light contralto voice, so that's what I decided to run with, was dressed in a long-sleeved, dark green shirt over a flat chest. Below that she had white pants with some kind of elegant emerald stitching around the shins. White gloves completed the outfit and left only the skin of her neck and head exposed.

The skin was definitely alien, being a light grey in color, aside from the slighter dark shade to her lips. Above those was a flat but recognizable nose, a pair of brilliant emeralds for eyes, but... she didn't have hair, or normal ears. Where the latter should have been were a pair of back swept, flesh covered... horns? Cones? Simply weird ears? She had *something* that seemed to run from the backs of her cheeks past where her ears would be, the narrow tips a good eight inches behind the rest of her bare skull.

One of them actually twitched up and down as I stared at her, the muscles visibly rippling across her face as it did. Thin golden chains were wrapped around each, and they jingled slightly with the motion, making light glisten off of emerald gemstones set into the links.

An alien was sitting next to my bed.

A bed inside of a room I couldn't remember ever seeing before.

"Uh..."

There was another little twitch of her horn, her lips curling into what looked like a smile. "Yes, I quite understand."

Her English was shockingly clear, if a little clipped, and I swallowed against my dry throat. It was a fight to gather my scattered thoughts into something a bit more intelligible, but I sort-of managed it after another half-minute of blank staring and confused gaping. "Uh... um, I'm... where.. am I?"

"I suppose that is the most pertinent question from your point of view." She allowed, "But I must ask you a few questions before I can answer. Do you remember your name?"

I had to wet my lips a bit, but I was able to nod a little and reply, "Cieran Kean."

It wasn't exactly the manliest of names, and I'd gotten a lot of grief over it when I was younger, but the alien only gave me a tiny little nod, "Good. Your species and place of origin?"

"Um... Human, Earth." I shook my head slightly. "Uh, from Arizona."

"Good." She repeated, "Now, what is the last thing you remember?"

I opened my mouth, closed it and thought furiously, trying to think through the pain, through the sheer wrongness of the situation. "I... was in a hotel. Traveling... on my way to..."

Fuck. Where had I been going? It hadn't been for work, I was pretty sure of that much. Well, I wasn't exactly sure, but it didn't *feel* right. It hadn't been a vacation either. I'd...

"...volunteered." I managed as things slowly came back to me. Bits and pieces fell into place as I kept talking, "I'd volunteered, been picked as a technician on..."

"A cryogenic ship." The alien finished for me when I trailed off again, watching as I nodded slowly in agreement. "What do you remember about it?"

There wasn't any change in her polite tone, but despite the pain my head was starting to clear. As it did my apprehension grew in time with my memories trickling back from wherever they'd been.

It hadn't been the first exploration ship Humanity had sent out into space, headed towards a nearby star. I hadn't been nearly important, wealthy, or talented enough to be on that one. I hadn't made the cut for the second one either. But by the time it had come for the third ship, *Pegasus*, to go out, enthusiasm had dwindled significantly and I'd scraped my way in as a ship-board technician.

I hadn't had much to lose when I'd volunteered. My parents had died in a car crash a few years ago, and I'd grown apart from my friends in the aftermath of that event. Getting the chance to start over on Earth's attempt to build a colony in another solar system had seemed ideal, even if the planet itself was supposed to be a pretty miserable little ball of ice. My specific job had been as a computer tech on the ship itself, to be part of the skeleton crew keeping it running during the initial colonization phase, so I wouldn't really have been on the surface much anyway.

The ultimate fresh start.

I could remember showing up at the spaceport in New Mexico, checking in at a hotel the night before the big day. I'd been more than a little panicky and nervous over exactly what I was volunteering to do, and I'd ended up avoiding almost everyone else out of sheer nerves. Sometime after midnight I'd fallen sleep wishing I'd been able to drink myself into a pleasant buzz, and then...

Then there was a giant blank spot in my memories.

"What happened?" I asked quietly, trying to lever myself up a bit and faltering at once. Whatever she'd done to hold me down was gone but my body still wasn't cooperating. "Where... am I? Who are you?"

She took in a deep breath, her sort-of-horns quivering once again. "You may call me Matriarch. We are currently in the River District of Atrix, on the world named Alum if that tells you anything."

It didn't. "Never heard of it."

"I suspected." Green eyes slid up and down me for a moment, assessing, "You are wary. I can not blame you for that, and I fear that what I have to tell you will not improve your mood."

Sucking in a breath, I managed to get a hold of the sheet covering my body and throw it back. Even that much effort made me gasp, something that made more sense once I got a better look at myself. My lanky frame was never exactly filled out, but now I was practically skeletal. You could count my ribs without trying, and my stomach had shrunk to the point where my hip bones were clearly the only things keeping my plain shorts on.

The lack of strength was easy to identify as well; my arms were little more than pale twigs, and my fingers trembled even as I stared at them. "What the hell?"

Motion made me turn to see the alien, the Matriarch, rise from her chair and take a step forwards. Up close I guessed she might have been five and half feet tall and well muscled, at least in comparison to any Human woman her size. That was all I had time to notice before four fingered hands got hold of my shoulder and effortlessly hauled me up into a seated position.

"Thank you." I murmured as I carefully settled myself, doing my best to move as little as possible. Even that little motion had sent my head pounding again and I wasn't eager to make it worse. "I'm... guessing things went wrong."

"You would be correct." She supplied as she returned to her chair. "I cannot say as to when your primitive ship departed your planet, only that it never made it to its destination for several factors beyond your control. The most pertinent reason being that your system was invaded and overrun by the Empire of the Homeworld a century ago."

That didn't exactly make me feel any better, and I gave her a somewhat numb stare. "How bad?"

One of her horn-cone-things twitched as she rolled a shoulder in a little motion, "Casualties were rather minimal if I remember the details correctly, though the occupation has been rather less civil. There is some kind of ongoing rebellion but there is little I can say beyond that. That planet is quite some distance from here, and truthfully is of minimal import to most."

Well, she'd been right, the news was definitely not improving my mood. But... well, at least I hadn't stepped into some kind of horror movie where I was the last living Human or something. Small mercies.

I did some more thinking as the throbbing in my head slowly began to diminish once more, and then took a guess, "You're... not with this Empire group?"

"I am technically a citizen, though the sordid details are not ones I care to share." She stated firmly, but without any heat or edge to her words. "Your own affairs are the reason I am here. Suffice it to say that your vessel never made it to its destination, as I said, though not through any fault of the Empire. During the chaos of their assault a great many of your people were able to flee. With them went information, and not all of them were able to keep the data to themselves as time passed."

A sinking feeling once more made itself known in my gut. "Who found us?"

The Matriarch did her odd little pseudo-shrug thing again, "A pirate organization with whom I have a personal enmity. They had already taken the first two vessels and were in the process of dismantling the ship you were upon when I caught up with them. They had already removed the passenger section, but we were partially able to prevent them from taking the crew zone. Unfortunately most of the others of your kind were killed during the firefight that followed."

"Did..." I swallowed against my still dry mouth, "Did anyone else make it?"

"The pirates took five, perhaps six. You and another technician were all my team was able to recover. Unfortunately..." Her chin twitched in a slight shake, "...both of your pods were damaged, as you can no doubt tell from your emaciated state. Your species' specific health requirements were not known by my personal medics and we were in deep space. They did their best to stabilize you both, but we had lost the other by the time we returned here and were able to access the Imperial DataNet."

"Oh." I fumbled for something else to say, but could only come up with, "Oh."

"If you are concerned over your security and well-being, I assure you that you will be safe here." She continued as if I hadn't tried and failed to say anything, "This home belongs to a young member of my own kind who owes me for favors past. She will ensure your recovery and employment moving forwards."

I blinked at the sudden shift and tried to recover, "Um, you... you mean you're not sending me back to Earth?"

Her voice turned dry, "Did you already forget my statement that it is currently in revolt? I doubt you wish to undergo physical therapy in a war-zone."

That... was kind of a fair point, but still! "I'm just going to be left here?"

"I rescued you from a short and brutal life of enslavement, Human." The Matriarch's tones hardened frighteningly quickly, "And I am not even asking for anything in return. Most beings would be appropriately grateful."

"I'm sorry." I quickly got out, flinching a little from her sharp gaze, "I didn't mean it like that. It's just... God, I'm just... this isn't what I thought I'd..."

"Thought what you would awaken to?" She asked, words still more clipped than they had been at the start of the conversation, "Obviously, and I do sympathize. However your emotional state will not affect the reality of the situation. I have little ability or desire to transport you all the way to your home planet, talk my way past an Imperial blockade, and then have to talk my way back out again. If you truly wish to go there you may do so after you have recovered and secured sufficient funding for yourself."

I swallowed yet again and nodded shakily, "I understand. I, um, thank you, for saving me."

That had evidently been the words she'd been waiting to hear because she took in a deep breath and settled back in her chair, once more calm and collected. "You are welcome. Now, I have some little time before I am due to depart. I will answer what questions you have regarding your situation."

I managed another nod, breathing slowly as the headache oh-so-slowly continued to recede. "Where, exactly am I? I know you said the name, but where is it?"

"It is a border world of the Far Reaches, near the Imperial Outer Colonies." She supplied, "By agreement between various parties it serves as a way-station and neutral planet between the various groups of the Reaches and the Empire. My own species predominates here, though you will see others passing through or living in small enclaves."

"Other Humans?"

Another very minimal shake of her head, "Your kind is relatively rare in the Reaches, aside from a fleet of exiles that escaped during the Imperial invasion. They generally keep to themselves while doing their best to aid the rebellion on your... Earth, you called it? There is the occasional envoy or merchant, but never more than a few dozen on the world at any given time."

Well... shit. I had a feeling this was going to be a very awkward way to restart my life. Maybe I should have just taken my cousin up on his offer to travel the world for a bit, calm myself down and recover that way. Then again, who the hell knew what had happened to him whenever these 'imperials' had invaded. Maybe I was the lucky one.

That cheerful thought spurred my next question, "Do you know what year it is, by the Earth calendar?"

She seemed about to shake her head again, paused, then lifted an arm up. I looked and saw a thin kind of mesh with a few metallic rectangles covering her left wrist, and a swipe of a finger across the top caused a quiet beep. A second later and the entire thing began to glow with various colors, a two-dimensional box flickering to life above her arm like a floating screen.

My eyes widened, more than a little impressed, as she used a gesture from her free hand to shrink it, then used another gesture to call up some kind of keyboard filled with alien lettering. She typed rapidly even with only four fingers, and after a couple more seconds the display updated.

"Twenty-one eighty-nine." She provided. "By the records of the Ark Fleet. It is Twenty-Two Sixty-One, Month Five, Day Eleven by the Imperial calendar if or when that becomes relevant to you."

I forced my sluggish brain to do some mental math, "I volunteered in... twenty forty, we were supposed to go into cryo that year, but the ship wasn't going to leave until the next. You said the Imperials invaded a century ago?"

"Yes, approximately."

So it had been close to fifty years after we'd left that the invasion had happened. At least everyone I'd known had been able to live fairly full lives before everything happened. That was... good. That was good. "We'd still have been in deep space, wouldn't we? Was it really that easy to find us?"

"A lone ship with no weapons, a frozen crew, and with no way to call for help?" The Matriarch twitched an, I decided to just call them ears, and rolled her shoulder again. "Even pirates can do such simple calculations once they had the appropriate data. Your kind remains new, exotic, and so they were well motivated. You would have fetched a rather high price in the slave markets on less savory worlds."

I winced. "This isn't one of them, is it?"

She let out a sound somewhere between a snort and a huff, looking genuinely amused, "Ease yourself, Human. The Empire is expansionist but they do not condone slavery. They would have obliterated this world long ago if the Board of High Families was stupid enough to allow it. There is a form of legalized servitude for those desperate enough to enter themselves, but it is a willing practice. You should have no need of such a career choice."

I'd started to calm down at the start of her words, only to grimace at the last bit. "What will I be doing, exactly?"

"Trenah'laria, the woman whose home we are in, owns a small repair and refurbishment facility downriver." She provided, "You will be her new assistant. I am led to believe it will primarily be technical work."

Well that sounded better than being stuck in some kind of fast food job, though the whole alien-technology thing was probably going to be a pretty big obstacle to overcome. Speaking of aliens, "I'm guessing not many people speak English?"

Her upper lip quivered and she leaned forwards. I froze when she reached an arm out, but all she did was tap something on my left ear.

Reaching up, I carefully felt around as well... and found an earpiece literally taped to the side of my head.

"That was not meant for your species but one of my people was able to re-purpose it." As she spoke, I focused on the way her lips moved, and felt stupid when I realized they weren't in sync with the words I was hearing. "There is another on your other ear. They will serve, though I would recommend learning our language for yourself sooner rather than later. It will make things far easier for you."

"Yeah, probably smart." I murmured as my hand dropped back to my side, trying to think of what else to ask and coming up with approximately a million questions. A rumble from my stomach made me flush a little when the Matriarch twitched her ears several times, "Um, can I eat your food?"

"With a few exceptions. You received the required inoculations while you slept so you should not have any adverse reactions. I instructed Trenah'laria to retrieve a meal, she will be returning shortly."

As if summoned by her words there was a dull chiming noise from somewhere in the ceiling, followed by another feminine voice calling out that she was back.

"And so she has." The Matriarch rose, "I'll send her in to assist you."

I – II

Trenah'laria turned out to be, well, 'stout' seemed to be the closest word that applied.

At best she was five feet tall, and while I'd thought the Matriarch was fairly well built, Trenah looked like she did physical labor on daily basis. I made a mental note to figure out which of the two was closer to normal for their species, and their gender, since from the shape of her arms she could have easily beaten me in arm wrestling even if I'd been healthy.

After that, I'd have probably called her 'casual'. While the Matriarch had been dressed in something that stated she was wealthy and refined, Trenah was wearing a red t-shirt with alien lettering across the chest, and had plain tan slacks covering her legs. Her exposed arms were covered in blue tattoos from her wrists to under the sleeves. Not words or images, just intricate patterns that caught my eye.

Though brightly colored eyes were apparently a species trait, because hers were an impossible shade of turquoise.

"So the Human managed to finally wake himself." She greeted me as she strolled into the room, "That ancient thing says I'm supposed to help you walk your pale ass to the food."

I blinked a little. I'd more or less expected someone kind of like the Matriarch, and was very much taken aback by... whatever the hell she was. "Uh, yeah. I think I can walk, just not all that fast."

"Oh yeah? You're not even fucking standing up yet, Human."

"Cieran." I corrected her, just a bit of irritation creeping into my voice as I settled my feet onto the floor. There was a soft rug covering most of it, but the floor itself looked to be made of the same polished stone as the walls. "My name is Cieran."

"See-ran?"

"Sigh-ran." I enunciated carefully.

She did the same ear twitch shoulder roll combination that the Matriarch had, and I was increasingly sure that was their version of a shrug. "Fine, you're Cieran then. Come on, bread and soup are going to be cold by the time you get out there."

I glowered at her a bit, then glowered some more when she walked over and offered me her hand. I took it after a few seconds, pride losing to practicality, and she hauled me upright without any apparent effort. The fact that my tall frame absolutely towered over her made it easy to lean on her shoulder, especially when it became clear I might have been overestimating myself.

Standing on my own would probably have been difficult but possible. *Walking* on my own would probably have seen my face bouncing off the floor after a couple of feet or so. As it was I made it about three short, shuffling steps before I had to give up and let her take nearly all of my weight. She did so easily, wrapping an arm around my waist and dragging one of my own over her shoulders, taking care so that I didn't hit the ear-horn-things as she did.

The height difference had to be at least a foot, which made it a little awkward. Thankfully by the time we got to the doorway she seemed to have adjusted and wasn't having problems hauling me along.

The room opened into a hallway that ran in both directions, a few open but dark doors to the left being other bedrooms or maybe bathrooms, while to the right there was the cheerful glow of sunshine and the quiet sounds of movement. Trenah promptly pulled me in that direction, the stone floor cool under my bare feet.

I managed to keep my head up through the trip, something I regretted when I found a mirror at the end of the hall. It was the only bit of decoration on otherwise plain walls, and it really drove home just how pathetic I was.

My black hair had been roughly cut away from my ears, leaving room for the taped-in-place translators, and it was long and matted everywhere else. Someone had tried to shave my face at some-point. They'd done a slightly better job about it, but they'd still left tufts of hair around my jawline. To complete the image my dull green eyes were sunken and lifeless.

Breathing quickly, I looked away before I could have some kind of break-down.

"...sorry about the fur." Trenah murmured as we shuffle-stepped into a fairly open dining space, her voice lower and gentler than it had been earlier. "Never had to cut that kind of crap before. Kept thinking I was about to rip your skin open."

"It's fine." I shook my head a little, looking around. The space was... shockingly normal. A wooden table with six chairs scattered around it, a broad but high window letting in light, and a few open archways leading to yet more rooms. I could have been at any respectable little home on Earth but for the alien next to me. "But it's hair, not fur."

"What's the difference?"

I opened my mouth, closed it, then sheepishly admitted, "I honestly don't know."

She let out a soft, almost barking sound that I hoped was a laugh, then helped me sit before my legs gave out. The cushioning on the chairs looked old and hard used, but they proved to be surprisingly comfortable. I'd barely settled into place before Trenah walked away, presumably to return with food. She passed the Matriarch coming in my direction, the taller woman looking me over as she approached.

"Regrettably I will not be staying to eat." She informed me. "I have other matters to attend to. I will return in a few local days to check in on you and see how you are recovering, then I will be departing this world."

I blinked once. "Oh. Already?"

There was a slight nod. "The groups that attacked your vessel remain active despite the setback my people gave them, and time is of the essence. If I am able to locate any more of your crew I will, of course, inform you. Even if I do not, I will likely return sooner or later, so do not think of this as our only meeting."

"Oh." I said again, more quietly. "Thank you. And... thank you again for saving me. Do we... shake hands or anything?"

Both of her horn-ear-things twitched once and her lips curled into something resembling a smile, "Most of my kind are rather touchy, but personally I prefer a simple bow or nod of farewell."

Smiling faintly, I gave her a deep nod since I couldn't really do more while sitting. She gave me an almost courtly little bow in return, then turned and left the way she'd come. I heard her say something to Trenah, and the other woman replying, then more footsteps.

A door shut in the distance just as my new caretaker returned with a large tray held in both hands. On it were a pair of steaming bowls with some kind of dark liquid in each, along with a plate of equally dark bread. I had no idea what any of it was really made of, but it smelled delicious and my mouth was watering before she'd even settled it on the table.

"Right one is yours." Trenah informed me as she took the chair on my left, her brilliant eyes narrowing as I carefully took one of the bowls. It took a lot more effort than it should have to pick it up and put it in front of me, and only the rich smell kept my spirits from faltering at just how pathetic I was. "Try not to burn your tongue."

"...probably smart." I agreed, "What's the bread made out of?"

"Whatever it is that bread is made out of?" She gave me another little twitch and shrug combination, "I'm a mechanic, not a cook."

I couldn't help but smile a little. "Fair point. Safe for me to eat?"

"According to the DataNet." Trenah picked out two large slices and put them on a plate for me, then took the rest of herself. "I'm also supposed to stop your furry ass from over-eating at first, so this is all you're getting for now."

I would have complained, but the first bite of bread distracted me rather thoroughly. It was warm, rich, and tasted more or less like bread, though there was an odd aftertaste that I could only hope was normal. The soup was, like she'd warned me, close to boiling, and I had to carefully blow on it before it cooled down enough to even take a spoonful. Various strings of some kind of meat and orange vegetables tasted like nothing I'd ever had before, though not in a bad way.

"So," I said, after my second effort had informed me that it was definitely not cool enough to have yet. "I feel like I should ask what species you even are."

"The old thing didn't tell you?" When I shook my head, she twitched both of her ear-cones. "We're Trahcon."

"Trahcon." I tested my own pronunciation, evidently to her satisfaction because she gave me a quick nod. "I'm guessing you have translators on too?"

In response she tilted her head slightly and lifted a hand to indicate a tiny bit of plastic wrapped around the tip of her ear-cone. "And the sooner I don't have to wear the stupid things the better, so starting tomorrow you're getting full immersion in Caranat. That's our main language."

I nodded and tried my soup again taking care not to burn myself. "I'll do my best. Can I keep these in case I need them?"

"Not like I can wear them." She pointed out.

That was definitely true. "Yeah, um, about that. Are those your ears?"

"My tarah?" Trenah reached up and lightly touched one of the ear-horn... one of her 'tarah' apparently. "Yeah, we hear with them, and they're packed with a bunch of other crap. You pinch one of mine and I'll punch you wherever the net says it hurts the most."

I quickly held my hands up in surrender, "Tarah. Sensitive. No-touching. Got it."

She let out a low grunt, nodding in approval at my reaction, "They're what lets us manipulate energy. We call it sorcery, no fucking clue what your kind calls it."

My mouth fell open. "Uh..."

"Limited kinetic movement, blockage and impacts for the most part." Turquoise eyes rolled in a very Human way at my expression, "Little bit of fire, but in general our species is pretty limited compared to a few others."

"...can you?"

She seemed to sigh, both of her tarah twitching, then she lifted a hand and narrowed her eyes. The same whiff of ozone that had come when the Matriarch had pinned me down abruptly filled my nostrils...

...and the remaining bits of bread slowly floated up off the table.

I gaped like an idiot for a dozen seconds or so, then she lowered her hand and the bread returned to its plate. "Wow."

Trenah snorted and gave a slight shake of her head. "Crap like that takes a lot of focus, easier to just shove it away violently. And we get the worst fucking headaches if we do too much of it. Mostly its easier to just get up and grab whatever it is. Or you know, use fucking technology. These days it's only priests trying to keep the art alive, and some commando types who want flexibility who learn anything but the basics."

The little display only gave me about a million more questions, and I started asking them as quickly as I could while I worked on my soup. Apparently it was some kind of ability to summon and manipulate energy from another reality, tied to the same devices and realm that allowed faster than light travel. They'd evolved it naturally, along with damn near every other major species on their home-world, though there was some limited success in using cybernetics to do the same things.

That brought up the question of their home-world, Zulflara, which was apparently some kind of oceanic death-world that practically no one else visited. Evidently the fact that super-hurricanes were a common occurrence made tourists a bit rare on the ground even before you considered the telekinetic wildlife.

"Not that Alum is great either." Trenah continued, her eyes narrowing a little when my head bobbed. Eating and talking together was tiring me out a lot faster than I thought it should have. "It's an overheated bitch of a planet, we're up on the coast of a polar ocean where it's mostly temperate."

"So plenty of sun?"

"Until winter." She grimaced. "Which isn't far off, so get ready for plenty of darkness."

"Joy." I muttered.

Trenah gave me another quiet bark of laughter, "Yeah, well, at least I'm not going to be suffering by myself this year."

I felt my lips twitch a little as I started to warm up to her, "Misery loves company?"

Her own mouth shifted into a recognizable smile, showing brilliant white teeth pretty much the same as my own. "Fucking right it does. Now finish your damned soup."

Once more I held up my hands in surrender, one holding my spoon, and then I got back to work filling my empty stomach. I made it about two thirds of the way through the bowl before the creeping exhaustion really began to make itself felt. My arms felt like lead weights as I did my best to keep eating, my head bobbing while I fought off the urge to close my eyes.

"If you fall asleep here I'm not dragging your tall ass back to bed." Trenah warned me when she saw my head rise and fall for about the fifth time. "And you should probably relieve yourself since I'm *not* dealing with that."

Tired as I was, I still managed an awkward laugh. "Yeah, I understand. Help me up?"

She did. We made our way back into the hallway, then to one of the darkened doors where Trenah hit a small button to bring up some lights. To my vast relief most of what was in the bathroom looked recognizable enough, and I let my eyes linger a bit on the very large tub.

Trenah thankfully didn't feel the need to 'directly supervise' after I promised I wouldn't fall over and crack my head open. It took me a little bit to figure out how to flush and clean up after myself, and I *did* nearly fall over when I stood back up. Once I recovered and got my shorts back into place, I called for Trenah and she cautiously came in, only calming down once she was sure it was safe.

"I'll wake you up for dinner." She said once she'd gotten me back to my room and helped me into bed. "Try not to die in your sleep or anything."

I tried to give her a vague wave of acknowledgment, but only managed to twitch an arm before I was asleep.

I – III

I liked to think that I adjusted fairly well to living with an alien roommate, all things considered. That was important because I didn't manage to adjust to a routine involving children's learning shows, how-to-read books, and extensive physical therapy nearly as well.

Trenah's general good humor and support through the first couple of weeks was probably the only thing that stopped me from snapping as home-sickness really began to set in. The first couple of days were actually the easiest, mostly because Trenah had temporarily closed her shop until she was certain I could survive a day in her apartment without burning it down or killing myself.

We spent those days setting up the pattern that would follow for my first month on Alum; my mornings and early afternoons were dedicated to language training, then the rest of the days were spent improving my body and working on more practical matters. Mostly how to cook and do basic household maintenance without breaking anything.

Once she returned to her day job she still called it quits a bit early in the afternoon, meaning I really only had to work on learning the language on my own. Caranat proved to be easy enough to read in terms of picking up the alphabet, but a real pain in the ass to speak. It's a very terse, verb-first language where experienced speakers often rolled the words together into an almost steady stream that made it difficult to grasp compared to English.

And if I never had to listen to children singing about a shark chasing a fish down a river again, I would live a long and fulfilling life.

As a result Trenah usually found me somewhere between irritable and irate when she got home, then subjected me to exercise equipment setup in the spare third bedroom. Despite my frustration with my physical weakness, the exhaustion of working out usually left me in a better mood afterwords. Once I'd bathed we often spent the evening lounging on her battered but comfortable couches watching various programs.

I didn't end up seeing the Matriarch again before she left, though she did stop by Trenah's shop, which left my roommate as literally the only person I knew on the entire planet. That made it a bit of an event when Trenah finally decided I was healthy enough to go out, thirty or so days into my recovery.

I'd been able to look out at the distant skyline from the windows, and I'd seen a few other Trahcon when Trenah decided ordering dinner was preferable to cooking, but that was the first time I was actually going to be out and about in public.

"I want to reiterate that I feel weird wearing women's clothes." I stated as I made sure my translators were secured to my ears. "Are you sure you couldn't find anything else?"

Trenah scoffed, both of her tarah quivering in amusement. "You're eight inches taller than any Trahcon guy I've ever seen, and six inches shorter than any Thondian one. Consider yourself lucky there's enough tall women around that I found clothes for you at all."

I gave her an arch look that bounced off of her thick skin, and once more glanced down at myself.

Despite my complaints it wasn't actually that bad. Trahcon fashion evidently went for loose clothing, and they didn't do skirts or dresses for either sex. The shirt was normal enough, a plain black thing with the name of a local Strike-Wave Team stretched across the chest, while equally dark pants were the more ill-fitting part of the outfit. They fit length wise but were obviously intended for someone with far wider hips than I possessed... though I did kind of like the stylized blue waves that decorated the shin area.

Plus, unlike Human women's pants, they actually had real pockets.

"The belt's keeping them on, stop fucking worrying." She reached up to give me a light slap on the shoulder, "Let's go."

I sighed and followed her, carefully picking up the steel cane she'd gotten for me last week. I didn't think I needed the thing, but I knew she wouldn't let me out without it.

Trenah's place opened into a broad open-air walkway, the doorways to other apartments on this side and a stone railing on the other. A few short steps was all it took to be able to look out over a fairly bustling river-front, with shops, stalls, and what looked like small gardens stretching out in both directions. Above and beyond that I could see distant towers reaching into the sky, along with glistening shapes that rose and fell even as I watched.

"Welcome to the River-District." Trenah said as she moved next to me, leaning her arms on the railing. "Not a bad place, is it?"

"No." I said quietly, a little taken aback by the almost riotous level of colors on display. Nearly every building in sight was painted up with artwork, and equally decorated statues seemed to be found every dozen yards or so below us. A quick glance over my shoulder showed that the outside of the apartments were coated with similarly bright collages. Trenah's in particular was covered in patterns that matched her various tattoos and I made a mental note to ask her about them later. "Wow. Is the entire city like this?"

"This district? Sure." A tarah twitched and a shoulder rolled as she shrugged, "Rest of Atrix? Ashahn's ass no. The Ocean-Front's nice enough, and the Core District ain't bad, but the Industrial District is about as fucking pleasant as it sounds. The Outskirts are about as bad in the nicer areas, and a lot worse in others."

"Slums?" I guessed.

She grimaced. "Don't know how your kind defines the word, but probably the right one to use. Lot of aliens come in from the rest of the Reaches, try and make lives here. Most don't do so well and they end up in those areas just trying to survive. My shop is right on the border between the River and Industrial, so it's not always in the best area."

It didn't take a genius to read into what she was trying to tell me. "That's why you haven't had me go with you when you're working, isn't it? Gangs? Thieves?"

"There's always idiots who think they can steal shit." Trenah pushed away from the railing and motioned for me to follow her. I did so, and she kept her pace mercifully slow. "There was a big fight in the Outskirts, race wars between a couple of gangs. Most of it wrapped up last year but there's still a couple of half-drowned idiots running around."

"Just not around here?"

"Not around here." She agreed. "I'll start giving you shit to work on at home in a couple weeks, then soon as you're healthy enough to move around all day I'll bring you with. I've only ever had one problem in the decade or so I've been in the area, but I'd rather not take chances when you can't even manage a damned jog."

I nodded slowly, not taking the comment personally. I was doing better, but that didn't mean much considering how bad I'd been originally, and it wouldn't do me any good to deny it. "Think having me around would be too tempting to certain idiots?"

"I think I've invested too much of my time in a gangling idiot of a Human to see it wasted because some bloody child decides he's an easy mark."

"Idiot?" I demanded as we neared a stairwell, my lips twisting in displeasure at the sight of them. "I thought you said my pronunciation was getting pretty good, and I made breakfast on my own this morning."

"True," She slipped around me to my left side, taking my free arm as we took each stair one at a time. "But you're male, and regardless of species that means you're an idiot by default."

I gave her a mild scowl and tried to whack her shin with my cane when we reached the bottom, only to end up scowling more deeply when she dodged and snickered at me.

Trenah led me on without any more words after that. Her place was apparently on the third floor, but thankfully there was a long ramp that connected the second down to the ground so I didn't have to deal with any more stairs. I kept my head on a swivel as we descended, the general rumble of conversation growing louder as we walked.

The river was a fairly broad one, with arching bridges stretching across it every hundred yards or so. Both sides seem to have the same kind of open air boulevard, with apartment buildings like Trenah's built up behind them. Strangely there seemed to be almost no actual vehicles in sight, apart from the occasional flying cars that took off or landed from the tops of the apartments.

Oh, and there were Trahcon. *Lots* of Trahcon.

We were surrounded by some kind of lunch rush as soon as we reached the ground, the crowd politely flowing around our slower pace. I did my best not to gawk while taking in everything around me.

Oddly enough the first thing I noticed was that it was really hard to tell the men and women apart. As my own clothing could attest, they pretty much dressed the same, and the lack of breasts and hair meant it took me a little while to start picking them apart. Even then it honestly felt like I was guessing at first.

The biggest difference seemed to be in the hips, and how they walked. Trenah may have been built like a tank but there was something feminine about the way she moved that told me her gender regardless. Once I started focusing on the movement it got a bit easier, leading to my next realization; there were a lot more women around than men.

Most of the females seemed to be more in line with the Matriarch's body shape than Trenah's. Next to none of them were as short as my companion either, and a few were nearly eye-to-eye with me. In contrast the men were a lot closer to Trenah's height though none of them looked to be as well muscled as she was. Hell, if anything the men seemed to be pretty slender in comparison to the girls.

Realization number three was the fact that, just as I was noticing all of them, they were all noticing me in return.

It was... an experience.

Like how being an exotic animal in a zoo was an experience.

So far as I could tell I was the only non-Trahcon in sight, and I became increasingly aware of that fact as we walked. They were anything but subtle either, nudging one another and glancing my way. A few outright pointed and murmured we walked past them. Thankfully most seemed curious instead of hostile, which lessened the effect a little... but only a little.

"Yeah." Trenah said as I unconsciously moved to walk a bit closer to her, "We're not really a subtle kind of people. Or quiet either. You're gonna have to get used to it."

I tried to think of something glib to say, faltered, then simply sighed. "Here I thought you were just unusually chatty."

My roommate gave me a flat look, her tarah tilting down to help display her displeasure, and then nudged me hard with an elbow. "Ass."

I took the blow and smiled slightly. "Ask you something?"

"That's part of the point of this trip, isn't it?"

"There's a lot more women around than men, aren't there?"

She grunted, the sound a tad bit surprised. "You're observant, aren't you? Don't think most aliens pick up on that right away. Yeah, we're not one of the even-up species. Figure three or four of us to every idiot."

My second attempt to hit her with my cane didn't go any better than the first. "So how does that work?"

Trenah snorted as she moved back next to me from where she'd dodged away, "You mean do the idiots get to have three or four women in their bed every night?"

I felt myself flush slightly. "I meant relationships in general."

"Sure you did." Her tarah twitched as she smirked, then stilled when she shrugged. "You want the short version or the long version with explicit details?"

I coughed slightly. "Uh, the short version."

"Prude." Trenah's smirk widened before she took pity on me, "We only reproduce in our first century, after that we're usually infertile. Once we're past that age people will end up with whoever they like, or not end up with anyone if they don't feel like it. We don't care much about the genders involved after we're done making eggs."

"First century?" I eyed her, "I really thought that one book was exaggerating. How long do you live?"

"Longer than your kind, and it's fucking rude to ask a woman's age." I actually stopped walking and stared at her, earning a barking laugh. "What? You think you were the only one doing fucking research on the net? I had to be prepared."

A hand rose so I could rub tiredly at my forehead. Of course Trenah would look up random things like that. "...you're trying to distract me from the fact that everyone is staring at me."

"It's fucking working isn't it?"

It was, so I merely shrugged and got my tiring legs moving again. "So how old are you?"

"Such a rude asshole." She shrugged in return, "Hundred and fifty three imperial."

Imperial years didn't line up with Earth ones, I knew that much, even if the exact math was beyond me. Still, I was vaguely sure Imperial years were *longer*, not shorter, which meant she was even older than that by my standards.

"Holy fuck." I muttered, shaking my head. "Wish I could look forwards to that many years."

Her smile faded completely, "Yeah, it's definitely got its perks, but living a long fucking time isn't all smooth sailing either. You see a lot of shit you'd rather not."

There wasn't much I could say in response to that. A ton of questions I could ask, maybe, but it seemed inappropriate considering we were in public... and considering how much I owed her. Thankfully we were apparently at our destination because she steered me towards an open-air restaurant situated on a pier stretching out into the calm river.

We found a small table and claimed it, and I found myself depressed at how good it felt to simply sit down.

Dammit, we hadn't even walked all that far. Stupid weak and exhausted body.

Trenah distracted me again, this time by making me try and read the menu out loud and order when the waitress came over. I managed the first one, even if I only understood about one word in five, but botched the order. The translator-less waitress had managed to keep her composure until I'd blushed, which had made her start giggling madly. My embarrassment wasn't helped by the fact that I could understand her just fine thanks to my ear pieces.

Apparently my skin turning red made me 'adorable'.

Eventually, and with more than a little kind help from her, I managed to get the words in the right order to make it clear I was asking for water, bread-sticks, and soup. After that Trenah had taken pity on me and handled ordering the main course.

Thankfully pretty much everyone else present was more interested in eating and getting back to work than they were in staring at me. I got a couple of double-takes and intrigued looks from our fellow diners but not much more than that.

"So," I spoke up once we'd gotten our drinks and appetizers, "I'll be getting actual work in a couple of weeks?"

Trenah noisily sipped from her soup, twitching a tarah in acknowledgment. The damn things were really expressive once you got used to them. "I've got a couple of small things you could probably help with, kind of shit that's mostly just manual labor at first."

"Like?" I prodded. "You haven't exactly told me what you usually do besides repairing stuff that people bring in."

"That's because that's pretty much the only shit I do." She retorted,

"That and contract work from Xerol."

"Who?"

A hand waved, "Thondian businessman, he pretty much runs the little enclave they have, you'll meet him eventually. Right now he's got me working on a pair of aircars, plus refurbishing a dozen armored chest-plates."

I blinked. "Armor? Oh, he has his own security forces or something?"

"Or something." She said in a tone that told me she wasn't telling me everything. "That's actually what you'll be working on. Gotta pry them apart to replace a lot of the interior crap, and that's easy enough to do. You can help me when I get the new shit in to upgrade them too, it'll help you learn."

"...you get a lot of orders to repair body armor?"

"Not really," She admitted, "Mostly I get cars or the bigger electronics, the kind of crap people have a harder time fixing on their own. That or side projects people don't want to spend their own time on."

I sipped some of my soup and nodded, "Sounds interesting."

Trenah set her bowl aside and leaned back, "It's not the worst job, that's for bloody sure. Once you're healthy enough we'll figure out what I'll need to pay you."

"Unless you're going to charge me rent or make me buy my own food, I really don't know what I'd need a lot of money for."

She gave me a flat look and let out a tiny snort, "You're shit at negotiating Cie."

I smiled slightly, "Well, you're literally the only friend I have right now, don't want to strain the relationship."

"We'll have to work on that." There was a slight shake of her head, "Not going to be easy if you want to know people who aren't Trahcon. I don't think there are many other Humans on planet, and most Thondians don't really like your species that much. Some fucked up shit between them and the

31

Ark Fleet."

"Oh." I pursed my lips, "Well, not really looking for romantic relationships or anything, especially since I'll be lucky to make it back to the apartment without falling over. I guess I'll just have to make do with a short little Trahcon woman for a friend."

Trenah's spoon tumbled to the ground as she sat bolt upright, her mouth dropping open while her tarah began quivering madly. "*What*!?"

I blinked in surprise at her reaction. "Um, was I not supposed to notice that every other woman I've seen is taller than you?"

"You... I am *not* short!" She snarled. "You over-sized furry, idiotic, savanna thing!"

Someone nearby let out a stifled bark of laughter, and a glance showed me a man and woman hiding smirks and twitching tarah behind menus. "Sensitive much?"

Trenah growled loudly enough for me to hear her even over the rumble of conversation, "Soon as we're home I'm going on the fucking net and finding the most humiliating shit I can do to you."

"Trenah." I smiled lightly, "Such revenge is beneath you. Literally."

"One more fucking word and I'm throwing you into the river!"

"...is this a bad time?" Our waitress interjected, holding plates of some kind of pasta in both hands. "Is the alien being rude?"

I didn't know much Caranat yet, but I knew enough to be able to cut in with my broken speech before Trenah could say anything. "She short is. Angry."

Trenah growled again... then the waitress giggled, reached out, and patted her on the shoulder. "Don't worry. You're very cute when you're angry."

My companion stilled in surprise, then glanced up and tilted her head as if seeing the taller woman for the first time. "Cute huh?"

The waitress slid our food onto the table, then gave Trenah a little smirk before turning away with far more hip action than was actually necessary. Even I couldn't help but watch for a few seconds as she walked off before shaking my head. I turned back to find Trenah not quite drooling as her gaze lingered.

"Think those ear pieces of yours will cancel noise?"

I just... stared at her for several seconds. "Please tell me you aren't serious."

Trenah gave me an arch look. "I haven't gone out in a bloody month, Cie, and did you see her ass? I damn well know you were looking at her ass too."

As much as I wanted to deny that, I really couldn't... which probably didn't say much good about me. Trahcon women were very much not Human ones, but that particular part of their body was definitely... ugh, I really needed to stop thinking about it. "You're seriously going to try and pick up our waitress?"

"Didn't I just fucking say that I was?" Her bright eyes narrowed. "And didn't you just say that I was your only bloody friend, and that you weren't going to strain our relationship?"

I stared at her once again, then sighed and shook my head, "Touche."

"What? That didn't translate."

"Well played." I clarified, "I'll keep my mouth shut and... I don't know, listen to music loudly or something."

"Good." She smirked. "I'll be right back."

"What about your..." Trenah rose and strolled off before I could finish, heading right for the waitress who was leaning against the bar, apparently waiting for her. "...food. Oh god, what did I just agree to?"

I – IV

It was three months into my life on Alum when things really began to change. Summer was ending, the days getting shorter and cooler, much to my and Trenah's mutual appreciation. Neither one of us really enjoyed the heat, and we began taking longer walks in the evening as my strength came back.

More personally I finally had a half-decent grasp on the local language, I was starting to learn how to actually do my job, and I felt sure that Trenah and I had progressed from roommates to being close friends.

And then I killed someone.

I'd been going with Trenah to her shop for about two weeks, and time had started to roll by pretty quickly. The shop itself was a pretty nice little building, basically a small warehouse a bit bigger than most auto repair joints on Earth, decorated in the same bright colors as her apartment's outer wall. She was vague about how she'd gotten it, but I didn't really bother asking that many questions. It was downriver, about a ten minute flight from our apartment complex, where it sat between a salon and a restaurant.

Trenah was just as much of a laid back boss as I could have guessed. At least so long as I made good progress on the various tasks she gave me and so long as I actually seemed to be learning. I was still mostly doing manual labor tasks but she let me look over her shoulder and talked me through what she was doing.

In theory I'd be ready for a few small projects of my own in a week or so.

Which I was kind of looking forwards to. The job wasn't proving to be all that different from what I'd expected my various tasks on the colony ship to be. Hell, if anything it was *more* interesting since Trenah got to work with both Trahcon and Thondian tech. Both were far beyond what we'd had in my time, though it seemed like the Trahcon were generally a few steps above the Thondians.

"I've got a lunch date with Xerol Shaaryak next week," She told me as

34

we were slowly wrapping up for the day, hauling her torso out of the engine space of an aircar. "Figured I'd drag your pale ass with, finally meet our biggest source of employment."

I glanced up from where I'd been putting various tools away, "Oh? He coming out here or do I get to see this Thondian enclave?"

"Koshun Minor." Came the reminder. "And yeah, it'll be out there. Think he's got a new big contract for me, probably another set of armor to get refurbished. Maybe even some weapons."

A slow whistle came out of my lips. "Is he having gang problems out there?"

I'd started to get better acquainted with the local news as my grasp of Caranat had improved. True to what Trenah had told me, there were several gangs that were causing problems in the Outskirts and the Industrial Sector. The biggest group of idiots were called the 'True Sons'. They were a collection of aliens who generally hated the Trahcon for, well, pretty much everything wrong with their shitty lives.

Given the fact that the local government, a majority of the population, and the largest mercenary corporation operating from the planet were all dominated by the Trahcon... such attitudes didn't usually go to well for them.

"Fucking everyone seems to be having problems right now." Trenah griped as she shut the engine panel, "Crescent is actually moving around on the streets, True Sons are all riled up, and even more idiots are trying to form up their own little gangs. News says the Imperial Ambassador is bitching up a storm to the High Families."

I shook my head and stretched out my arms, enjoying the fact that I wasn't exhausted after a day of fairly low-key work. I was still a bit leaner than I'd have liked to have been, but I wasn't a walking scarecrow anymore. Progress was good. "Huh. I thought that local station said the Sons were way down on territory."

"They are," She shrugged and stretched as well, "But idiots like that tend to get desperate instead of smart when they get shot at."

As usual, Trenah was entirely correct.

The True Sons were pretty desperate.

Desperate enough for a couple of their younger members to try and rob a random shop in fact.

The gunshot that blew the door control panel apart was painfully loud. I flinched and all but fell out of my chair in shock at the hideous noise.

I jerked my head around and got a brief glimpse of a tall figure kicking the door open, body illuminated by the streetlights outside. Then Trenah made a snarling sound in her throat and threw a hand forwards, ozone filling the air as she forced the door to abruptly reverse direction. It slammed shut over a deep bellow of pain, itself followed by the sound of several bodies slamming violently against one another, drawing more shouts and curses.

"Get over here now!" Trenah's voice had gone flat and hard, and the sheer command in her words had me up and darting towards her before I even realized I was moving. She kept one hand thrust out, holding the door closed mentally, while her other yanked open a drawer on her desk.

I got to her just in time for her to shove a curvy gun into my hands, my eyes staring at it, then at her when she pulled a monstrous pistol out for herself. "I-"

"Safety is the green button." She snapped. "Push it and don't point it at anything you don't want to shoot. Get behind the car and kneel down."

"But... ah... what are... what..." I could barely get the words out in English, my Caranat failing me entirely. I'd only ever fired a gun at a range before, and even then only two or three times. Never in an actual life or death situation.

A gray hand seized my shirt, jerking me down so that she could glare at me from just a few inches away. "Turn your safety off, when they come back in, you shoot them. Got it?"

"Y-yeah." I managed to secure the weapon in both hands, vague memories making sure I kept my finger alongside the trigger rather than on it.

She gave me a rough little shove and I staggered to where she'd told me to go, falling painfully to a knee and letting the weapon rest on top of the car's hood like I'd seen in too many movies.

That was all I had time to do before Trenah had to release her hold on the doorway with a little growling sound, the steel promptly giving way as our attackers charged in.

The first figure proved to be a Thondian male, probably the same one I'd glimpsed earlier. He was at least six and a half feet tall, with tanned skin and long, elfin ears stretching away from his bald scalp. Ivory teeth were on full display as he stormed inside, some kind of shotgun held in his hands as his black eyes swept from left to right.

Which was the exact wrong order to do things. We were on his right, and he'd started his sweep from where I had been less than a minute before.

Trenah shot him before I could even move my finger, her monster pistol making my ears ring as it barked. The first round slammed into a shield, drawing what sounded like a foul oath from our guest. But he didn't even make it another step before a second metallic round ripped right through his weakened defenses and into his left cheek. As if not noticing the fact that his brains were now decorating the ground behind him, he managed two long steps forwards before pitching forwards.

The entire event took maybe three seconds.

Two more forms shoved their way into the room behind him, and it felt like I had a lifetime to look at them. One was another Thondian, wearing bulging clothes that were obviously concealing armor. His face was decorated in tattoos proclaiming his gang allegiance to the point where I could barely tell his original skin color, and he was likewise clutching a shotgun in both hands.

Right on his heels was what I only vaguely recognized as a Naule; a low-slung, ape-like being with four arms and shaggy black hair partially covered by cast-off orange clothes. Three of the arms were on the ground, helping his legs propel him at surprising speed, while the last held a pistol up and at the ready. His sunken eyes took in the corpse of their leader, and moving faster than I thought possible, he all but bounded over the body and began moving laterally, pistol swinging into line.

But fast as the alien was, I was already pointing my gun more or less in the right direction. Desperately trying to remember every short lesson I'd had on firearms, I slid my finger onto the trigger and gently pulled. The little gun began barking at full automatic, making my forearms strain as I fought against the pull.

Whatever shields the Naule were evidently as cheap as his dead friend's. The first couple of rounds only drew sparks, but then there was an abrupt spray of black blood as bullets traced their way from the center of his chest to where his right arms met his body. I quickly let go of the trigger, watching as the body crumpled, the wide, fanged mouth open in pain and shock.

I was only vaguely aware of the other Thondian crying out, his weapon being ripped from his hands by a telekinetic yank to clatter into a corner. I jerked my gaze away as the Naule's body gave a final shudder, and found myself watching as Trenah advanced in stalking motion towards the final attacker.

In any other circumstance it might have been comical. The Thondian was close to seven feet tall and absolutely towered over her, but he was the one shakily holding his hands apart as she gave him a look that could have frozen water.

She nodded slowly at his reaction, then before he or I could react, her aim dropped and she put a round into each of his shins with another double-hammer blow of noise.

His screams were probably loud enough to wake any neighbors we had, assuming the gunshots had not already done so.

"Cieran?"

Then again, did we even have any neighbors? This was pretty much a business only area, and I was pretty sure we were open the latest. The salon had to have been closed and the restaurant's construction team was probably already done for the day too.

"Cieran!"

That was probably why these guys had tried to rob us. Or kill us. Or robs us then kill us. Wait, why rob us before killing us? It would make more sense to kill us and then rob us. Unless they were worried about the local police, in which case the other way around might work.

Pain rocketed across my face when a gray hand whipped across it.

"Snap out of it!"

"S-sorry!" It was hard to gasp that out, and I belatedly realized that my lungs were screaming at my brain that I needed to breathe. The tightness of my chest eased as delicious oxygen began to reach my system, and I all but gulped down air while I staggered back against the car.

"It's all right," Her hand gently touched my shoulder, though I noticed that she kept half an eye on the wailing survivor. "Just put the gun down, and try to breathe."

That... seemed like a really good idea.

It was a lot harder than it should have been to force my fingers to loosen up, and I had to focus on the process before I could let the gun clatter to the aircar's hood. Somehow I managed to push the safety back on, then I had to plant my hands beside the weapon to keep myself upright.

Everything was trembling. That was... probably bad.

"Stay there. I've got him covered." Trenah was apparently still worried about me, and about our still breathing guest, though I didn't think she really needed to worry about him. He was too busy sobbing, rolling around, and clutching at his shattered legs. Now that I could actually take the time to look at him, he seemed... young. He had the same gangling, mildly awkward appearance that a Human teenager might have had. "You all right now?"

"I... yeah... yeah." I took a few deep breaths and nodded slowly. I was still shaking, and I wanted to throw up, but things seemed to be slowing down. I managed to speak in her own language, though my words were still a bit halting. "I'm good. Sorry."

"It's all right, you waited until it was over at least. Could have been a lot worse for your first time."

"Thanks... I think."

Her mouth twitched into a little grin, "Security should already be on there way. You think you can cover this guy while I check out his friends?"

No. "Yes."

It was another struggle to get the gun back into my hands, pretty much putting paid to the idea that I was actually all right. I more or less aimed it at the wounded man though I kept the safety on. It seemed best considering that I had to rest my arms on the vehicle to make sure they didn't quiver madly.

Trenah gave me a concerned look but said nothing, keeping her own weapon in hand as she carefully picked her way over to the two bodies.

"True Sons. Fucking figures. Only they'd be stupid enough to send three kids to rob a machine shop. Ashahn's ass, what the fuck did they think they were going to get from us? Don't suppose you could answer that?"

The Thondian moaned and rolled around some more.

"Didn't think so." She gave a soft sigh, "By all the fucking Aspects, we didn't need this kind of crap today."

She went through the dead men's pockets, not finding all that much. A few identification chips, some loose credits, shield bandoleers that practically fell apart when she yanked at them... the dead Thondian didn't even have a wrist-comp, and the Naule's was at least twenty years out of date. She was just tossing the sleeve-like mesh aside when the sound of sirens began to grow in the distance, and she motioned for me to put the gun down again.

"They can be kind of touchy, best to keep it away."

I hesitated slightly, "What about... oh."

Trenah hadn't even waited for me to finish before reaching out with her sorcery once more, the Thondian slowly flattening across the ground the same way the Matriarch had pinned me into my bed all those months ago. "I can hold it long enough for them to get their asses in here, have some faith Cie."

"Yeah... sorry." I carefully set the gun down again, then slowly fell back and collapsed into her desk chair. "Not... not at my best right now."

"Don't worry about it, first time's rough on everyone. Least you haven't puked your guts out like I did." her little nose wrinkled, "I can still *smell* that stupid Regnon sometimes... you don't know just how bad something can reek until you've had to deal with a disemboweled Regnon."

As I tried and failed to deal with that mental image, and the fact that the smell from the two bodies was growing into something awful, the first cops had managed to arrive. A loudspeaker enhanced voice boomed from outside, flashing blue lights strobing in through the ruined door. "*Attention in the shop! This is Internal Security, can you confirm your identities?*"

"Trenah'laria, shop owner." I winced slightly at how loud she managed to shout that out, "And my Human assistant. I've got two dead gang members and a third that could do with medical aid and a nice cell!"

There was a long pause, enough for someone to look up something. "*Confirm your identification!*"

Trenah promptly rattled off a set of numbers and letters. Evidently they satisfied the authorities because the same woman called back, "*Verified. Keep your hands in sight, we're moving in.*"

My friend quickly set her pistol onto her desk and moved next to me, her arms carefully spread apart as the police quickly darted in to join us. They were all in some kind of dark blue armor, though none were wearing helmets, and their own pistols were quickly lowered when they saw that we'd been telling the truth.

Two of them headed in our direction, while others began to pile in so they could check over the wounded man and his dead companions.

"What happened here?" the one who approached me asked the question half a second after Trenah's asked her the same thing.

"Um.." I stammered. "Well.."

"I've got this." Trenah cut in, "You're my employee, no responsibility so long as I take it."

I blinked at that. "Really?"

"Fucking Alum." Trenah said sagely, actually drawing a snort from one of the two cops, and both of them actually seemed to relax a little at her casual attitude. From there it didn't really take too long for her to tell them the full story of what happened. One of the two brought up a floating screen from her wrist-comp to enter notes, while the other simply ran Trenah through the whole thing twice to make sure they had it straight.

"So... are they going to take us in?" I asked when the two had backed away to converse with one another.

She snorted before stretching out her arms and yawning massively. "Why would they bother? They're all marked as gang members, and the damage to the door speaks for itself. They'll probably call someone to fix it for me, and the worst I'll have to do is fill out some paperwork for the insurance that they'll mail me later."

I practically gaped at her, "What? We just... they're dead! And there's just... *paperwork*?"

One of the other cops, a slim little man with some kind of rank insignia on his armor, barked out a laugh at that. His voice wasn't quite as deep a a Human guy's, but it was noticeably more so than any of the women's despite his more slender build. "New on Alum? I can tell. Fuck, if I was off duty I'd buy you a drink for taking out a few of these pathetic bastards. Racist little washed up shits."

There was a rumble of agreement from his comrades, and whatever tension was still in the room vanished as a couple of them hauled out the wounded teenager none-too-gently.

The same man nudged one of the Naule's limp arms with a boot and nodded slightly before looking at me again, "You had the automatic, didn't you? Not bad shooting at all, you let off the trigger before you could shoot up your own shop. Don't see that often, especially in young aliens."

We'd just killed two people, crippled a third, and the police were just... going to let us wander off. Hell, they were *complimenting* us for doing it. Praising how we'd shot them to pieces without causing damage to the little shop we'd been fighting in.

It was really in that moment that I fully realized I wasn't on Earth anymore. That I wasn't surrounded by other Humans. Until then I guessed that I'd still been operating under some kind of delusion that the aliens around me were basically Humans. Maybe a different race of Human, different language and culture, but not really... *alien.*

I think I went into a kind of shock around then. I sort of remember Trenah speaking with the man, apparently some kind of detective, about getting the door fixed and blood cleaned up. Him saying it would be handled overnight and that they'd call her when they were done. At some point after that Trenah gently got me upright and moving, more cops praising us and muttering about how the gangs were getting reckless as we left.

Reality slowly came back into focus when we were in her aircar, a battered, gold colored thing that she flew with ease. I slowly looked around and realized we weren't following the river traffic back towards her apartment, "...where are we going?"

She gave me a concerned glance; she'd probably already told me where we were going. "Fuck. You're really out of it, aren't you?"

"...yeah. I'm sorry."

"Stop fucking apologizing." She shook her head, "Ashahn's blood it's getting annoying. Nothing that happened is your fault, Cie. Those idiots would have killed us both and your brain knows it."

"...I know that." It just wasn't helping right now.

Trenah let out a quiet sigh, "We're going to get some drinks is where we're going. I need one and you *definitely* need several. There's an old bitch I know who runs an honest tavern down south, the kind of place you just go for drinks and company instead of dancing or crap like that. It'll help calm you down, and maybe I'll find someone to bring back with us."

"...really?"

"What? You can't tell me your people don't mix sex and violence too, I fucking know better than that." She gave me a small smile, clearly trying to cheer me up, "Or were you hoping for me to pick out someone for you this time?"

I groaned a little at our most-repeated argument. "I'm not going to sleep with some random stranger just to make you happy."

"Why not sleep with a random stranger to make *you* happy?"

"Because Trahcon women don't really do anything for me, and I'm not into men."

One of her tarah twitched, "What about a nice Thondian girl? They've got those stupid chest orbs that your kind likes to drool over."

I felt my cheeks heat up in spite of everything. "Trenah... just... ugh. Just get us there and get us drinks, please."

She let out a little cackle but thankfully refrained from further teasing.

It didn't take us all that long to arrive, her car settling down between two far more weather-beaten models. The bar was pretty recognizable as a bar, even to an alien like me, though it had the same kind over-the-top architectural style that seemed to be the Trahcon's default option. In this case the owner had gone with water-like stone carvings set into the walls, all of them in a deep blue that went oddly well with the neon signs in the various windows.

"Welcome to Forever. Don't ask why she called it that, don't fucking know." Trenah talked as we walked, entering through a door that slid open automatically.

Inside proved to be a nice little place. Neither fancy nor run down. The lighting was low, highlighting several large screens showing various programs; mostly sports. There was a reasonable number of booths, only a few of which had occupants, but the bar itself ran the length of the main room.

Behind said bar was a towering woman, practically my height, and she looked like she was just as built as Trenah was.

44

"The littlest Laria." Her voice was a bit gravely, and she spoke with a heavy accent. Her consonants were a lot softer and her vowels longer than I was used to. She gave us a grin as Trenah lead me over, a teasing lilt creeping into her words. "And her new pack-mate. Looks young to me, even for a Human. He even old enough to drink?"

"I'm twenty five, that's four years legal by my people's laws." I spoke for myself, drawing an almost impressed look when she flicked bright blue eyes to me, a single tarah tilting up in interest.

"Slow in your pacing, but not bad." She noted, "Shame you got the local flavor, not a very attractive accent to be honest. Name's Ashul'tasir, I own the place. What brings you two out here? Hope it's not sex, haven't got the time today and the fur is too much of a turn off."

My friend rolled her eyes and twitched her tarah up and down. "Like we'd want to fuck an arthritic old fish like you. My usual, and something hard for Cie."

"Hard huh. What's your taste like in our drinks?"

I shrugged, "I have no idea. Maybe a mix, something smooth."

"One of those. I'll get something up."

She moved away, leaving the pair of us sitting on the Trahcon style stools. Which were quite similar to Human ones, except they had only a single bar sticking crookedly up from the back to lean against. Sounds painful I know, but once you get used to it it's actually rather comfortable.

"You all right?" Trenah kept her voice low as I settled back, staring vaguely at nothing.

Sitting down again had probably been a mistake, it made a wave of exhaustion and stress kind of roll over me. "...I'll live."

"Remember that they would have killed us, all right? Well, killed me. They'd have given you the join or die speech."

"Good to know that stupid speech transcends species... and yeah, I know."

We both said nothing when Ashul... dammit, no, it was Tasir until she gave me permission to use her personal name, returned and set drinks in front of us. Trenah had gotten something in a jet black bottle, I got something kind of grayish-blue. Which turned out to taste like tropical punch, with a pleasant little kick of something like rum at the end.

"So how do you know the old fish over here?" I asked, desperately trying to think of anything besides the black blood and stunned features of the man I'd killed. "And why is she bar-tending? Thought old Trahcon just kind of lounged around and offered unwanted opinions."

"Old bitch isn't as old as she likes to pretend to be." She replied with a rolling shrug, "Used to be some kind of Imperial big-shot from what I've heard, retired out here after some project she was running ran into a fucking hurricane. Taught me a couple of tricks when I was younger, gives advice once and a while, and she makes damned good drinks."

"This is pretty good." I admitted quietly, taking another sip. "How long she been doing this?"

"Too fucking long kid." We both jumped slightly, jerking our heads around to see her sipping from her own drink not more than a yard away. "But I doubt you're here to talk about me. You got that look."

"Look?" I asked.

"Don't be obtuse. You got into a fight and you had to kill someone, and you feel bad about it." I bit my tongue and let her keep going, "Even though they'd have probably offed you and Trenah, you still let yourself get all mopey like you aliens always do."

My friend promptly rose to my defense, "He's never been in a gun fight before, it's fucking normal. Especially for his kind."

"Had to happen sometime with how this place is these days," Her muscled shoulders shrugged, "Better it happened when you could walk away and come here to drink. Gangs?"

Trenah exhaled and nodded, "True Sons."

"Little bitches" Tasir shook her head, "Bunch of morons. How hard is it to case a place and realize that there's armed people inside?"

"It's Alum, everyone is fucking armed."

"Only the smart ones, only the smart ones." There was a flicker of pain in her eyes "And not enough of us smart ones left these days... drinks are on the house tonight, so long as the Human doesn't freeze up next time."

How did...

I shook my head, I didn't want to know how she could tell. Instead I picked up my glass, took a nice long pull, and began trying to forget everything that had just happened.

I – V

The week after the incident passed by fairly quickly.

I didn't have as many nightmares as I thought that I would, which was a bit of bright news. The few that I did... well, they weren't pleasant, and I'm pretty sure Trenah knew when I had one because I threw myself entirely into work those days. But for the most part life was turning out to be life as usual, just on a different planet.

Wake up, throw things at Trenah to wake her up as well, exercise together, eat whatever we had laying around for breakfast, and then fly to work. If the day was rough, or if I was in a more depressive mood, she'd drag me off to Forever for drinks. Ashul'tasir wasn't always there, but the other bartenders were companionable enough to talk to for a while, which I usually ended up doing alone while Trenah tried to find someone to go home with.

Those nights she went out for casual sex, or brought someone back to her room, I spent laying around on my own. Reading the DataNet on my brand new wrist-comp was quickly becoming my main distraction, learning everything I could about the various projects we had waiting for us at the shop. I'd always prided myself on my ability to learn quickly, but Trenah constantly lamented that I had a long way to go.

Which meant I was more than a little taken aback when our delayed trip to meet with Xerol Shaaryak came with the news that I was going to be getting a solo project.

"I really don't think I'm ready for something big, Trenah." I said for the fifth time, my lanky body stretched out in the passenger seat of her car as she flew us northeast. "Especially if you're funding the initial part of it."

"Pretty sure I told you to shut the fuck up about that." She groused, her nearer tarah flicking in irritation. "For the last time, you can read just fine, you can speak clearly when you don't stop to think about the shit coming out of your mouth. That means you can look crap up on the Net and ask me questions. And this will keep you too busy to mope."

"I was *not* moping."

Trenah scoffed but let it go. It had gotten pretty clear that, while she definitely cared and worried about me, she didn't really understand the kind of shock and depression I'd gone through after killing the idiot. Trahcon apparently didn't get hit in the same way.

That or just being a hundred and fifty-seven years old made it hard to relate.

Still, she was doing her best, so I couldn't really bitch too much. "You don't get to complain when I screw things up."

"So long as you fix whatever you wreck." Her head tilted forwards, "There's the district. Koshun Minor."

The architectural difference was so blatant it practicality smacked you in the face. The bright color and wildly variable styles of the Trahcon gave way to elegant but uniformly white buildings with dark red roofs. I picked out a large mansion complex set into the center of the area almost at once, the buildings surrounded by a wide park. Even from a distance its size was impressive. The thing had to be at least as large the entire apartment building that we lived in... probably larger.

I let out a slow whistle, "The mansion belong to him?"

"Him, his niece, and two cousins." Trenah provided, "Plus a couple dozen staff. You do a good enough job on this we may even get invited inside. It's fancy as hell, not really my thing, but his cooks make some damned good food."

My head shook a little as she slowed and began to bank, "Where are we landing today?"

"The Boneyard."

I gave her a look, then glanced out the window again before snorting as I saw the area she was steering towards. It was right at the edge of where the small Thondian enclave bordered the looming structures of the Industrial District. "He owns a junkyard?"

"He owns this whole damned district, remember what I told you about Thondians."

"Right, right. I'll remember, and I won't insult anyone." When she gave me a flat look I had the decency to correct myself, "On purpose at least."

"Just don't get us shot." She commented as we came down for a landing.

I gave her an annoyed glance but stayed silent as the engine's whine quieted and then cut off. The door swung upwards at a push, leaving me free to clamber out and get a good look around.

A Thondian who had to be Xerol Shaaryak was standing just outside of the entryway, two guards from his own species lurking behind him. He approached even before Trenah was fully out of the car, leaving me to face him mostly alone. Which was... just a little bit intimidating.

He was close to seven feet tall, and was built proportionally to his massive frame. Like the few other Thondians I'd seen, he had long ears that were almost exaggeratedly elfin, though his were bedecked with golden earrings from their bases to their pointed tips. His skin was a rich, dark shade of brown, save for the sand colored sections on the sides of his throat and chin that were raised slightly. They were a kind of cartilage that served as natural armor, if I remembered my very brief look-up on his species.

Still, in the end it was the eyes that were the strangest; Thondian's had black where Humans or Trahcon had white, leaving the brown irises shadowed. And the fact that he was wearing a dark blue suit that probably cost more than Trenah's car also helped with the whole intimidation thing.

"Ah, Cieran Kean." He spoke Caranat with booming tones, lips pulling back from ivory colored teeth in something like a smile. The extra sharp canines made him look almost vampiric, adding further to my nerves. "How good to finally meet Trenah's new companion."

"Lord Shaaryak." I replied as politely as I could, bowing slightly at the waist and tilting my head to the left as Trenah had told me to do. "It is good to meet you, sir. I hope that your day is profitable."

His laugh was as deep as his speaking voice, and he gave me a much shallower bow with a right-leaning tilt of his head. "A Human taught proper manners by the least polite woman I have ever met? This world never ceases to surprise!"

"Oh fuck off you sand-born ass." Trenah called, though she did it with a grin on her face and her tarah tilted in amusement. The pair of them exchanged quick bows of their own, though both kept their heads level which I thought meant that Xerol didn't consider her inferior to him... or something.

Dammit, I really should have spent more time researching Thondian culture and less time poking at various electrical systems.

Xerol quickly beckoned us forwards once our greeting was complete, walking beside Trenah while I trailed a bit to stay out of their way.

"I take it you are here for the research project you proposed last week?" He said as we reached the entrance, "I do believe all of the materials remain in place, and I will of course pay handsomely if it proves to be of worth. Though I feel as though I should warn you-"

"I know, I know." Trenah waved him off, "It's all old and beaten up, you already told me."

I felt my steps falter a little, less at Trenah's words and more at the dark expressions both of the guards were giving me. Trenah's warnings that Thondians and the Ark Fleet didn't get along rang in my head, and I carefully slowed my pace further and gave them a similar bow of greeting to the one I'd given their boss.

Both of them started in shock, then almost hastily replied with shallow-right bows of their own.

Feeling like I'd done something right, I lengthened my strides a bit to catch up with the others as they meandered through the yard. The place was overflowing with equipment in various stages of dismantling, and even as I watched a small horde of Thondian and Trahcon workers were doing their best to rip apart the rest of it. Small personal speeders and large aircars seemed to predominate, though I also picked out several orbital shuttles being pried apart.

There didn't really seem to be any division of labor between the species, both groups being treated more or less equally. The closest thing to a split seemed to be a small section of better dressed workers seated at various tables; working with hand tools to inspect or dismantle more delicate equipment.

Xerol led Trenah and I past the main working area, through a collection of gutted flying trucks that had been reduced to just their frames, and then slowed to a stop near an oddly shaped pile of metal.

"And here it is." Our host waved at the thing, "I assure you that it is in better shape than it appears."

"It looks like a rusted pile of driftwood." Trenah noted, kicking part of it with a boot before waving me closer. "What do you think, Cie?"

It took me a second to realize what I was looking at, then my eyebrows rose.

The mound of rusting metal was actually some kind of slumped over exoskeleton, legs sprawled out, both arms hanging limply at its side. There wasn't any exterior plating, and even to my inexperienced eyes it looked like more than a few pieces were missing. Still, the dark gray ropes of artificial muscles seemed to mostly be intact, and the main engine housing in back hadn't been disassembled either.

It honestly reminded me of the kind of power armor you might have seen in video games, albeit far blockier, exposed, and stained with orange streaks.

"I think it's going to take me a year to do anything with this." I replied as I dropped to a crouch, trying to get a better look. "Where did you even get it?"

Xerol chuckled darkly, "This piece came from Koshun itself. One of my competitors had hoped to use it and several others in the construction business. "

There was a snort from Trenah. "Moron."

I smiled a little, understanding that much at least. Trahcon didn't exactly need powered exoskeletons to help with construction; when even a young member of the species could move things around with their minds you tended to be able to cut corners.

"He was not a shining example of my people," He brought his hands together, his finger tips touching in a gesture I was unfamiliar with, "Alas, he was compelled to depart for Terminus, leaving much of his equipment and work force behind."

That time I joined Trenah when she snorted again, easily translating the polite phrasing to know that Xerol had both driven the man out of business and off-world.

"So what's the plan going to be?" I asked, rising back up. "I'm guessing fixing this back up to factory spec isn't what you want from it?"

"Indeed not." Xerol agreed with a small smile, "Several weeks ago, at roughly the same time as the incident at dear Trenah's shop, several groups belonging to the True Sons attacked various businesses within my sphere of influence. While my security guards were able to deal with those specific events, we have seen them continuing to scout around the edges of the district."

I felt myself grimace. "...oh. I get it."

"You do?"

"I think so." I shook my head and waved a hand at Trenah, "They hate Trahcon, blame them for everything wrong with their lives. You work with them, employ them, and make a profit trading with them. So you're worse than being an alien, you're a traitor. They want to make an example of you."

His teeth showed and he gave me a slight nod of acknowledgment. "They also likely believe my operations to be an easier target. Internal Security has only a small presence here, and I am no friend of either the Crescent or the Board."

My lips twisted a little as I turned back to the exoskeleton. "You want me to weaponize this thing. Give you something to intimidate them with."

"He doesn't, I do." Trenah corrected me. "He's got a dozen or so of them rusting around here, but not the time or staff to tinker with the fucking things. It'll be a good project for you, and if it works out, he'll pay us to do the rest of 'em. Plus a fat bonus for the schematics and procedure."

"And if it doesn't you're not really losing anything since you don't really pay me anyway." I noted.

She gave me a lazy grin, "Pretty much."

Exhaling, I lifted up my hands and ran them through my hair. "Guess that puts a little less pressure on me, so thanks for that, but I still don't-"

A gray hand and smacked the back of my head before I could flinch away, "Cieran, shut the fuck up and help me look this thing over."

I sighed. "Yes ma'am."

We worked while Xerol politely observed, the pair of us picking at the remains of the suit. Trenah decided to make the process the first part of my learning about it, challenging me to make observations and take notes as we dug into the thing.

"The engine is over-sized for the size of the suit, which means it's either inefficient and we'll have to replace it, or it'll be able to handle anything we throw at it." I said once I'd managed to pry open the heavy mount on the suit's back. "Wait, shit. The casing is cracked, we'll need a new one."

Trenah grunted, "We'll want something top-end enough to handle moving it, plus powering any weapons or shields we put onto it."

I pursed my lips and nodded. I had only the vaguest idea of how shielding actually worked, but she'd walked me through the basics of weaponry in the aftermath of the shop-incident.

Some species went for more exotic styles, but most stuck with either a rail or coil gun that fired very small projectiles at rather obscene speeds. That had the advantage of making it easy for a clip to hold a lot of ammunition; even pistols could fit anywhere from dozens to hundreds of rounds depending on the caliber. Extremely advanced batteries handled the power, but keeping those charged was one of the general considerations when it came to fighting. And since the weapons could generate a hellish amount of heat, coolant systems were also critical.

In theory mounting a gun directly the suit could help with a lot of that. Power could be drawn from the core, coolant brought in from the suit's own systems, and an ammunition feed would enable a lot of bullets to be thrown down range with few reasons to ever let off the trigger.

But I could already see a few problems with that.

"You want to attach them right onto it?" I asked. "I thought keeping the hands free would be better. Gives us more options for what it can carry."

"True." She gave me a Trahcon-style shrug, "But I was thinking pistols built right into the arms. There's more than enough damned space."

"I could see that working." I admitted, glancing at the massive rectangles that served as the forearms. "Still, I think we should focus on getting it running at all before we bother trying to think of how to shove guns into it."

Another shrug. "Your project."

I smiled and we kept at it, eventually ripping out a dozen or so ruined bits of equipment and noting down everything I could think of that it might need. Then Trenah had added a good three times that many extra bits I'd either missed or simply hadn't thought of, and Xerol had dispatched a few of the employees to start grabbing it all for us.

"I'll wave the costs for now, these items were merely going to be dismantled regardless." He spoke as I vainly tried to clean my hands off with a small towel. "Of course if the project goes anywhere the material costs will come out of the final sale price."

"Yeah, yeah." Trenah shook her head, "You're blessed by those stone circles you worship."

Xerol's sudden smile reminded me of a shark honing in on its prey, "Speaking of the Sacred Pillars, the Day of Carving approaches next mid-week."

Trenah's tarah tilted down and quivered once. "The last time I went to one of your parties you made me dance with your niece and the tall bitch tried to break both of my wrists."

"That is because she loathes you." He replied with amusement, "And you were drunk and insisted on placing your hands where they should not have been."

I gave my friend an amused smirk, "I had no idea you were into cross-species hookups too."

"I was fucking drunk off my ass." Trenah growled, "I don't even *remember* that night except for waking up with my wrists in braces."

"How good that you will have an assistant to spend the required dance with." Xerol cut in smoothly, "In either case, Ashul'tasir will be handling the catering as usual, so do try to avoid imbibing quite as much liquor this year."

"I'll have to if you expect me to dance with this ugly idiot."

"Hey!"

Turquoise eyes rolled, "You're trying to grow a dead animal on your face."

I reached a hand up defensively, touching the french beard I'd started to grow out. "I'll have you know I look better with facial hair."

Xerol interrupted just as Trenah was opening her mouth, undoubtedly to continue needling me. "Not that I begrudge you finally finding someone who can handle your unique personality, dear Trenah, but I do have other engagements today. I trust I will see you both next week."

Trenah gave him a dark look but nodded, and then we got to work finalizing everything.

I had thought that rebuilding a powered exoskeleton would be complicated. I had been wrong about that.

It was *insanely* complicated.

The suit had not been well maintained even before it had gotten dumped into a scrapyard. Worse, it had been designed with a brawny Thondian pilot in mind. Since they tended to be between six and half and seven and a half feet tall, it made it impossible to adjust to Trenah's size and difficult even to allow me to fit in properly. Thankfully the suit wasn't actually intended to match up perfectly with someone's body; the wearer's feet actually rested just above its ankles, and the hands slid into waldo units in the forearm.

It gave the whole thing a very gangling appearance once we got it upright, with its comparatively shorter upper arms and legs, but with a day's work we managed to adjust it enough for me to fit inside.

Then I spent seven days pretty much ripping the rest of it apart, cataloging all of the broken and corroded pieces that would need to be replaced. Once that was done I started doing my best to figure out how it all actually worked.

"We're going to be late if you keep messing around with that stupid thing." Trenah crossed her arms as she watched me triple-check the new power core I'd spent the last day installing. "And you're going to smell like oil and metal."

"So are you." I replied, twisting hard on a bolt and nodding to myself when it didn't move. "Or are you just bitching because we may not have time to clean up?"

"How the fuck am I supposed to find a partner if I'm covered in engine grease?"

"There's a fetish for everything." I said philosophically, pulling my head out of the suit's engine mount so I could glance back at my friend. "Can you bring a light over?"

She gave me a skeptical look, "What's wrong with your wrist-comp?"

"I need that hand to hold myself in place."

Her eyes rolled but she wandered over, flicking a finger along the device on her right arm. She'd gone with a red for her light where I preferred blue, but it did its job of illuminating the shadowed spaces in and around the suit's power core.

"Besides," I continued, checking over the various hydraulics and artificial muscles to make sure I hadn't damaged any of them during the day's events. "I can't remember the last time you tried and failed to find a fuck buddy for an evening. You looking for a guy or a girl tonight?"

"Whoever is sexy, willing, and who doesn't act like a drowning idiot." She answered with an audible shrug, "The better question is who are *you* going to bring back tonight?"

"Trenah..."

"You've been here for months now." Trenah stated impatiently, "And you haven't even *tried*. By the Highest fucking Aspects it's just... unnatural. I'm starting to think there's something wrong with you."

I sighed. Don't get me wrong, I liked Trenah, a lot. She was incredibly patient, a surprisingly good teacher, and she could be very fun to hang around with... but she was also a sex-maniac to the point where I'd seriously begun to wonder if there was something wrong with her.

Most of the other Trahcon I'd met or spoken with didn't seem nearly as focused on the subject as she was. Sure, as I'd said, she rarely slept alone if she didn't want to, but with a very few exceptions it was almost always her initiating the conversation.

"I don't go for men, so my options are Trahcon women who don't really do anything for me, and who think I'm ugly because I have hair and I'm taller than they are," I replied as I made a final check of the suit's back bracing. "Or Thondian women, who think I'm ugly because I'm shorter than they are, and I'm also a caste-rejecting Human heathen."

"You're slender enough." She countered, "If you shaved that stupid fur off you could find a tall girl who might go with you. Ashahn's ass, Tris likes you enough, she'd definitely sleep with you if you did that."

I pulled myself free and glowered at her, "For the last fucking time, I'm not shaving my beard *or* my head. And didn't I just say that you don't do anything for me?"

She twitched her tarah outwards in disgust and killed the light on her wrist, "Fine, fine, but don't think I didn't notice."

I frowned as I turned away to grab a towel. "Notice what?"

"You said you didn't find me or other Trahcon women hot but you didn't say shit about Thondian girls."

I felt myself grimace at the slip.

Thondian women were just Human enough to be exotic really. Sure, they were universally above six feet tall and a bit overly built, but unlike Trahcon women they actually had small breasts. Add in the very feminine hips, the exotically long ears, and even with the lack of hair you could easily mistake them for some kind of dark-skinned fantasy elves.

Which I found enticing enough to be intriguing, and stereotypical enough to feel a bit guilty for being intrigued.

Not that it was really relevant since even a week's worth of glancing around on the Net told me that the enmity between Humanity and Thondians was more than a little vicious. Thondian culture was some kind of hybrid feudal/caste based system that had evidently rubbed the Ark Fleet the wrong way, something that had blown up when a couple of Human visitors had done something illegal and gotten themselves sentenced to terms of enslavement as a result.

The resulting diplomatic explosion had kicked off a minor war that hadn't lasted long, but the follow-up sniping, state-sponsored pirate attacks, and generally vicious cultural posturing had gone on for several decades in the aftermath.

"No Thondian women would touch me with a ten foot pole even if I was intrigued." I shook my head as I started cleaning my hands, "And for the twentieth time, I'm not really into casual relationships."

"Prude."

"Personal preference." I corrected.

She sighed and shook her head, "Did you even have someone before you volunteered to be turned into an ugly ice sculpture?"

It had actually been most of three years before then. "That's none of your business."

"Unnatural." She repeated stubbornly.

"Look on the bright side," I told her, "At least you've got me around to help *you* find company."

"Heh, true." She allowed, "Come on then, we've barely got time to get cleaned up if I drive like a maniac."

I snorted and followed her as she headed out. Despite her words she didn't fly any more recklessly than usual, and within an hour or so we'd taken turns showering, changing, and then were back in the air and headed for Koshun Minor.

My clothing options remained generally limited since I didn't want to order custom, keeping me restricted to the sections devoted to particularly tall Trahcon women. For that night I'd picked out a blood-red Strike-Wave jersey with the local team's clenched fist logo on either shoulder. Black pants offset the shirt, with the flared ankles decorated with red clouds and lightning, mostly covering the simple boots I hadn't felt like upgrading.

"I still can't believe you're wearing a fucking River-District jersey." Trenah shook her head as she guided us towards a small business complex a few blocks from the mansion, my own eyes flicking over the lights of the city.

"Rather hypocritical of you." I tugged on the hem a bit, making sure it wasn't tucked in. "I remember you bitching that they didn't have one in your size."

"You would have thought they would have." She groused as we landed on the side of the street, fitting neatly in between two other vehicles. "Lazy fucks."

I eyed her as we got out, as despite her words she was hardly all that dressed up either. I assumed most of the Thondian women inside would be wearing actual dresses, but Trenah had gone with the a plain turquoise shirt, black silk pants, and had a blood red sash riding down from her belt and around her upper hips. It was simple, striking, but most of all, was very... her.

It also did nothing to hide the hand cannon on her belt.

My own gun was a bit more concealed behind me, and I still didn't feel comfortable wearing it, but she'd insisted.

"You sure we won't have to turn these over when we go inside?" I asked as we started walking, following the other few late arrivals.

She snorted, "Ashahn's ass no. Half the bloody guests will be armed, it's not exactly a quiet holiday. If the True Sons are getting stupid in their ambition it would a great thing to hit."

That didn't exactly make my anxiety about going to an alien party thrown by some kind of noble-born millionaire go away, and I hadn't calmed down at all when we reached our destination.

"Ah, Trenah, Cieran." Xerol Shaaryak boomed out his greeting from the doors as we approached. Our host was dressed in an immaculate white suit that made us both look hilariously under-dressed, and even had a cane with a solid gold head clutched in one hand. "So good of you both to come."

We exchanged polite head tilts of respect, his to the right, ours to the left, before he cheerfully ushered us inside.

I'm not sure what the building was supposed to be but Xerol had turned it into a respectable little ball room. Most of the place was filled with small tables and chairs, packed to the brim with individuals from several species. Thondians predominated, but there was a sizable minority of Trahcon present, and I even caught a small group of Naule sequestered off on their own.

Shockingly I was the only Human present, but I was getting used to that.

More importantly, despite Xerol's outfit, neither of us had ended up being under or overdressed, which was a relief. At least half of the crowd was as casual as we were, with the rest falling above or below us. Only a few Thondians had apparently gone all out in their appearance, much like our host had, which probably marked them out as the rest of the local nobility. Highborn, I abruptly remembered from one of the cultural files I'd read.

My eyes were naturally drawn to a long bar which had been setup all along one side of the room. Behind it Ashul'tasir was directing the chaos while other bartenders raced around to fill orders.

"Feel free to mingle as you wish." Xerol gave a broad wave towards a large open area, "There will of course be dancing later, once dinner is completed."

Dancing... yeah, no thanks.

Apparently Trenah had the same thoughts on that as me, because he made a point of giving us both an ivory toothed grin, "It is traditional, as you well know. I will have to insist."

We exchanged a quick glance that earned us a deep chuckle, "Do not even think of it, either of you."

Trenah's eyes widened innocently as her tarah tilted up. "Think about what? Cie, you know what he's talking about?"

"I have no idea." My hands slid into my pockets as I did my best to look nonchalant, "No idea at all."

The cane thumped hard against my chest before I could dodge it, drawing a surprised grunt from me, and a similar one when he whapped it against Trenah's thigh, his smile never fading. "If you even think of leaving before I see you out there, I will beat you both until you can't walk."

Somehow I didn't doubt him for a moment.

"Enjoy the party." His grin widened as he nodded once to each of us before he strolled back towards the entrance, probably to greet any other fashionably late guests.

"By all of the fucking Aspects but I hate that man sometimes." Trenah shook her head at his back, "Every damn year he makes me dance with someone. I think he gets off on making me uncomfortable."

"Really?" I couldn't help but ask, "You've never tried to get out of here before that point?"

There was a deep wince and her right hand rose to rub her left shoulder, "Yeah... the first time."

I winced, "That bad?"

"Bastard had his bodyguards grab me the next day. Jabbed me with that stupid stick in the shoulder till it bruised, then made me spend the entire day watching recordings of... well... I'd rather not say." Her entire body shook as her face twisted, "I've had to deal with some bad shit, but by all of the Aspects it was awful. I wanted to claw out my own eyes *and* tear my tarah off by the end of the first hour. Swore by Ashahn herself I'd put up with one lousy dance if it meant never going through that again."

Well shit. "Think we could pretend to spin each other around call it done?"

She jerked her chin towards the bar, "Last year he made me dance with his bitch of a niece. What do you think?"

"Fuck." I sighed and followed her.

After that bit of news I needed a drink too.

It wasn't so much that I hated dancing, I didn't, but I'd gone into the night dead-set against anything even remotely resembling romance. Partly because I just didn't think I was mentally ready, partly because I had no real interest, but mostly because my stubborn pride insisted that I had to prove to Trenah that I didn't need feminine company to have a fulfilling restart to my life.

63

We fought our way through the crowd, making judicious use of our elbows and ability to completely ignore the dirty looks everyone threw at us.

The bartender, a thin rail of a Trahcon named Tris'ren, who was fine with her personal name being used, shook her head and tossed down our usual drinks without a word. A good ten or fifteen minutes of companionable drinking followed, both of us enjoying our refreshments while chatting with her after the rush abated a bit. Once the crowd had mostly dispersed to the tables or into smaller groups standing around randomly, a few others at the bar joined us. Strike-Wave was the main topic of discussion, particularly after a Naulian had noticed what I was wearing.

"Seriously, the River District?" He rumbled, his lower hands rubbing together while his upper set held onto his drink. His lips pulled back to show his sharp teeth, head shaking a little to make his long red hair move. "You mean the only Strike-Wave team on Alum to make the championship game and *lose* five years in a row?"

"At least they made it that far." I countered, "And from the superior, condescending tone, would you be a Core City fan?"

Laughter that sounded far less ape-like than I expected from his appearance bubbled up as he replied, "As if. Try Irrail."

A strangled, choking sound was enough of a warning for me to jerk my arm away before Trenah finished coughing up the beer that she'd practically inhaled. "Irrail!? They haven't made the post season in decades!"

The poor man had the good grace to look embarrassed, "We almost made it this year."

I jumped in before Trenah could really dig into him about the historically awful team, "Yeah, I remember watching the finals last month. That game was a fucking disgrace. I can't believe they haven't proved that official was bought off."

There was a rumble of agreement from the crowd around us, someone else agreeing more loudly. "Criminal is what it was."

Even Trenah had to give a nod to that. Popular consensus had it as the worst officiated game in the last century, and that had cost Irrail their spot. Not that they would have gone anywhere, but it was the principle of the thing.

That of course started everyone going further on the subject of the game, and we even roped Ashul'tasir in for a while. Eventually our little group split up, and Trenah had predictably found someone to slip away with. She normally seemed to prefer her own gender, but tonight she'd picked out a young man close to her own height. From the way his features were a bit flushed he'd already had a bit much to drink, but she was wasting little time in pushing more beer into his hands.

Which left me alone at the little stretch of the bar, save for Tris, and that suited me just fine. She wandered off to take other orders soon enough, leaving me free to just people watch.

It was kind of interesting, comparing them all to Humans, and to each other.

I made a game for myself trying to pick out the Thondians by their social ranking using just their clothing and attitude, and thought I got most of them right. Most of them were dressed just a bit above Trenah which I took to mean they were in the middle-class. A smaller number in the guise of staff lurked in corners or bussed tables, and I assumed they were all low-born. The two groups didn't interact at all, and Shaaryak and the handful of other dressed up Thondians likewise seemed to ignore both groups unless they had something to say.

The Trahcon were just as overly social as I could have guessed they would be. Members of both genders were happily chatting up anyone who happened to walk close enough, often without even bothering to see how interested they were in the first place. Other Trahcon energetically joined in whatever conversations began, while the Thondians largely held an air of weary acceptance.

In contrast, the Naule were pretty much all sticking with one another around a small group of tables in a corner. They left only to get more drinks or flag down a waiter, and only really seemed to interact with a small handful of Thondians who I guessed were co-workers of some kind.

I was amusing myself watching a very drunk Thondian trying to hit on a tall Trahcon woman who looked like she couldn't decide if she wanted to throw him out a window, drown herself in booze, or simply break down laughing, when someone new moved into the empty bar seat beside me.

The Thondian woman that settled into place was obviously upper-crust, highborn or whatever, I could tell that just from her clothing. She had the same rich brown skin as Xerol, and like him wore white, though her layered dress certainly revealed more skin than his suit. It made it easy to trace her very shapely hips and the slight bust, and also revealed plenty of the sand-colored bits of natural armor on her shoulders, neck, sternum, and arms.

Though... if anything the different coloration added rather than detracted from her exotic appeal.

Gem crusted earrings dangled from each of her pointed ears, reflecting the light as she turned her entire body to stare back at me. Her dark eyes narrowed as I unconsciously flicked my gaze up and down her slightly, and in spite of myself I felt my mouth go a bit dry.

Of course my burgeoning attraction more or less died when her lips twisted in distaste, her head tilting to the right in what I vaguely recalled to be a demonstration of superiority. She didn't even bother waiting for me to try and bow in reply before straightening and giving Tris an equally annoyed look.

….rich brat alert.

I'd mostly been good about keeping my head level and not accidentally insulting anyone, which I'd taken as a win considering how much alcohol I'd consumed over the last hour or so. I broke the streak by leaning a bit into her view, forcing her to notice me again, then I casually tilted my own head to the right before spinning my stool away as if dismissing her from reality.

My inner child, who I'd begun picturing as a tiny version of Trenah, drunkenly clapped their hands together in glee at the furious hiss she let out. "Hey Tris, can I get a refill?"

Tris glanced between us, tarah twitching madly, then she smirked and leaned a hip against her side of the bar as she likewise turned her back on the new arrival. "Sure. You want another Moonrise or you want to try something new for once?"

"Well I don't know," I spoke over the infuriated "*Bartender!*", "What do you think of that wine from Heshenna? Trenah won't shut up about it."

A gray hand rose to cup her chin, "It's not bad for Naule work," she had to raise her voice over a "*Hey! You!*", "Don't know if we have anything that's not newer than seventy though."

"Damn, I think she was mostly raving about the sixty-one." A hand clamped firmly on my shoulder and yanked me around to stare into a pair of furious eyes.

"Are you done *lowborn?*" The Thondian woman's voice was low but surprisingly melodic, and would probably have been pleasant to listen to if she wasn't furiously biting off each word. "I'd like to order a *drink*."

I let myself hesitate for a long moment before shrugging, "Order away."

"Get me-where did she go!?" Both of her hands hit the bar in anger, propelling her halfway to her feet as she looked both ways before finding Tris already working on my next Moonrise, her attention entirely occupied. The other bartenders were easily twice as far down, and were legitimately serving other guests.

"You know, you'd get a lot farther in life if you were more polite." I took a long sip from my still half-full drink as she turned that anger back towards me, "After all, it's never a good idea to insult the people who make your food and drinks. You never know what they might slip into them."

There was a long, seething sound somewhere between a sigh and a snarl, revealing her teeth. Most of them looked normal, if ivory colored, but up close it was easy to tell that her canines were longer and sharper than a Human's. Not quite as vampiric as Xerol's but very noticeable. "Do you have any idea who I am?"

"Nope." I had a pretty good idea, but I wasn't about to admit as much considering her attitude. "Do you have any idea who I am?"

Her eyes narrowed. "Someone with an overinflated sense of self importance for a lowborn alien. Obviously."

"Nice." I said, honestly a bit impressed. "Good reply there, I should have opened with something like that."

There was a long silence as she continued to glare at me, her fingers drumming on the bar as she waited for something. At first I thought it was just for Tris to come back, but it wasn't until I realized that she'd kept her eyes firmly on my face that I figured out that she was waiting for me to ask her name. It must have been some kind of cultural pride thing, where she couldn't simply offer it.

Trenah was a horrible influence one me. That or I was more drunk than I thought. Or maybe there was just something about her obvious upper-crust attitude that set off the sarcasm I usually kept inside my own head. "So, who do you root for?"

The woman blinked. Of all the possible things I could have said, she clearly hadn't been prepared for that. "I... what?"

"Who. Do. You. Root. For?" I enunciated each word carefully, just in case she was hard of hearing. And to help make my somewhat slurred Caranat a bit more understandable. "In Strike-Wave. You must have heard of it, *everyone* loves the game."

Her teeth showed again as she almost snarled. "You are insulting me, and I will not tolerate such disrespect from a lowborn alien."

My left arm waved expansively, "By all means then, leave the lowborn Human to his drinking and inflict your unpleasant attitude elsewhere."

"How.. .you..." She let out a seething, whistling sound between her teeth, "How *dare* you!"

"How dare I what? Be myself? I know, it really is quite daring of me isn't it. Most people can't handle the insanity, but I have to say you're holding up all right." I gave her a wink and fully channeled Trenah. "We're getting along *so* well. Perhaps we should dance later? Maybe find a secluded corner and indulge ourselves?"

I realized I'd stepped into something the moment her expression went from one of murderous rage to cunning calculation, brown and black eyes shifting to the slowly filling dance floor before snapping back to me.

"Since you've asked." And damn me if she didn't blink and look down demurely, tilting her head to the left slightly, the very picture of an apologetic lady as she slid out of her chair and bowed. "I must beg your forgiveness, and insist that you allow me to take you up on that offer of a dance."

"What?" My buzzed mind whirled as she shifted gears. "Ah, actually I-"

I frantically tried to find Tris, hoping that she could help me get out of this.

"Excellent." A strong hand practically yanked me upright, not giving me the chance to get away. Upright she proved to be a couple of inches taller than me, and her fingers were like steel traps wrapped around my arm. "You do know how to dance, do you not?"

"Well, not to your kind of music, so why don't I just stay-"

"Then I shall lower myself to guide you." She trapped my hand in the crook of her arm, dragging me away from the bar. I cast a desperate glance around, trying to find Trenah in the hopes that she might save me, only to see her already on the dance floor and drunkenly lurching around with her boy-toy of choice for the night.

I did my best to escape, and briefly got free at the edge of the dance floor. I had no idea what the hell her plan was, and even buzzed I was getting an increasingly bad feeling that I would be in trouble if I didn't figure it out. "All right, all right! Fine! You win! Who are you?"

"Hand, here." My right arm was grasped firmly into hers, "Other hand, here." And my left onto the side of her strong waist, more near her stomach than her back. "Now, we dance."

And we did. Not particularly well, considering I had no idea what I was doing and she growled at me every time I tried to say something. Thankfully the current routine was slow enough that I was able to avoid stepping on her, though it gave me plenty of time to be mortified every-time I saw Trenah lurch past with her partner half-hanging off of her.

We went through three dances, and I started to relax and even sort-of-enjoy myself towards the end. Especially since whatever my partner had planned didn't seem to be working out for her. She held her polite smile through the first song, but it became strained in the second and she started to look unsure of herself the longer I simply gave in to what she wanted.

By the third she was definitely frustrated and my enjoyment was back up to full strength.

My smirk was my final mistake because it set her off again. Her dark eyes narrowed to slits as the song began to wind down, and she pulled me closer against her body and spoke quietly enough that I had to stay there to hear her.

"My name is Nynsi Shaaryak." She murmured.

When my mouth opened to tell her that I'd guessed that, she abruptly yanked me closer with a flex of her arms and pressed our lips together.

It was... wildly different from kissing a Human woman. She had a discernible taste beyond that of her own drinks, something... strong, like earthy herbs in an entirely pleasant sort of way. The kiss lasted just a handful of moments, then she pulled back and glanced around before her own smirk returned.

"Enjoy explaining this to my uncle and cousins." She all but whispered. "Maybe next time you will respect your betters, Human."

I flinched and cautiously glanced over my shoulder.

To my left, Xerol was staring at me with no real expression on his face, the fingers of both hands wrapped around his cane. To my right, two Thondian men a bit shorter than he but far more muscled were wearing dark blue suits... and both of them were blatantly displaying their seething anger.

My heart practically stopped, the momentary rush from her kiss vanished, and her grin only grew wider at the resulting expression on my face.

Oh... well... shit.

I – VII

I managed to escape from the holiday party alive, though mildly panicked.

Nynsi had slipped away quietly, leaving me free to retreat while her cousins and Uncle had stared me down. There must have been some kind of disturbance at the entrance, because one of his guards had moved up to talk in Xerol's ear before all three of them had headed in that direction. I hadn't wasted a moment after that, running off to find Trenah so that we could get the hell out of there.

Trenah and her date, both of them laughing at nothing in particular, had guided me out to her car through a side exit and gotten us home before anyone could come to kill me.

I'd collapsed on the couch with headphones in place when we got back, Trenah shaking me awake after they'd finished and she'd kicked her one-night-stand out. That had let me zombie-shuffle off to bed without hearing things I didn't want to hear, and by the time I'd woken up I'd half-convinced myself that the entire sequence had been a weird dream.

That hope had lasted until I'd checked my mail and saw a message from Trenah saying I wasn't to wake her up for anything short of a natural disaster.

Which left me waiting for the inevitable really.

I prepared as best I could. I made myself a heavy breakfast, double checked that the door was locked, that Trenah's security system was running, and then I settled down to try and enjoy the day.

Needless to say, that plan didn't exactly go well. I jumped at almost every loud noise from the television, found myself pointlessly checking the door cameras, and overall scaring myself stupid.

Still, I really only had myself to blame. I really shouldn't have gotten that drunk, or needled her as much as I had.

I was staring into the fridge, wondering what I could eat for lunch, when the doorbell finally chimed. My throat went dry as I slowly got my wrist-comp online so that I could check the cameras. The terror flipped over to confusion when I saw who was there, and I kept frowning until the bell rang again..

Padding over, I opened the door to stare flatly at Nynsi Shaaryak. Her dress was a casual light blue number that hung on her powerful frame, although this time I wasn't nearly as tempted to check her out. What's more she didn't look nearly as hungover as I was.

Totally unfair.

"Do I want to know how you knew where I lived?" I asked by way of greeting.

Her dark eyes narrowed as she glanced warily over my shoulder, neither of us bothering to tilt our heads or bow or anything. She was probably making sure Trenah wasn't present. "My uncle... has instructed me to apologize."

When I'd woken up in a panic, *that* wasn't something I'd imagined I'd hear today. "I... what?"

There was a little growl, "May I come in or are you going to make me stand out here?"

My own eyes narrowed, a spike of annoyance driving the confused stutter away. "Here is fine. I spent all night worried that Xerol or your cousins were going to kill me."

"Rehat and Chehat desired to do so." She admitted, making my jaw clench a little.

"What stopped them?" I asked.

"My uncle. He... chastised me for my behavior. I should not have made a spectacle of you on the dance floor. I should not have tried to inspire my relatives to go after you." She bared her teeth in obvious irritation, showing off the sharp canines once more. "Does that make you happy? You left quickly enough that he couldn't interrogate you, so he cornered me before I could depart. I cannot lie to my own Patriarch, not well enough anyway, so he received the full story."

"Oh." I felt lighter almost at once. "All right, then yes. I'm a bit happy."

"Sufficiently happy to allow me to leave?"

"We've been over this, I'm not stopping you." My hands waved as her familiar attitude came back, this time without the alcoholic filter that had made it seem mildly amusing. "Go inflict yourself on someone else."

That murderous expression returned in an instant, but whatever she was going to say in response was cut off when I slapped the control panel to shut the door in her face.

I'd just turned away when the doorbell rang again. Her voice was muted thanks to the steel, even though I was pretty sure she was shouting over another ring. "Open up! Please!"

Part of me wanted to leave her out there, but the doorbell wasn't exactly quiet. If she kept at it she would definitely wake Trenah up. Growling a little, I reached out and slapped the button again. "What the fuck else is there to say?"

She still looked plenty mad, but she jerkily dipped her head to the left and managed to force the words out. "Do you... do you accept my apology, friend of my uncle?"

"Yes, fine. Whatever." I tipped my head just enough to acknowledge what she'd done. "I accept. Anything else?"

"Why do you have to be so *aggravating* Human?" Her hands flew upwards as she gave another one of those seething, whistling sounds, "I'm *trying* to apologize."

"First, my name is Cieran, not Human. Second, you're doing a shit job of it." I shot back, "You were trying to get me beaten up, or killed! How many of your people were at that party? You think they'd have taken me at my word that I wasn't trying to force myself onto you?"

"I... fine... all right, I'm sorry, I've already had to apologize to my uncle for having to explain to my cousins that you did not press yourself on me." There was definite pain there, she wasn't enjoying the fact that she'd gone a bit overboard and was being forced to admit that she'd done so. "I should have thought of that before I did it."

"Fine..." I blew out a long breath and forced myself to calm down. Yes, she'd set me up pretty badly last night, but she was at least trying to apologize. And I hadn't exactly been a gentleman at the party either. Nor was I being one right now, and I didn't even have the excuse of alcohol to fall back on.

Sure, she was a bit uptight, but I dealt with Trenah on a daily basis. I could deal with Xerol's niece.

I took a few more calming breaths then tilted my head to the left slightly, hoping I looked appropriately apologetic, "I'm sorry as well. I shouldn't have lost my temper just now, and I probably went a little overboard last night."

Her eyes narrowed slightly, then she also seemed to relax. "I accept, friend of my uncle."

Friend seemed like a strong word, but I didn't feel the need to correct her. "So... are there any Thondian customs for apologies I should know about? You don't have a sniper on me right now do you?"

"Regrettably I do not." I didn't quite gape at her, and her lips twitched into something like a teasing smile. "Here I thought you could handle mere barbs."

"Ha fucking ha." I replied flatly.

She smirked and then shook her head, "My only company is one of my uncle's Harath'krem."

I blinked and took a step forwards, glancing around. My best guess was that the term referred to some kind of bodyguard, and I found her after a few seconds. She proved to be a Trahcon woman of average height lounging against the railing a few yards away. Her armored vest and dark uniform made her stand out even before you got to the pistol and sword combination on her belt.

"Huh." I shook my head and slipped back inside, not quite sure what to make of that but doubting that Xerol would have left his niece's security to someone incompetent. "She with to make sure you apologized?"

Dark lips quivered slightly, "Something like that."

I groaned as it clicked, "To make sure that we *both* apologized?"

"Yes. He indicated he was less than happy with how you handled your liquor."

"Of course he was." I sighed and rubbed tiredly at my face. Way to make a good impression on Trenah's main supplier of work and the man who'd be evaluating my own project. "Well, we both did."

Her head tilted directly forwards in the tiniest of nods, "We did."

"So." I shook my head and leaned against the door-frame, "Not going to storm off in an aristocratic huff? Not desperate to get away from lowborn scum like me?"

"Well you *are* Human, so you're not truly lowborn. Merely alien, I misspoke in my anger." Her arms crossed, "And I already asked to come in."

I blinked. "Why? You're not going to try and get me in hot water with Xerol again are you?"

"By the Fourth Pillar I swear that I shall not," Her arms uncrossed, hands coming together in what seemed like a religious gesture. "I merely wished to make you lunch to complete my apology, away from my uncle's Harath'krem."

"Wait, you *want* to spend time with me?"

The Thondian woman gave me an amused look, all of the tension visibly gone from her body. She still held herself a little stiffly in my opinion, but that seemed to just be how Thondians were. "Are we going to have this conversation standing in the doorway, or while we eat food?"

That was a fair point. "Are you going to try and poison me?"

"Would you like me to?"

"No, not really." My first instinct was to say no, but I also didn't want to insult her again, and by extension piss off Xerol. Not right after we seemed to have patched things up and hopefully avoided any kind of problem. I wasn't really sure what her abrupt shift in attitude was about... and some curious part of me wanted to dig deeper into whatever was going on. "I suppose that'll be fine. Come on in, Trenah's sleeping off her hangover so try to keep your voice down."

I stepped aside to let her in, and made a point to shut and lock the door after her. While she walked deeper into the apartment, I watched on the cameras as the guard came into sight. She settled herself into place against the wall next to Trenah's apartment. I half expected her to knock and ask to come in, but she simply bowed her head as though content to wait.

Bemused, I turned around and followed Nynsi Shaaryak through the small living area and towards the kitchen, "So, is this some kind of religious tenet? You're obligated to cook a meal for someone in apology?"

"Hardly. This is me trying to avoid my uncle for a few hours." She was already poking around the fridge, having apparently wasted no time, "And while you're hardly my first choice of company, you are more companionable than Ghai."

I snorted. "That sounded dangerously close to a compliment while still managing to insult me."

"A particularly lovely tree is probably better company than she is." She paused for a moment, then shook her head. "That is unfair, she is extremely capable as a fighter and trainer, but you're more likely to find water in the desert than hear her speak a dozen words in a day. It is hardly her fault, she has a lingering injury, but it makes spending time with her... trying."

"There we go." My head shook as I smiled, "Wouldn't want to think you actually wanted to be around me now."

"You may be surprised," She offered, glancing at me. Her motions were a bit odd, she rarely turned her neck at all, instead twisting at her waist to regard me. It had to tie into the whole head-tilting to indicate respect thing, and I made yet another note to do more research. "You're nothing like I would have expected from one of your species."

That made me blink. "In a good way?"

"In a curious way, if nothing else. You intrigue me."

"Huh." I offered quietly, really not sure what to say to that. Evidently I wasn't the only one confused here. That was probably part of why she'd elected to stick around.

Nynsi turned back to what she was doing. "We will discuss it later. What does your kind prefer to eat for this meal?"

A hand waved vaguely at the fridge. "If it's in there I'll eat it, otherwise why would we have it?"

"Must you answer everything with sarcasm?" She yanked out a few containers of a local fish harder than was strictly necessary, and moved on to grabbing a few potential sides. "Where are your spices?"

"Right, two cabinets down. Knives and cutting board are in the one to the left. Your other left. There you go."

The rest of the meal preparation went smoothly enough. I stopped needling her, she stopped antagonizing me, and between us we managed to make a reasonable little lunch. She'd done a pretty good job on the fish itself, not burning anything and using a pleasant combination of spices. The noodles and little shrimp-like crustaceans she'd done on the side weren't quite as I preferred to make them, and not as good as Trenah's, but were hardly bad.

"So..." I asked after a few minutes of silent eating had passed, my curiosity forcing me to start talking, "Why are you avoiding your uncle? Besides last night."

"That is largely the reason." She replied, stabbing at a cut of fish with her fork. "He can be extremely overbearing when he believes someone has made a mistake, and I have had my fill of being lectured. May I ask you a question in return?"

I sipped some water and waved a hand in permission.

"This is Laria's apartment, is it not? Why do you live with her?"

I blinked a little, "Xerol didn't tell you? I assumed he knew."

"He likely does but he did not see fit to tell me." Her eyes abruptly narrowed, "You are not... *with* her, are you? I would lose all regard for you if you are."

That made me snort a little, "That's a bit harsh, but no, I'm not. I don't particularly find Trahcon attractive. We're friends and she lets me live here in exchange for me taking less money as her assistant."

"Hn." She hummed noncommittally, her body shifting a little as she took a quick look around. "You said she is asleep? At this time?"

"Sleeping off her hangover." I reminded her. "I overdid a little last night, but she went way overboard."

She took another, longer glance around. It was hard to tell with the lighting and her dark eyes, but I was pretty sure she focused heavily on the hall leading to the bedrooms. "I see. How did the two of you meet? Laria has a reputation as somewhat of a shut-in."

I could only guess that Trenah was considered as such only by her own species, or maybe by Thondians. Filing that away, I alternated between eating the rest of my lunch and telling my very brief life story up until this point, glossing over most of my life on Earth. I still wasn't quite comfortable remembering my first life, much less talking about it with someone I barely knew. Thankfully the Thondian woman seemed content to not ask questions about that part.

But it also felt... strangely good to talk with someone who wasn't Trenah.

"Fascinating." She murmured when I finished, her hands folded primly in front of her. "That certainly explains things, and I can see why my uncle wishes to make you a friend of the family."

"Friend is a bit strong," I admitted. "I mean, I've only met him a few times. I'm *friendly* with him sure, I'd hardly want to insult the leader of a community. Especially when he provides a good portion of my boss's work, but we're not exactly close."

Her voice turned a bit dry, "Cieran, I entirely expected you to lash out at me verbally at the bar, to physically remove me from your person when I dragged you to the dance floor, and then to react with disgust or violence when I forced myself on you. The fact that you did none of those things is more than enough to make my uncle intrigued, even before the fact that you are the assistant to his favorite freelance mechanic."

I winced slightly. "I read a little, I knew things between our species were bad, but *that* bad?"

"The only Humans I met before you only ever referred to me by various slurs." She stated, voice a bit flat. "They were deeply unpleasant beings and left me with a less than positive opinion on your species. I hope that somewhat explains my initial reaction to you."

It rather did. Didn't really excuse it, but it definitely explained it. "So that's why you're having lunch with me, make sure I'm not hiding some kind of hatred for you?"

"You are disturbingly perceptive." She tilted her head a little to the left, something about her smile telling me she was impressed. "Quite so. My uncle was certain that you could not have held back any such... opinions... considering how much you drank last night, but I wanted to be sure considering the nature of your assigned project."

...and Xerol's niece knew what I was working on for him. "You know about that?"

"Come now, Cieran." Nynsi chided me. "Did you really think my uncle handles all of the family business personally?"

"Fair point." I shook my head a little, "Is that mostly what you do? Help him?"

"I primarily run security as well as handling various export businesses." She set her fork on her empty plate and leaned back slightly in her chair. "In truth it is less interesting than it sounds. I vastly prefer-"

I didn't get to find out what she preferred because Trenah shambled out of the hallway just then. My guest closed her mouth with an audible snap and tensed while my friend seemed oblivious to her presence. She lazily finished pulling a shirt on while shuffling towards the kitchen, which made it easy to tell when her brain caught up with reality.

Trenah froze in the act of turning away, and only slowly came back around to stare at the table.

"Cieran." She said in a flat, even voice. "I know I've said a lot of crap about finding someone, but *please* tell me you didn't fuck this uptight bitch."

The Thondian woman bristled, her head tilting down and to the right at once. "Laria. As uncouth and unpleasant as ever."

I sighed and felt my vague hopes about making a second friend go up in flames. "Can we please keep this civil? My head is still pounding a bit."

Both women started to say something at the same time, stopped, then Shaaryak spoke before Trenah could try again. "It is quite all right, I will take my leave. Cieran, I would like to continue this discussion later. Perhaps at Forever tomorrow evening? As my uncle's head of security I am interested in your concepts for the project."

When she phrased it like that, I didn't really see what choice I had. "Sure, when?"

She gave me a time, gave me a quick little bow, and then abused her long legs to stride out the door before Trenah could do more than glare at her back.

"So you want to tell me what the fuck that was about?" I asked once I'd heard the door shut behind my guest.

"No." Trenah said flatly. "I'm going with tomorrow. That woman is a massive pain in the ass, you'll see."

I shook my head. "She seemed fine enough, once she calmed down."

"You'll see."

I – VIII

Trenah refused to say anything more on the subject of Nynsi Shaaryak for the rest of that day as well as the next. Part of that seemed to be her general anger that I'd let the other woman into *her* apartment, but mostly it seemed to be her desire for me to see whatever it was for myself.

Despite her opinion, Trenah had joined me in wearing nicer clothing than we normally would have for a simple trip to the bar, both of us in the same outfits we'd taken to Xerol's holiday party. And, just as then, we were both armed, though I remained just as uncomfortable with the small sub-machine gun attached to my belt.

"We'll need to get you something more appropriate." Trenah said as she noticed me fiddling with the gun. We were about halfway to the bar, her hands steady on her car's controls. "Maybe a small pistol of some kind, or a technical launcher."

I glanced at her, "What would I need specialized grenades for?"

"Disabling people without killing them." She suggested, "Figured you'd prefer that."

"Ah." That was true. "I thought those were mostly incendiaries or shield breakers."

There a small snort. "Those are just the most popular. There's stun models, ones that discharge electricity, gas types... if you can think of it someone's fucking made a type for it. Think there's even a kind that spits out some kind razor-wire to flay people."

The mental image made my stomach churn. "Who the fuck would want that?"

"Slavers." Her tarah tilted down and out in disgust. "Fuckers like to make examples of people to scare everyone else into line."

I shook my head. "Ugh. Remind me to thank the Matriarch again, whenever she shows up."

"Can't blame you." Hands slowly pulled the throttle back and pushed the main wheel down as we began to descend towards the bar's parking lot. "Looks like we're early."

I made a vague sound of acknowledgment. We still had some time before the appointment, and I rather hoped that Shaaryak would be fashionably late. The longer Trenah had to sit around in a bar, the more likely it was that she would wander off to start hitting on someone. In a perfect world she'd be too busy trying to get laid to pick a fight with the Thondian businesswoman.

I had exactly no hope that lovely plan would work out, but it was a nice dream to have.

We parked in the lot and headed inside to find the place mostly empty. Tris was lounging behind the bar, and the only customers were a small party occupying one of the regular tables. Two Trahcon women along with a single man were sipping from beer and talking in low tones, picking at appetizers.

After considering the various booths and tables for a moment, I decided to head for the bar instead.

"Cieran." Tris greeted, "Trenah. You're in early today."

"Meeting with Xerol's niece." I said before Trenah could say anything. "My usual, please."

Both of the bartender's tarah angled up and out in intrigue, then she nodded once and glanced at Trenah. After getting a nod in return, she stepped away and started making our drinks. She was still about halfway through the process when the front door opened, and Ghai the Harath'krem stepped inside.

She was dressed and armed the same as she had been yesterday, both of her hands resting on her weapons. After a quick glance she nodded once and got clear of the doorway, letting Nynsi Shaaryak enter.

The tall woman had evidently felt like dressing up as well, her dress replaced with the same kind of business suit I'd seen her uncle wearing. Hers was a charcoal gray in color, and perfectly tailored to show off the body beneath while still looking professional. I mostly managed to not check her out beyond a cursory glance, keeping my eyes on hers as she strode confidently past her bodyguard.

There was the tiniest hitch to her step when she saw Trenah, but she kept her expression pleasantly neutral as she walked towards us.

"Cieran." She greeted me with a small smile, giving me a tiny but direct nod that I returned after a second or two.

"Miss Shaaryak." I replied easily. "Did you want to get a table or booth?"

Trenah spoke before she could, "Not until I have a word with her about the fucking storm she tried to call down on your furry head. Privately."

I grimaced when the taller woman pressed her lips together into a thin line. "He and I have already spoken and exchanged apologies for what occurred. I fail to see what you may have to add at this point."

"Well I have crap to add all the fucking same." Trenah growled, "You want to do this now, or you want me to show up at Xerol's place tomorrow and do it in front of him?"

"Trenah..." I tried to speak up only to receive a sharp enough glare that I held my hands up in wordless surrender.

The Thondian woman looked like she'd rather cut her own hand off than go with Trenah, but the threat was apparently sufficient to force her into going along with it. She gave my friend a tight nod and waved towards the exit. The two slipped out, the door closing just as Tris set my drink down in front of me.

I took a heavy pull from the Moonrise and tried to let the alcohol calm me down a bit.

A bit of motion on my left made me glance over as I set the glass down. Ghai the Harath'krem settled onto the stool there, her eyes proving to be an electric blue, and her features were actually rather elegant. Almost delicate and far more feminine than I was used to seeing from her people. I mean, I didn't really think of Trahcon as being all that attractive, but the woman next to me was probably the closest I'd seen to a beautiful one by Human standards.

"They aren't going to get into a fist fight or anything, are they?" I asked, trying not to stare more than was appropriate.

Ghai pursed her lips before speaking. Her voice was almost inaudibly quiet and rasping, and I abruptly understood what I'd been told the day before. "Unlikely. Dislike, not hatred."

I needed a few moments to turn her short words into a full sentence in my head. "Uh, you sure? Because Trenah really seems like she hates her."

She reached out to take the Blood Tide that Tris had made for Trenah and smiled faintly, "Bluster."

My head shook a little but I didn't stop her from sipping from the glass. Her head tilted a little bit at the taste, letting me glance down at her neck... and making me wince in sympathy. While it was mostly covered by her high-collar shirt and the armor, I could see the edges of a vicious scar along her throat.

Which definitely explained her ruined voice.

Some curious part of me wanted to ask what had happened, but instead I simply lifted my own glass to my lips again. That seemed far too personal a question to ask the first time I spoke with her. So instead of talking further, I simply stayed quiet, something that seemed to suit Ghai just fine as she likewise continued to sip from her own cup. Tris came back from the kitchen with some bread, twitched her tarah on seeing Ghai with Trenah's drink, then put the plate down and wandered off to check on the table.

The pair of us managed to eat a slice apiece before our respective companions returned. Neither of them seemed to be any happier than they'd been when they'd left, looking anywhere but at one another as they walked back to us. The Thondian woman used her longer legs to come up on my right side, forcing Trenah to choose between sitting next to her or Ghai.

Trenah, as could be expected, chose the latter. She squawked furiously on seeing her drink halfway gone and promptly began a one-sided argument with the thief in question. Which at least distracted her and let me swing my stool over so I could face Nynsi Shaaryak without twisting my body uncomfortably.

"So..." My voice trailed off.

"It was as expected as it was unpleasant." She replied, her voice somewhat flat. "Our relationship has never been a positive one."

"Do I want to know why?"

"It is of no matter." A hand waved dismissively. "Allow me to get a drink and then we may begin our discussion."

I nodded agreeably before turning to wave so that Tris knew we had more work for her. A couple of minutes later Nynsi had a glass of dark blue wine in one hand, and the pair of us were settled at a table a bit away from the others.

"On to business." She stated to open the conversation, "How much progress have you made with the exoskeleton?"

"Not much." I admitted, "I tore out all of the damaged parts, adjusted the interior so I could actually test it, and installed a new power core. I can walk around inside of it but not much more than that. Everything else is just vague plans and too many pieces taking up space in our shop right now. I'm guessing you have requests?"

Nynsi nodded, "Indeed. First and foremost, how confident are you of providing a viable combat asset?"

I gave her a somewhat helpless shrug. "This is my first real project of any kind, and I'm dealing with technology I've never touched before. I understand the basics and the Net is full of articles I'm stealing ideas from, but at the end of the day I'm still an amateur working with second-hand parts. A supervised amateur maybe, but I've got limits."

"I see." There was a small sigh, "I do not believe we require anything overly advanced, nor impossibly complicated. Speed and dexterity are not priorities, we need symbols of power and authority more than a failed attempt at creating a truly mobile battle-suit."

Meaning they needed big, hulking, intimidating guards more than they needed something actually capable of running around and fighting.

"Hmm." I hummed softly, looking over as the only other party in the bar rose from their table and headed for the exit. "So you want something with a lot of armor and shielding, maybe a bunch of back-up systems. Walking speed is all right?"

"I would prefer something faster if possible, but if not it isn't a deal-breaker." She assured me, likewise glancing at the departing trio before returning her dark eyes to me. "Consider defensive ability and reliability to be the foremost requirements, followed by firepower, and speed only after that."

A hand rose to rub at my still-growing-in beard. "I'm pretty sure it can haul a lot of armor plating considering the power-plant and the skeleton. I'll have to do research on shielding. Trenah and I had a few ideas on the weapons, I was thinking some kind of standard hand-held equipment with coolant lines, she was considering putting some kind of pistol in the forearms."

She took a sip of wine before replying, "A technical launcher would be superior in regards to built-in weapons, if that is possible."

"It might be." I shrugged a little, "I'll read up on the subject."

"Good." While she had more questions regarding the suit, my relative inexperience and the fact that I'd only been working on it for a week rather limited my responses. She caught on to that fairly quickly and, after making sure I knew to record absolutely everything so that my work could be replicated, she changed the subject.

"Let us speak more personally now that business is done." Nynsi said, regarding me with the same kind of curious interest she'd had at the apartment. "What kind of being are you, Cieran Kean? Beyond a Human who holds no antipathy for my people."

"That's a rather vague question." I noted with an amused shake of my head. "I'm guessing you want me to say something more than the fact that I'm a Human male in his mid twenties from a desert city on Earth."

Her lips twitched, "What are your interests? Beyond Strike-Wave, as I believe I can assume you're a fan of the Talon-Fists."

I tugged a little at the jersey I was wearing, "They seemed an appropriate team to root for, considering it's where I live. It's a fun game to watch, though I do wish there was a non-Trahcon version. Are there Thondians who can play?"

"You mean are there any who can manipulate dimensional energy?" She asked before shrugging, "Naturally? No, but there are a few cybernetic procedures in the Ascendancy that can enable us to use abilities similar to what the Trahcon can do. It's rather unpredictable however, not everyone responds... well. So far as I know it's limited to military volunteers."

I winced and nodded, "So not exactly something they do just so people can play a sport."

"Not really." She agreed, "What about your own species?"

"I honestly have no idea if there's anything like that."

Nynsi shook her head and smiled again, "Of course, my apologies, that was an ill-thought question."

My eyebrows rose as I caught something in the way her lips curled. "Was it?"

When all she gave me was a polite expression, I elaborated, "Was it a poor question, or are you testing me to see if I'm really from a cryo-ship?"

"You are disturbingly perceptive." She mused, punctuating her words with a sip of wine before continuing, "Far more so than those others of your species I have met. It is more like-"

I never found out what it was like, because at that moment the fucking entrance to the bar exploded inwards, sending bits of wooden shrapnel flying through the place.

The reactions of everyone present were rather mixed. Apart from the pair of us, the only other people present were Ghai and Trenah at the bar, and then Tris wiping down the table the other party had used. The three of them all brought their hands up in pure reflex, ghostly blue-white barriers appearing between them and the entrance as they summoned up shields.

I pretty much froze until a hand seized the side of my jersey and hauled me out of my chair as Nynsi rolled out of hers.

"Get to the bar you two!" Tris shouted, her free hand yanking a pistol out from under her uniform.

I managed to recover enough that the Thondian woman didn't have to drag me along with her, the pair of us scrambling up to our feet and running for it just as the attackers began to push their way inside. Guns began to boom and bark as I instinctively ducked my head, planting my hands and vaulting the bar in a move I couldn't have possibly pulled off without the adrenaline in my system.

Nynsi followed me within a second, a pistol appearing in her hands so fast that it looked like she'd simply summoned it into being there, "Who!?"

"Fucking True Sons!" Trenah snarled as her monster pistol fired several times in sequence, and then she, Tris, and Ghai were all piling in behind the bar with us. All three were shooting half-blind towards the door, and I forced my shaking hands to finally grab my own weapon and pull it from my belt.

I flinched as an incoming round shattered a bottle above me, then managed to get my head up just enough to take a quick look.

One of the gang members, a Thondian, was already laying face-first just inside of the door, a puddle of blood spreading out around him. Just ahead I saw another member of the same species throw himself inside one of the booths, the young man screaming his head off for his friends to help him while he fired blindly around the half-wall.

I flinched back as one of the random shots came too close for comfort, getting my gun up and vaguely aimed just as his help arrived.

Two Naule surged in through the doorway, moving just like the one at the shop had, using their extra arms to propel them faster while their upper hands clutched guns. They were fast, faster than I thought physically possible, but they were coming in through a narrow doorway with five armed people on the other side.

I pulled the trigger but I honestly don't know if it was my bullets that killed them. The first poor bastard barely made it through the doorway before tumbling down, his dark blood spraying everywhere. His companion made it maybe a yard past him, mostly because his friend had absorbed most of our shots, before a round blew his head apart into bits of flesh and brain matter.

My stomach churned horribly at the sight, but I clenched my jaw and did my best to keep the drink and bread from coming back up.

"Tris!" Trenah shouted as Nynsi and Ghai kept the only gang member who'd made it inside pinned down, "Is there anyone in back?"

"Handle it!"

She didn't bother replying, darting down the length of the bar and vanishing into the kitchens. Ghai gave Nynsi a quick glance, jerked her chin in that direction, and then was off without a word. She moved even more smoothly and quickly than Trenah, actually drawing her sword with her free hand as she disappeared into the kitchen with my friend.

They'd barely left when our uninvited guest shouted from his hiding place, "Hey! Grays! We've got this place surrounded, give up the old bitch and no one else has to get killed!"

The old... Ashul'tasir?

I exchanged a confused look with Nynsi before the idiot kept going, "I promise we'll let the rest of you go if you just drag her out here!"

Instead of replying Tris reached under the counter and grabbed a rectangular block of metal. A quick jerk of her fingers expanded it out into the shape of a short-barreled shotgun. She rose and fired in a single smooth motion, the weapon far louder than the pistols everyone else had been using.

I had no idea why the bar had bullet-proof materials in the booths, but whatever had been installed hadn't been intended to deal with the massive round the shotgun put out. The man let out a surprisingly high pitched yowl of surprise when wood and metal exploded into shrapnel, then dove out of the booth when Tris pulled the trigger a second time.

My finger tightened as he tried to scramble to his feet, my rounds hammering down some kind of shielding before Nynsi's pistol barked and tore his throat apart.

"Slide down." Nynsi gave me a firm shove with a shapely hip. "We'll have better fields of fire from the end."

I nodded, trying to not twitch as my heart hammered wildly. "Right."

Tris nodded as we darted past her, both of us staying below the level of the counter until we reached the end and set ourselves up again.

I licked my lips nervously as gunfire sounded from the back, a male voice screaming in pain before being abruptly cut off. So at least Trenah and Ghai were keeping that entrance clear for us, leaving us free to watch this one.

Something clattered down the floor from the way we'd come, and I jerked when a metallic box hit the side of my leg. I glanced up to see Tris nod impatiently at it, "Technical grenades! Grab a few and throw them at the doorway, they'll attach automatically."

"How many weapons do you have here?" I called back as I knelt, trusting the two women to handle watching while I inspected the box.

"Enough." Tris replied. "Three grenades, I'll trigger them!"

I nodded and focused. It looked like the box was some kind of launcher, with a tiny barrel sticking out from one side, but thankfully it had large lettering indicating where I could pull it open. Inside were small discs, each as large as an old fifty-cent coin, all of them stacked neatly atop one another. I pulled one out, turned it around in my fingers once, then at an impatient motion from Tris got up and threw it towards the door.

It flew straight, more by the design than any skill on my end, and collided with the wall just above the open doorway. I waited for it to fall but true to Tris's statement it seemed to stick in place. Shaking my head, I quickly grabbed another and tossed it just as someone new started shouting from outside.

"Hey!" A deep-throated woman, maybe a Naule, maybe a Thondian, called. "In the bar!"

"What?" Tris raised her voice to shout back, "You done already?"

"Hardly bitch! Turn over the gray named Tasir, and that traitorous Shaaryak whore, or we burn this place to the ground with you in it!"

Nynsi's lips pulled back to show her teeth when Tris let out a barking laugh. "Good luck with that you fucking drift-water scum!"

"They're going to rush us soon." Nynsi murmured into my ear, "This bar isn't in an active area, but someone will still have heard the gunfire even if we didn't get an alert out. If they don't hurry up security will be all over them."

I nodded to show that I'd heard, trying to stay focused. This was hardly like the last time. Then it had been bang-bang-bang. Literally. Door open, door closed, people entered, people died, that was it. No thinking required until the aftermath.

Now... there were three corpses staining the tile flooring with their bodily fluids, and we were waiting for an unknown number of enemies to charge us. Our position was good, but there just wasn't enough space between the doorway and the bar to make a good killing zone.

And if even a few got inside we would be easy targets stuck behind the bar. One grenade would probably be enough.

Fortunately for us our attackers weren't exactly the military elite. Rather than bursting in silently, or worse, using more explosives to open a new door, they came yelling and screaming straight in through the tiny front entrance.

Two Thondians died first, too concerned with getting over the bodies rather than shooting at us. Another pair of Naule took more of an effort to kill, a few of their shots blowing out more beer bottles and a couple even catching Nynsi. Whatever shielding she had under the suit kept her alive, but it still made her growl what were probably unladylike curses in her own tongue.

Tris set off the grenades just as three more people began to come in, two more Thondians with a shorter figure behind them. The tiny bombs went off with surprisingly muted flashes of fire and dull whumps of noise. Both men went down screaming, their skin audibly sizzling as their clothing erupted in flame. Nynsi killed them both as they frantically tried to roll around to put the fires out, leaving me as the only person ready to shoot the last target.

The Naule who surged in was clad from head to toe in dark gray armor, a rifle held in her upper arms while her lower hands yanked two objects off of her belt.

I barely had time to realize that it was a pair of grenades before Nynsi all but tackled me, smothering me under her as Tris let out a snarling sound. She must have deflected one with her sorcery, but the second hit the wall above us and detonated with a crackle of electrical discharges.

Nynsi let out a yelp as her body shuddered, convulsing as she slid off of me. I felt my heart clench and all but flew to my feet as anger and rage chased away the nausea and fear. The Naule had ducked into a booth, only to come surging back out when Tris put a shotgun round right through the half-wall protecting them.

I opened fire as soon as I had a good shot, the little gun bucking in my hands as I held the trigger down. Sparks and ricochets flew as the rounds impacted whatever shielding the armor had, then the colors shifted as they broke through to start hammering at the actual plating. None seemed to penetrate but it drew the Naule's attention away from Tris and to myself. I had to let go of the trigger as the pull of my gun drew my aim too high to hit my target, leaving her free to take her time as she brought her own weapon around.

The sight of the rifle barrel swinging in line with my forehead had me throwing myself back down the ground, my momentary courage failing me as gunfire blew apart bottles and glasses, showering me in fragments and booze.

My own yelp of pain came just Tris pulled the trigger on her shotgun one more time, and then something heavy clattered to the floor.

I let out a quiet groan, wincing as I felt stinging pain in my shoulders and somewhere near the back of my head. Damned glass must have cut me. The ringing in my ears got worse when Tris shouted yet again. "Trenah! You two alive back there!?"

Trenah, thankfully, called back at once. "Yeah! We're a bit singed but all right! How's the front?"

"Everyone's alive! Shaaryak got hit by a Discharge, and the kid's got some cuts, but everyone's alive!"

I shook my head and glanced at Nynsi, finding her groaning but likewise collecting herself. Her voice was low and hard as she muttered to herself, "What in the Paragons' names was this about?"

"I don't know." I replied quietly. "But I think we'd better figure it out."

I – IX

Needless to say Internal Security didn't just let us leave on our own that time.

Self defense though it was, the bar was technically a public area, and since the owner wasn't present to take responsibility we were stuck trying to explain what the hell had just happened.

Thankfully none of us had been seriously hurt, which boggled my mind. Trenah had some light burns on her left arm from a grenade that had gone off a little too close, but apart from that there was just the cuts I'd gotten from flying glass and the shock that Nynsi had received. The medic with the cops had extracted anything that needed to be removed and patched me up with some kind of binding gel, checked over Nynsi and informed her she was fine but would be sore, and then...

Then the questions had started.

The detective was a different man from the one who'd responded to the attack on the shop. He was average height for his gender, maybe five feet and an inch or two, and had lean, wiry build. Apparently he was stupidly handsome by Trahcon standards because he'd had to give up on interviewing Trenah after she'd done nothing but try to flirt with him for twenty minutes straight.

Which meant he'd been questioning Nynsi and I for the last hour.

"All right, so you have no idea why the True Sons would attack a bar out here in the outskirts, looking for an Imperial citizen who has all but disappeared from public life?" It was the tenth or so variation of the same question. I was pretty sure it was some kind of interrogative technique, and that it probably worked. It also probably spoke well of him that he'd been nothing but polite and apologetic. Of course that would have counted for more if I wasn't exhausted, possibly in shock, and too damned annoyed about the constant questioning to care what I said anymore.

Fortunately Nynsi was still in control of both her brain and her mouth.

Her fingers tightened painfully around my forearm to stop me from saying anything before she spoke once more, "That is correct detective. We are acquainted with her, as many in the local districts are, but we cannot say that we know her well enough to answer such a thing. As I have already informed you. Multiple times."

Both of his tarah twitched at her tone, vivid emerald eyes narrowing. "I see. Well, until we can track her down and get some answers you are both required to stay on planet. And since we don't know if any of the Sons relayed who they were fighting before they died, I'd recommend you both volunteer to go into protective residencies under I-Sec supervision."

"Fuck no." I winced as fingers dug deep enough to leave bruises, "I mean, uh, we can take care of ourselves detective."

"I'm sure." His wrist-comp shut down as he stood up from the stool he'd been sitting on. He didn't look particularly surprised at the answer, and I wondered how many people actually took them up on that kind of thing. "I'm Detective Wear'ahn, look me up in the Security directory if you change your minds or if you recall anything else. I'll be in touch if we have further questions."

Without waiting for us to respond, he visibly steeled himself and turned back towards Trenah. My friend openly licked her lips and lifted her tarah as the officer made his way over to her, clearly ready to resume.

"You need to learn when to *not* run your mouth." Nynsi whispered harshly in my ear, though her fingers finally loosened their death grip, "You could have gotten us both dragged to the district station for even more pointless questioning."

"Sorry." I murmured back, ducking my head sheepishly. That brought my shaking hands into view, and I shoved them both into my pockets before she could see them. "I mouth off when I'm stressed, it's a bad habit."

"I have noticed." She shook her head in a tiny motion. "Still, his advice is at least partially sound. If the True Sons can't track down Tasir herself, they may well go after her known associates."

I exhaled and nodded tightly, "You're saying we should all head home and fort up until we figure out what's going on."

"I think it would be best if we all returned to my family estate." Nynsi corrected me, "The two of you included. As the detective said, we have no way of knowing if they had any active transmissions going out, especially that last attacker. That level of equipment was not the kind of gear one sees in random gang members."

My stomach churned a little at the implications of all of that... and at the smell inside the bar. The officers had removed the bodies but the place still stank of blood and worse, the combination not doing anything positive for my state of mind. "You think they'd come after Trenah and I? We're just customers."

"It's unlikely, but as the detective asked, what are they doing attacking a bar to begin with?" She spread her hands apart and tilted her head. "Further, why attack a machine shop in the River District?"

I thought about it, and it didn't take me long to understand what she was getting at. Xerol had all but confirmed that he was a priority target for the gang. By extension that meant the various people he contracted work to could also be targets. Practically everyone I'd met had noted that Trenah was one of his favorites, and if that was public knowledge...

"...the attack may not have been as random as it looked." I said quietly. "They could have been after Trenah in specific. She's a Trahcon, so natural enemy, and a favorite of Xerol, who they want to kill as an example."

"It's more than merely possible." She responded just as softly. "I don't like the woman, but my uncle does, and she's disgustingly competent. She may live quietly but she's very well known in certain circles. Worse, her home is publicly registered and hardly located in a secure compound. I think the security of the mansion is the best location for all four of us."

Sighing, I reached up and rubbed tiredly at my face. The motion tugged at the various cuts I'd gotten, and I quickly stopped with a wince of pain. "I think I agree, but I don't know if Trenah will."

"I can handle that." Nynsi tapped the wrist-comp on her left arm, "Or rather, my uncle can."

As Xerol seemed to be the only person I'd met who could intimidate her, I had to agree. At a slight gesture from Nynsi, I stood up and followed her to the shattered entrance. The cops there made us stop for a quick check with Detective Wear'ahn to confirm that we'd told him everything we knew, then they waved us out.

The air outside was clean and crisp, cooling as the sun began to fade despite the early hour. It seemed like every day we lost another minute of sunlight, and I wasn't really looking forwards the constant darkness that winter would bring.

Maybe a dozen other officers in their blue armor were keeping a perimeter, though their posture was generally relaxed. They must not have been too worried about a follow-up attack, especially as the pair near the parking area were more interested in ogling Nynsi's vehicle than watching for more gang members.

Since the long sleek aircar was covered in silver plating, with golden symbols I took to be Thondian lettering on the doors, I didn't really blame them. It was at least half again as long as any other model around, with an extended engine block in the back and an elongated nose decorated in more gold lettering. In comparison, Trenah and Tris's more weather-beaten cars looked like they were ready for the scrap yard, and I couldn't help but admire it like the work of art it was.

"Close your mouth Cieran." Nynsi all but purred, visibly pleased at my reaction. "It is unseemly to gape."

I gave her a half-hearted glower. "I wasn't drooling."

"Did I say as much?" She murmured, waving me towards the passenger side. "Please enter, we will wait for our companions."

The interior of the car proved to be just as luxurious. Leather seats molded themselves to my body as I sat, the sheer comfort nearly making me groan. Various computer screens and projections fired up when Nynsi took the driver seat and engaged the engine. Music promptly began to play, a Trahcon orchestra composed mostly of low drums and strings that was soothing to listen to.

I let my head fall back and exhaled as the sounds washed over me, hands folding in my lap as I made sure they were secure and unable to start twitching. The fine craftsmanship had momentarily distracted me, as had the endless rounds of questions, but now...

Now I had nothing to focus on, and I could almost feel my muscles beginning to tremble and twitch. The phantom smells of the blood and guts of the dead people abruptly filled my nose. It was all I could do to not throw up in a car that probably cost more than the entire building I lived in.

Thankfully Nynsi was distracted with calling her uncle, giving me the time to get myself under some vague semblance of control. She muttered something to a feminine voice, probably a secretary, who then transferred her to Xerol. The two of them began a rapid conversation in their own language, something more rhythmic yet also harsher sounding than Caranat.

I did my best to focus on her voice and the words, using it to further distract my punch-drunk brain from the fact that I'd just helped kill several people. In strange ways I felt both better and worse than I'd had after the attack on the shop.

It might have had something to do with the relative dangers. I mean, sure, the attack on Trenah's place of business had seemed awful at the time, but in hindsight I hadn't really been likely to die. I could have cowered on the ground and let Trenah handle them without seriously hurting our chances of survival.

Today though... that had a been a lot of attackers, and that last one...

A new distraction came when two figures emerged from the bar, Trenah and Ghai heading in our direction. Nynsi waved for me to stay sitting, Xerol's face still hovering above her wrist, and then slid out of the car to approach the two women.

I watched as they held a quick conversation centered around the open call, then the light cut out and all three of them came over to pile into the vehicle.

"You all right Cie?" Trenah asked the moment she was behind me.

"Tired and cut up, but I'm all right." I replied.

She made a quiet noise of disbelief and leaned forwards, sticking her head over my shoulder to get an up close look at me. A hand promptly began to run through my hair, making me hiss as she tugged at the closed cuts. "Looks like they're all sealed but your fur is disgusting. Blood and dried up alcohol is a shit combination."

"Scalp wounds bleed a lot." I grumbled, trying to bat her hand away. "I'll clean it when we get there."

There was a grumbling sound and she reluctantly fell back into the seat behind me. Ghai sat quietly beside her, watching attentively as Trenah continued, "But how are you *doing*?"

The emphasis on the critical word made my lips turn down slightly as I turned away from her. "Better than last time so long as I don't think too much about it."

Nynsi had been plotting out the route on the car's computer, but her her fingers stilled at that. "Are you not used to combat?"

"No." I said flatly, hoping she got the hint to drop it. Hadn't I just said I was fine so long as I didn't think about it?

Thankfully she seemed to pick up on my tone and instead focused on getting us airborne. The car proved itself to be more than just a showpiece because the acceleration made us leap up off the ground in a matter of heartbeats. The inertial compensators stopped us all from being flattened against our seats as Nynsi put us into a spiraling climb, leveling out and heading for Koshun Minor once she'd reached the appropriate altitude.

The flight was silent for a few minutes, save for the quiet music, and then Trenah got bored. She shifted her ass over until she was practically pressed up against Ghai's side. The taller woman gave her a somewhat surprised look as she tried to lean back a bit, then wordlessly waved towards the pair of us when I turned around to frown at them.

"Hey, you agreed at the bar." Trenah poked her chest with a finger. "And Cieran's polite enough to mind his own fucking business, right Cie?"

"I am." I agreed, "But we're in a *car*, Trenah."

She turned to give me a somewhat blank look. "What's your point?"

"His point," Nynsi stated flatly, "Is that I will disable the compensators and put us into a dive if you attempt to seduce my uncle's Harath'krem."

"Oh she's already seduced." Trenah countered, drawing a commendably dramatic eye-roll from Ghai, "We just haven't had the chance to rip each other's clothes off yet."

"No sex in the car." I said firmly, taking Nynsi's side. "I'm not ready to be emotionally scarred."

Trenah glowered at me, her tarah twitching up and down several times, then she said, "Fine, no sex in the car."

"Good." I sighed, "How did-"

Before I could finish asking how the fighting at the bar's back door had gone, Trenah had turned around and shoved her mouth against Ghai's. The taller woman's eyes widened briefly, then lazily drifted shut as her arms wrapped around Trenah's muscled torso.

"Please tell me they aren't doing what it sounds like they are." Nynsi sounded disgusted, and she was very firmly keeping her eyes facing forwards. I could only sigh and watch as Ghai hauled Trenah into her lap, both of them seemingly oblivious to the fact that we were still present. "By the First Pillar, they are, aren't they?"

Turning away I shook my head and resolutely kept my own eyes on the city line as the various lights began to come on. "Don't ask questions you don't want to know the answer to."

Her dark lips twisting in a disgusted expression, she reached out and pushed the throttle up several degrees. Thankfully it wasn't a very long flight, we were coming in for a landing inside of five minutes. And, despite their rather heavy make-out session, the two Trahcon had managed to keep all of their clothes on and hadn't progressed beyond kissing and caressing each other's tarah.

We'd barely set down in a cavernous garage when Trenah had shoved the door open and all but ripped Ghai's arm out of its socket in her haste to pull her out of the car with her. By the time I'd unstrapped myself and gotten out as well she was already vanishing through a doorway, pushing Ghai ahead of her.

"I would have thought she'd have cared more about your condition than for finding a sexual partner." Nynsi shook her head tightly as she likewise got out, "But then I suppose she has always been uncouth in that fashion."

I shrugged a little, looking around with interest. "Trenah is Trenah. You get used to it."

The garage was massive, the size of a small hangar, and contained at least two other cars just as nice as the one we'd arrived in. A good six or seven more typical models were parked in neat rows off to one side, and a glance upwards showed several more suspended in some kind of rack from the ceiling. Tool cabinets and work benches lined the walls, everything neatly organized and spotless, though I was a little surprised at the lack of a welcoming committee.

While I looked around Nynsi input some kind of command on her wrist-comp, drawing my attention when massive doors slid shut in the distance.

"Heavy doors." I noted quietly. "Where is everyone?"

"The garage staff works earlier hours than the remainder of the mansion, and most of the building's employees are likely on errands in the district or are otherwise occupied." She replied, long legs carrying her around the car as she made a gesture for me to follow. "My uncle is currently inspecting an industrial facility, and both of my cousins are meeting with business associates in the Ocean-Front."

"Huh." I shook my head a little as we walked to the nearest exit, "So what's the plan?"

"First to find Rane'li, our communications specialist on staff, to see if there is any news." She blinked when I took a few steps forwards to open the door for her, her expression curious before she nodded and moved through. "Second, to find you a guest suite so you may clean your fur."

"Hair." I corrected.

That earned me another blink, "Ah. If I may ask what the difference is?"

I sighed, remembering Trenah asking the same thing, "I honestly don't know."

She visibly smothered a smile and patted me on the arm, "Very well, we will find a shower so you may clean your *hair*. Then I believe food will be in order, followed closely by sleep and rest."

"I can't argue against that plan." I said, "In fact it sounds perfect."

A genuine smile and another pat on the arm was her answer, and then I mostly focused on not being obvious in my gawking as we walked down halls. The mansion was nicely decorated, to put it mildly, and I appreciated that if only for the fact that it let me concentrate on something besides what had just happened at Forever.

Tasteful art, mostly landscapes focused on desert imagery, was spaced every couple of yards. Broad windows would have let sun shine in during the other seasons, but artificial lights still shone on collections of flowers and potted trees set near benches. Closed doors were usually opposite them, and Nynsi answered my unspoken question by saying we were passing the servant's quarters.

A left turn followed by another walk eventually brought us to an open door, and inside was... well, some kind of command center.

The room was circular, with an elevated platform of the same shape in the center. All around it were various screens and work stations, while atop the central area was some kind of holographic table. It was currently switched off, but I could easily picture Xerol or Nynsi pacing above everyone else, giving orders and direction as they did.

"*Kasha* Shaaryak." A trio of Thondians were hard at work in front of various screens, but all three rose and bowed with their heads tilted left when we entered.

Nynsi gave them a more shallow, right-leaning bow in return,

"Rane'li, a report."

Two of the staff, one man and one woman, returned to their work, but the third remained standing. She proved to be even taller than Nynsi, maybe six and a half feet, and her skin was nearly the color of black ink. It made the sand-colored sections of armor along the sides of her neck stand out even more, even as it made her eyes harder to follow. Still, she had pleasantly balanced features, and I had to stop myself from letting my eyes drift below her neck to see how well the maroon uniform fit her.

I would not give Trenah the satisfaction of seeing me stare at anything with breasts dammit, even if she wasn't present.

She began to speak in her own language, only for Nynsi to cut her off at once, "Caranat, please. Our guest does not speak either the High or Low tongues."

The woman blinked, but dutifully changed so that I could follow the conversation, "Of course, Lady Shaaryak. Your honored Patriarch was able to contact Ashul'tasir, she is at one of her other businesses in the Core District. She is quite safe, if unhappy to learn of what happened, and has sent instructions for Trenah'laria and her assistant to remain here until further notice."

That made my eyes narrow, "She's *ordering* us to stay?"

"That was the implication of her message." The staff member agreed, "Patriarch Shaaryak informed her that Trenah'laria would not take such a command well but she merely repeated herself before indicating she would be here tomorrow to discuss matters in person."

Nynsi let out an angry whistle before shaking her head in a sharp motion, "Under no circumstances is Laria to be told of this instruction tonight, we will deal with Tasir tomorrow. Did my uncle have any further direction?"

"No, my lady."

"Very well. Instruct the kitchens to prepare a dinner for myself and my guest, ensure it is safe for his species and then send it to the guest suite nearest to my rooms. We will take our meal there before retiring for the evening."

Rane'li bowed to the left again. "Of course."

Nynsi did her own, more shallow bow again, then motioned for me to follow. I paused before doing so, speaking to the staff-woman, "Thank you. I don't suppose you could also send of a change of clothes for me?"

The tall woman tilted her head a little to the right and nodded, "It will be done, honored guest."

I tried not to wince at the flat tones and right lean to her head, and quickly bowed my own head to the left hoping that it made me look contrite, "Thank you again."

From the way her head rocked back in surprise I figured I'd either over-done it or shocked her. In either case I had to catch up with my host so I didn't stick around, instead quickly ducking outside and then falling back into step with Nynsi once I'd caught up with her.

"I'm not going to get killed in my sleep, am I?" I kept my voice down, making sure my once-again shaking hands were hidden in my pockets.

"Of course not, I have declared your status as a guest." From the way she tilted her torso and eyed my arms she'd noticed my reaction this time, "You're safe here, please do not worry about it."

That was far easier said than done. Still, I kept myself reasonably calm as we walked to yet another wing of the mansion, then up a flight of stairs to enter what Nynsi referred to as 'her' section of the massive building. In addition to her suite it also had rooms belonging to the various members of the security staff, and somewhere below us was the mansion's armory.

I rather hoped I wouldn't have to visit the latter as she guided me into a guest room. It was nice enough, the size of a small apartment with a well furnished living area. Beyond was an equally well appointed bedroom and, more importantly, a full bathroom.

By the time I'd carefully cleaned the dried blood out of my hair, dinner and new clothes had arrived, though to my lack of surprise none of it was my size. I settled for putting my own pants back on, then picking some kind of blue silk shirt that mostly fit me once I'd tied it closed with a cloth belt.

"I apologize, all we really have is feminine wear for you." Nynsi said once I'd emerged, still gingerly toweling my hair. "I will send someone tomorrow for your own clothes if this proves to be an extended stay."

"I'm used to it." I said as I sat at the small table, "All I own are Trahcon women's clothes, not really a market for Humans here. Or at least not for Humans of my height. The food looks great by the way."

She gave me another curious look as I focused on the meal, some kind of pasta with red and orange sauce that smelled delicious. "...you are a very curious being. No Thondian man I know would be comfortable in feminine clothing."

I shrugged a little and took up my fork, "I complained a bit about it at first, but honestly it's not that different from what I'd normally wear. Plus I got used to it, don't even think about it anymore... but I would definitely draw the line at wearing a dress."

That drew a genuine laugh, "True, you lack the *kasini*... ah, hm. This language lacks the proper term... let us say that you lack the proper upper chest to wear such an ensemble."

"I definitely do." I agreed, doing my best not to glance at that particular area of her body, "Thank you for all of this, by the way. And for keeping me company, you didn't have to stay."

"You are my guest." She stated as though that explained everything.

I brought some pasta to my lips, felt the heat of the sauce, and thought better of it for the moment. "So is Trenah but you aren't eating dinner with her."

"Laria," She shook her head and blew a little on her own food, "Is being tended to in other ways."

My cheeks heated up a little, "I... uh, yeah. I suppose she is."

Thondians apparently didn't blush like Humans, but she seemed to lose a bit of the steel in her spine, slouching and glancing away a little in a way that I guessed meant she was likewise embarrassed. "Quite. Let us not speak of whatever the pair of them are up to."

"Agreed." I nodded, blowing on my fork until I thought it safe. It was far less spicy than I'd have guessed from the smell, which was good since all I had to drink was water. I sipped some and spoke again, "What does being your guest mean, exactly? Besides not getting my throat cut while I sleep and having you eat dinner here."

"It means I am obligated to protect and care for you so long as you offer no insult or harm to me in return." She paused to eat some of her own food, then resumed, "I am not obligated to eat dinner with you precisely, but I thought it best not to leave you alone as you seemed in an ill state of mind."

My stomach turned a little and I quickly focused on my food once again.

"You were not a warrior on your world, were you?" Nynsi asked quietly. "This is new to you."

I rolled a shoulder in my best approximation of a Trahcon-shrug. "This was only my second time. The attack on Trenah's shop was the first." I didn't mean to continue past that, but something in my brain short-circuited and my mouth just kept moving, "She killed one, right away, and took care of the third. But the second one... some stupid Naule kid. Don't even know how old he was. Came sprinting in like the ones at Forever, and I just... cut him down with a single burst. Took him across the chest."

Warm fingers brushed against my hand, and I jerked a little in surprise at the contact. "That explains a great deal. Your kind are not like the Trahcon, I know that much. It takes some adjustment before you get used to it."

"I'd rather not get used to it." I said around another sip of water, shaking my head as some of the tension left me. I must have really needed to actually say some of this out loud. "But I'm afraid I won't have a choice."

"You likely won't." She agreed gently. "The Far Reaches are dangerous, and though Alum is the most civilized world within them, there remains conflict. Maybe if your benefactor had given you to another Trahcon you would have been spared some of this, but Laria was involved with my uncle long before you came here."

"I know." My fork clattered down as I lost my appetite. I had no idea why I was talking with her about this, I barely knew her, but I just couldn't stop myself. "I know I'm not responsible and that I only defended myself. I know Trenah's involved, and I'm not going to abandon her to deal with whatever the fuck is going on. But knowing all of that just... fuck, it doesn't help like it should. I have nightmares."

"Laria doesn't help?"

"She tries but..." I shook my head and fought down a yawn, "I guess you'd know more than I would. You said Trahcon are different."

There was a quiet sigh, "They are. For the most part they have vastly different reactions to stress or trauma than most other species, and they have a difficult time understanding others in turn. Are you finished eating?"

"...yeah." She nodded and rose, motioning for me to do the same. I started to then found myself sitting again, shaking my head blearily and trying to figure out why my legs had given out. "...huh?"

"I will have to speak with our doctor, I believe he gave you something stronger than I requested. He must have thought I meant for your physical pain."

I blinked some more and then managed to glower as I realized what she meant. "You... drugged me."

"A mild sedative in your water, to help you sleep." She corrected gently as she walked around the table. "I had hoped it would be unnoticed, merely something to make you drowsy. Don't worry, he is a Trahcon and has no issues with your species. I merely wasn't clear in my instructions."

"You are... not a good host." I glowered some more.

She gave me the embarrassed little pose again, then recovered and settled onto a knee beside me. Before I could even try to stop her she'd gotten an arm under my legs and another under my arms, then hauled me up into a bridal-carry with only a quiet noise of effort.

I tried to be embarrassed but I mostly just felt fucking exhausted... and besides, whatever perfume she had on her neck smelled amazing. She let out a breathy hiss, kind of like a giggle, and I dimly realized I must have tickled her with my beard.

Then I was cold and laying in a bed, feeling someone pulling blankets over me.

"...rude." The word was more like a groan. "Bad... host."

"You will thank me in the morning." Came the distant reply.

There was a ghostly touch of warm fingers across my forehead... then I fell into a dreamless sleep.

I – X

I woke up feeling far better than I'd felt in a while, which left me simultaneously grateful and annoyed.

My mood shifted towards forgiving Nynsi when I exited the bedroom to find a breakfast of bread, cold cuts, and juice waiting for me on the table. Next to the chair was a bag that contained a set of brand new clothes in my size, both the shirt and slacks proving to be dark blue with red patterning.

There was a small note attached apologizing for the fact that it was still Trahcon women's wear, and wryly noting that I'd been entirely correct in the lack of options for beings of my height and build on planet.

Smiling, I'd settled into a chair and wolfed down my breakfast before taking another shower. I'd just finished dressing in my new outfit when there was a single knock at the door.

"Come in!"

The door slid aside to reveal Rane'li, the towering woman taking an almost cautious step inside before she realized that I was the only one present. She gave me an almost studiously neutral bow, and then again rocked back when I carefully bowed a bit deeper and to my left.

"Ah..." She seemed to shake herself, then spoke in an almost embarrassed rush, "The Lady Shaaryak requested I wake you if you still slept, and to direct you to join her and Lady Laria in one of the meeting halls once you were prepared."

"Thank you." I said politely, "I don't suppose you could give me directions?"

The member of the mansion's staff did so, and gave me an oblique look that I thought showed her confusion when I thanked her again. Then she was gone, leaving me to finish cleaning up after myself. I wasn't entirely sure what to do with yesterday's clothes, so I simply folded them and left them on a chair so I could grab them later.

My walk proved to be a quiet and fairly quick one, the conference room I'd been directed to was on the level directly above me. The third floor seemed to be much smaller than the others, and was apparently dedicated to various meeting areas. Rooms one and two proved to be virtual auditoriums with floor-to-ceiling windows and reclining chairs, but both were otherwise empty. Room three was far smaller, about what I'd expect from a corporate office, but was likewise well-lit.

Nynsi was seated at a long table, wearing another charcoal gray suit, with a similarly clad Ghai on her right. A far more disheveled looking Trenah, wearing clothes several sizes too big for her, was sprawled on Ghai's right in turn, her head resting against the taller woman's side. From the way her hands were clutching a small cup of tea, and the sunken eyes Ghai was sporting, the pair had managed to find time to drink in between their other activities.

"Morning everyone." I said, rather loudly. My reward was both of the Trahcon women flinching at the noise and then directing glares at me. Hangovers were apparently the same regardless of species, something I'd taken a grim delight in abusing whenever I wanted to tease Trenah. "Long night?"

"Fuck you." Trenah growled, all but curling into a ball in her seat. "Go fucking drown yourself in the nearest shit filled river."

Nynsi gave her a less than impressed look before turning back to me, "Good morning, Cieran. I am glad to see you looking well rested."

"Yes. I..." I sighed, "Thanks, I needed the sleep. And the food."

"No thanks are required between guest and host, but you are welcome all the same." She replied, her gaze returning a thin tablet in her hands. "Ashul'tasir is on her way along with my uncle. I believe the plan is to discuss yesterday's events and then determine the proper reply."

I nodded and walked over to the table. After a brief moment of hesitation I moved around where Trenah was again using Ghai's shoulder as a pillow to take a seat across from them. I wasn't entirely sure how the whole left-right dynamic worked beyond the bowing, and I didn't want to end up insulting Nynsi by having her on my right.

None of them seemed to really care about my choice of chairs, so I took that as another win and did my best to relax.

"So," I said far more quietly, "I see you managed to get drunk on top of everything else."

Trenah cracked an eye open and gave me a tired glower. "I don't remember needing your permission to have a fun night. Especially after all the shit that happened yesterday."

Both of my eyebrows went up at that. I'd meant my words to come out a bit teasing, hoping to start some of our usual banter. "...well, yeah, but you know I didn't mean it like that."

Her single open eye narrowed a little, then she seemed to deflate. "...not looking forwards to this crap."

Considering her mood that was probably the closest I'd get to an actual apology, and I nodded, wordlessly accepting it. "Is anyone?"

Apparently no one was, since no one bothered responding. Nynsi kept reading whatever she was reading, while Ghai and Trenah shared tea and did their best to recover. That left me to lean back in my chair, watching the three of them and trying not to think too hard about what had happened yesterday. Instead I tried to focus on what was coming up with mixed success.

I didn't have long to chew on it, five, maybe six minutes going by before echoing footsteps began to approach. Xerol breezed in first, followed closely by one of Nynsi's cousins. After them came a tired but alert looking Ashul'tasir, all three of them in professional wear, and the last two with weapons openly hanging from their belts.

It was a little depressing that I didn't even bat an eye at the guns. It was sad what you could get used to.

"Good morning, honored guests. Niece." Xerol greeted as he walked past me, electing to take the seat at the head of the able. The other Thondian male sat on my side but next to the family head, leaving about five empty seats between us. To my surprise Ashul'tasir sat next to me, the older woman giving me a slight nod that I returned after a confused beat.

"I believe," Xerol continued once everyone had settled, or in Trenah's case, straightened up. "That some quick introductions are in order. Lady Tasir, this is my cousin, Rehat Shaaryak, and my niece, Nynsi. Rehat, the young Human is Cieran Kean, Miss Laria's assistant and protege. I believe that both he and dear Trenah will be staying in the mansion for some time."

Trenah and I exchanged a quick look before she spoke up, "That's fucking news to us."

Our host tilted his head a little to the left and bowed in Tasir's direction. "If you could please explain, as you did to me earlier this morning?"

Tasir twitched both of her tarah outwards, her expression grim. "I've got a couple of contacts in Son territory. According to them everyone in this room has some kind of order put on them effective yesterday. Little Shaaryak and I are supposed to be captured, everyone else has a kill bounty on their head."

I flinched and spoke before Trenah could explode. "*What*? In the name of God *why*?"

"The Shaaryak's control the largest organized group of aliens on planet," By which I assumed Tasir meant non-Trahcon, "Which makes Koshun Minor the True Sons' priority target to take over in the wake of their set-backs last year. In their minds it is prime recruiting territory and a far better area in which to operate. My best guess is that they want to kill all of the Shaaryak men so they can force the girl to marry some idiot and sign over control."

That made my jaw clench and I glanced at Nynsi, "Could that actually happen?"

"I would kill myself first." She stated with terrifying levels of calm, "But the laws of the Ascendancy and its culture are strictly Patriarchal, even if the direct laws of Alum are not so. By our people's standards I could only control the estate if every male in line before me is killed, and even then only until my first-born son reached the age of majority."

I could only shake my head in shock and mild disgust. "How... archaic."

That earned me a sharp look from all three Thondians present, though it was Nynsi who replied, her voice suddenly cool. "I will not disparage your own species nonsensical culture if you refrain from doing the same, dear guest."

"...my apologies." I said as I quickly shook my head once more, "I meant no disrespect, I was merely reminded of the time period in which my own people had similar practices."

It wasn't much of an excuse but it seemed to be enough to temporarily mollify everyone, and Nynsi nodded, her tone slowly returning to normal. "However, there is a flaw in their plan. While the majority of our workforce are exiles or the children of exiles, our family was re-instated due to my uncle's actions in setting up the district here. By Ascendancy law my cousins and I can only marry non-exiled highborns, and I can assure you there are none within the ranks of the True Sons."

"I'm getting there." Tasir growled, looking a little annoyed that we'd interrupted her. "To finish up the crap I started with, you two," She nodded at Trenah and then at me, "Are to be killed for different reasons. Trenah-"

"I'm a Trahcon and it's well known I work for Xerol." Trenah interrupted, drawing a glare that bounced off her thick skin, "Fucking easy enough, but what in Ashahn's bloody name is Cieran doing on their kill list? They can't have fucking added him just from yesterday."

Tasir pointedly stayed silent for several long moments, clearly making her stew in revenge, then spoke about an instant before Trenah could erupt. "He wasn't, the bounty we found was post-dated a week ago. They must have had people watching your shop. According the text he's been targeted for being a Human who is such a traitor that he'd work with both of his species' natural enemies. There's a bonus in it for anyone who brings him in alive so they can make a public example of him."

I flinched even as Trenah growled. "He the only one?"

"The only Human? Yeah." Tasir rolled a shoulder and twitched a tarah in a shrug, "But his bounty went out with about a dozen others that are pretty similar, most of them Naule or Thondians, plus one Xenthan of all things. All of them work with or for our species. Someone in their leadership wants to start a fear campaign against anyone like them. Another set of bounties went out the week before, and I wouldn't be surprised if another one goes out next week."

So at least I wasn't being singled out, though that didn't really make me feel any better. At the end of day I still had a fucking price on my head.

"It's not all that much money, couple hundred credits," She continued, "But it's enough that broke idiots might make plays for him. And your bounty, Trenah, is a couple thousand."

Trenah's face twisted in muted anger, her tarah quivering with the emotion, "You really think they'd try shit in the middle of the River District? Even if I couldn't kill a dozen of those assholes without trying, which I damned well can, my fucking neighbors would drown any leftovers."

The older woman's voice sharpened, "Yeah, until some smart little fuck shows up and sets your damned apartment on fire, or just crashes a car into it. Even if they aren't smart enough to do that you'd putting your neighbors at risk and Internal-Security will eventually haul you into some safe-house in one of the southern arcologies. You want to go down and bake in those jungles?"

"...Ashahn's bloody ass." Trenah muttered, deflating a little. "I fucking hate it when you make sense."

"I know." Tasir replied dryly, "So until they're dealt with, safest for the two of you to stay here, surrounded by trained guards, reinforced walls, and armored glass."

Though her words had included both Trenah and I, her eyes and remained on my roommate, which more or less made sense. I wasn't really the important one here, I was just the tag-along. It was Trenah's safety she and the others were more concerned with... or, at least, everyone but Nynsi was more concerned with.

Said woman spoke up in the short silence that followed, "If I may ask, what form of contacts do you have to give you that intelligence, and just why are *you* on their capture list in addition to myself?"

Tasir's body went rigid, both of her tarah tilting upwards in a warning. "That's for me and your uncle to know, girl."

"Fuck. That." I blinked in surprise as Trenah supported Nynsi, "We almost got killed in your own goddess-damned bar, I think we're owed some kind of explanation."

"No." Tasir's voice was as unyielding as stone. "You aren't."

I frowned at her reaction. It had seemed like a fair enough question, and not an unreasonable follow-up. I mean, sure, I'd entirely expected her to deflect and refuse to tell us anything, but not so sharply.

Turning my chair a little, I took a closer look at her. It wasn't hard to tell when a Trahcon was feeling stressed out or exhausted, and I started noticing the signs the moment I looked for them. Her tarah were shaking from the effort of being upright, making her cheeks twinge where the muscles strained to not let them droop. Her posture was a little too forced as well, and she was surreptitiously leaning an elbow on the chair's armrest so that it could take most of her weight.

It wasn't until the silence became awkward that I realized that everyone had stopped talking in favor of watching me as I watched Tasir, who turned around to glare furiously at me as she realized where everyone else was looking.

"What, Kean?" She demanded in a low voice.

I licked my lips and leaned cautiously away from her, my mind racing to connect the various dots, remembering everything I'd ever heard about her. She was from the Empire, formerly a big deal there apparently, but no one really seemed to know why she was here. She owned at least several bars in multiple districts and routinely changed which one she was personally running. She had contacts in the Outskirts, in the True Sons' turf, and for some reason they'd decided to target her for capture directly.

And she was very stressed out about that fact, more so than anyone else in the room, despite the fact that we all had monetary value attached to our lives.

"How large is your bounty?" I asked, curiously.

"That's none of your-"

"Fifty thousand." Xerol spoke over her, his expression perfectly neutral. "Twenty thousand more than my nieces or my own."

I thought about that some more, connecting it into everything else I knew, and then I smiled a little. "Oh. Oh that's kind of clever really."

Trenah had evidently been on the same mental wavelength because she tilted her head and snorted about a second after I spoke, "...that explains a lot of shit."

Xerol's lips seemed to curl and he gave us a vaguely respectful nod while Tasir's expression darkened. "What is clever, and what explains things?"

I shared a look with Trenah and she waved a hand in my direction. I nodded once and spoke for us both, "Tasir, you're some kind of Imperial agent, aren't you? You use your bars to gather information, keep track of things. Someone in the True Sons figured that out too, and they want to kill you to hit at the Empire. How did you figure it out, Xerol?"

"Background searches when she purchased several buildings in my district some ten years ago." He replied while Tasir glared some more, "When I learned that she privately owned more than fifty otherwise unconnected taverns, bars, and diners around the city. It became somewhat more obvious when I realized she had a similar network in Irrail, and even a few locations in the southern arcologies."

Tasir sucked in a slow breath between her teeth, her tarah tilting into another warning display. "That information doesn't leave this room, understand?"

"Who would I tell?" I asked, honestly puzzled. "Apart from Tris, literally everyone I know is in this room."

The icy look she gave me made me shrink back a little, and made Trenah start to growl. Tasir whirled on her, my friend flinching away from that glare as well. "What I'm doing here is none of your concern, and you *will not share your theories.* Understand?"

"Yes honored elder." I said very, very quietly, using the most polite term I could think of. Trenah echoed me a beat later, her voice far more sullen than mine even if her posture told me that she was just as cowed.

Rehat, Ghai, and Nynsi all bowed their heads quickly when that ferocious expression was turned on each of them, but even then Tasir didn't seem to relax.

Instead she simply sucked in a breath and spoke in a tight, irritated voice. "...to answer your unspoken question, Kean, I have no fucking idea how a small-time gang managed to figure it out. I don't advertise my position and the majority of my businesses are officially owned by others or by assumed names. It took Xerol most of a year to even suspect what was happening."

"Three to confirm it, at great expense." Xerol murmured. "Though I like to believe I would have done so far more quickly if circumstances then were similar to those currently ongoing."

She waved an irritated hand and continued, "Regardless, my best lead is the fact that they've recovered too quickly from last year's push to get rid of them. Internal Security and the Crescent tore their guts out and they're already back up to similar numbers if not the same level of territory. That means they've got some kind of off-world backer bringing in new idiots, and that particular river-fork is going to be my priority. Xerol and the rest of you will be handling the other."

That made everyone turn to the man at the head of the table, and he gave a polite nod before speaking, "The information we have is largely general, the names of their current targets, some of their holdings, and one of their upcoming events. We must rectify the lack of detailed knowledge."

Rehat finally spoke, his voice a slightly deeper copy of Xerol's, "Ahhh. We are going on the offensive. It has been too long, honored Patriarch."

"I quite agree." Nynsi murmured, "When and where?"

"In two days," Xerol brought his hands up as he spoke, pressing the tips of his fingers together lightly. "Supposedly there is some form of exchange taking place at a warehouse in the Industrial District with several leaders of various rankings present. Our objective will be their capture, or failing that, the seizure of any and all materials they are moving."

I frowned and cautiously spoke only when he paused and glanced around, clearly checking if any of us had questions, "What could they be moving? Isn't pretty much anything legal here?"

"With the appropriate permits, yes." He agreed, "However, I find it less than probable that the True Sons will have bothered to pay the appropriate committees for the correct documentation."

"Fair point."

It was Nynsi's turn to make sure that I wasn't about to speak further, and then she asked her own question, "Who will be undertaking the operation?"

"You will be in overall command with Team One." Her uncle instructed, "Rehat will act as your second with his own team, and Teams Four and Five will likewise operate alongside you. The remainder will stay here to ensure our own defenses. Trenah? I don't suppose you will consent to participate? Your experience and skills would be most welcome."

Trenah's tarah tilted down a little at his last few words, but after a few seconds she gave an almost cautious nod. "The racist little shits should know what kind of sharks they're poking, I'm in. Can I have Ghai?"

He considered that in return and turned his attention to the woman in question, "If she wishes, though I will have to recall Iyaht from her vacation if she goes with."

Ghai let out a quiet snorting noise, her rasping voice producing a single word, "Lazy."

"I will tell her you said as much." He gave her a smile that showed off his sharp canines, then, to my surprise, he turned to me. "And yourself? Will you accompany the team as well?"

Trenah spoke before I could find my voice, "He doesn't have any training or combat experience."

"True," Xerol agreed, "However he seems to have quick thoughts and a mind for detail. Even if he does not partake in the actual fighting I would request his presence to aid us in evaluating whatever we find."

That... didn't really make much sense to me. I mean, sure, maybe I'd impressed him and Nynsi with some of the things I'd worked out, but I couldn't have impressed him *that* much. Trenah had figured out Tasir's occupation once she'd had the same information for example. And someone like him had to have plenty of people on staff who could handle investigations like that.

I was about to politely decline when I caught sight of Tasir looking at me from the corners of her eyes. Her gray lips were pressed in a firm line, her expression somehow... evaluating. Disapproving. Something in the way her bright eyes tightened and her tarah lowered a fraction of an inch told me she wasn't happy with the idea of me going with.

A glance back at Xerol saw him looking... encouraging. There was a small smile on his lips and he rolled a hand in a tiny gesture that seemed to tell me to go along with it.

So one mildly terrifying person wanted me to stay behind. One mildly terrifying person wanted me to go with.

"I..." I coughed quietly and looked at the table, trying to find some kind of middle ground. "...I guess I can help look at things afterwords? Maybe mind the car or something?"

Trenah's brilliant eyes narrowed to slits, clearly unhappy, but after a few seconds she glanced between Xerol and Tasir before nodding slowly. She probably saw the same dichotomy I did, and understood why I'd agreed. Tasir frightened me... but I was living in Xerol's home now. Best not to anger him.

"Guess we'll have to find you some armor then." She said.

"Yeah... guess we will."

The meeting had hardly finished before Tasir rose from her seat and stormed out.

For our part, Trenah and I both stared at Xerol in wordless question only for him to spread his hands lightly. "The matter is between Tasir and myself. I will elaborate only when it becomes relevant."

"He's involved." Trenah growled, pointing a single finger at me. "It's fucking relevant."

"You are both involved." He corrected her as he stood, "If I am correct, it will not be relevant in the end, and so I will not waste further words or time upon the subject. Ghai, dear? I need you to accompany Rehat on his rounds today. I will handle recalling Iyaht."

Ghai nodded once and rose, patting Trenah fondly on the shoulder before she and Rehat Shaaryak made for the door. For his part, Xerol likewise began moving, though he continued to speak as he did, "Nynsi, please introduce Kean to the armory and see that he is properly equipped. Trenah? I have one of my security teams waiting for you in the garage to assist in retrieving anything you may need from your home and place of business for an extended stay here."

Trenah's glower was starting to become etched into her face, and her tarah had to be hurting from much they'd been twitching. "I'll do it because it makes sense, but fucking remember that I'm not one of your employees. Or your social subordinate."

The man paused, then turned back and tilted his head a little to the left. "You are quite right, my dear. I will ensure to ask appropriately next time."

"You'd better." Came a dark mutter as my friend stood up, what was probably one of Ghai's shirts reaching down to her thighs and making it hard to tell if she had anything on under it. "Fine, I'll go get Cie's project and my gear. You need anything besides clothes?"

She'd directed the last at me, and I shook my head after thinking about it. "I've got my wrist-comp, can't think of anything else I really need."

That earned me a slight nod, and then she was out as well, leaving just Nynsi and I to slowly get to our feet. My new friend gave me a somewhat appraising look that somehow managed to keep her chin mostly level, and then waved for me to walk with her.

"So that went well." I muttered as we exited the conference room. "Why does your uncle want me to go with, and why does Tasir want me to stay here?"

Dark lips pressed into a thin line, "I'm not sure. He didn't confide in me, if you are attempting to ask that indirectly."

I shook my head once, "I'd have just asked that if I thought you knew. Mostly thinking out loud and trying to make sense of this."

"Mmm." She hummed, "Perhaps she believes you to be some kind of spy from the Ark Fleet, or from your home-world's rebellion."

"...and my grand plan involved starving myself nearly to death, and then living with a short, foul mouthed mechanic whose only real ambition in life is to see how many times she can get laid?"

Nynsi let out an almost startled laugh. "That *is* quite the defense. Perhaps she wants to hire you and use you as some kind of agent among your own kind? You involving yourself in combat would be detrimental to such a plan."

I smiled a little at her reaction, and then gave me a mild shrug. "That's a little more plausible, and I wouldn't mind going back to Earth, but why me? I'm pretty much a nobody, with no relevant skills, and everyone I knew is long dead."

"A nobody can become anyone." She pointed out when we reached the stairs, the pair of us slowly heading down. "But again, I agree with your point. Perhaps she's merely being paranoid after a gang worked out her posting."

It was my turn to hum quietly. "Mmm... that sounds right, I think. She was really stressed out. What kind of off-world group could rattle her like that?"

She was silent as we reached the second floor, then continued down towards the first. "The Empire is not a nation to be trifled with. The Guild Federation certainly has the power, but they're on the far side of the Empire from us and historically do not bother with the Far Reaches. Not when the Near Reaches are so much closer and more strategically important to them."

"My own species?" I suggested. "Maybe that's why she wants me out of this."

"The Ark Fleet is certainly resourceful and cunning enough," Nynsi agreed, waving an arm to the left when we reached the ground floor. "And they have enough petty hatred for the Empire to sponsor a gang whose core belief is a hatred of Trahcon, but where would they get the resources and personnel? So far as I know their attention is entirely on supporting the rebellion on your Earth or else plotting to retake Xentha. My own people have no love for them, and none of the Warlords in the deeper Reaches would give them support either."

I sighed, "They really made that many enemies?"

"To some extent, but it is safer to say that the Warlords only have varying degrees of enemies. Some, perhaps, would be willing to aid the Ark Fleet, but not without obvious and blatant payment."

Which the Empire would presumably notice. "Your people then? The Ascendancy you called it?"

Her patrician features turned down into a grimace. "Plausible. It is known that only the distance between them has prevented the Empire from seeking to absorb the Ascendancy as it took the Naule's state, and it is believed that the invasion of your world was intended as the first move towards closing that distance. Causing unrest near the Imperial border could be a plot the Ascendancy would support."

"But it doesn't explain why Tasir wants me to stay out of it."

"It does not." Nynsi agreed. "We will simply have to trust my

123

Patriarch. By the Paragons' wills, it will prove to be irrelevant as he stated."

Being a pessimistic person by nature, I didn't think I'd be able to simply set my worries aside.

Of course a few moments later we reached the armory, and the little worries about Tasir faded when compared to the very large worries about what I'd agreed to partake in.

I was going to be in a battle. An all out assault on some kind of gang meeting. Seriously, what the fuck had I been thinking? I should have just risked disappointing Xerol and turned him down. At least Tasir and Trenah would have both appreciated that.

The armory looked... well, like an armory. A fairly large one.

Weaponry was lined up against the walls in neat rows by type, with small shelving units containing what looked like parts for yet more guns. There had to be at least three dozen rifles of varying models, a similar number of shotguns, and then two or three times that amount of pistols and submachine-guns. And that wasn't counting the various armored boxes that probably held explosives from the warnings plastered across them.

I let out a slow whistle as I followed Nynsi inside, looking around. "This is a lot of guns."

She let out another little laugh, smiling as she beckoned me to follow her. "I suppose it is, but I don't believe you need a replacement. You seemed capable with the model you have. I am more concerned about getting you fitted with the proper protections and a technical launcher."

"I don't have the faintest idea how to use one." I pointed out as we walked from the weaponry part of the room into the body-armor part of the room. "And will any of these even fit me?"

"Considering the difficulty I had locating mere clothes for you? Doubtful, but we should be able to re-size it in time."

I groaned, "Please don't tell me I'm going to have to model armor that doesn't fit me. I still have *some* pride left."

"As amusing as that would be," Nynsi gave me a small smirk her head dipped a little to the left, a foot shifting as she sort-of leaned in my direction. "Measurements will be enough. Please stand right there. I'll take some scans and consider what we have available."

I had no idea what that particular posture meant, and said so as I walked to the spot she'd indicated. "I feel like I should ask about the whole left-right posture thing that your species has. The few files I found were pretty limited in their descriptions but I don't think I was looking at the right sites."

A blue wrist-comp snapped to life above her left arm, and she held it steady as her fingers moved across the holographic display. "The right side of our body indicates dominance, the left, submission. We usually display it through the motions of our head, the direction we lean, or how we bow, which you seem to have generally picked up on."

"A little." I shrugged. "I'm guessing not leaning in either direction means something neutral? Is that why you all hold yourselves so stiffly?"

"From my point of view you sit and stand as though your spine cannot support your weight." She replied, although there was enough amusement in her tone to make it clear she was teasing me. "But I suppose I can see your own viewpoint. In general body language is a part of our actual language, the words we speak are accented by how we hold ourselves."

That made me grimace. "Hard to learn?"

"For aliens, generally so, though the lower tongue relies more on verbal spacing than physical presence. It is usually the only one aliens bother with. Please hold still." I did, and she continued speaking as she walked a slow circle around me. "In the case of how I looked at you earlier, I was displaying silent amusement at the idea of you modeling armor for me, and showing that I enjoyed you speaking in such a casual fashion with me."

"All that in one motion?" I asked, genuinely impressed.

"Do not worry about it." She said as she finished the circle, bringing her wrist up so she could view the data without tilting her chin down. "As an alien you won't be expected to know. If anyone claims you insulted them with how you hold yourself, simply bow to the left and state that you meant no offense. If they are less than intelligent and push you, contact me and I will handle it."

"I'll keep that in mind." I said, trying to look at what she was doing on her floating screen. "Rane'li seemed surprised when I bowed to the left to her earlier."

Nynsi blinked rapidly. "You did? When?"

"Twice." I shrugged, "Yesterday and today. She didn't seem thrilled to help me, I thought it might make her think I wasn't some conceited alien who hated your species. It did seem to help... or it just really confused her."

"...I suppose I can understand your reasoning." She allowed, "But please bow in neutral fashion to her and the rest of the staff moving forwards. Doing as you did means that you are implying that you are below them in the social structure."

I blinked, "Aren't I?"

Her lips twisted in a very Human display of displeasure, though the odd way her body shifted to the right was very alien. Very Thondian I supposed. "Technically yes, as you are an alien and a Human in specific. But as my personal guest I would prefer you did not display submission to anyone beyond my family."

"I'll try to remember that."

She regarded me with her dark eyes, then nodded very slightly. "I trust that you will. Now, I will need your assistance in locating the proper sections of equipment."

The next couple of hours passed in a kind of mind-crunching blur as Nynsi had me pull out several different types of armor, compare and contrast them, and then pick out the pieces that would actually work for my particular build.

For its part, the protection itself was kind of interesting. It was basically two layers; the first looked like tight, tile-covered black clothes. Shirt, pants, socks, gloves, the works, each with clasps that ensured there were no gaps once I had it all on. Each tile was apparently filled with a thin anti-ballistic gel along with ceramic plating over vital areas. Of course the vital areas didn't exactly line up for me compared to the Trahcon woman it was all meant for, but it was generally close enough.

From how Nynsi described it, the material would slow and lessen the damage from actual guns, but its main purpose was to protect me from fragments and shock-waves from explosions. The real body armor was a set of, well, *armor* that went over top of the undersuit. There was a chest plate, shoulder pads, grieves, back plate with a power core for the suit's shields, a full helm with digital displays inside... it was impressive as hell.

My personal set ended up being a mismatched collection of Trahcon sized pieces, only a few of which came sort-of close to fitting me initially, along with a Thondian helmet that featured a narrow X-shaped visor. Once we'd gotten it all laid out, she'd entered a series of work orders into the system while I poked at the various bits and pieces, and then it was on to the technical launchers.

Those had the potential to be insanely complicated, but for a novice at my level the basic instructions were: point your wrist comp at the person you want a grenade flung at, push button, watch grenade fly at said person, hope they don't dodge.

Nynsi spent most of two hours walking me through that, and the far more important settings I needed to know in order to not blow myself up. We were just finishing up with that when Xerol called for her, summoning her to some kind of business lunch out in the district. Which left me free to wander back to my now-permanent rooms and resume thinking too much about what was going on.

That was where Trenah found me poking at my lunch when she returned an hour or so later. She'd found the time to change into her own clothes, and looked far less hungover. More importantly she had a bag containing what few outfits I owned, which she tossed onto the floor as she strolled in.

"How'd it go?" She asked in lieu of a normal greeting.

"Well I managed to shoot six dummy grenades down the length of the armory without blowing myself up." I shrugged and tossed my fork aside. The pasta Nynsi had arranged to be sent up for me wasn't bad by any means, but I didn't have much of an appetite. "So that's something. I might even have a full set of armor ready in time too."

Her tarah lowered when she grimaced, "I'd rather they didn't so you wouldn't have to come with."

"Worried about me?"

"Of fucking course I am." She shook her head, "You survived two fights so far but you're no fucking soldier, and don't lie and pretend that you are one. Ashahn's ass but this is way beyond your level Cie."

I quickly held my hands, "I know! I know, but it seemed like the right thing to say at the time. I don't... fuck. I don't know."

Trenah's brilliant eyes stared at me for several seconds, then she seemed to slump back and sigh. "Xerol's a fucking bastard, putting you on the spot like that. And don't bother asking me what in Ashahn's bloody name is wrong with Tasir because I don't fucking know."

"I figured." I said. "Neither does Nynsi."

There was a quiet grunt as her tarah twitched in anger. "Well at least you'll just be guarding the cars with the sharpshooters, could be in far deeper fucking waters that's for sure. And I've got two days to try and teach you how to shoot straight."

That made me sigh, "I'm guessing that's going to be all I'm doing for the rest of today?"

"You bet your pale ass." She waved a hand, "I won't be that hard on you, not with it so close, but I want to at least make sure you know how to shoot from cover. And go over what I want you to do if you see idiots running away, which they fucking should once we start handing them their asses."

"Shoot them with technical grenades and bullets?" I suggested dryly.

My friend snorted, "Yeah, but preferably in the legs. Questioning living idiots is hard enough, can't get anything at all out of dead ones."

Despite the fairly morbid nature of the conversation I couldn't help but smile a little, "Did you already eat lunch or did you want the rest of this before we get started?"

Trenah waved a hand and I obligingly slid my plate and utensils over. She didn't quite inhale the food but it wasn't for lack of effort. Then... then my crash-course in combat training started.

I – XII

I was sitting in the back of a aircar with Ghai, trying desperately not to poke and prod at my armor, when the call finally came in.

"We have confirmation that the True Sons are on site." Xerol's voice came from speakers in the back of my helmet, making my already nervous stomach clench a bit more. *"May the Paragons who stand above the Pillars watch over you all."*

Our vehicle begin a sharp bank as Nynsi brought us around, already giving orders. She was doing it in her own language, but one of the many nice things about my new helmet was the automatic translator. "All teams move in. Team four will remain with the vehicles, all other teams will move into the warehouse as soon as we have cleared the landing zones."

The other three teams leader spoke over one another, two men and a single woman all acknowledging what she had said.

For my part I tried not to show my nerves as Trenah and Ghai began to check over their gear. Like me they were in pitch black armor, though their helmets had a distinctive downwards-fan on the back to protect their tarah. Unlike me, with just my little Watcher sub-machine gun and a technical launcher on my belt, the pair of them were armed to the teeth.

They both held carbines in their laps while heavy pistols rested on their waists. Each of them had enough grenades to blow us all up a dozen times over, and Trenah had even joined Ghai in carrying a sword on her belt.

Which struck me as a bit excessive for fighting a bunch of dirt poor gangsters, but then again they were the ones actually trained for combat. Two days had really only been enough to make it clear how out of my depth I was, giving me the minimum amount of experience required to wear my armor and shoot technical grenades in a given direction. Usually.

Trenah leaned around as she finished her inspection, the blank visor of her helmet finding mine. "You all right Cie? Remember your job?"

I gave her a tight nod, "Stay with the car, disable or kill anyone trying to get out or approach. Watch my back to make sure they don't have help coming. Once it's all done I get to go inside and help you all figure out what the fuck is going on."

"Good." She nodded sharply, "Remember, if your shields break, get your furred ass into cover. Armor's great but it's not without its weak points."

"I remember." I said dryly, "And for the last time, my ass is not covered in fur."

There was a snort as she turned away, "Right, it's covered in *hair*, whatever the fuck the difference is."

I was ready to reply with an insult of my own when Nynsi cut us off, "Focus, we're approaching the target."

She was already putting the car into a steep dive, and a quick glance out of the window showed several other cars pulling out of the usual morning traffic lanes to descend as well. A few of those, containing the squads assigned to maintain the perimeter, were already ahead of us and landing. I had enough time to notice that, but not enough time to really think about what was happening because Nynsi kept the engines roaring until the last possible moment.

The ground rushed up at us as we dove, then the car abruptly leveled out, the deceleration slamming me back into my seat.

A vicious jostling served to announce that we'd landed relatively hard. The vehicle hadn't even finished shaking before Ghai and Trenah had popped their doors and vanished into the dim sunlight. Nynsi was a half moment behind, making sure that the engine had stopped, and I was a few seconds behind her.

"*Sharpshooters are in place.*" Rehat growled across comms as I shut my door behind me, "*Half a dozen guards on the roof, figure as many at the main door.*"

"*None at the side entrances, looks like they've kept them locked for us.*" The leader of team four, a woman named Marn, chuckled darkly, "*I'm sending a runner to keep them that way.*"

"Good, begin the advance!" Nynsi ordered, racing towards a bit of cover provided by an old truck, our two Trahcon companions already lurking behind it.

That left me alone and free take a few quick steps so I could shelter behind the car. Once I was in my assigned position, such as it was, I tried to take stock of everything while struggling to keep my breathing even.

The first gunshots began to crack through the air just as I got settled. I glanced up in time to see a figure collapse in a spray of red mist on top of the warehouse, the body tumbling over a wall. There were ten or so more rounds fired in deliberate sequence after that, the harsh sounds intermixed with one very high pitched scream.

Then the hidden sharpshooters ran out of targets, and everything went silent for a few heartbeats before it all went completely to hell.

"Roof clear, shifting to clear the main entrance." Rehat reported calmly.

I did a quick count as chaos erupted, the tiny warm-up giving way to the actual fight. We'd landed at the edge of the building's parking area, with others putting down to block streets and alleyways, though I assumed that the sniping teams had landed on nearby buildings. Thondians in heavy black armor were running in from every direction, rifles and shotguns up as they charged forwards.

Against them, against *us,* was maybe two dozen men and women in plain clothes, spread out in little groups. A few were gaping in confusion, some were drawing weapons from coats or pockets, and a smart minority was turning tail and sprinting for the warehouse's open doors.

I hesitated as the next round of gunfire began to cut them down, then brought my left hand up. Getting my fingers to form into the command gestures when my wrist-comp came online was a lot harder than it had been at the mansion's practice range. It took me two false starts and I had to change targets once, but I eventually managed it.

A final flex of my thumb towards two Naule who'd taken cover behind a beat up car of their own was enough to release the grenade. The launcher on my waist spat out a blue disc that shot across the open lot with only a small flicker of light, reaching the pair before detonating in a pulse of electrical energy.

They must not have had shielding because the Discharge sent both of them staggering, their limbs convulsing as arcs of lightning snaked out from the grenade to run through them.

"Good aim." A chipper sounding man spoke as he slid to a stop nearby, rifle up against his shoulder. It chattered in two quick bursts, both of the Naule going down in sprays of black blood. "Not bad for a Human."

"Thanks." I said, watching as Trenah dismissively waved a hand to send three gangsters flying into the side of the building hard enough to break their necks. She and Ghai were out in front of everyone else, and seemed to be ignoring what little gunfire the True Sons were managing to throw at them. "You're... Chen?"

"Leader of team five." He agreed, settling down onto a knee and resting his rifle on the car's nose. "You mind if we join you on perimeter watch?"

I felt my lips tug a little at the corners in spite of the situation. "If you have nothing better to do. You always this cheerful?"

Chen let out a rumbling laugh, his free hand making a series of gestures that saw seven others began to move from one piece of cover to another. "Not all of us are dour old bastards, but if you tell any of the Shaaryaks I said that I'll shave you."

"They won't hear it from me." I promised as the other teams began vanishing inside. The gunfire that had begun to trail off picked back up, rising to a nearly constant barrage of sound.

I had to rely on the sound since I couldn't really see much. The warehouse's hangar sized doors may have been open, but we'd landed at a poor angle to the entrance. I could pick out eight or so armored Thondians taking cover behind a crate, then several of them threw grenades over the top, muffled explosions proceeding their advance.

"So." Chen asked, his deep voice still amused. "What in the Paragon's sacred names is a Human doing running with us?"

"Short version? I'm Trenah's assistant."

He let out a low chuckle. "If there's a short version I'm guessing there's a longer one."

I sighed. "There is. It's complicated. I'm not from the Ark Fleet if you're worried I'm secretly an asshole out to kill you in your sleep."

The chuckle turned into a barking laugh, and a hand struck my shoulder hard enough to bounce my chest against the car. "Good. I'd hate to have to kill the lady's guest."

A groan and a cough to clear my battered lungs was about all I could manage in reply, something that just made him laugh more before his attention turned back to the warehouse. Inside the gunfire once again began to trail off, then like a switch being flipped it abruptly rose back up to a full barrage. Something massive crashed hard enough to make the ground shake, everyone tightening our grips as we tried to figure out what was happening.

"*Bring the other one down!*" Nynsi snarled the words, making me flinch and then blink as I realized what she meant.

Some kind of large transport, like a floating semi-truck with its engine at the back but its cab up front, began nosing its way out of the warehouse. Its underbelly was being shot to hell by everyone inside, and I could only assume its engines were getting punished just as badly. The thing was already starting to dip towards the ground when Chen and his team opened fire with their scoped weapons, aiming for the glass windshield in front.

They started cursing on the open channel almost immediately as their rounds simply ricocheted off.

"Fucking armor!" Chen snarled, "Aim for the lift engines!"

Very belatedly I started to bring my gun up to join in, then felt myself frowning as the truck's sputtering engines got clear. But rather than tilting back to try and get some altitude, or even just accelerating as best it could to gain distance, the thing began a ponderous turn in place.

It clicked after a couple of seconds, "They're going to block the doors!"

"He's right!" Chen shifted his aim, "Engine block! Now! Human, technicals!"

I jerked my left hand up as everyone else changed their aim yet again, this time going for the rear engines as they became more visible. At least half of them were already out but the extra rifle fire began to shred the remainder while I got my wrist-comp ready. The second time went far more smoothly than my first effort, somewhat helped by the massive target.

My fingers curled and then relaxed in sequence as I repeated the command motion, blue discs whipping out with each movement as I joined in the barrage.

The Discharge grenades I had loaded were mostly intended to rip at shields, or to stun unarmored opponents. But they were also very useful in messing with unshielded electronics in general, and while the truck apparently had armor plating, it didn't have shields.

While I couldn't claim total credit for bringing the thing down, I definitely did my part. Electrical arcs and muffled blue flashes came as the grenades streaked out to detonate beneath the truck, ripping at the various engines keeping its long body upright. The ones on our side began to fail in sequence as the second and third grenades arrived, making the truck tilt dangerously.

Combined with Chen's sharpshooters crippling the turbines on this side, the thing's acceleration and tilt pushed it into a hard swerve before the driver could get it in place to block the warehouse entrance completely. Instead it crashed down with another titanic roar of noise, coming to rest at an angle that would still leave everyone able to move around it.

I was opening my mouth to ask what we were going to do next when the truck's doors actually blew outwards, letting figures leap clear and begin sprinting in our direction.

There were six of them, all of them Thondian by their height and build. Four were in the same dark gray armor that the Naule had been wearing in the attack on the bar, and brought shotguns up to their shoulders to pin us down as they charged. I started to duck as the shots came in, taking in the pair bringing up the rear as I did.

Their armor was bright white with blue accents, a swirling, almost tribal pattern covering their upper chest.

"White Storm!" Chen shouted as he disdained taking cover, firing a few precise shots as he reported to Nynsi, "Fucking White Storm!"

"We're pursuing, hold them!"

A heavy round hit the man in his armored shoulder, sparking off his shields but still driving him down to a knee. "Fuck! You going to use that or what Human!?"

I flinched, sucked in a breath, and then forced my body to rise up so I could level my own gun across the car's hood. They'd crossed about half the distance to us, though at least one of their number was laying limply on the ground. From the sounds of it at least one of our own people was badly injured, and the breathless cursing across the radio made it harder to focus.

Both of the ones in white were heading right for Chen and I, and I settled my aim onto the leader of the pair. His own weapon was shooting at someone to our left, and he seemed to jerk in surprise when I managed a short burst that hammered against his shields. His head and shotgun swung around as I reset my aim and fired again, his response coming with the speed of a professional.

It hit me somewhere in the chest, my helmet's various displays lighting up like a Christmas tree as my shields plummeted, and like Chen I fell onto a knee as I fought to keep my balance. I managed a third burst but that one was a lot less accurate, only a couple of the rounds hitting his shoulder before pulling up and away.

His second shot wasn't as inaccurate and finished the job of breaking my shields. Something in my chest cracked as the breath rushed out of me, leaving me gasping while a small display helpfully told me just how badly my armor was compromised.

Chen had already recovered by then, and he fired off a quick salvo of his own. He must have gotten at least one of them because the other was alone when he vaulted the car and planted both of his feet into the squad leader's chest. Chen went down hard, but twisted as he did, avoiding the coup de grace aimed at his head. The motion threw the other man off of him, and by all rights should have sent him stumbling to the ground.

Instead the bastard somehow managed to land on his armored boots, recover his aim, and put a shotgun blast into Chen's torso. His shields broke in a series of sparks, his armor cracked but held, keeping him alive for a few more seconds.

Time enough for me to lunge forwards and shove my small weapon against the back of the enemy's knee and yank hard on the trigger.

Shields don't really work against things that close, and joints are always a weak point in any armor. Blood exploded out in time with a guttural scream as I more or less cut his leg in half with a long burst of fire. He tipped back as he fell, cracking the back of his head against the car, losing his gun.

I didn't give him a chance to recover it. Scrambling forwards again, I pushed my gun against his chest, then put another too-long burst into where I thought his heart was.

My gun clicked in protest after the tenth shot or so, a small section on the side venting steam as it tried to cool the overheated components.

I was only vaguely aware of the gunfire around me slowly trailing off, the sounds of active battle being replaced with questions, reports, and calls for medical attention. At some point Chen managed to drag me off to one side, propping me against the car and telling me to stay put before he ran off to inspect his people and help finish off the remaining gangsters.

Which suited me just fine.

"Cieran." Nynsi's voice broke me out of my fugue state a few minutes later, my eyes blinking open to find her kneeling beside me. "I see you've already broken the armor I gave you."

I smiled even if she couldn't see it. "Thank you for making sure it was high quality. I feel like I just stopped a car with my chest."

"It rather looks like you did from the outside as well." Her helmet shook once, fingers reaching out to carefully touch my armor before she shook her head a second time. "A heavy round from a quality weapon. Are you injured?"

"Don't think so. Bruised maybe. Everyone else?"

"Five injured, only two severe." She paused, "Laria is not among them, she... fought well."

I smiled a little more. "You really don't like her, do you?"

Rather than respond to such an obvious statement, she simply stood up and offered me a hand. I took it and she hauled me up with as little effort as it had taken her to carry me, only letting go once she was certain I wasn't about to fall over.

"We've counted roughly three dozen True Sons, not counting the armored team. None were well equipped and all are now dead." Nynsi spoke as she guided me around the car, walking towards the warehouse. Presumably so that I could do my actual job of poking around. "That last group was likely their leadership. I would have liked to take at least one alive, but I cannot fault my people for not taking chances."

I made a sound that was meant to convey agreement, but mostly just showed how numb I was. Another dead person to my name... it had been faster, like the time in the garage, but I still felt out of it.

"The presence of White Storm agents is... extremely concerning, though it likely answers just who is supplying them with arms, equipment, and training." There was a slow, almost seething whistle as we approached the crashed truck. "And their contraband."

The last word managed to get through to my punch-drunk brain, and I shook my head a few times as I did my best to focus. "Contraband? What *were* they smuggling in to a planet where almost anything is legal with the right paperwork?"

"The only thing that isn't." She replied simply.

It didn't really click until we stepped around the truck to the side facing the warehouse, and found the vehicle's cargo door forced open.

Trenah, Ghai, and more than a few members of Nynsi's private army were entirely occupied helping... people.

Nervous aliens dressed in little more than rags were being carefully brought out, many of them clutching injuries that had to have come from the crash or stray rounds penetrating the armor plating. Most were Thondians, their heads universally ducked low and to the left, though there more than a few Naule among them. The simian aliens were unkempt, their long hair greasy and unwashed, and all but a handful needed to use all six of their limbs to walk.

The ones that weren't were using one or more of their four hands to help guide down a tiny group of pale skinned Humans, all of whom were thin and shaking as they stared at the aliens surrounding them.

"Oh." I said quietly. "That's... that's not good."

"That," Nynsi sighed, "Is an understatement."

II – I

The weeks after our raid on the warehouse were exciting for everyone but me.

To my immense disappointment Internal Security bundled up the rescued slaves and rushed them to a treatment facility before I could even talk to the few Humans among them. I understood why, they needed medical and psychological help far more than I needed the company of my own species. But that didn't stop me from being childishly irritated, and then becoming annoyed with myself for my reaction.

Not that anyone noticed my morose mood given how hectic things became. While I was occasionally brought into a meeting so that Trenah and Nynsi didn't have to waste their time telling me what was going on, mostly I was told to stay in the garage and focus on my personal project. Nothing motivated like a crisis, and I'd made quite a bit of progress. Especially since Nynsi had told Rane'li and a mechanic named Ullika to help whenever they had a spare moment.

In truth that wasn't all that often but every little bit helped. Especially since Trenah also stopped by whenever she wasn't running missions with Ghai, or when she wasn't arguing with Nynsi about the best way to deploy the various security teams. Xerol spent his time refereeing between them whenever he wasn't meeting with Internal Security, his various underlings, or the one time he was called to personally speak with the High Families.

Which weren't actually families in the way I understood the word. To the Trahcon they were more like corporate CEO's... or maybe mob bosses. Or both. What mattered was that the High Families were the planet's nominal rulers, and when they told Xerol to show up and explain what the hell was going on, he didn't have the option of saying no.

That summons had come just when the True Sons launched an all-out retaliation campaign across Koshun Minor. Vandalism and arson were their most common forms of attack; they did their best to avoid any further pitched battles. There were few if any actual casualties, but it was a pain in the ass for everyone to deal with all the same.

We enjoyed ten days of that before they changed it up. A diversionary attack against the district's tiny spaceport distracted everyone and let them grab a pair of Thondian lawyers right from their office.

The broadcast of their subsequent executions had sent Xerol into a cold fury. He'd called up Ghai and her partner, sending them out with orders to return with high-ranking prisoners of his own. The pair had vanished for four days and left me with even fewer people actually willing to talk about things not related to my project.

Down to a whole two of them in fact.

"I take it they were successful?" I wiped my grease stained hands on a towel, glancing to where Nynsi was politely waiting. She was really the only Thondian I could call a friend, and she remained the only one who actively sought my company.

"Indeed." She replied, keeping herself and her white suit a respectable distance from my disheveled work area. "They located two White Storm officers. Sadly only one of them survived the return trip."

I did my level best not to grimace at that. I *thought* I was starting to get used to what was going on around me, but there were still things that my friends and allies did that I'd rather not know about. "One of the mercenaries helping out the Sons? I thought you said they'd ditch the gang after being exposed. That the Crescent would come down hard on them for being on planet at all."

Nynsi had excellent control of her expression, but something in her dark eyes told me she was fighting back irritation. "Evidently I was wrong, as was my Uncle. According to his Harath'krem they found a squad giving weapons to at least three times as many True Sons. The numbers involved are becoming worrying."

141

That time I couldn't stop my grimace.

Between the attack on the warehouse, the various firefights around the city, and Internal-Security conducting their own raids, everyone was sure that the True Sons *should* have been going to ground after all the casualties they'd suffered. Instead it seemed like ten more were popping up for every one that was killed or arrested. No one was really sure how large the problem was, and that was making Internal-Security very conservative in their response. Until we, or their own detectives, could provide hard data they were sticking to the core districts to make sure the violence didn't spread to the more affluent areas of the city.

"How did they get their prisoner out?" I asked as I finished cleaning up. "I didn't hear any of the squads getting deployed, and Trenah crashed on my couch last night. That's a lot of people for two of them to take on alone."

Nynsi gave me a little shrug, and proved to have noticed my earlier discomfort because she neatly glossed over the details. "My uncle's Harath'krem are experts at infiltration. They had little difficulty, it was nothing they have not done before."

"Huh." I offered as I tossed the towel aside, the two of us starting for the door. "I knew they were good but that's pretty impressive. Oh, reminds me, I've been meaning to ask you what their title even means. I looked it up on the DataNet but every site I went to said it was something different."

"It is not a straightforward position." She admitted. "The direct translation of 'ennobled soul' describes the general purpose. It is a means to elevate a single lowborn or midcaste without having to bother with the process of elevating an entire family. Which is extremely rare and difficult to do."

"Guessing the title is a bit less rare?"

There was a quick shake of her head as we exited the garage, Nynsi leading me towards one of the wings I hadn't visited yet. "Not rare at all, extremely common actually. Most Highborn families have at least one, possibly more. It's the *reason* they were elevated that tends to vary wildly. Traditionally they serve as bodyguards or advisors, elevated to the position due to their loyalty or exemplary service."

I nodded slowly, "And not traditionally?"

"Particularly wealthy members of the midcaste are able to purchase the position from time to time." Patrician features scrunched up in distaste, "Worse, it is becoming common to use it as a means to raise illicit lovers from the lower castes. It makes them more socially acceptable, and gives any illegitimate children a claim to a higher caste."

"Ah." I coughed lightly, "I'm going to assume that Ghai and Iyaht are the first type, and that aliens are allowed the title?"

"It's the only title aliens are legally allowed in the Ascendancy, the only way for them to become citizens." She shook her head, "My people are not quite as xenophobic as your own. Sadly that means little, those in the Ascendancy are hardly welcoming."

"They're not exactly welcoming here, either." I said, taking care to lower my voice as I did.

Nynsi's already rigid back straightened further. "Have you been harassed?"

"Not really, I think everyone is too terrified of you and Xerol." I paused and considered my words before shrugging, "I'm mostly ignored unless I step right in front of them and make them pay attention to me, which I only do when I *really* need something. They're quick to help when I do, and just as quick to ignore me the moment it's convenient for them."

"I will speak with the garage staff." Her voice lowered as well, "They are supposed to provide you with all possible assistance."

I felt flattered at her apparent anger, and a little alarmed at the same time. "They're actually the best, I think because I'm around so much. Rane'li spent yesterday re-writing the suit's display code for me, and Ullika has been helping with some of the hydraulics when he's not busy with the cars."

My words seemed to calm her down. "Good. I'll speak to the others. I will see about pulling in Trahcon staff from our other operations if things do not improve."

I opened my mouth to protest only to see her tilt her head to the right, eyes narrowing. The order to shut my mouth and let her handle it was practically audible, so I simply held both of my hands up in silent surrender.

That earned me a prim little nod and we fell silent as we entered a stairwell, heading down into a basement I hadn't even known was there. Though instead of being dark and ominous like some kind of bizarre dungeon, it was as brightly lit as any of the hallways above.

A turn into a side-hall and a short walk brought us to something like a police interrogation room. Numerous holographic and console displays were mounted against one wall and hovering above a single conference table. Most were showing various news reports on both White Storm and the True Sons, while a few others showed our prisoner.

Trenah and Rehat were both seated at the table, but they and the room were less interesting than the two-way mirror dominating the entire far wall.

The prisoner, a Trahcon woman in bloodstained white and blue fatigues, was tied to a metal chair on the far side. She had several bruises on her face, turning her gray skin something mottled and unpleasant, but she seemed mostly intact beyond that. Behind her was Ghai, leaning casually against the wall with her eyes closed, while in front Xerol was slowly pacing back and forth.

"Now," Xerol's strong voice came from hidden speakers, Trenah impatiently waving us in to join them at the table. "You have a few options available to you my dear. The most pleasant of which is to simply tell us everything you know."

The bound woman tried to twitch her tarah and flinched in pain. A closer look let me see some kind of bar-like device locked around them both, holding them immobile and presumably stopping her from calling up any energy.

I added yet another research item to my ever growing list.

"And be killed by my employer?" She shook her head once, "No thanks, and don't bother offering me sanctuary. You're about to drown and I know it."

He nodded slowly, "Then I will see you in three days, I am led to believe you can survive that long without attention."

That statement clearly took her aback. "Wait, what?"

"Were my words incorrect? You seem to be an intelligent woman. Torture through pain is rarely effective, so I must trust more reliable methods. Regrettably they will take time." And our host did look regretful, which was a credit to his apparent acting talent. "It is not a pleasant thing to watch a being starve and thirst, unable to sleep or move, forced to sit in their own refuse, but our questions must be answered."

Her shoulders tightened at each word of what would be happening to her. "White Storm is a legally registered corporation. You can't torture me, they'd take you for everything in court."

"Perhaps." Xerol allowed, "My Harath'krem's extraction was not as clean as I would like, it is possible your superiors will learn of your situation. But will that console you while you are locked in this room? I am told that your people do not handle the dehydration process very well. Perhaps I will leave a pitcher of water on this table, just beyond your reach, so that you will be reminded of what you will receive for cooperating."

I shifted uncomfortably, less certain that Xerol was merely acting.

The imprisoned mercenary licked her lips once, then exhaled. "If I do, will you let me go, or at least send me to Internal-Security?"

"You trust an organization that blatantly takes bribes from the Crescent, your corporation's largest rival, over myself?"

"Yeah." She replied bluntly.

Xerol's back was to me, so I couldn't see his expression, but he waved a single hand after a short pause. "My word that you'll be given to them, with my recommendation you be moved to protective custody in a southern arcology."

The prisoner stared up at him with bright blue eyes, then nodded once and seemed to sag in her restraints. "Ask your questions then."

"Tell me about yourself first. Are you a recent hire or an experienced agent?"

"New hire." She provided tonelessly. "I used to train corporate security, White Storm offered half again my usual salary with a future position as an officer if I did well."

Xerol thumped his cane on the floor, "Strictly as a trainer? And why bring you in, considering that the True Sons loathe your species?"

"No. Once the stupid aliens were trained up I was going to be moved to a combat team, and my bosses told the aliens to drown themselves when they bitched about it." Her expression started to darken, then she winced when her tarah tried to move to show her emotions. "I wouldn't have taken the contract if I'd known. Nothing's worth the kind of shit those idiots said. Or tried."

"Then why bring you in at all?"

"To remind them that my bosses are the ones who tell them when and where they can fight." She rolled a shoulder as best she could, "Little bastards have been sailing with their own winds a bit too much, our commander's been putting his foot on their necks to knock them back into their place."

There was a slight nod, "And your commander's name?"

"Arrogant Naule bastard named Yarrath. Didn't give his clan name and I didn't like him enough to ask." Another attempt at a shrug, "He was angry about not being involved in the other operations, he hated having to waste his time teaching baby fish how to hold a gun."

Xerol tilted his head to the right and thumped his cane once more, "To what end? Why is your corporation involved with a minor gang on Alum?"

To my lack of surprise, the woman had no real idea. She wasn't nearly high enough in the corporate food chain to know the full plan. What she was able to provide was plenty of information on the True Sons themselves and none of it was good. Her first big drop was confirmation that all of the idiots she'd been training had been shipped here. Most had come from Terminus, but others had been recruited on smaller colonies. Unpleasant news, but nothing we hadn't expected.

That turned the conversation to the people we'd accidentally rescued... and resulted in everything becoming far more complicated.

"The slaves?" Our prisoner grimaced, "I don't know all that much about that, but I do know that's supposed to be the main focus of our operations. Pretty sure a couple of True Son leaders got their throats cut for moving against you early, they weren't supposed to until later. When things escalated."

"Escalated?" Xerol inquired. "And how would such a thing happen? A gang openly bringing in off-world aliens as slaves is merely a gang who will cease to exist once revealed."

"They're aren't keeping them." There was a short pause before she corrected herself, "I don't *think* they're keeping them. Too many are coming in for them to hide it if they aren't moving them somehow. I think they get brought in, processed and clean up, then get sold off to someone else."

Xerol pressed her on that, but she either didn't know more or was unwilling to say more. Given how quickly she'd caved earlier I was betting on the former, and that left us debating among ourselves while he began to run her through it all a second time to verify her story.

"Who would be foolish enough to buy slaves on Alum?" Nynsi pursed her lips, "The High Families have always eliminated anyone who crosses the line between contractual servitude and open slavery."

"Hn." Rehat agreed, a broad hand rising in a little gesture I wasn't familiar with. "They have to. Empire would send one of their warlords if they didn't."

I cautiously spoke up, "What's the point of even owning slaves really? I mean, what would they be used for?"

Rehat seemed surprised that I'd spoken, but after a moment he gave me an almost cautious nod and explained. "Depends on who owns them. If it's a single person it's about what you'd expect; sex and household servants. Not usually practical but in certain circles owning slaves is a means to inflate one's social ego. Businesses use them as workers, farmers, things like that. Usually the up-front cost means only the big players get involved, at least in places that consider themselves civilized."

Trenah grunted, "You get farther out in the Reaches and the waters get bloodier. Some colonies are more than half slave, especially the ones the old-school Naule settled after the Empire grabbed their homeworld and obliterated their culture. Lot of Thondians get off on the idea too. The Ascendancy is filled with slaves."

Tellingly, neither Nynsi nor Rehat denied it, leaving me to grimace and thank my lucky stars that I'd ended up on Alum instead of almost anywhere else.

"So we're either looking for rich idiots with more greed and lust than good sense," I said, "Or corporations with money to burn and no morals to speak of. Isn't the latter more likely if lots of people are being moved?"

"Yes," Nynsi agreed, "However, as my cousin stated, it is a suicidal maneuver. A ban on slavery is one of the very few requirements that the Empire enforces on High Families. Knowingly enabling the practice is grounds for an invasion, and everyone knows that the Empire is always looking for an excuse to start a new war."

I frowned, "Is that what White Storm wants? An imperial invasion?"

The Thondian woman shrugged, "I don't see how that gains them anything. The Crescent is occasionally erratic but they aren't *that* foolish. They would evacuate in advance of any such attack, probably to the old headquarters at Cathia. An annoyance to be sure, but not a crippling blow. Hardly worth the White Storm's effort. And the True Sons would just as obviously never support such a plan. The Empire does not leave after it conquers, the Naule and your own species know that well enough."

Rehat made a sound that was somewhere between a hum and a growl, "What about-"

A chair abruptly slammed backwards as Trenah shot to her feet, her tarah angling as high as they could go while she spat a non-stop stream of curses. I took a quick step backwards in surprise, while Nynsi and Rehat both reached for weapons that weren't on their belts, stilling somewhat awkwardly when their brains caught up with them.

"-Ashahn's Aspect-fucking bleeding-"

"Trenah!" I reached out and grabbed her shoulder before she could start pacing, "What the fuck?"

"Those fuckers are trying to fucking jump-start a gods-damned hurricane is what!" I flinched as she all but shouted in my face. When I merely held my free hand up in confusion, and Nynsi and Rehat glanced at one another, she growled and elaborated. "If we're a side-show that means this slaving crap is the main event, and it's supposed to escalate things to point where a reinforced gang could take this district."

I nodded slowly as I let her go, "All right, I can get that, but how?"

She waved an impatient hand, "White Storm knows the little alliance they put together out in the Reaches can't take the Crescent directly. It's too fragile a confederation, and the Crescent has too many big ships, so they're trying to summon up a bigger shark to do it for them."

It abruptly clicked in my head. "Fuck. That's... disgusting but kind of clever."

Nynsi narrowed her eyes, "Would the pair of you please explain yourselves properly?"

We both turned to her, though it was Trenah who replied, "It's exactly like you fucking said. It's a suicidal maneuver guaranteed to bring in the Empire unless the High Families crack down the instant they find out about it. White Storm knows that, so they set up a scam. Bring in slaves, clean them up, sell them as contracted servants. If any of them bitch that they're not willing most people will just assume they're trying to get out of their contract. Not like idiots don't already try that."

"But as I also said, the Crescent is hardly that..." She paused, then let out a very unladylike curse of her own. "They don't sell them to the Crescent, they sell them to sub-contractors and allies. Groups that the Crescent needs to support their operations."

I nodded, "And when the moment's right they reveal everything and chaos erupts. The High Families would lose everything if the Empire invaded, so they'd have to be fast and ruthless. White Storm probably has a bunch of people ready to take advantage however it turns out, and if it doesn't work they don't really lose much. Couple of squads, some investments, but not much more."

Trenah made a sound of agreement, "This is probably less about them actually gaining anything and more about them giving their rivals a hard punch in the throat. Distracting them from something else at worst, getting the Crescent booted off Alum at best. That'd be one insane coup to pull off, they'd go from middle-tier to the highest tables on Terminus with one operation."

I wasn't quite sure what the latter meant but Nynsi swore again and glared at nothing in particular.

"A plausible theory." Rehat rumbled after a few moments, "But unless we have proof beyond inference I'm afraid it won't mean much. The High Families have no love for my Patriarch, and Kolkris would sooner kill all of us than listen to what we have to say."

I blinked at the name and glanced at Nynsi.

"The leader of the Crescent." She provided, exhaling and visibly calming herself. "A madwoman by any species' standards, but an exceptionally dangerous and intelligent one, I doubt we will get anywhere with her. Better to locate further evidence to provide Internal-Security so that we can convince the Families."

"Well we'd better get on that shit." Trenah grumbled, turning back to where Xerol was running the prisoner through her story for a third time. "If

we're right, those assholes will do everything they can to drown us the moment they realize what we're up to."

The good news was that Xerol agreed with our theory. Within a day he'd called up contacts in Internal-Security, agents of the High Families, and gotten a hold of Tasir just before her ship departed. The last had grasped what he was saying before he'd even finished and promised that checking out the White Storm enclave would be her first priority when she got to Terminus.

The bad news was that none of the local authorities agreed. According to Nynsi, the High Families thought the whole thing was some kind of power-play from Xerol. A scheme to remove several business rivals so that he could take the lucrative contracts the Crescent tended to dole out to their long-term suppliers. They'd shut the door in his face and were ordering the Internal-Security branches in the richer areas of the city to not lift a finger to help us.

Equally bad was that the local Internal-Security groups believed it plausible, but their pride was on the line. They didn't want to admit that slave smuggling could have been happening under their noses for weeks, months, or years. Instead they believed the operation we'd interrupted to have been a first effort in a plan now likely abandoned, and were planning to focus on containing the fighting rather than launching more raids.

Which led to the worst news, at least from my perspective.

"I still can't believe they're *drafting* me." I complained as I forced a bit of armor plating on my exoskeleton's arm. "The only thing I've managed to do in fights is not get horribly killed. And that was thanks to dumb luck, not skill."

From her place at a nearby console, fingers tapping away as she updated a few of the armor's settings, Rane'li hummed in agreement. "It does make the Patriarch seem rather desperate."

"Desperate?" Ullika let out a deep grunt from behind the suit. "I don't think that word is strong enough, *kallithas.*"

"Don't call me that." It was probably the tenth time I'd heard her say that, and neither one of them would tell me what the damn word meant. It hadn't been in the dictionary I'd downloaded to my wrist-comp, which probably meant it was slang. "And by his species' standards you must admit that this one is surprisingly tolerable."

The man poked his head around, revealing skin just a few shades lighter than Rane'li's almost ink-black tones, his head tilted to the right. "Hrn. I suppose that for a fur-covered *chenethic* he's not all bad. Plus watching him fall on his face every ten steps was funny as shit."

I sighed. *That* word I had figured out, and it wasn't a very polite one in any language that I knew. "I didn't fall down that often, you can stop bringing it up any day now."

Ullika barked out a laugh and retreated behind the suit once more, "Right, it was more like every twelve steps. You looked like a drunken fool staggering and moaning about how your furry ass was bruised."

Rane'li was too polite to laugh along with him, but she made a strangled noise and kept her body posture rigidly neutral when I threw a disgusted look in her direction. That merely made her turn her chair away, leaving me muttering to myself as I tried to focus on what I was doing.

It turned out that learning how to walk in a powered exoskeleton was awkward as hell. I was suddenly a good twelve inches taller, eight inches wider, and even with the various gyros helping to keep it steady the entire suit shifted awkwardly every time I took a step. To make it worse, the range of motion on the arms was limited by the bulky metal around them. That made keeping my balance even more annoying.

Nynsi had been quite pleased that it was as far along as it was, though Trenah had noted it was long way from being usable as anything but a decoration.

Which was harsh but true. The weight had been even more than I'd anticipated meaning the thing was god-awful slow. Not much faster than a brisk walk even after I'd gotten used to the strange gait. And as far as combat went... it had no built-in weapons, the shields were installed but failed half the tests we put them through, and even external weapons were iffy since its hands weren't sized for normal guns.

In short it wasn't likely anything would come of the idea beyond the prototype when it was finally completed. Even for a glorified door warden it was just too slow, it would be too time intensive to configure for another user, and Nynsi had admitted the only reason she still had me working on it was the fact that it wasn't really costing her anything.

Still, in theory the thing had enough armor to qualify as a small tank. More than enough to deal with the ramshackle collection of guns used by the True Sons. And since it was already configured for me Xerol had decided I could use it in combat if needed. Only as one of his 'emergency guards' of the mansion estate, I wasn't to be assigned to any of the actual security teams, but it had still left me rather unhappy.

Trenah pointing out that we didn't really have a choice, being guests in his home, hadn't helped.

"At least you won't have to run anywhere." Rane'li said when she managed to get a hold of herself, once more turning to face me directly. "You are to be just a reserve asset, are you not?"

I nodded and inspected the arm I'd been working on, checking to make sure I hadn't interfered with the range of motion. "So far as I know."

"A glorified statue next to the front door, something for those flying lizards to aim at." Ullika snickered. "When you aren't busy catching bullets for the rest of us."

I sighed again, "If the back cover is secure then you're pretty much done. So, you know, go do something else. More productive. Far away from here."

There was something like a snort before the taller man threw his hands up and walked off without saying anything further. Something I'd assumed to be rude the first time he'd done it, but from what I'd learned since was actually considered polite by Thondians. Something about not needing to waste time with further words, with farewells reserved for when you seriously meant them.

"He doesn't like you." My other temporary assistant informed me the moment he was out of earshot.

"I know." I replied, "The insults give it a way."

Rane'li shook her head before returning to her code. "Ullika considers himself above you. If it weren't for the Patriarch's orders he'd sooner throw you out a third floor window than speak with you."

I started to reply but pursed my lips before any words could get out. I really hadn't gotten that bad of a vibe from him, but then again I only had the barest understanding of how Thondian posture interacted with their language. It was possible, probable with Rane's words, that he was being a lot ruder to me than I thought.

"What about you?" I asked without looking over. "Do you want to strangle me every time you talk to me as well?"

"I would not say that I wish to strangle you," She audibly hedged, "And you are strangely... tolerable for one of your kind."

Yet another sigh made me shake my head and fall silent as I got back to work. Rane'li evidently didn't feel the need to waste further words either. She stayed quiet for the rest of the hour, and didn't offer any goodbyes when she wrapped up for the day.

The rest of the garage staff departed around the same time as her, leaving me alone in the cavernous room.

I spent most of another hour distracting myself with work. Mostly just getting the rest of the armor plating attached to the left arm and then the left leg. Once that was done I didn't really have much else to do since I couldn't test the shields by myself, or start on the weapons. The latter was scheduled for tomorrow morning with Trenah supposedly going to spend all day helping me get a technical launcher into the right arm.

In truth I probably could have gotten started, at least in prepping for that project, but after a full day of tests I wasn't really in the mood for overtime. So instead I wandered out of the main doors to go looking for my best friend.

It was already twilight out, damned approaching winter, and the estate's lights had probably been on for an hour or so. Statues and flowers

155

alike were illuminated to show them off, while hidden emitters along the ground made sure the paths were clear enough to walk along.

I took my time, enjoying the ambiance and the cooling air. About ten minutes later I found her in the southern section of the gardens, stripped down to a pair of loose shorts with a sword in her left hand. Her bare back glistened slightly with sweat, highlighting the tattoos that covered everything from her neck to her waist with images of storms and lightning. The body art moved with her muscles as she ran through some kind of exercise, sword whistling as it cut the air.

"Done already?" She asked without pausing.

"It's an hour past the garage closing." I noted, crossing my arms as I watched, a little intrigued. Not by Trenah's body, there remained no attraction there, but by the weapon and movements.

I'd never seen her with the blade she was working with before. It was something like a kukri, but thinner and longer. Different from the straight sword I knew she'd taken from the mansion's armory.

"Nice sword."

Her tarah twitched outwards. "It's an old piece of driftwood is what it is."

"Doesn't look that old." I frowned, taking a closer look. She paused and stepped closer, turning it so I could see an extremely worn grip along with a battered cross-guard. Some kind of circuitry was visible along the sides, along with lettering similar to but distinct enough from Caranat that I couldn't read it. "Family weapon?"

"You know Trahcon don't have families like your kind." Trenah slide the blade into a sheath before turning and heading for the shirt she'd left on the ground. "Aside from a few crazy fish. This battered thing is from the man who trained me back when I was a stupid little huntress. And don't you say shit about my height."

Since I'd been about to make a comment on that very thing, I gave her a sheepish grin and shrugged. "This what you've been up to all day then? Figured you'd be out on a mission for Xerol or hanging out with Ghai."

Both tarah quivered again, this time showing agitation. "Don't mention either of those fuckers. I'm sick of them both."

That took me aback. "You are?"

"*Yes.*" She hissed, yanking her shirt on in quick, angry motions. "Fucking Xerol keeps forgetting I'm not his damned employee, or one of his little bodyguards. Ghai is sexy and the best fuck I've had in years, but she won't stop trying to get me to officially join up. I'm ready to smash both of their heads together."

I blinked. "She wants you to join up? Like, as an employee?"

"As in one of her aspects-damned *pack.*"

I'd learned enough about Trahcon to know that was a big deal. Like a fucking huge deal. Like a combination of an adoption and a marriage proposal kind of deal. "She likes you that much?"

"Fuck if I know!" The snarl came as she paced back and forth a few steps, not looking at me. "I've met her on and off over the last decade but we don't fucking know each other *that* well. I'm pretty sure it's the same shit that Tasir has been bitching about for the last two decades. Treating me like I'm some wounded little huntress who needs a safe nest to crawl back to."

Oh boy. This was touching on things I'd never dared ask about. Things I'd generally done my best to avoid even thinking about, as if even doing so was an invasion of Trenah's privacy.

Trahcon lived with their packs, groups as large as a dozen or more. In pairs or trios at the bare minimum. Always.

Trenah lived alone in an apartment meant for three to six people. Apparently had for decades.

"Trenah-"

She cut me off before I could even try to calm her down. "I don't even know why I'm bitching to you. Aliens don't fucking understand."

I winced. "Trenah..."

"I'm fucking sick of this place." She practically spat the words. "Of this palace and all the little fish bowing to their every whim. Sick of having to deal with Thondians day in and day out. Of Tasir sailing off and leaving us with her tides-cursed mess. Sick of Ghai and the others staring at me like I'm some broken fucking thing they have to fix."

Her volume had risen as she kept rolling, and I didn't like the idea of anyone nearby hearing this. Bracing myself, I took a few steps forwards and gently touched her shoulder. She jerked at the touch, spinning around to glare up at me. Both of her tarah were angled as high they could go, quivering madly with anger, and I could smell ozone in the air.

Something electrical crackled when I pulled my hand away. The motion made her eyes narrow, then she exhaled and half closed them. A few moments later the invisible energy seemed to dissipate, the sounds and smells fading.

"Sorry." The word was a sullen mutter, but she took a small step forwards before pressing her forehead against my chest. "I'm an Aspects-damned Guide. I should have better control."

I let out a slow breath then cautiously wrapped my arms around her stocky frame. "Sounds like you've been keeping that bottled up for a while. This why you've been sleeping on my couch the last few days?"

There was a deep inhalation and then a puff of warmth against my shirt as she let it out. "More or less."

"There something else?"

"There's always something else." Another tired sigh came as she finally returned the hug, squeezing me tight enough to make me wince before letting go. I let her step back, watching as she rolled her neck. "I don't like that Xerol is dragging you into this storm, Cie. I can't say I know Humans, but I think I know you, and this isn't the kind of thing you should be involved in."

"I don't really want to be involved." I admitted, shaking my head. "But I'm not going to abandon you. I owe you for everything you've done, and you're my friend. One of two that I've even got."

She smiled for a brief second. "And I appreciate you not sailing off, I do, but this... shit. We're living here and it would be stupid as fuck for you not to help defend the place, but you've got to be careful around Xerol. And his bitch of a niece."

"Nynsi isn't-"

"I know you like her." Trenah growled, "And I know she actually talks to you like you're a person, unlike practically everyone else here. But Thondians don't do charity. Or casual friendships or whatever you've think you've got with her. If she's being nice to you she's doing it for a bloody reason. There's always a motive with them. It's how they're wired."

I blinked. "What kind of reason could she have? I'm an apprentice mechanic with no real combat experience, no contacts, and no wealth."

"True, but you've got a quick mind and an attention for detail." There was a shrug, "Maybe she just wants you as a cheap adviser or contact. Or maybe she's got some kind of fetish for furry things."

I sighed. "Really?"

Trenah managed a smirk, looking almost like her normal self. "Just saying to be careful around her and to actually think with your head instead of your dick. I know how you men are."

"Of the two of us, I'm pretty sure you're the one with a one-track mind." I countered. "Don't think I didn't notice you checking out that shuttle pilot yesterday."

"Illyahn." A glazed look slowly crept over her face. "Mmm, did you see her muscles?"

I rubbed at my forehead, amusement and exasperation at war. "Good to know that a tight ass is all it takes to make you forget about any serious conversation we have."

Her left tarah twitched downwards once. "It's a lot more fun to talk about and you know it."

"I... fine, fine." I shook my head, "But promise you'll track me down and vent if you need to? You scared me there for a bit."

Trenah's turquoise eyes stared at me a for a few long seconds, then she exhaled and nodded once. "I'll try. Not really used to having anyone around *to* vent to in the first place, but I'll do my best. Now can we get some food and work out a plan that ends with me fucking someone in your bed?"

"Why *my* bed!?"

She smirked. "Because it'll be fun."

I growled and muttered, mostly for show, and we started on our walk back to the nearest door.

In typical fashion, we'd just gotten back inside when the alarms started up.

II – III

We found Nynsi in the garage, the tall woman yanking armor on over her business suit. Other members of the staff were doing the same, maroon uniforms vanishing beneath ceramic and metal plating. I didn't think many, if any of them, had the tiled under-suits. That would limit how much protection they actually had, there'd be vulnerable openings, but it would be a hell of a lot better than nothing.

"What's happening?" Trenah demanded about a millisecond before I could.

"Evidently taking prisoners was a line we were not meant to cross." Nynsi replied, "The local Internal Security building is being attacked as we speak, as is the district's spaceport. Fortunately one of them was stupid enough to make an unsecured broadcast, so we know that those raids are intended to divert our resources to allow for an attack on this mansion."

I sucked in a breath, "How many are coming?"

"Unknown, but they must believe they have enough to overwhelm us or they wouldn't be bothering."

Trenah let out a frustrated breath, "Couple of dozen at least. Maybe more. How many teams do you have here?"

"One." Was the grim reply.

Eight guards to defend a building the size of a small high school. Even if I included the three of us, plus Ghai and her partner, that didn't really improve our odds. But... this was why all of the staff had guns so that they could act as a reserve, the same group I'd been assigned to.

I just really wished I hadn't been called up quite this soon.

"Outnumbered again then." I glanced between them and tried not to look nervous. From their combined expressions I didn't really manage it.

"What's the plan?"

Nynsi pulled a gauntlet on and gave me a level look while she did. "Defend our home. Laria, my Patriarch requests that you assist Ghai in defending the entrance hall along with what guards remain. I will defend the garage with most of the reserves and Cieran. Iyaht will take the rest to defend the good doctor and will be on alert for any secondary breaches."

After the conversation we'd just had, Trenah's unhappy twitch at the mention of the other three prominent Trahcon in the estate didn't surprise me. Personally I'd only exchanged a tiny handful of words with Iyaht or the doctor, a slim man named Urrast'Rae, and they'd seemed pleasant enough. Better company than the rest of the mansion staff, that was for sure. But if Trenah wasn't happy with them, I felt obliged to take her side.

I shook my head once. This wasn't the time to try and distract myself, "Um, what do you want me to do?"

"Is your armor functional?"

"Technically." I hedged, "The shields sort-of worked the last time we tested them, and all of the armor is on. But it still doesn't have any built in weapons. It can't use mine either."

The Thondian noblewoman let out a sharp whistle, her species equivalent of an explosive sigh from what I could tell. "Can it at least interface with a standard gun?"

I nodded once, "If you have one with a large enough grip, and Rane's code works, yes. The coolant feed is definitely functional so unless I burn through the entire ammunition clip I can fire as long as you need."

"Good. I will send a runner to the armory, please prepare the suit. You'll be in the back acting as fire support." She resumed latching the rest of her armor in place as she spoke, ignoring an agitated Trenah as she did. "I don't anticipate that they will have anything that can breach the armor plating so you will be safer than if you were running around with Laria."

That made Trenah's jaw clench and her tarah lift, "...fine, but I'm having a long fucking talk with your uncle when this shit is done with. I want to know what in Ashahn's fucking name you think you're up to."

Nynsi stared flatly at her, then turned her dark eyes to me. I could hear the wordless question and could only roll a shoulder in a silent shrug.

"Very well." She said after another moment, "I will schedule something if we all survive the next hour. Now if you could please...?"

There was a huff then Trenah bumped me with her shoulder as she headed for the door. I watched her leave, and only when Nynsi gave me an impatient look did I turn away and jog over to where my project loomed in a corner.

A finger-swipe on my wrist-comp brought it online, a second's work linking it to the suit's systems. Another gesture sent the open command; hydraulics pushing the chest plating out and swinging the box-like head upwards and backwards. From there I had to plant a foot on one of its knees and climb up onto the shoulders.

Then I had the fun of slowly lowering my body into the thing without hurting myself.

Fingers slid into the waldo units that connected them to suit's actual hands, while padded clamps secured my feet just above the suit's ankles. Then it was quick nudge of my chin against the power button to kick the core to life. The hydraulics hissed and within a few seconds I was cocooned in armor and steel.

"Secure." I reported as the various displays started up, camera boxes giving me a much better view than the thin vision slit. "Looks like everything's working. For now."

"Good, I'd have hated to waste my time helping a savanna make something that didn't work." Ulika's deep voice came from the speakers behind me, his armored form approaching from my right. He held an unusually long rifle in his arms; the thing was better than five feet long. I had no idea what species could have even used it comfortably, and rather hoped none of them were among the attackers. "Here you go."

"I can't exactly-"

He dropped the weapon onto a nearby workbench and turned away before I could finish, striding off to join the others moving cars into defensive positions. A vaguely disgusted sound came across the comms, then Rane'li stepped away from where she'd been standing next to Nynsi.

Without a word she helped link the coolant feed from the suit's right arm into the base of the weapon, as well as connecting the secondary cable that linked it to my targeting system. My displays promptly updated to give me something like a video game screen, complete with a heat bar, an ammunition counter, and a little targeting reticle that moved wildly around as I took the weapon in over-sized hands.

"Thank you." I said once it was in place.

"You are welcome." Rane'li informed me in her usual neutral tones. "Lady Shaaryak requests you move to the rear to clear space for additional barricades."

I nodded, not that she could see it given the fact that the suit's head was anchored in place, sunken into the shoulders. It gave the whole suit a very hunchbacked appearance but it had let me slap extra armor on to help protect my skull. And given the choice between looking cool and staying alive, I'd choose the latter every time.

Besides, the tiny cameras feeding me video meant there wasn't really a need to turn my head around anyway. Unless they all got damaged, in which case I'd be mostly blind except for a tiny view forwards... but I did my best not to think about that.

It didn't take me long to lumber over to where Nynsi was directing the placement of the last of the aircars. They'd moved most of them off to the side, but four were parked in a rough line a few yards in front of the back wall. Bumper to bumper, a pair directly in front of the door, the others with their noses pressed up against the walls, leaving small avenues for us to move through if we needed to advance.

Everything else, including the crate they'd originally brought my armor with, had been shoved against the wall opposite the cars. That left a wide open space about twenty yards long. It was blatant enough that even I could tell that the True Sons would have to be insane to try and come straight in at us.

"We're leaving the main door open?" I asked Nynsi, "Are you trying to lure them into doing something they shouldn't?"

Nynsi nodded, light reflecting off the visor on her helmet. "The more we can entice to die here, the better. Ulika, Rane'li, take your positions on the far right. Cieran? I want you firing over the car on your left. I'll be just across, if we have to retreat I'll cover your egress from the suit."

"Got it." I replied quietly. My heart was starting to speed up as my everything got tense, and it was hard to keep my voice even.

Distracting myself in the time I had seemed like a good idea, so I started testing my range of motion. The cables didn't seem to get caught on anything when I swung the gun left to right, then up and down. I'd still have to be careful to make sure they didn't get torn or stuck on anything, since if they got disconnected my aim would go straight to hell.

A quiet ping from the speakers told me someone was broadcasting on the main channel, Trenah's strong voice coming across a moment later. *"Everyone in the mansion, get your fucking asses moving if you aren't in position already. We've got six trucks and a dozen aircars breaking from traffic and heading straight here. Good news, the mansion's barriers should stop them from just crashing in and killing us all in a blaze of fucking disaster. Better news, everyone is drowning the stupid fucks so we'll be getting reinforcements soon."*

There was a long pause and a muffled sound before she spoke again, *"Xerol wants to say something, probably fucking poetry."*

A long sigh came through, making my lips twitch into a grin. *"Please forgive our heathen companion my friends, she lacks the ability to properly appreciate our culture. I ask that you all remember the five Pillars of Strength upon which we stand. Power, Knowledge, Heart, Kin, and Unity. May the Paragons who stand above them guide us as we defend our home this night."*

Nynsi and the others murmured something together that sounded vaguely spiritual.

"Right... poetic, like I said." I could practically see Trenah's irreverent shrug, *"Ashahn can smite the stupid fuckers if her sacred ass isn't too busy fucking the lazy fish on the homeworld."* I had to bite my tongue to stop from laughing. *"Anyways, looks like they're making their final approach... cameras show three trucks to the garage, two for the front door. Last is setting up to circle with the aircars. If they've got better troops with I'd bet all my fucking money they're in those."*

"Expect contact in moments." Xerol spoke through another sigh, this one sounding like it came from Ghai's raspy throat. *"Call out at once if you require reinforcements, respond with readiness if you please."*

"This is Iyaht." Ghai's soft spoken partner sounded off first, *"The good doctor is safe and my team is ready to run around when you need us."*

"This is Nynsi. The garage team is secure and prepared." She stated formally.

I blew out a long breath, sliding into place behind my aircar. I was a good two feat taller than it even when I crouched. The servos whirred quietly as my right knee struck the floor, my left foot settling aside to help me keep my balance. Holding the awkward weapon in a single hand, I laid it along the roof of the car and tried to brace myself for what was coming.

Nynsi took up her place to the right and resumed giving orders as she did. "Ullika, Bolz, you are our reserve. Hold fire until they approach within the garage itself. Rane'li, Cieran, you will provide cover fire. Pin them down even if you do not have a direct target. Everyone else concentrate fire on anyone with proper equipment or anything that looks like a heavy weapon. We cannot afford to lose our cover."

Or me. I resisted a shudder and muttered a quiet prayer to whoever might be listening that the enemy didn't have any. I had no confidence in the suit's shielding if anyone showed up with a rocket launcher or the alien equivalent. Considering that the armor wasn't exactly built for easy escape, even a glancing hit could result in some fairly ugly injuries for me.

"All teams prepare, they are landing." Xerol's disturbingly calm voice came just as a floating truck buzzed into sight, coming down in a rapid hover

landing. It was about half the size as the ones we'd seen in the warehouse, probably liberated from an honest delivery service.

The first driver was, to be blunt, a fucking idiot. He spun the vehicle around so that the people leaping out of the back could sprint directly into the garage. Which would have been all right if there hadn't been anyone inside waiting for them.

But instead all he managed to do was to give us a shooting gallery straight into his vehicle.

I settled my gun, putting my left hand onto it as a brace, and fired off a quick burst. Nynsi opened up with her scoped pistol at roughly the same moment, quickly followed by Rane'li and her automatic rifle. Slower shots came from everyone else as they fired only when they had clear targets.

There were a few screams as bodies tumbled out, bloody mist puffing into the air as the gang members died. More shouts and cries followed as those behind tried to push their way forwards, realizing that they had to get out or die.

My first burst surprised me by how little I noticed the recoil... as in, not at all. I'd automatically tried to compensate for what I'd come to expect from my normal gun, and managed to track the few rounds down and to the left rather than letting the gun remain steady. Still, it didn't really matter given the situation, so I quickly adjusted my grip and let go at full auto.

What followed was a very rapid slaughter.

I found myself wincing soon after easing off the trigger to let the gun cool down. We were maybe twenty seconds in and there were a good dozen True Sons dead or bleeding out in the back of the vehicle, a few quiet cries barely audible over its rattling engine. The cabin itself must not have been armored because it slurred drunkenly to one side, digging a soft divot into the soil as it dropped the last foot to the ground.

A few of the quickest might have made it to either side of the garage, but not more than that.

"Well," I said, "That's done with."

Nynsi managed to convey exasperation even through her helmet, but at least one or two of the mansion's reserves chuckled loudly. "This is the garage, first truck is down. Amateurs."

"Confirmed. First assault on the entrance hall was repulsed without losses." Trenah reported back as we all waited for the next targets to arrive. *"Fucking morons just rushed in the front doors. Cameras show them spreading out now, so make sure your asses don't get flanked."*

"Understood. Both remaining trucks landing!" Nynsi's voice rose a bit as the next two vehicles appeared. Showing that even these idiots could learn from their mistakes, one moved out of view entirely, probably to set down out of our sight, while the other swung around so that the already downed truck would cover its people as they disembarked.

"They can learn." I muttered, not looking at the mess from the first truck in favor of focusing on the new targets. A single burst chased someone back behind the wreckage, while a second person tried to run out from the other side. Rane'li cut them down before they got more than a few paces, a Naulian body tumbling to join the corpses already littering the garden.

Directly to my left, a man whose armor only partially covered the uniform of the kitchen staff, spoke up. "Hey, savanna... Human, I mean. You hear me in there?"

"Yeah." I fired off bursts in a slow rhythm, making sure no one got adventurous on our side of the fight. I wasn't sure if that was the best tactic but it seemed to be working. "Is this the best time to chat?"

"Considering I have no idea why you're here, probably not." He laughed, the sound swallowed by him cutting loose with his own weapon. "But I was wondering if you could try that truck. Doesn't look bullet proof to me."

"Hn. Good idea." I let out a quick breath, adjusted my aim, and then held the trigger down.

It would seem that the truck's walls were *not* bullet proof. Or even bullet resistant. A new chorus of screams went off as I liberally sprayed fire into the general area I thought the gang members might be, the shots tearing through the thin skin and into the equally thin flesh behind. The guy I'd shot at earlier emerged, frantically trying to clear the area, only to be brutally cut down by my newest acquaintance.

The weapon's heat forced me to ease off after ten seconds or so, coolant flooding from the suit and into the gun. While I waited for it to cool I had too many heartbeats to see what was going on and none of it was pretty.

Blood, mostly the dark red and nearly black of Thondians and Naule, coated the ground. Bodies and moaning forms were piled all around the first truck and to either side of it, and I could make out screams of pain coming from behind the truck I'd just shredded.

How many people had I just killed? A few? A dozen? More? Part of me wanted to be sick, but I forced my stomach to behave. I could throw up as much as I wanted when this was done, when people weren't trying to kill me and the few people I knew.

While I was having yet another internal crisis, the survivors apparently chose that moment to sprint for better cover. A group broke from behind the trucks, racing for the opposite side of the garage from where their companions were sensibly keeping themselves concealed. All of them fired at full automatic as they ran.

It's hard enough to hit something when you had armor and linked weapon systems. Trying to hit targets in cover, while running, with guns that qualified as scrap metal was next to impossible. Their shots went wild, sending sparks flying as they struck the floor, ceiling, cars, and walls behind us. Everyone but me opened up, and our side's shots weren't as inaccurate as theirs.

One of them, a Naule, made it. The rest were dead long before they could cross the few yards to safety.

"At least two on the left." I reported as I got my brain back into working order, firing slow shots to keep them pinned down. "They're skittish."

"As expected." Nynsi paused before changing channels. "Patriarch, the garage remains secure, what is your status?"

"I remain secure, dear niece. Trenah and Ghai hold the entry hall still, and Iyaht has dealt with a single effort to beach the servant's doors. So far only the rank and file of the gang have been seen, no mercenaries or elites."

"The same here, Patriarch. What is the status of the last truck and cars?"

He didn't respond at first, and she began to repeat the question only to be cut off. *"They have just broken from a circle and are coming down at speed. Internal Security has completed their own defense and are sending officers our way. Be prepared for a rapid assault."*

The word was barely out before the last truck roared down. This was no inexperienced driver, slowly bringing the vehicle down. They came in like they were falling from orbit, the engines roaring at the last moment to prevent a crash. I'd hardly begun to shift my aim when the back doors were flung open, and armored forms in dark gray dropped out, each bearing the mark of the True Sons on their chests.

It would seem that the veterans had arrived, and they'd brought the real fight with them.

II – IV

If their arrival hadn't made it clear that these were the actual soldiers amongst the wider gang, their immediate actions in the moments after they landed made it plainly obvious.

The first trio in sight dropped to their knees and started firing at full auto, the fire accurate enough that everyone besides me had to duck. Behind them, more leaped out of the truck's bed, dashing left and right to get into the cover provided by the sides of the hangar sized garage.

"Dammit." I muttered, firing off controlled bursts at the group providing covering fire. A second curse came out when my shots merely sent sparks flying from shields.

A third swear word came out when I realized that I'd just announced my status as the only person shooting back at them. All three ceased their fire for a bare second, adjusted their aim, and then cut loose in my general direction. Some of the rounds went wide, snapping past me or slamming into the car, but more than a few pinged off of my own shields. I twitched my eyes up to see the damage, and ground my teeth as each hit made the percentage drop... and it was dropping a lot faster than I thought it should have.

"Fucking finicky shields." I growled, returning fire as best I could.

"Up, up! Concentrate fire!" Nynsi snapped out, suiting actions to her words and putting shots into the enemy I was still trying to put rounds into. Her aim was better than mine, her monster of a pistol breaking through the weakened barrier and tearing the man's neck apart on her third shot.

The chef on my left rose and joined Rane'li in cutting loose, the others following their example after only a short delay. Everyone aimed at the exposed pair still covering their fellows, tall figures reeling as a wave of bullets washed over them. Both lurched upwards and tried to run for cover, one even dropping his overheated rifle in the process.

Neither made it. The first died after just a couple of steps, and the second fell just a yard shy of safety.

"Too many reached cover." Nynsi snarled, "Cieran, status? Could you lead a counter-push?"

I winced at the idea. "My shields are at forty percent and aren't recharging."

She inhaled sharply enough for her mic to catch it, then seemed to force herself to speak normally. "Very well, we hold here. Patriarch, we have at least ten enemies with modern weapons and armor outside."

"Confirmed, I am diverting-wait." A short pause, *"No reinforcements available, they are pushing the entrance hall as well as attempting to breach the servant's wing."*

Anything else he or Nynsi could have said was left unspoken as our local problems elected to begin their advance inside. At each corner of the entrance grey forms appeared, leaning out just enough to cut loose with suppressive fire.

Rane'li and I retaliated in kind and drew most of the attention. She took at least one ricochet to her helmet that saw her duck, leaving both enemies to concentrate on me.

My shields were gone faster than I could blink. Rounds started hammering at the armor, sounding like a hellish hail storm, and I did my best to protect the lines connecting me to my gun.

Unfortunately that forced me to turn more to the right and gave them an opening on the left, something they took advantage of immediately. The poorer gang members broke from cover and sprinted towards us, firing wildly as they came on. That worried me a lot less than the professionals who came in behind, moving with calmer, steady motions that kept their weapons level as they advanced.

"They're coming!" I shouted when I realized practically everyone else was still keeping their heads down or were firing blindly over various cars.

"Up!" Nynsi barked again, "Cut them down!"

I turned back to the left as the enemy's cover team overheated their weapons. That helped inspire everyone on our team to get up and cut loose, but it came at the same time as two or three gangsters pulled pins on large grenades and tossed them forwards.

Smoke and white sparks began spitting out at once, flares leaping up and popping off like fireworks. Flashing gray clouds formed almost instantly around each of the bombs, merging into a bank of fog lit up by the random lights.

It wasn't fast enough to save the unarmored idiots leading the charge, the mansion's reserves put them down without effort, but it was enough to cover the veterans as they advanced. Everyone, myself included, fired blind shots at a slow pace as we tried to find them, but the bastards were disciplined.

None of them shot back to reveal themselves. Not until a series of blue streaks and several bouncing canisters came our way.

"Grenades!" Someone screamed just before the Discharge technicals went off with rapid pops and arcs of electricity. I'd had enough foresight to make sure the exoskeleton could absorb the effects without systems blowing out, but my allies' partial armor couldn't hold up. More than half of them went down, filling the comms with swearing as they convulsed, twitched, or banged their heads onto the cars as they fell.

The flash-bangs that bounced off the cars before blinding everyone probably didn't help either.

I'd need to buy Rane'li something nice because the suit's cameras snapped to black just as the blinding light began to flare, then cut back in even as I blinked furiously. I still had a few spots in my vision but I could see armored figures racing towards us.

Their plan was obvious. Everyone but me was stunned or prone, it would be easy for the True Sons to simply jump up onto the cars and fire point-blank into them. Then they could stroll right into the mansion while the professional team was distracted holding the other entrances.

Some sane part of me knew I had to do something about it.

Some insane part of me was already doing something.

My left leg straightened, pushing me back up to my full height. I tightened my finger and kept the rifle firing at full auto as I simply walked into the car to knock it aside rather than wasting time going around. The noise of the collision was fairly incredible even over my gun going off, and I knew that I'd just drawn the attention of literally everyone in the garage.

"What the fuck!?" An armored True Son stumbled back in shock, practically tripping as the size of my armor became apparent. "Focus on it!"

"No! Focus on-" One of the others tried to give orders, probably to tell them to bypass me and kill everyone else before they collected themselves.

The part of me that wasn't freaking out focused on him as a priority target, and I swung my gun into line with him. He recoiled as shots ripped into his shields, stopping him from finishing his command. Everyone else agreed with the first man because they skidded to a stop and aimed right at me.

What followed was ten times as terrifying as being in cover had been. The suit literally vibrated around me as bullets slammed into armor plating, displays flashed as the gyroscopes did their best to keep it upright. The feeds connecting the gun to my arm didn't last more than a few seconds, snapping as full strikes or ricochets tore them apart to leave me firing without any real accuracy.

"Get up!" Nynsi's voice was deafening from my speakers as she screamed, "Pillars and Paragons crush you! Get to your feet and fight!"

I mostly managed to keep the gun on my first target until he went down, but when I turned to fire at a Naule on the my right it exposed the long weapon. A full burst caught it and left me with a broken, sparking club. I didn't even have time to try and swing it at anyone before a round got through the armor to smash something in the suit's left elbow, awkwardly locking the arm at an angle.

They'd have probably swarmed me and done some fairly awful things with grenades or point-blank shots if everyone else hadn't recovered their wits. Erratic gunfire from behind me picked up as the mansion's defenders rejoined the fight, then rose to a crescendo when Nynsi simply vaulted her car to rush into the smoke. Everyone else wasn't about to let the highborn woman charge in alone and followed suit, creating a wild melee in the fog.

I lumbered around as best I could, something that got harder when something seized up in my left leg, but I managed to break the remains of my weapon over an attacker's head. He went down and didn't get up while the fight whirled around us.

On my left I saw the cook shove his rifle into another Thondian's gut and rip it apart with a burst, then fall himself when a Naule put two pistol rounds into his back. To my right, Rane'li trampled a wounded gangster to tackle one drawing a bead on Nynsi, the two of them rolling out of view as they fought over a knife.

Tossing the broken grip of my rifle aside I tried to wade in with just my fists. I managed to scare two of them into jumping back, leaving them open for someone else to kill them, but with the servos in my left leg damaged I was too slow to catch them. My left arm being locked up didn't help either, leaving me to do a lot of slow flailing.

A wounded Naule wrestling with Ullika drew my attention off to the right. I'd just begun to move that way when a bit of motion made me glance left in time to see another one of the four armed aliens toss something at my chest.

There was an audible clink as a technical grenade attached to the armor, and I felt my lips move without input from my brain.

"Oh shit."

The explosion didn't actually pick me up off my feet, the exoskeleton was far too heavy for that, but it did send me flailing backwards to crash onto a car's hood. All the while my primitive alarms shrieked warnings about how badly I was fucked. A dazed look at my main status display showed that more of the suit was an angry red than a healthy blue, something that didn't surprise me at all.

Things got a bit blurry after that single moment of comprehension. There was a lot more gunfire and screaming. At some point I managed to roll off of the car and onto the ground, then shifted so that I was sitting against the vehicle I'd just wrecked.

I came back to my senses as the fight wound down, just in time to see Rane'li enthusiastically trying to beat a man to death with her bare hands. I didn't think she was getting anywhere, even as big and strong as she was, but she was giving it a credible effort.

"Stop! Take him alive!" I saw Nynsi vault a car on the edges of my main view screen, quickly stepping up to grab the other Thondian woman just as she was about to bring her armored fists down again. "Rane'li, we need him alive!"

She managed to pull her off of the unconscious form, calling out more orders as she pushed the taller woman back. "Loram, check Bolz. Ullika, check on Cieran. Everyone else finish off the remainder."

"I'm... all right." I managed after a shake of my head. "Didn't penetrate. Think I'm a bit out of it, and my armor may need some work. But I'm all right."

"Some work." The mechanic chuckled as he approached, squatting down in front of me to get a better look. "I can see you in there short-fur, and you're sparking like a broken transmitter."

Short-fur? That was a new one, though I had no idea if it was casual slang or an outright insult.

Before I could manage a reply, Trenah's voice came across our comms. *"Shaaryak, we've got a problem. Lost contact with the guards in the east wing, Ghai and I are moving but we need a team to come at them from your side."*

Nynsi moved into my view, her chest turning as she swept her helmeted gaze over the wrecked garage. There'd been a bit more than a dozen of us to start with, but I was pretty sure less than half were still upright.

"I will take a team immediately." She said before gesturing. "Ullika, watch the prisoner and ensure that he remains alive. Rane'li, assist our guest in extracting himself from the suit, then the two of you will secure the garage. Everyone else is to follow me."

A couple of desultory gunshots ended the lives of two crippled attackers, but after that three figures trailed after Nynsi when she headed into the mansion proper.

I watched them go, the last of them slapping a control to start the process of closing the heavy hangar doors. As it began its slow slide I let out a long breath and began to relax.

I'd survived. Again. Somehow. I'd even been useful, though I was sure I'd throw up the moment I got out of this stupid thing. God but the place was a butcher's shop even without all of the bodies in the garden.

A stretch of my neck let my chin nudge the release button. Behind me the power core obediently whirred down to a low idle, but the hydraulic system didn't start up. I frowned and nudged it again only to get a minor warble from the motor for my efforts.

I glanced at the screens and felt my frown deepen. The armor was shredded and the left arm was definitely fucked, but none of the egress systems were showing as damaged. "Hey, Rane'li?"

"Yes?" Her visor glanced over at me from where she'd taken up a spot leaning on a car.

"Mind coming over here and checking the suit? I can't get out of this bloody thing. It might be a fragment lodged somewhere that my read-outs aren't reporting. Maybe in the back, near the power supply."

She shrugged, but straightened all the same. From the stiffer than usual way she limped over she must have strained something in the melee. "Please warn me if you see someone get up."

"Not a problem." I assured her, keeping an eye out as she walked around me. Ullika was busy dragging her former victim through the gap between the other set of cars. The guy's helmet was battered and dented, and I made a mental note never to get her pissed off at me.

"What are you two up to over there?" Ullika called out after dropping the legs of his cargo, reaching up to take his helmet off once he'd done so.

"Damage is even worse than it looks." I sighed. "You sure all of them are dead?"

"Hm? Oh yeah, this one should be the last of his group." He shrugged, casually hefting up his shotgun onto a shoulder. "Hey, *kallithas*, you see anything back there?"

"No." I felt the armor shudder as she started jerking loose plates aside to get a better view of my left shoulder, "He wasn't even hit in the back. I can see some of the system, it looks intact."

"Well what the hell is causing this then?" I grumbled, hitting the button for a third time. When nothing I happened I swore under my breath and glared at the display telling me it should be functional.

"How would I know?" Rane'li muttered. From her unusually impolite tone she probably didn't intend for me to hear that, especially as she sounded normal when she poke a bit more loudly. "Maybe something in the chest itself? Could we simply rip it open?"

"Feel free to check, it'll give me a good view of your ass." Ullika suggested brightly.

Her helmet didn't stop her from giving the man a withering look, though for my part I'd started to frown. Ullika wasn't normally this blatant from what I knew, and he still looked... tense. His weapon up on a shoulder like he was ready to drop it and fire at a second's notice, and his dark eyes were locked on us instead of the prisoner he was in charge of.

That worried me since said prisoner was starting to twitch.

"Fine." Rane'li ducked under my stiff left arm, regarding the mess that was my chest plating and pointedly keeping herself upright. "What am I looking at?"

"Ullika," I tried, "The prisoner is waking-"

The shotgun round hit Rane'li in the back, her body bouncing off of my chest before spinning to the ground. She lay there limply while my heart tried to slam its way out of my chest in sudden panic.

"Not looking behind you, obviously." Ullika lowered his gun, his sharp teeth gleaming as he grinned. "Stupid bitch."

"What the fuck!?" I half-screamed, jerking my chin to the other side to hit the power-up button.

Nothing happened.

He kept smiling and brought his left arm up, a gesture bringing his wrist comp to life and showing me... showing me a copy of the same displays in front of my face. "Seriously, short-fur. You didn't even double-check the work I did for you. Though I suppose you weren't the only naive idiot since she didn't either."

My teeth ground as I frantically tried to work out what the hell I could do.

"Don't bother calling for help either, I had three different run times in place to take your comms out." He chuckled again, turning to regard the unconscious prisoner. "Stupid shit, getting beaten up by that tall brat. She wouldn't even sleep with me you know, turned me down half a dozen times. Prudish whore."

There was nothing I could do to stop him from casually aiming his gun and blowing our prisoner's head into fragmentary pieces amid a spray of red blood. From the color he might have been Human under the armor, but it didn't really matter anymore.

"Stupid bitch, like I said. Then again, that upper caste whore is sleeping with a Human, so I'm not really sure why I'm even surprised anymore."

I blinked. "Wait, what?"

"Don't bother denying it." He sneered, body tilting right. "Everyone knows Xerol's niece is whoring herself out to you. Sleeping with an alien is disgusting to begin with, but one of *your* kind? It's a betrayal of our species."

My brain whirled. He thought Nynsi and I were a lot more than friends, probably because he couldn't grasp the idea of a Human being a friend with a Thondian. And if he wasn't exaggerating, if that was actually a rumor going around, then that could probably turn out badly for me. Though not as badly as whatever he probably had planned this very moment.

I had to keep him talking and hope that Nynsi came back with her team, or Trenah came over to check on me after finishing up in the servant's wing.

It was a fucking slim hope but it was all I had.

"So you're with them." The suit didn't have enough power to stand when idling, but I could still move my right arm. Planting on the ground I shoved over a bit to try and cover Rane's still form. It was hard to tell but she might still have been breathing. I hoped she was still breathing. "The True Sons. For how long?"

"These fuckers?" He gave the corpse a kick, "As if I would lower myself to work for this scum."

"So other Thondians then. Who?"

"You'll find out soon enough." He promised, "And I'll be fifty thousand credits richer with a new set of identification chits that will let me get back into the Ascendancy. Here I was worried about how hard this would be, instead you practically gift-wrapped yourself for me."

In my rear view, Rane'li twitched, her body slowly curling as she struggled to breath. I let out a gasp of relief of my own, then shifted again. A desperate plan slowly began to form as I heaved the exoskeleton over a few more inches to make sure he couldn't see her.

"Don't worry about your whore." Apparently now that I was at his mercy, he just couldn't shut up. Not that I was about to stop him. "I'm not the only one here who remembers what species he is. I'm just the insurance plan

180

in case they fail, but what do I care? So long as I get paid."

Oh shit. There was someone else here to grab Nynsi too. Or kill her. Either would be bad.

My eyes flicked back and forth between him and my view of my only ally. He was using his wrist-comp to scan the various aircars, no doubt trying to figure out which had the least damage. Rane'li was still coming around, but there was still a lot of blood on the ground her. I had no idea if she was even capable of what I hoped, but I couldn't think of any other options. Besides waiting and hoping, which was a bad plan to begin with.

I shifted again, turning so that my right leg was close to the car. "So, now what? You pick a car, tell me to get out, then drag me away?"

"Something like that. I don't know if you're armed in there and I'm not taking chances, so you'll get some of the good drugs I stole to keep you docile," he patted a pocket, "You'll be in dreamland before I pull you out of your shell. Ah, this one will do."

Of course the fucker chose Nynsi's work of art, the car having somehow escaped the battle with nothing more than a couple of dents and a few scorch marks. "I think I'll be keeping it, a worthy bonus for a job well done. Still, I suppose I should be thanking these lesser things. Without their attack I might never have had such an easy time of it. I was worried I'd have to convince you to take me on a training run somewhere."

"I'm surprised you didn't make your move right when they first attacked." I tried to keep the bastard going, keep him enjoying the sound of his own voice. "Wouldn't that have been even easier?"

He was scavenging through his pockets, pulling out familiar looking syringes. "Maybe it would have. But how could I pass up the chance to kill those creatures? Ugh. Even worse, I might have been forced to share the reward with them. That's a good reminder though, short fur. I really should demand more payment for shutting up the prisoner before he could talk. I'll try and convince them to kill you quick if they give me an extra bonus."

Rane'li rolled slightly, a hand reaching out to touch my back. Her other slid across the floor, fingers curling and then relaxing. I twitched my left arm as best I could, hoping that she'd take it to mean that I'd seen her.

"Well, can't take too much more time. Not with that gray bitch so fond of you, I'd rather not tangle with her."

"She'd tear you apart." I agreed, swallowing and really hoping that this worked. He walked towards me as I spoke, one handing keeping his shotgun against his shoulder while his other kept the syringe ready. "I suppose you'll just shoot me a few times if I try to resist?"

"Just once." He grinned to put his ivory canines on full display. "Can't have you dying on me."

My voice was definitely unsteady but I managed to keep the banter going as he came closer, "Yeah, be a shame to cost you all that money."

The moment he began to swing around, his eyes focused on the gaping hole in my chest armor, I made my move. Sucking in a breath, I slammed my right elbow back into the car and managed to break off part of the front panel. He jumped backwards as I made a grab for it, but the sluggish suit wasn't able move that quickly.

Metal rang as it bounced off my fingers and clattered away. I tried to lunge for it, sweeping my locked up my left back as I did, but all that I managed to do was unbalance myself. The suit tipped and shuddered onto my right side as more systems failed, eventually groaning as the power dropped to critical levels.

Ullika stared at me before grunting out a laugh, "Seriously? Was that supposed to-"

Rane'li, holding the rifle I'd just managed to kick back into her arms, heaved her bleeding body up and over my sparking form. She cried out in pain as she did it, in time with Ullika's frantic curse as he tried to get his weapon back into line with her again.

Unfortunately for the traitor, her gun was already aimed.

A thunderous burst took him in the waist, just below the heavy chest plating he wore. Dark red blood and lighter bits of his organs tumbled out in a disgusting shower. Ullika managed a choked off scream, weapon and syringe falling as he instinctively tried to clutch at himself.

All that did was expose his face for her second blaze of automatic fire to turn his head into an equally unholy mess.

"Fucker." She gasped as his body collapsed. "*Chenethic.* I always... hated you."

I gasped in relief as the tension faded out of me yet again. "Are you all right?"

"No." Her voice was shaky as she lifted a hand, touching the side of her helmet. "Reporting in... Ullika betrayed us. We're alive. Injured. More traitors... inside. Be ready."

Apparently listening to a reply, she heaved herself forwards, letting the rifle clatter to one side as she slowly crawled to the corpse. "No. Suit hacked. Trying... to get him... out now ...yes."

I waited until she was silent for a longer period before asking, "Is it over?"

"Yes." She repeated as she reached Ullika, grabbing a limp arm and tugging at the wrist-comp there. "Internal Security... is here. Several wounded... Laria is one."

My slowing heartbeat began picking up speed again, and my stomach twisted. "How badly?"

"Don't know... shut up... please."

I had to bite my tongue but I managed to stay silent as she fumbled the device around in her hands. It hadn't locked so she was able to start trying various applications right away. A minute, maybe two passed before she found the right one. The suit rattled but opened, letting me frantically worm my way free.

All things considered I was out in record time, shaking myself as I crawled over to where she'd gone limp after sending the command.   I wanted nothing more than to sprint out of here and find Trenah, to drag her to the nearest doctor and force them to heal her... but she would be with Ghai. And Nynsi. And others.

Rane'li had just saved my life, and she had no one but me.

I hesitated on reaching her, swallowing as I saw her lower back. Her ink black skin had been torn apart, and... I could see things you weren't meant to see inside a living person. Worse there there was enough dark blood to make me worry I was already too late to do anything for her. "Oh god. Uh..."

"Canister." Her words were a quiet rasp. "Right... thigh. Medical..."

I found it and pulled it free. It was covered in the runes that Thondians wrote in, but a quick turn showed the other side labeled with Caranat's alphabetic script. "Pull then apply... cover and provide additional heat to ensure..."

The muttering stopped once I realized I was doing it. After a couple seconds I managed to aim it as I pulled the small lever attached, a watery gel spraying out to coat the deep wound. It seemed to fizz then foam, sucking in blood and firming up as it did so. I had no idea what it was but after three or four long sprays the entire wound was covered and her pained breathing had eased.

Lacking anything else, I jerked my shirt up and over my head before pressing it gently against the wound. The woman let out a quiet groan before falling still again. I spread my hands apart and hoped that my body heat would do whatever the gel-foam-crap needed to work.

"Cieran?" Nynsi's voice brought my head spinning around. She'd ditched her own helmet, and her dark eyes were narrowed in concern as she raced into the garage. I hadn't even heard the door open. "Are you wounded?"

"No, she is." I turned back and shook my head once. "Bad."

Rane'li managed something like a rasping chuckle. "...bad... he says."

Armored feet came to a stop beside me, Nynsi stooping down to take a look for herself before letting out a sharp hiss. "Take her feet, I'll take her shoulders. We need to get her to the medical suite."

I nodded, "Everyone else?"

"Not now." She admonished me gently, "Once we're there. I swear."

I bit my tongue again, and then forced my shaking hands to grab onto the wounded woman's legs as I prepared to help carry her.

II – V

The chaos of the aftermath was somehow worse than the chaos of the actual fight.

Internal Security swarmed the building with a small army, and I heard later than they killed or captured a good dozen True Sons who'd tried to make a run for it at the end. Once that was dealt with, the cops moved into guard positions and began assisting with the wounded. There were plenty of the latter, but only one of them really concerned me.

Unfortunately Trenah had already been airlifted out before we'd gotten Rane'li to the medical suite. That told me her injuries were severe, but my attention had been distracted by helping the wounded Thondian woman. Rane'li had stayed just long enough for the doctor to pump her full of extra drugs to help stabilize her, then she had also been rushed out, leaving only those lightly wounded to be treated at the mansion itself.

Even once I'd found a shirt and gotten Rane'li's blood off of my hands, my efforts to find out Trenah's condition hadn't gone anywhere.

Nynsi had been dragged off to help Xerol liaise with Internal Security before she could tell me anything, and I wasn't about to interrupt either of them. I couldn't find Ghai, the only other person I really knew, and as usual most of the staff seemed to be studiously ignoring my existence. Doctor Urrast'rae probably knew, but he was understandably busy.

So in the end I'd ended up in one of the dining rooms, slumped in a chair and staring vaguely at the wall. Frustration, concern, anger, nausea, depression, and a few other emotions left me feeling too drained to even think about what had just happened.

All that mattered was Trenah.

I couldn't lose her. She was my closest friend. The only person on this planet I trusted without reservation, especially since it seemed like Nynsi had been keeping a few things from me. Although for all I knew Ullika might have been lying, traitors were hardly reliable sources of information. But still... there was something more going on here. Something that had nearly resulted in me getting drugged and carted off, and *had* resulted in Trenah getting wounded.

Wounded badly enough she needed to be evacuated on the very first run.

If Trenah... if she died...

Ghai found me still sitting in a morose slump an hour or so later. She announced herself by ghosting into the room and setting a black bottle in front of me. I jumped at the noise, blinking as I came back to reality, taking in her expression and the beer.

"That bad?" I asked.

She settled down in the chair next to me, her own drink in her hand. She took one pull than pointedly flicked her bright eyes between my bottle and my face.

Grimacing, I picked up mine and drank as well. I wasn't really a beer guy, but whatever was in the bottle was surprisingly good. Like warm bread with only the smallest hint of alcohol, though it had the usual odd aftertaste Trahcon food tended to leave behind.

"How bad?" I asked again.

Ghai inhaled slowly, her tarah drooping before she quietly rasped out a few words. "Bad. In the back. Several rounds."

I felt my jaw clench. "Another traitor?"

There was a slow nod. "Several. Iyaht too."

My bottle rose as I took a long drink from it. I hadn't really known Ghai's partner very well, or at all really, but Trenah had spoken well of her. She'd been tall and kind of aloof, but I'd also seen glimpses of a dry humor the few times I'd run into her. And of course the fact that she actually spoke to me willingly had been a plus in comparison to the Thondian staff.

"Dead?" I asked quietly. I was more worried about Trenah but I wasn't heartless. I had no idea how long Ghai and Iyaht had been working together, but anything from years to decades seemed likely.

"No. Burned." Ghai took a heavy drink before adding, "Badly."

"Shit." I whispered, looking down. "Are they going to make it?"

Her long pause and third pull from her bottle was telling enough even before she added, "Don't know."

I closed my eyes and tried to focus on my breathing. It didn't exactly even out so instead I tried to drink myself into a calmer state. Ghai seemed content to try the same thing next to me, at least until our bottles were empty. When I eyed them morosely she rose without a word, vanished into the kitchen, and then returned with several more in her arms.

We opened them and I lifted mine towards her in thanks. The gesture made her tarah twitch in amusement before she awkwardly returned the motion. Then we both tipped them back and resumed our prior activity.

I didn't speak again until we'd finished the second set and she was opening her third, "Will I be able to see her?"

Ghai paused, tilting her head in consideration. "Why?"

I frowned. "She's my friend. My best friend, why would I not want to see her?"

Gray lips pursed, then she let out a long breath before forcing out a full sentence. "She will be unconscious for several days even if she lives. There is no point to seeing her before she awakens."

I stared at her in surprise as she winced, reaching up to rub her throat with a single hand. After a few seconds I recovered, filing away the fact that she evidently could talk normally, just with a lot discomfort on her end. "It's... you don't want to be there, when she wakes up?"

She blinked once and then shook her head. "Human thing?"

"I guess it is." I took my third bottle, opened it, then stared at it for a few seconds before asking. "Will I?"

There was a slow breath before she confirmed my fears. "No. Not in her Pack. No one is."

"Meaning?"

Her left shoulder rose, "Privacy laws. Need her permission."

So we'd have to wait until she was awake and capable of calling us. Or ordering her doctors to tell us what was going on... and who the fuck knew when that would be. Days? Would they keep her in a coma or something if it was bad enough?

I brought my beer up and drank a good half of it in one go. When I spoke again it was to change the subject before I lost it completely. "The traitor in the garage, Ullika. He said was going to get fifty thousand for me, plus a trip back to the Ascendancy, and it was specifically for me alive."

My drinking buddy had just tipped her beer back when I'd started, and she promptly began coughing when I got to the amount. Her electric blue eyes were very wide as she tried to clear her lungs, but I continued before she could speak. "According to him, there are rumors going around that I'm sleeping with Nynsi. And those rumors are the reason there's a bounty on my head larger than hers. Or even Xerol's."

Ghai's tarah quivered as she caught her breath, "...complicated."

"Don't give me that." I snapped, the alcohol fueling my anger. "A prisoner is dead and Rane'li might be dying just because I'm not a racist dick to Nynsi, and because I consider her a fucking friend. And apparently that's enough for someone in a foreign nation to want to abduct me. Was that the same reason Trenah was targeted?"

"No."

I glowered at her. "Ghai."

She quickly lifted her free hand, "Mistake. Myself, Iyaht. Xerol after."

The need to turn her brief words into full sentences in my head put the breaks on my temper, especially as it made a kind of sense once I thought it through. Xerol was clearly a primary target to the locals, and whoever was running the True Sons evidently knew what was going on inside of the mansion. Anyone that clued in would know he had a pair of Trahcon bodyguards, or Harath'krem or whatever they were called, and that they'd recently abducted one of their drill instructors.

And that they'd done it alone, probably killing a whole lot of people in the process.

If I'd been on the other side, getting rid of Ghai and Iyaht would have been high on my priority list too.

"Trenah went off to back up Iyaht, and you took a different route?" I guessed.

Ghai eyed me, then nodded once. "She checked halls. I checked medical."

I grunted and finally took another sip of beer. Ghai was taller than Trenah but still short for a Trahcon woman, an inch or two below five and a half feet. It wasn't implausible, especially if the traitor was in a rush and attacking from behind. Which any Thondian with a brain probably would be, considering that an angry Trahcon could bounce them around with just their mind if they had a few seconds warning.

From what little I knew shielding could protect against a Trahcon's talents, but only the security teams had full armor. The partial sets used by the reserve staff probably wouldn't have saved them, and whoever was wearing them would have known as much.

"Caught them." She continued, making me twitch in surprise. "One of them. Prisoner below."

I pursed my lips. "Will Internal-Security take them?"

Two fingers rose and touched her closed lips, then she reached out and pressed them against mine. I got it after a second, nodding as she pulled back.

The authorities hadn't been told, and I was to keep my mouth shut about it.

I held my bottle up in salute again, and this time she easily mimicked me before we both drank. The quiet drinking that followed was relaxing for the thirty seconds it took before I started worrying about Trenah again. I'd seen what modern guns could do in the garage, and the idea that Trenah had been hit in the back by more than one round was...

My empty bottle clinked as I set it down besides its brethren. "Where's the rest?"

"Second fridge."

"Want more?"

When she nodded, I stood up and felt the room shift a little around me. Breathing slowly, I took a few experimental steps while Ghai watched, then shrugged once I was sure I was merely buzzed and reacting to standing up too quickly.

That wouldn't do at all. I needed to be drunk enough to stop worrying about Trenah. And about Ullika's words.

Of course my grand plan collapsed when I returned with a case of beer to find Nynsi standing next to Ghai. The tall woman was still in her armor, arms crossed over her torso, though her expression was perfectly neutral.

"Hey Nyn." I greeted as I carried the drinks over. "You here to stop us or join us?"

The shortening of her name got a reaction, a sharp narrowing of her eyes. "Cieran. I see you remain impolite when intoxicated. Do not shorten my personal name ever again."

"Yes ma'am." I drawled in English, which drew further narrowing when I set the case down. My effort to pull out a bottle got an answer to my question when she took a quick step and grabbed my wrist hard enough to make me wince.

"You've had quite enough." Nynsi informed me flatly. "Ghai, please see to my uncle while I escort our guest back to his suite."

The Trahhcon bodyguard angled her tarah out and down in apology, rose, then grabbed a final beer before heading out.

Nynsi and I held a short staring contest when I used my other hand to pick up the crate of drinks and tuck it under my arm. "I'd really rather be drunk right now."

"And I," She informed me as she tugged me into motion, moving her hand from my wrist to my shoulder to make sure I couldn't escape. "Find you far less interesting when you are drunk. I am need of a conversational partner, not a sarcastic and impolite alien."

I grunted, adjusting the beer so the box wasn't poking me. "This where you finally tell me about the rumors about us?"

Nynsi had one hell of a poker face, but I was too close to miss the tightness around her dark eyes. "If you wish to know."

"I would have liked to have known to begin with." I managed to keep my irritation out of my voice. Sort of. Kind-of.

Well, not really.

Her lips pulled back from her teeth in an expression I didn't recognize, but something about the slight droop to her shoulders made me think she was chagrined. "I did not think it relevant at the time. The staff knew that I had declared you a guest, that you had agreed to assist in the defense of our home, and Xerol informed them all that you and Laria enjoyed his most enthusiastic support and defense."

"Didn't help." I muttered darkly.

"No." She said, anger bubbling in her own voice. "It did not."

"...are you going to answer the question?"

Her breath came out in a quiet whistle. "In private, I would rather not let Internal Security hear sordid rumors about my personal life."

I grunted, eyeing a pair of cops standing guard at the base of a stairwell. "Fair point. Maybe we shouldn't be walking like this in public?"

The warm body pressed against me grew even stiffer, her grip on my shoulder tightening. "Am I that repulsive?"

"Not at all." I said quickly, "I mean, you're not Human but you're... um... I'm not sure what the right word are but you're nothing close to repulsive. I just meant that it might fuel these rumors."

"I believe it is too late for that." She noted with a single shake of her head.

It was hard to argue with that, and with the hand keeping me awkwardly pinned against her as we walked along. Thankfully we only passed Internal Security agents on our way to my rooms, and most of them were busy checking windows, talking with one another, or recording data to pay any real attention. I felt like a prisoner being marched to a cell, which struck me as the inverse of what should be happening.

I was the one with the questions, but Nynsi was clearly the one in charge at the moment.

She only let me go once we'd reached my suite and closed the door behind us. I set the case down on my small table and pulled a bottle out. Her body language remained hard to read, but something in the way Nynsi looked at me told me I was on thin ice.

So instead of opening it I just set it next to the box before collapsing into a chair. My companion made a low sound that might have been approving, then settled with far more poise into the other chair. I watched her for a few moments, then sighed and let my head fall back until I was staring at the ceiling.

"What are we really caught up in, Nynsi?" I asked without looking at her. "I thought we already hit peak danger, but it seems like I was wrong."

There was a long silence, then a quiet hiss before she spoke. "Tell me what Ullika said, as closely as you can recall."

I did, giving her the blow-by-blow of what had happened after she'd left. It didn't take long, and when I finished she let out another angry whistle between her teeth.

"Rane'li will need a sizable bonus for dealing with that creature in an appropriate fashion." Her words were low, furious. "Though I do wish she had been in a condition to take him alive so that I might have done it myself."

One of my hands waved slightly, "I understand being angry, but I'm hoping for a reason *why* it happened."

Her second whistle was much longer, louder, and almost seething. "I am far beyond being merely *angry*, Cieran. Five of our people betrayed us, brought harm to others in our employ, and harmed our guests. Had my uncle not stopped me, I would have ripped apart our prisoner's chest with my bare hands to feast on his heart."

I... didn't have much I could say to that.

Maybe fifteen seconds passed with nothing but furious breathing, then Nynsi seemed to get control of herself. Her breathing steadied though her voice remained lower than usual. "Regarding events in general, our theory in regards to the True Sons and White Storm is accurate so far as I know and believe. There are a few additional details that my uncle and I did not believe to be relevant at the time, though I will admit that they are so now."

Part of me wanted to snap at her for still being evasive and taking her sweet time. The rest of me was still too unsettled to say anything.

"The bounty on your head was likely posted by my father." She continued, her words almost a growl. "He is a ranking White Storm officer. I imagine he wishes to torture you to death on a live broadcast. He would ideally do so before he kills my uncle and cousins, then sells me to a supporter in the Ascendancy to finance his further ambitions."

That was something close to what I'd expected, but hearing it said aloud still made the dark weight in my chest drop a little lower. I'd assumed the motivation for my capture had to be personal given the stupid amount of money that Ullika had been bragging about. And since I didn't have any personal enemies of my own, that meant they'd have to be enemies of my few friends by default.

In the time I'd been here the topic of Nynsi's parents, and why she lived with her uncle, had never once been brought up. It had never even been hinted at. I'd assumed that they were either dead or badly estranged as a result. The latter was apparently correct, though apparently the word 'estranged' probably didn't even begin to cover it.

"So this whole thing is just a family dispute turned up to eleven?" I asked quietly.

"I do not know that turn of phrase, but I do not believe that the entire affair is solely due to the bad blood between my father and uncle if that is what you imply." She replied, "The White Storm are thugs, but they are professional ones. The benefit to my father is likely secondary to the core plan. It's possible, even likely, that he is acting beyond his actual orders for his personal gain."

I let out a slow breath. "That explains that, at least. Guessing Ullika or one of the other traitors was passing the rumors to him. Why would he believe them though? I mean, it's not like we really spent that much time together, or slept in the same room. It would be easy to poke holes in any stories they told him."

"My mother and a second uncle were slain by your people." I finally let my chin drop in time to see her shake her head once, "During one of the many raids and counter-raids that occurred shortly after their exile. My father is quick to blame your kind for anything and everything as a result. He may have believed such rumors even if we had only interacted in a business setting."

That weight in my guts settled further and made my shoulders slump. "So I'm just in the wrong place at the wrong time. Seems to be the story of my life."

Our chairs were close enough that she could reach out and rest a hand on one of mine. "It was never my intent to see you involved in this. Nor for Laria to be wounded. I truly did not think that the rumors needed to be repeated, or that my family's... politics would reach you."

"And now that it has?" I asked, not pulling my hand away. I was annoyed with her but not much more than that. Trenah's injuries hadn't had anything to do with not knowing that family detail. And personally, whether or not I'd known that I was a target probably wouldn't have affected anything. Sure, I might have double-checked Ullika's work... but I could have just as easily not grasped the danger.

Christ, it had taken me until *today* to really get that Ullika had actually despised me.

"I will need to improve your combat training." Her fingers squeezed once, "And find more trustworthy assistants to help you repair the exoskeleton. Then, if Laria recovers-"

"*When* she recovers." I put a harsh emphasis on the first word.

Nynsi paused, then gave me a polite nod and corrected herself, "When Laria recovers, I will ask her to provide any and all assistance with those programs."

I let out a slow breath. "And if we decided to leave instead?"

"I would recommend against it. You were both targets before, you are greater ones now. Despite recent events," That barely hidden rage crept back into her voice, "This estate remains the safest place for you, unless you wish to emigrate to the Empire or throw yourself at the mercy of Internal Security."

Even if I'd wanted to, I didn't think Trenah would go for either option. And since I wasn't about to leave her that made my choice fairly obvious as well. Still, Trenah was stubborn, so it was possible that we'd still be finding a new place once she was out of the hospital. Or maybe once she recovered, however long that might take.

Since that train of thought made me start worrying about Trenah once again, I did my best to focus on something else. Something not related to her or the many people I had just helped kill. The drinks right in front of me seemed like a good place to start.

When Nynsi let go of my hand, I reached my own arms out to pick up the drink I'd left behind. Her lips turned down at the corners when I opened it, then parted in surprise when I pushed it in front of her and took a second for myself.

"I have duties to attend." She informed me.

"Sure you do." I smiled a little. "That's why you're in here answering my questions and telling me what's going on instead of being off with your uncle doing anything else. I do appreciate that, even with everything."

Her voice turned wry, "And so you elect to repay me with my own drinks?"

"I don't have any of my own to give you. And if we're both drinking maybe we can think of something more pleasant to talk about. It'll leave you in a more relaxed mood when you go back to work."

She seemed to consider that, then calmly reached out and picked up the bottle. After a polite sip she asked, "And what could we talk about, Cieran?"

I thought about it while drinking from my own. "I have no idea. Something that will make me stop worrying if Trenah will still be breathing come morning, and will stop you from wanting to eat people's hearts."

An expression close to a smile flickered across her face, "Ah. That was perhaps more severe than I intended."

"Maybe, but it was honest." I took a longer pull from my drink. "What's the plan moving forwards? I assume you and Xerol want to strike back."

"Obviously, but talking business is unlikely to calm me." She noted, "It is... difficult to not take my anger out on anything at the moment."

"I noticed. Something fun then? Relaxing?"

She started to shake her head, then paused as her lips curled on one side. "Perhaps we could discuss your fur. It is growing far more quickly than I would have thought. Is that common for your people? Those I met from your fleet all had short strands or had removed it entirely."

I self-consciously brought a hand up to my hair, "It's not like there's anywhere for me to get it cut."

She seemed surprised by that, "You cut it? I thought... does that not hurt?"

"There aren't nerves in it." I shrugged, "I mean, it would hurt if you tore it out but that's it. Cutting or trimming doesn't cause pain or anything."

For some reason she seemed a little disappointed. "You cannot feel it touched at all?"

"Well, kind of? I mean, I feel where it tugs on my skin so I suppose in that way I can feel it when someone touches it."

Nynsi nodded slowly, her tones diffident. "Ah. And does that cause pain or is it pleasant?"

"Only if you pull hard at it, otherwise it can be nice." I felt myself frown. "Why the fascination?"

"It is an academic interest. There is little on the DataNet about your species, less on the Xenthans, and the Naule are not of any real interest to me." She said.

I wouldn't have thought much about it if she hadn't added the last bit. Blinking, I set my beer down, tilting my head as I peered at her. "...Nynsi?"

Her body language seemed to tighten up defensively, "It is an academic interest."

"Yeah..." I tried to think of a tactful way to say it and failed miserably. "Did the rumors get started because you actually have a fetish of some kind?"

"No." Nynsi's voice lowered into a warning growl.

"Just an academic interest?"

"*Yes.*"

The sheer defensiveness packed into that word brought a laugh out before I could even try to stop it. Which drew more angry looks and a rushed explanation about how she'd been fans of a few Human and Xenthan fighters in some kind of Terminus dueling circuit when she'd been young. How she'd 'gotten over it' when she had grown up, how she certainly did not have anything like a 'fetish', and how incredibly aggravating I was when I was drinking.

I kept laughing, and for a little while, I didn't think about how my best friend was fighting for her life.

II – VI

No amount of teasing and conversation with Nynsi could make the next week a pleasant one.

True to her word I spent almost all of time in combat training that she organized and directed. Not that she was with me, she spent nearly all of her own time with her uncle going over their options moving forwards. Instead I was mostly with Chen, the squad leader's loyalty being impeccable according to my hosts.

Just as importantly he was the only member of the security staff who seemed to genuinely have no problems with my species. He had an irreverent sense of humor, and I got the idea from everyone else that he was a bit strange by Thondian standards. That was a probably a good thing since he was far easier to talk to than anyone else. Not that there was much casual conversation, Chen was relentless in working me through various training scenarios and physical exercises.

Whenever he was out on assignment I usually ended up in the basement's shooting range trying to improve my aim. That or back in the garage trying to work on the sabotaged wreck that was my make-shift power armor. All of which was a long way of saying I was doing everything in my power to not think about Trenah, or the fact that no one at the River District Hospital would tell me anything beyond the fact that she was alive.

The eighth day after the attack saw the next change-up to my life, the day when Nynsi finished vetting my new assistant.

Who was... not quite what I was expecting.

She was a giant of a Trahcon. Literally. She was six and a half feet tall, built like a linebacker, and wearing the maroon uniform of the staff tightly enough to show off every muscle she had. Her dark gray features were surprisingly pleasant, not quite as comely as Ghai, but the pair of blue diamond tattoos bisecting eyes of the same color gave her a bit of flair.

It hadn't taken her long to spot me after getting out of the car, and she'd wasted little time in wandering to my little section of the garage. Sadly it had taken me a while longer to gather my wits after wondering just what the hell she'd been fed as a kid.

"So... you're Illyahn'donah?" I asked, shaking myself after several long seconds of awkward silence.

She gave me a grin, and her voice proved to be very melodic for her size, "So far as I know. Since I don't see any other savanna's here, you must be Cieran Kean."

"Human." I corrected absently, using the English word. "I don't really like the Savanna People thing, though I'll admit it's better than short-fur. And you can call me Cieran."

There was a quick nod, "Then you can call me Illyahn, boss. I hear I'm supposed to help you with some kind of project?"

I jerked one of thumbs over my shoulder, indicating the compiled wreckage that was my exoskeleton. "We get to rip that apart and rebuild it. All those crates on the left should have most of the new parts."

She turned and twitched her tarah once in amusement. "That's a lot of parts."

It was. It was, in fact, enough parts to replace practically everything except for the suit's core frame and skeleton. Originally I hadn't really thought about fixing up the stupid thing up at all, but Nynsi had insisted after Chen bluntly told her I'd be a below-average rookie without it. Since it was practically wrecked anyway, and since its shortcomings were largely caused by the second-hand parts I'd been using, she'd also decided to actually spend money on it this time.

The beat up old power core was being replaced by one with nearly double the output, which would go a long way to powering the new muscle strands and shield generators. Supposedly we'd also be getting high grade armor to replace the old shuttle plates I'd cut up, giving similar protection for less weight. In theory the suit would be able to get up to something close to a fast jog, making it far more useful.

It would still be an ugly hunchbacked block of metal, but if it continued to keep me alive I wouldn't complain.

"If you're all right just jumping into things," I continued, "I'd like to get most of those emptied and everything organized today. And maybe run you through a few questions in the mean time."

"No problem boss. Where do you want to start?"

We ended up spending most of the morning cracking boxes open, checking items off checklists, and talking. Well, it was mostly me asking a question or two while she told me her experience as a shuttle mechanic. It didn't take me long to decide that she was far more experienced and qualified to be doing this than I was. Not at Trenah's level, but I'd be able to pick up things from her while we worked.

It also didn't take me long to realize a few other things.

"So..." I asked while she carefully began to work the new power core out of its box. "I feel like I have to ask about the height."

"Towering Branch Syndrome." She replied at once.

I blinked. "Eh?"

"Your species have something where you grow up way too large?"

"Oh, gigantism." I shook my head once, "Sorry. Was that rude to ask?"

"Nah, you were polite about it." She rolled a shoulder and waved towards the other end of the garage. "Besides, most people are more confused that I actually know who my little sister is."

That made me blink again and look in that direction. Sure enough, Nynsi was giving some kind of speech to a dozen or so new arrivals who'd showed up around the same time as Illyahn. The replacements for the staff who'd been wounded or killed were mostly Thondians, but another shockingly tall Trahcon woman stood out among them. It was hard to tell from a distance, but she might have had an inch on her sister, though with far less muscle.

"Erana." Illyahn provided. "And yeah, she's got the same thing. Our mother apparently didn't believe in gene screening before she popped our eggs out."

"Huh." I provided, not really sure how to respond. "To be honest I still don't get the whole communal raising of kids who don't even know who their parents are thing. No offense meant."

"None taken." She grinned over her shoulder before turning back to her work. "There's a few groups out here who like to live like you aliens do, but to be honest I think that's pretty weird. No offense."

I snorted and tossed the tablet I'd been taking notes on onto a work station. "None taken. Looks like we got everything except for new weapons, I'll have to go talk to Nynsi about that. How are you at coding? Since we're gutting the power system we'll have to reconfigure everything Rane'li put in, and I don't think I can manage that."

Tarah quivered in amusement though she didn't turn around. "I can make a display window change colors."

That made me sigh. "Well, too much to hope you were perfect then. You have to move into your room still, right? Go ahead and get the rest of it unpacked then you can call it a day. I'm going to go see if I can summon up a programmer to go with a new rifle."

My titan of an assistant turned, brought two fingers up to an eye in some kind of salute, then got back to work. I felt a little bad about sending her straight to it while I wandered off, but I really did have to get those things handled sooner rather than later.

Nynsi was dismissing her new minions when I approached. She glanced me, nodded once, then waved for me to follow her to a quiet corner of the garage.

"Does she meet your expectations?"

"I've known her for all of two hours." I leaned against the wall and crossed my arms, "But she seems to know her stuff as far as mechanics. I'll need a programmer though. And guns. And maybe you could pick someone Trenah didn't have a crush on next time."

Nynsi let out a quiet huff of breath. "Cieran, all of our Trahcon employees stare at Donah. Height is considered extraordinarily attractive and she is likely one of the tallest members of her species alive."

I glanced back in time to see the giantess hauling heavy pieces of the new engine out with no apparent effort. Just beyond that I could see at least two more Trahcon, probably more replacements. Both of them were men, and both had identically glazed looks as they stared. A second look found a young Trahcon woman of average height leaning slightly around a car so that she could watch Erana depart the garage.

"Huh." I pursed my lips to stop from laughing. "And you had to bring both of them in?"

She gave me a very tiny shrug. "Your assistant requested her sister be assigned here instead of taking a pay raise. The girl has potential as a secretary, and I need a replacement as Rane'li will be bed ridden for some time. In truth I am more concerned about their age."

My amusement faded quickly, "How old are they?"

"Forty and thirty eight respectively."

That drew a slow whistle from me. It made them easily the youngest Trahcon I'd ever met, and if I remembered correctly, put them on the dividing line between their versions of childhood and becoming teenagers. Leaving the Stage of Growth to become Hunters. Or huntresses, I supposed, though Caranat didn't differentiate for gender.

"Suddenly the staring is less funny and a lot more creepy." I murmured, shaking myself. "That's like ogling a fifteen year old."

Nynsi pursed her lips as if doing mental math, then nodded slightly. "Perhaps slightly older, Illyahn is at least at the age of consent for her species. Still, I take your point and will be making our personnel policies very clear. I am more concerned about keeping them both in line and focused. According to my uncle, Trahcon of their age can be... troublesome. Even more so than someone like Laria."

The mention of Trenah made me slump a little further. "Still no news?"

"No." She said quietly. "I am sorry. I may not like her but I will of course tell you the moment I hear anything."

"I know, and thank you." I blew out a tight breath and tried to focus. "Uh, work. Right. The shipment didn't have a new rifle in it, and I'll also need a programmer."

Dark eyes blinked. "Is there something wrong with Rane'li?"

"You said she's on bed rest." I noted.

Nynsi gave me an amused look. "Her hands and brain remain functional, and she will have a great deal of time with which to do little."

"Maybe," I said, "But she had a giant hole in her back the last time I saw her. Isn't that the kind of thing you need some time to recover from?"

"We do not heal as completely as Trahcon if that is what you are asking. She is stable and being transferred back to the mansion as we speak. I will have our technical staff setup a station for her." She paused in consideration, then exhaled through her teeth. "In regards to weapons, I'm afraid the model destroyed last week was the only Regnon rifle in our armory. Chehat was quite upset at its loss."

I grimaced. "I wondered why he upgraded from ignoring me to glaring at me."

"Yes... I will have to purchase a replacement in addition to weapons for your suit. Do you have a preference?"

"Not really." I'd gotten somewhat used to the submachine gun Trenah had given me, but even a larger version didn't seem appropriate given my probable role in the back ranks. "Something rapid fire? I'm guessing I'm going to be providing support if we're attacked again."

Nynsi gave me a slight nod and brought up her wrist-comp, typing out a quick note with her free hand. "I will pick something appropriate. If there is nothing else I need to prepare, there is a mission this evening."

I shook my head. "That's everything at the moment."

Another nod, then Nysni's expression went carefully neutral. "My uncle would like you to observe the raid in the command center with him. He wishes to discuss recent events since he has not had time to speak with you, and he also hopes that you may see something we miss."

That took me a bit by surprise. Mostly because, as she'd said, I'd barely spoken a word to Xerol since I'd moved in. "Is that an offer or an order?"

"An offer." She assured me. "My uncle is... cognizant of Laria's irritation with him, and of the cultural differences. He has no desire to damage our working relationship with either of you."

I hummed softly, thought about it, then shrugged. The actual mission would be well after working hours so I wouldn't really lose any time. Might miss out on a bit of sleep but I wasn't getting much of that lately anyway. "I suppose I could, sure."

One of her strong hands rose to gently touch my shoulder as she nodded, "Thank you. In the meantime I have a further favor to ask while I am occupied preparing. Please meet with Rane'li when she returns and explain the situation. Inform her that she is to serve as your assistant until further notice."

"Another assistant?" I shook my head, my lengthening hair briefly falling over my eyes before I irritably brushed it aside. "Two in one day? Trying to spoil me?"

Nynsi gave me a grin as her body language shifted into something I couldn't read, leaning to her right and forwards with arms crossing high on her chest. "Perhaps."

She turned and departed before I could even try to puzzle out what she meant by that. The warnings and rantings that Trenah had given me the day of the attack came back to me as I watched her depart. Nynsi was very definitely my friend, I was certain about that, but I was beginning to think that she also had some kind of agenda.

...and after a few seconds, I realized that I'd let my eyes drop further than they should have to admire a specific part of her body.

I reached up and pinched the bridge of my nose, exhaling sharply. The lack of Human women for company was starting to get to me, and the last thing I needed right now was for someone to catch me staring at Nynsi's ass. No matter how pleasantly her suit framed it.

Returning to my station, I watched Ilyahn work for a few moments, then moved on to get started on ripping the suit apart. In truth it was a lot less fun than I'd thought the controlled destruction would be. Probably because the number of scorch marks and dents from bullets made my stomach clench every time I found one.

I stopped counting after the fiftieth but I was pretty sure there had to be at least a hundred. It was enough to make me seriously second guess exactly what I was doing here. No number of expensive new parts would change the fact that I'd be the largest target in any fight I got involved in. Ullika had been an asshole of the highest order, but the bastard had been right about one thing; the suit was a bullet magnet.

I'd gotten lucky once. I might not get lucky again.

By the time a heavy shuttle carrying some of the wounded arrived I'd managed to work myself into a fairly morose mood. Illyahn departed for her own rooms around then, leaving me to wait for my other assistant to be offloaded while being studiously ignored by most of the staff. A few, two of which I knew had been in the garage during the attack, gave me polite little bows that I returned with care.

But for the most part I was still persona non grata, something I was sure was adding to my depression. Following janitors and various technicians as they carried men and women on stretchers didn't do much to help either. Especially since they took them to their rooms rather than to the medical suite like I'd expected.

Neither of the men carrying Rane'li spoke to me when I followed them, or even acknowledged the fact that I'd wandered into the woman's room behind them. Her suite smaller than mine, lacking even the tiny living space, and she apparently wasn't the type to decorate. The only thing of note was an extensive work station with six monitors and an expensive looking chair set in the corner.

While I observed, the men gently deposited her into bed, setup some kind of IV line on a stand nearby, gave me suspicious looks, then left in the same silence they'd worked in.

"Kean." The tall woman rasped once the door closed. Her skin tone made it hard to tell if she was pale or not, but there was a sunken nature to her features that would have told me she was wounded even if I hadn't seen her get shot. "Are you here to demand repayment for saving me?"

"You saved me too." I said as I turned her working chair so I could settle into it. The thing was as stupidly comfortable as it looked, and I let myself slump back to enjoy the small luxury as much as I could. "There's no debt."

She tilted her head with a quiet huff of effort, then exhaled through her teeth. "We'll see. You have instructions for me?"

I nodded slowly. "I... well, Nynsi says you're to be one of my new assistants. Help with reprogramming the suit now that I'm building it with decent parts. Honestly I'm not comfortable with you working considering that you look like you can barely keep your eyes open."

Rane'li blinked once. Then twice. "It is not as if I am doing anything else."

Her words drew a sigh. "That's exactly what Nynsi said. Call it a Human thing, I guess. If you think you can work I'll get a remote connection setup so you can tinker with it. I won't push you though."

More staring and blinking, then she gave a tiny shake of her head and muttered something in her own tongue that I didn't pick up.

I waited a few seconds, but when she didn't say anything I could understand, I went ahead with my own question. "Will you recover?"

The fact that she was prone made her easier to read than normal. Probably because without being able to move her body she seemed to show more of what she was thinking in her expression... and I was pretty sure I was confusing the hell out of her. "...yes."

"Really?" My eyebrows rose. "I'm pretty sure a Human would have been screwed with how bad that looked."

"Your species is... fragile." She murmured diplomatically. "We have more secondary organs. I will be fine unless I take a similar wound to my other side. What work will you have for me, in specific?"

Her attempt to turn the conversation to the professional was blatant, but I didn't really mind. In the end we ended up talking for several hours as we went over what new items had been bought and how much damage the suit had taken. She managed to work me through a few programming basics on my wrist-comp, got exasperated at the fact that I couldn't read her species' runic script, and sent me a link to a proper translator.

Sleep took her while I was perusing that, her eyes shutting in the middle of muttered instructions to make sure I had it set to translate the lower-tongue only.

I quietly let myself out of her room, and made sure the door was shut and locked behind me. A glance at the time made me grimace, then start walking towards my own suite so that I could change. If I was going to be spending the evening with Xerol I'd need to be wearing one of the few nicer outfits that I owned.

"Time to dress up for my host." I murmured. "And time to be on my best behavior. Last thing I need is for anything else to go wrong."

I knocked on the wooden wall... and quietly hoped that no one else I knew would end up shot by the end of the evening.

II – VII

Xerol was alone when I got to the command center. The dark clothes I'd picked out were a little too close to his black suit, and the uniforms of his security teams, but they'd been the nicest things I'd gotten on my last shopping trip. Though I supposed I should have been grateful that feminine fashion for Trahcon wasn't nearly as bright as the clothing their men seemed to like.

"Cieran." My host greeted me, waving a broad hand towards the elevated circle he was standing within. "On time, excellent. Please join me."

I did as he tapped out a command on his wrist-comp. Glass view screens slid smoothly down from the ceiling, each one filling up with displays from helmet cameras. Thankfully each also had a label indicating who was who, though at the moment each one merely showed the interiors of vehicles packed with armored forms. Probably shuttles taken from the nearby starport.

"Sending out five teams?" I asked after doing a quick count. "Who got left behind?"

"Marn." He replied, "And before you can make a pithy comment, yes, she was highly displeased."

I smiled faintly, "You mistake me for Trenah. Usually I only offer sarcasm when I'm drinking, otherwise I try to be polite and keep those comments inside my head."

A deep chuckle came out at that. "Ah, my apologies. Would you object to speaking business while we await my teams' arrival at their targets? Thank you. My niece has indicated you have been given two of our employees as assistants."

"Yes... was she not supposed to?" I asked.

"They were her staff to assign." He replied, "Though I will admit that we have never loaned our people to an outsider before. It makes your place here even more complicated than it already was."

I pursed my lips, it wasn't hard to see where he was going with this. "You're saying that people are going to resent it."

"I have sent out a second copy of my prior instructions indicating that you, and Trenah when she returns, are my most honored and protected guests. That you have both sacrificed blood defending my home and my people." Xerol exhaled slowly, the same tic that Nynsi showed when she needed to keep her temper under control. "Sadly your species remains a problem for some of my employees. Those born here are less prejudiced, but many are exiles from the Ascendancy and they remember the battles with the Ark Fleet."

"Could we keep it quiet maybe?" I suggested, "I mean, Illyahn's not a Thondian so that might not go over that badly. Or would it?"

He flicked a hand in dismissive motion, "Any other year, perhaps. Or if you were a more established assistant to Trenah, someone who had been in and out of the district for some time. As it is the combination of what you are, and how unknown you are, will likely cause issues unless we mitigate it."

Something in his tones and the direction of the conversation abruptly clicked in my head. The way he was laying out the known problems as if he was preparing to lead me to a conclusion. He was going somewhere with this, and I was pretty sure I knew exactly where that was. And since it was a place I wasn't interested in going I moved to head him off as politely as possible.

"I'm not interested in a change of employers." I said firmly.

Xerol went very still, almost unnaturally so. Even his breathing didn't seem to cause him to move, not until his lips curled. "You are disturbingly perceptive at times."

"Thank you." I responded evenly. "But my answer isn't going to change. I respect you and Nynsi a great deal. Speaking honestly though, I'm still not very comfortable living here, much less working for you directly."

"I am sure the direct assault on your person did not help."

"No," I agreed, "It really didn't."

A deep and genuine chuckle made me grin as well, my host turning back to the screens while still chortling. "My brother always had a gift for ruining my plans when we were boys. I suppose it is only to be expected that he continues to do so."

I glanced at him before turning to try and find Nynsi's display. "It's personal between the pair of you?"

"In my experience familial battles are one of the few things every species has experience in." Xerol shrugged. "Even the Trahcon have their own variations despite their unusual cultures. Suffice to say that we both hold the other accountable for our original exile. That I was able to see my sentence rescinded for my work here did not improve matters."

"Ah." I considered indulging my curiosity for a few seconds before electing against it. Rumors and Ullika's actions aside, the last thing I needed was to get dragged even deeper into their family politics. "Do you think he's on planet?"

My host considered that as speakers began to relay the squad leaders' instructions. He adjusted the volume so that we weren't being bombarded by people speaking over one another, then replied, "Chacksin has many faults, but cowardice is not among them. He is here, somewhere. One of my hopes for this evening is that we may find a clue as to his bastion before he loses his patience and comes for us directly."

I frowned. "Would that be a bad thing? You stood off one attack before, and you didn't even have your private army here."

"I did." He agreed, "However my brother does not make the same mistakes twice. He'll have learned from the failures of his pawns. If or when he attacks this mansion again, it will not be in the same fashion."

I hummed, but before I could offer commentary he continued with a whistling sigh, "In truth I am not a military man. I am not helpless in a fight, and I believe I am reasonable at grand strategy. My expansion here over the past decade tells me as much, but direct combat tactics have always eluded me."

My knowledge of Thondians wasn't great but admitting weakness was something that always seemed to be difficult for them. "Nynsi seems all right at it."

A small grin briefly appeared, "Yes. She is quite skilled at whatever she sets her mind to That girl is her grandfather reincarnated, though some part of me wishes she had been born male. She would have done very well on Koshun as the familial Patriarch. Far better than either of the twins."

Discomfort made me shift my weight from side to side. I did understand enough about Thondians to know that they had very strict ideas of what men and women should be doing in a society. That Xerol gave Nynsi as much power as she had, that he allowed both she and Marn to command *men* in battle, made him a screaming liberal by their standards. And that was without getting into the strange mixture of caste and feudal system that they used in their home nation.

Sadly there wasn't really much I could think of to say. Anything I could offer would have been something he'd heard a thousand times before from Trenah, Ghai, and any other Trahcon he'd worked with. Plus... at the end of the day the man was still my host. The one who'd given me guns, armor, food, shelter, and helped us survive when people had come for us.

Holding my nose closed at distasteful aspects of his culture was both polite and probably wise. Not *right,* but... shit. Thondians weren't *Human.* I'd screwed myself up mentally treating the Trahcon around me as if they were Human. My already complicated personal situation would probably get a hell of a lot worse in a hurry if I started trying to treat Thondians the same way.

But still... it made me uncomfortable.

"May I ask you something? About your culture?"

That seemed to pique his interest, and he turned to face me directly. "You may ask, though I cannot promise the answer will be satisfactory to you. Our peoples seem to have rather deep rooted disagreements."

I exhaled, nodded once, then chose my words carefully. "The day of the attack, Trenah was worried about how you viewed her. How Nynsi viewed me. She said that you never do anything without an agenda. Is that true? Or was that just Trenah being Trenah?"

To be honest I expected him to be insulted to one degree or another. Instead he let out a low chuckle and turned back to the screens. "That sounds like her. Impolite and crass, yet not wholly wrong. The word *agenda* is not the one that I would use but I will admit that my people rarely act without some degree of self-interest. Even among kin and close associates."

I noted the absence of the word 'friend' and wondered, yet again, what the fuck I'd stumbled into. "Am I allowed to ask to what that is?"

He let out a low chuckle, "You may."

When he didn't elaborate further I gave a quiet laugh of my own, "Nynsi's?"

Xerol seemed to consider it, mouth still quirked on the sides, then he offered. "Consider what you believe my goals to be. Then note that my niece strives to exceed my own examples. Ah, they are arriving."

I gave him a half-hearted glower before pushing my worries aside in favor of returning my gaze to the screens.

"What are their targets tonight?" I asked. The screens seemed to bounce and shift as men and women piled out of the boxy cargo shuttles. It made it look almost amateurish, like a collage of home videos.

At least until the gunfire started.

"Two automotive shops that have been providing and repairing many of their vehicles, and an apartment complex they have been using as a barracks." Xerol replied. "Rehat and Chehat are both attacking the latter, while Nynsi and Horthan are dealing with the car depots."

"Chen?"

"In reserve in case any target proves to be more difficult that anticipated." Another small smile showed me his ivory teeth. "He was nearly as displeased as Marn."

I didn't have any problems picturing the man's irritation after the time I'd spent being drilled by him.

The gang members at Nynsi's target weren't the quickest on the uptake. I'd have thought that the noise of a sub-orbital shuttle landing in the street would be enough to put them on alert, but Nynsi had her entire team out and the craft taking off before anyone reacted. An orange haired Naule poked his head out of a door only to get a bullet between his sunken eyes courtesy of Nynsi's pistol.

Chatter picked up as the teams coordinated their attacks. Unfortunately for me everyone was speaking in their own language, and without a translator I couldn't even begin to follow any of it. Not that I had much to understand since the fighting stayed as one sided as it started.

"It's really hard to see these people as the ones giving us so much trouble." I murmured, shaking my head. "None of these are anything like a fight. Were you expecting harder resistance?"

"In truth, yes. This is a frustrating dichotomy, is it not?" Xerol mused as we watched the various teams gunning down people wearing rags. Some tried to fight back with weapons that were little more than scrap metal. Hell, a few of them tried to jump the armored soldiers with knives or clubs.

"Their morale is unusually high." He continued, waving to where one of the teams gunned down a dozen Naule who tried to rush them across a small parking lot and died to a man trying it. "But their tactics are poor and their equipment is worse when not directed by those in gray. Which, if our intelligence is correct, was the original coloration of the gang's markers."

I frowned at that. "The same color as Trahcon skin. Odd choice for a gang that professes to hate them."

A broad shoulder rolled in a shrug, "A way to reclaim it perhaps? In truth I try not to delve into the psychology of it. I merely note the difference in competency and ask for your opinion."

No pressure. Exhaling, I watched as Nynsi's team cautiously swept through a garage not much larger than Trenah's. Unlike some of the others, the True Sons in her location were smart enough to quit while they were still breathing. A handful died trying to hold the doorway, but after their corpses hit the floor the rest gave up. Weapons were tossed aside and hands rose, maybe a dozen survived to end up kneeling against a wall.

"The obvious theory is that we're dealing with two groups. Wait," I frowned in thought, "Three. White Storm, the True Sons in actual armor, then

215

the imported goons. The ones in armor are definitely the True Son leaders...
maybe all that's left of the original group that got hammered last year. White
Storm probably gave them the better armor and guns as a way to buy their
loyalty early on, then took over once the gang was in their debt."

"Making them tools to be used and discarded." Xerol crossed his arms
as we continued to watch. "I admire the strategy even as I despise the
complications it offers. They have both fodder and commandos, and we must
cut through the former to locate the latter. It fits with my brother's usual
strategy of layered assaults and distractions."

"So it's a matter of cutting through the idiots to get to him." I guessed
with a shake of my head, "What's your plan? Try and make the True Sons
resent their bosses by hammering their territory?"

Xerol nodded once, stepping to his right to take a closer look at a
screen. "That is the first step, yes. My brother will not risk operating openly,
he cannot know that the High Families and Kolkris did not believe me. The
True Sons will be fighting alone, and the more openly they try to retaliate the
more likely that Internal Security will act."

"Ah." I got it. "Making them fight low key, which your people are
better at since they have better gear and better training. If they want to have a
chance they'll have to commit their veterans, the same people you want to
capture to get intel on your brother's location."

My host grinned once more, though his eyes remained on a display
showing men ransacking a small office. "You are refreshingly quick on the
uptake. That is, more or less, my plan as we currently speak. I do, however,
wish to resume our discussion on your place within it."

That made me get defensive again. "I'm not a soldier. I'm an amateur
mechanic and a half-decent analyst."

"Who also possesses a suit of proto-battle armor that none of my
people can fit within. A suit that cannot be countered by the enemy's rank and
file." He interjected smoothly.

"I could modify it for someone else to use." I said quickly. "It only
takes a few days to get used to."

His left hand waved in a dismissive motion. "It is more than that. You are Human, and as you noted some weeks past, a greater traitor to your race than I in their eyes. Further my brother believes your relationship with his daughter to be... inappropriate. That anger can be used."

I was not liking how this was going. Not one bit. "You know nothing like that is happening between us, and I really don't want to be used as bait just to piss someone off."

"*Speaking* to Nynsi is inappropriate as far as Chacksin would be concerned. And you would be quite safe, assigned only to specific missions with at least two of my teams in support at all times." He said firmly. "A contract would be drafted, detailing this as a temporary employment, and you would be free to review and edit it as you see fit. You would be well compensated."

"Again, I'm flattered, but-"

Xerol interrupted me with a number.

I choked on my words.

"Per mission." He added, ignoring my rather unseemly display. "More than enough to allow you to return to your homeworld with a single assignment. Enough to allow yourself and Trenah to recover in moderate luxury for several years once all of this is dealt with."

I just... stared at him. My economic knowledge about the worth of a single credit wasn't great, but I knew that he was telling the truth. It was probably equivalent to five years of work for Trenah. Two or three such payments would be... a lot of money. More than enough to make sure I didn't have to work while I helped Trenah get over her injuries. Fuck, it was enough that we could hire people to run her shop for a year while still having plenty leftover.

Enough for us to go to Earth. Or any other planet where crap like this wouldn't happen to us.

Plus it would probably help my standing among the locals. Holding my ground in the garage had earned me the respect of the people who'd fought there, even if the rest of the staff still despised me. Going out with the security teams on counter-raids might be enough to earn me tolerance if not love. And tolerance might be enough to ensure the next time Nynsi's bastard of a father tried to hire someone to grab me, they might think twice about it.

Dammit.

"I..." Inhaling, I shook my head once. "I need to think about it."

"Of course." Xerol said politely, "The relevant paperwork is still being drawn up, I will have my niece deliver it to you tomorrow. If our enemies do not retaliate within the next week we will launch another operation. I would like an answer before then."

"Yeah... sure."

God above, I needed Trenah to wake up soon. I needed her advice. I needed to know if this was bad idea or a terrible idea.

Or if it was the only thing I could do to keep our host's respect and protection for as long as this storm lasted.

II – VIII

The next day Xerol decided that his secret prisoner had stewed for long enough. And, lucky me, I was cordially invited to watch the interrogation.

It was being held in the same interrogation room as last time, and again I found myself sitting in the observation room next to Nynsi. Unlike last time Xerol was seated in here with us while Ghai was the one who stepped into the cell with the former butler.

He didn't look very good. His skin was a lot lighter in tone than most other Thondians, a tan shade with bone-white armored sections. The combination made it easy to see the bruising across his chest and belly. On top of that the poor bastard clearly hadn't been fed in a while from the way his bones practically protruded from his body.

The combination must have affected his alertness because he didn't seem to notice the door opening and then closing.

Ghai brought him to his senses by using her telekinetics to slam him against the back wall hard enough to break the chair he was tied to. She waited for him to settle into place, then tossed an arm to the right as her tarah quivered, sending him flying in that direction. He'd barely struck that particular wall before she gestured again to hammer him into the ceiling.

Then the floor.

Then the wall again.

I winced when he started screaming and babbling in two different languages, begging for her to stop.

"For the love of the Paragons stop!" He was practically sobbing in pain from where he'd landed the last time, sprawled amid the remains of the chair. "I'll tell you whatever you want! Please!"

Ghai didn't bother responding verbally, settling instead for a disgusted sneer as she casually stretched out an arm again. He flinched and whimpered, but only slid slowly until his back hit a wall. Some instinct had him start to curl up defensively, then a long moan escaped as she brought her other arm out and mentally forced him to stay sprawled.

"Jesus Christ." I muttered, glancing away. "This is a bit much."

"He is the one who threw the incendiary at Iyaht." Nynsi provided, her own gaze not wavering.

That explained her anger but didn't make me any more comfortable with what I was witnessing.

"Reasons." Ghai's rasp came from the room's speakers, her voice more elevated than I'd ever heard it. "Now."

"I... I don't have anything against Trahcon!" He was practically blubbering, "Nothing against Trahcon!"

His interrogator sneered, continuing to show more temper and emotion that I'd honestly thought she'd had in her. "Iyaht disagrees."

"I... I panicked and thought she knew. I just... just threw the grenade and tried to run for it!"

Ghai took a single step forwards and growled.

The ex-butler shuddered and looked away, more words tumbling out. "Right... right... I... Chacksin ul Shaaryak contacted me a few months ago. He said Xerol was... was losing it. Was letting his nostalgia get the best of him. That his time had passed, that the family needed to be stronger now than it ever was before."

"Fool." Ghai said flatly.

Some tiny semblance of anger managed to work it's way into his voice. "I didn't really believe him at first. Xerol has done well by the Ascendancy, by our species. But then... that... that *Human* showed up. Danced with *Kasha* Nynsi. *Kissed* her. And he just stood there and let it happen!"

Xerol turned and gave Nynsi a very dry look. To her credit, his niece winced and wordlessly ducked her head to the left, accepting the blame for what she'd done the night we'd first met.

"I... I had to do something. The twins aren't from the core family, her firstborn should be the heir. Should return to Koshun. I couldn't sit there and let her get corrupted. Chacksin... left me a way to contact him. I did... told him what happened at the ball. And after. He told me... he told me he was glad there were still Thondians who knew who their enemies were."

Ghai shook her head once. "Hired Ullika, the others. You were the leader."

The man winced. "I... I just knew who to talk to. Chacksin was the one with the plans. The orders. Told us what to do. When the True Sons would attack to provide a distraction."

"Nothing we didn't already know." I murmured.

Xerol evidently agreed because he tapped a button on the table, transmitting his words to the small communication cones on Ghai's tarah. "We need details my dear. What is my brother's goal for his daughter?"

Ghai relayed the question and got an answer. "I... I don't know the details. I know he has a suitor in place. Someone from the Ascendancy, another old family. I don't know more than that. I swear."

"Do you?" Ghai murmured.

Another shudder. "I swear... an old family. Maybe one of the ones sitting in the Patriarch's council? I don't know. He didn't give details. Just swore it would strengthen the bloodlines."

She pressed him but he only repeated himself a few more times. After a few silent moments Xerol relayed his next question, a more pertinent one to the current situation. "How did you contact him? What other details did you provide?"

"I..." He managed to raise his eyes, "Promise you'll let me live. I'll tell you everything. Please."

"Xerol's call." The man's bodyguard stated coldly. "Talk."

He stayed silent for several seconds, but when her tarah began to rise and angle outwards his will broke permanently. "Live calls... from a restaurant in the district. Red Run. The owner is another contact. We... gave him what we could access. Were paid for the information on each business we told him about. About Xerol's contacts in the rest of the city."

"Laria." Ghai growled.

There was a vague nod. "Her shop's address. And her home's. Think there was going to be a kill team sent after her and the short-fur if they hadn't come here."

Nynsi seemed to recover a little bit of pride at that, giving me a pointed look. I sighed and nodded, waving a hand in admission that she'd been right about that. That evidently pleased her immensely because she gave me a prim little smile.

The rest came out in fits and starts. Information about the various payments he'd received caused Xerol to take steps to seize the various bank accounts where he could, and to have Internal Security lock down the ones outside of Koshun Minor. Details on how he'd recruited Ullika and the other traitors revealed just how much I was apparently disliked among the staff, depressing me thoroughly. Evidently there had been plenty of volunteers to be the one to 'get rid of the furry alien', but that enthusiasm had dried up quickly whenever they'd hinted about going after Xerol.

Which was probably a good thing for my host even if my own situation remained terrible.

About the only other thing of relevance was the method the six of them had used to smuggle extra grenades into the mansion, and how they'd communicated with the True Sons in the run up to the attack itself. Details that Xerol and Nynsi were musing over when Ghai slipped into our half of the room.

"That is all." Her rasp had gotten significantly worse the longer it had all gone on. It had to have been agonizing but she was gamely keeping her voice at something approaching a normal volume. "Anything else?"

"I quite agree." Xerol said. "Nynsi? Kean? Nothing? Very well. It gives us some insight and another traitor to deal with. I will handle that myself. You three may have the remainder of the day off to do as you wish, there will be plenty of work to deal with in the days to come."

We all nodded, Nynsi and I standing while Ghai turned back to the door. A hand fell to her belt, then rose with her pistol held in a solid grip.

I felt my breath hitch for a second, turning away before I could witness anything I'd rather not see. Sadly the turn didn't stop my ears from working, nor was the walk to the door long enough.

"...I told you every-no! Please! I told you! Xerol! *Tarath* Xerol! *Eshan kul ah-*"

A gunshot ended the pleading.

I made it outside of the small room, about ten steps past the door, then I had to stop and lean hard against the wall to stop myself from throwing up.

"Cieran?"

My left hand rose in a silent request for peace. Nysni gave it to me, letting me breathe and try and focus. The man had been a categorical traitor. He'd thrown what amounted to a napalm grenade at Iyaht and left her in a medical coma. He'd been the one to bring Ullika into his little conspiracy, making him indirectly responsible for the attack on me and Rane'li. He'd been the one to bring in the others, including the man who'd put bullets into Trenah's back.

He'd earned a bullet to the head.

I had to remember that, and not the desperation in his voice before Ghai relieved him of his life.

"I'm fine." I said finally. "Just needed a minute."

Nynsi said nothing. Instead she stepped closer and placed a strong hand on my back, gently guiding me towards the stairs. I expected her to lead me to my rooms, but instead she led me to the southern wing and up to the second floor's gallery. It was the most brightly lit hall in the building, floor to ceiling windows occupying an entire wall, while the other opened into the modest ballroom Xerol reserved for high level affairs.

To my vague surprise she nudged me to a small alcove with a bench, settling beside me once I'd sat down.

"I thought some sunlight would do you good." She provided. "We get little enough of it these days."

I couldn't argue with that. It felt like we lost more of the light every day as the fall season passed. "Winter will be weird. I was born in a desert... we saw the sun every day, even when we really didn't want to."

Nynsi was silent for several moments, then her voice turned wistful. "I was born here, in exile. I've never been to a desert, though I would like to see one some day. It is where my people come from."

"I know." I said quietly. The Empire was rather literal in its naming of peoples and places, even in the dead language they used for such things. Trahcon? River-People. Their word for Human? Savanna-People. For Thondians? Desert-People. Hell, even Zulflara, their home-world, literally translated as *home-world*.

An imaginative bunch, the Imperials.

"You are not used to these things at all, are you?" She asked quietly. "You seemed to hold up well after the attack on the mansion, even if you did not after the events at the bar."

I couldn't help but let out a rueful little laugh. "I haven't been holding up well at all to be honest with you."

My friend let out a frustrated breath. "You should have stated as much. It is as hard for me to read you as it is for you to read us. Your work has been unaffected, if anything you seem to be making exceptional progress."

"I said I'm not doing well but I don't think I'm falling apart. I've been tinkering with design programs at night when I can't sleep." I shrugged, "It let me plan things out ahead. And I'm well motivated all things considered."

"You haven't been sleeping?"

Another shrug, "Maybe half as much as I should be. Too worried about Trenah. Wondering if another butler is going to slip into my room and cut my throat. Hearing about how many of them wanted to didn't help. Or want to, maybe."

She was silent for several seconds, then a low, angry sound escaped her. "How difficult is it for those in the lower rankings to accept that we know what we are doing. That someone who bled for us is hardly an enemy."

I smiled. "Technically I didn't bleed at all in the fight here. I only got wounded defending Forever."

"During which you defended me. Therefore my statement was correct." Nynsi stated firmly. "Something I will make more widely known, especially after you join our next operations. Or have you decided against it?"

My smile faded as quickly as it had come. "...I don't see what choice I've got. I have to prove myself somehow just to stay safe here, and I don't have anywhere else to go. I don't have the money to hide in a new place, and Trenah's apartment is definitely being watched by those assholes."

Dark eyes regarded me, then she turned to gaze at the lowering sun. "I could likely provide payment for time spent on the project given the extra work, but that would not be enough for you. You would have to find further employment which would expose your new location, and my father is unlikely to give up. That or go into Internal Security's custody."

"No thanks." I muttered. The situation was fucked up beyond all belief but this was where my friends were. What few of them I had, anyway. I couldn't abandon them no matter how uncomfortable it all made me. "I can deal with it. I just... need to adjust I guess."

"Do you need sedatives to help you sleep?"

I gave her a wry look. "Are you going to slip them into my drinks if I say no?"

"Only if I believe it required." Though her expression remained perfectly neutral, she leaned in to give me a slight nudge with her shoulder in a way that struck me as teasing. "Though I will refrain from such things tonight in exchange for a favor."

"Is it a favor you'll use to keep distracting me?"

"It is my duty as a proper host and companion." She rose, offering me a hand, "The Donah sisters wish to travel to the Core City to expand their clothing options, and my uncle's instructions about traveling in groups remain. As I have a weapons shipment to sign off on, I will be their assigned escort with a few others."

I accepted the hand, no longer surprised at how easily she hauled me up to my feet. "And you want me with?"

"I believe you need to get out of this building for a night. I am led to believe it will be good for your state of mind."

That made me blink. "Led to believe that by who?"

Nynsi smiled... and said nothing.

"The whole not explaining thing that you and your uncle like to do? Kind of annoying."

Her smiled widened, displaying her elegant canines. "Are you declining my offer?"

I rubbed my bearded chin. "...getting out for a night does sound good. And I probably could do with new clothes."

"That you could."

II – IX

I didn't go on the next set of raids. Not because Xerol didn't want me to, but because the work on the suit wasn't finished in time. Illyahn and I made damned good progress, mostly thanks to her, but there were limits. One week just wasn't long enough.

Sadly it was functional enough for me to jump in when the True Sons launched a few counter attacks agaisnt Koshun Minor. It was a fairly awful evening listening to people fighting over the radio while I stood around the mansion's front door as an obvious guard. Easy work, but the longer I'd been out in the open the more uncomfortable I'd gotten.

Something really not helped by the fact that the suit's left knee had locked up as soon as I'd gotten out there, leaving me as more statue than sentry.

By the time raid three's launch day came around... it was fixed up and fully ready to go. Which was how I found myself buttoned up inside the exoskeleton, the computer systems compensating automatically for the movements of our shuttle. The uncomfortable sensation of the suit shifting my body to maintain its balance was a small price to pay for *finally* knowing something about Trenah.

"Run me through it again." I asked quietly, speaking into a private comms channel that Rane'li had setup during her rework of the operating system.

"*She's being kept in a medical coma to keep her stabilized and let her natural healing work without her tearing anything.*" Rane'li repeated, probably reading directly from the medical transcript that she'd somehow acquired.

She hadn't believed me when I said she didn't owe me. Evidently she also had a talent for hacking that she kept quiet. Not that I was looking a gift horse in the mouth.

"*Looks like it's on the recommendation of someone named Tasir.*"

She continued, *"Backed up by her medical record. Apparently re-injuring herself is fairly common... though a lot of her file is encrypted."*

I grimaced at both bits of news. "How the fuck did Tasir know to say anything from Terminus? Is there a steady connection?"

"She wouldn't need one. She's been on Alum for a week."

"How the fuck do you... nevermind, I don't want to know." I exhaled, wondering just what the fuck Tasir was up to. Was she still working with Xerol? If so why I hadn't I seen her around? Why hadn't Xerol or Nynsi told me she was back? Did they even know?

Christ but I wished I knew what was going on around me.

"Ignore the encrypted sections, that's not important and not our business. How bad are her injuries?"

"Three hits. First round hit her in the back, just above her hip. Broke her pelvis and tore
her intestines up pretty badly on its way through." Her normally flat voice softened noticeably. *"Second one was higher, mostly stopped by her armor but it was a larger round than her protection was rated for. It slowed but still broke several ribs. Several fragments nearly reached her right heart."*

Swear words in two languages came out before I could hope to stop them. "The third?"

"Right leg. Off center shot tore a lot of muscle away from her calf. Report says the only reason she didn't bleed out was because someone practically drowned her in sealant foam within a minute of the injuries."

I had to assume that had been Ghai. I gritted my teeth and split my attention long enough to make sure that Rehat was still busy talking with our pilot. I hadn't really wanted to ride with his team, but Nynsi's was using regular aircars, and Chen was going after another apartment complex. Not really the kind of target my over-sized metal ass would fit inside.

Once I was sure I had a bit more time, I pushed on. "Does it say her recovery time? When are they going to wake her up?"

228

"...looks like next week for bringing her around. Nothing in here about recovery time. I... don't know anything about their rate of healing."

"Something for us to research then." I shook my head as best I could inside the box-like protection surrounding it. "Thank you for this. I owe you."

The wounded woman made a sound that was half amused, half frustrated. *"Humans."*

I was about to retort when she cut the line, leaving me to mutter a few more obscenities before calming down.

Trenah was alive.

She was wounded beyond what I'd thought someone her size could survive. She'd probably need months, years, of recovery time. It would be far worse than what I'd gone through, and I didn't doubt she'd be even less patient than I'd been. Helping her heal would be somewhere between a nightmare and merely frustrating.

But she was alive.

My existential relief was interrupted by a polite knock on the armored chest of my suit. I blinked and focused in time to see Rehat wrap the back of his gauntlets against it a second time. "Yes?"

When he didn't reply I mentally kicked myself and made a quick gesture to get to the proper radio channel. "Sorry. Are we on final approach?"

"We are." He stated. "You are finished with your call?"

"Yes, apologies for taking so long." I replied, "I'm ready to go."

From the way his helmet tilted a little to the right he didn't believe me, but he didn't openly call me out either. He was polite like that, unlike his brother. Or most of the others not named Nynsi. "Very well. Team Two, check systems and report"

My eyes glanced over my new readouts. Shields were up and holding steady, the power drain that had crippled them in the garage fixed thanks to Illyahn. The Regnon built Visage support rifle was hooked up and prepared. All of the exoskeleton's core mechanics were similarly showing as functional, and thankfully nothing was overheating unlike the first few tests.

And actuators in the left leg weren't reporting any problems. Yet.

I waited patiently until the others had indicated their readiness before speaking, "Kean. I'm ready and good to go."

The words had barely cleared my lips before the pilot shouted back, "One minute! Lady Shaaryak is down and engaged. They report they managed to deploy their jammer before the enemy could call for help!"

"Excellent." Rehat rumbled, "Engage our own equipment as a back-up. All personnel prepare to engage."

I bit my lip, and not for the first time on this trip was glad that no one could see into the armor. This was very different than simply defending myself or whatever building I happened to be in at the time. This was a direct attack. And for everything I'd told Nynsi and Xerol about being ready for this... I didn't know if I was.

I was even more nervous now than I'd been before we'd hit the slave-holding warehouse. Back then, no one had expected much of anything of me. That I'd actually managed to be sort of useful, and had nearly gotten killed because of it, had been as much of a surprise to me as to everyone else.

But now I wasn't running around in light armor with just a submachine gun and some technical grenades. Now I was inside nearly a ton of moving metal, with enough shields for three of Rehat's people, and between the targeting system and the suit's own ability to handle the recoil, pretty much no reason to miss with my assault rifle so long as I kept my head.

People actually expected things of me now.

I wasn't really comfortable with that even before I got to the part where I was essentially killing people for money. Well, money and respect. That last helped keep me steady so long as I focused it. How it would hopefully lead to more acceptance and lessened chance of death in the mansion.

...dammit. What the hell was I doing?

"Hitting the ground in five... three... now!"

The shuttle door swung open, Rehat leaping out in a single, smooth motion. Sucking in a breath, I heaved myself out after him, the engines working as the pilot compensated for my departure.

My legs flexed slightly, knee and ankle actuators flashing yellow when I impacted the ground, but I didn't really have time to focus on them. Just as the pilot had said, Nynsi was already engaged.

Three aircars were settled in a tight formation to our left. Their frames created a make-shift bunker that her team was settled in behind, guns blazing away as True Sons began to fan out to counter-attack.

A far more professional response than usual from them.

"Kean! Suppress right! All others sweep left!" Rehat shouted, punctuating his words with a long burst from his rifle. A Naule jerked and tumbled with all six limbs convulsing before going limp, drawing the attention of everyone on this side of the fight.

And there was a lot of attention to be drawn.

Two dozen or so gang members were in the open. Unlike the usual rabble they actually had some armor and functional looking weapons. They also had the good sense to start shouting, pointing, and then retreating when they realized we were on their flank. Behind them, in the open doors of the hangar that was our target, I saw several more targets but didn't have time to keep gawking.

Settling my aim, I blew out a slow breath and opened fire.

It was distressingly easy to kill people.

I was slow in the suit but its bulk and level gait made it easy even for me to keep my aim steady. Add in the video-game targeting reticle and the coolant feed and I was able to put down three Thondians with three long bursts of gunfire. One of them died more or less instantly thanks to a pair of rounds hitting his head. The other two merely fell and began to thrash.

My aim stayed high as I focused on those that were still upright and moving. Not that it saved the two, one of Rehat's men finished them off before I could even think to suggest that we take them prisoner.

On my far left I could see Nynsi's group begin their own advance. Pistols, rifles, and shotguns flashed as the seventeen of us drove the enemy back towards the hangar. Blood of different hues puffed into mist as more True Sons collapsed, spreading across the ground in disgusting pools. Thondians and Naule predominated, but I saw at least two wide, squat forms that might have been Chezzek. Their bodies bled a bright blue that was distracting as hell.

Maybe eight or nine of the initial group survived to make it to cover. The rest were dying or dead as I lumbered past and over them, everyone else easily keeping pace.

"Cieran please take point," Nynsi requested across comms when I began to slow, *"We cannot let them close the doors."*

I winced but obediently began to accelerate, "Confirmed. I'll sweep right on entering... shit. I think I see someone in full armor, gray."

While I still had a hard time reading Thondian body language, especially with armor on, it was easy enough to see everyone straighten up a bit more at that report.

Nynsi brought a hand up and made a quick gesture that saw everyone else pick up speed. *"Confirmed, priority target. Team one, advance and move left. Secure all exits from the building. Team two provide fire support for ourselves and Cieran."*

"Confirmed." Rehat responded.

The gaping entryway came up a lot faster than I hoped it would, furtive forms barely visible as they darted from cover to cover while someone shouted commands. Even if I hadn't already spotted him, that much would

232

have confirmed that there was someone present who knew what they were doing.

So it wasn't a surprise when I ran into a wall of gunfire as soon as I crossed the threshold.

I instinctively flinched despite the armored cocoon I was moving around in, my shields dropping quickly as I moved right. I'd barely begun to return fire towards figures crouching behind a workstation when I collided with a much smaller form.

A Thondian in the dark gray armor of a professional True Son got the worst of the impact, falling onto her ass and letting out a vicious serious of curses as she scrambled to keep hold of her shotgun. She got her hands into place faster than I could swing the over-long arms of my suit around, her first shot slamming into my chest plate and finishing off my shields.

Her second came at the same time I retaliated. The shotgun round hit my left shoulder hard enough to jerk my aim for a second, making me correct as my own shots drew sparks from her barrier. Gritting my teeth, I stepped forwards and all but rammed the barrel of my gun into her belly, holding the trigger down the entire time.

As I'd exploited before, shields didn't work against things that close. Nor did her armor hold up for very long.

Blood sprayed out to coat everything. The gang member let out a choked up scream that cut off after a second or three.

Thankfully I really didn't have time to look at the body. There was a small set of buttons above the corpse that must have been for the hangar controls. A panel that the True Sons very much wanted access to.

There'd been a brief few moments where the gunfire in my direction had slackened, they might not have wanted to hit their friend or Nynsi and Rehat had been keeping them busy. Either way the moment my tiny duel ended the barrage resumed.

The hail like sound of small bullets slamming into the suit remained as terrifying as it had been the first time around. And just like then, there was

233

nothing I could do besides plant my feet, take the punishment, and pray the armor held up.

"I make a full squad." Rehat noted, *"Technical barrage, right to left. Clear out the unarmored types, then we focus fire on the hard targets."*

At least two of his people must have had launchers because the barrage was literally that. Discharge and Incendiary technicals streaked out in tight arcs, rising and then falling among the group who were trying to murder me. I got my rifle back around and joined in as they began to fall, cutting down the last Naule who survived just long enough to try and make a run for it.

The last group of mostly unarmored True Sons didn't last any longer against Nynsi's team. She preferred more traditional grenades, and it only took two to turn a parked aircar into wreckage while killing everyone hiding behind it.

Which left us with a small but professional group who retreated as their companions died, moving behind several more aircars that looked like they'd been in the process of getting armor welded over their frames.

I sent bursts after them, harrying their shields but not accomplishing much else. Glancing at my coolant levels I blew out a breath, adjusted my aim a little, and then went to full automatic before Nynsi or Rehat could order me to. I wasn't really hoping to hit anyone so much as I was trying to suppress them. It seemed to work out since the Sons kept their heads down and only fired blindly over the cars.

That wasn't nearly enough to slow or even inconvenience everyone else. Black forms advanced silently, some taking positions and joining my barrage, covering the others as they got closer.

We could all tell what was about to happen.

So could the True Sons, and they decided to take a chance as a result.

A rifle was abruptly pitched over the cars to clatter onto the ground. A pistol followed, then a shotgun as we eased off on our suppressive fire. Half a dozen more weapons came out quickly after that, as did several belts with grenades and knives still attached.

"We're done!" A man shouted into the silence, "It's all disarmed! We want to negotiate our surrender!"

Nynsi was silent for a few seconds, then shouted back, "Come out, hands down and spread. We'll discuss your chances then."

For a long moment I wasn't sure if they'd do it, then they started to come out. There were five left, two Thondians tall enough to be men, and three Naule who looked even more awkward than normal with all four of their arms spread away from their bodies.

"Rehat, advance and keep them covered." Nynsi ordered by radio, *"Cieran, advance and cover them as well."*

Advance and intimidate she meant. Still, I didn't argue, advancing behind Team Two as they approached. Sure enough the enemy's helmets all seemed to swing in my direction, only noticing everyone else when their guns were practically against their throats.

"I've got information." The speaker said again, one of the two Thondians. "I want to trade it for our lives. We'll give you our gear too, and leave the planet for Terminus."

Nynsi seemed to consider that, "Talk."

"We're True Sons. *Actual* True Sons." He seemed to want to make that very clear, whatever the hell it meant. "Look, I hate the White Storm as much as you lot do, but those Patriarch dick-suckers didn't give us much of a choice."

It was probably a good thing I was in armor, otherwise I would have shown how baffled I was. I mean, sure, I'd guessed some of that along with Xerol, but the insult meant nothing to me.

"Explain." Nynsi's voice was perfectly level, giving nothing away.

The *Actual* True Son actually seemed taken aback. "Wait. You mean you don't know?"

"I would hear your version of events." She replied.

The man didn't have her level of body control, shifting visibly before replying. "Right. We weren't always their fucking beasts, at their beck and call. They approached us last year after the Crescent tried to tear us apart. There was money, resources, recruits... everything we needed."

Muttered growls and angry fist clenching came from the others, settling only when he waved a hand towards them. That they quieted instantly told me that, whoever this was, he was a big-shot of some kind.

Had we really gotten that lucky?

"But in the weeks after we accepted, they basically just started taking over. Killed every boss we had that didn't kowtow to that exiled prick ul Shaaryak. Took all of our best guns, gear, and troubleshooters. Shipped them all off to Terminus for 'training'. Still haven't heard back from most of them."

Nynsi twitched her helmet left to right. "History is interesting but not currently relevant. Give me a reason not to kill you all."

He went silent for a second, then casually offered, "I can give you the facility where they're letting the slaves recover before putting them out on the market."

...oh boy.

Everyone, even Nynsi, went stock-still at that. Which was probably the wrong thing to do because his posture became smug, even with his face hidden by his helmet. "I thought that would be worth something to you. Here's what I want, you let two of my people get our private car from outside, me and two others stay. When they get back, I'll give you the address, and we part ways."

"How do we know you won't go running back to Chacksin ul Shaaryak?" Re'hat prodded.

"The Pillars can crush that son of a bitch for all I care." Either he was seriously pissed, or the guy deserved a medal in acting. "I hope you lot make

236

him suffer before you end his miserable life. Bastard's made us work with grays, treated us like fodder. I just want to get to Terminus and leave this shit planet."

It didn't take Nynsi long to make up her mind. "Agreed. Two of the Naule can retrieve your car. The rest of you kneel with your hands behind your necks."

She got no arguments from them. Rehat's team stayed nearby and alert, but for my part I relaxed and backed away to think. I didn't really have time to get anywhere because my system pinged almost at once, alerting me that I'd just been added to a private communications line.

"*Uncle,*" Nynsi spoke, "*We'll have to act on this immediately if it's valid. They may not go back to him but they will alert my father that we're coming. Cieran agrees.*"

I did but I didn't remember saying anything in the last couple of seconds.

Xerol let out a deep hum, "*Of course they will. Matters remain complicated... we will need to strike it as soon as all of our teams can be prepped. I will contact Internal-Security and see what forces they can commit.*"

I let out a quiet sigh, "Guessing I'm going with again?"

"*I will naturally count it as a separate mission in regards to payment.*" Xerol offered reasonably. "*But per our contract you are free to decline.*"

Because backing out after a single mission would make me look so professional and trustworthy. "No... I suppose I can go on another one."

"*Excellent. Dear niece, please recover the address and any additional information as soon as possible. It is probable I will send you directly to the target so be prepared to leave in haste.*"

"*Yes Patriarch. We'll be ready.*"

Well... shit. Looks like I'd been right after all.

This had been a fucking terrible idea.

II - X

The preparation for the second attack was a lot more rushed than anyone was comfortable with.

For the morning attack the team leaders had spent better than two days in conference rooms plotting, staring at maps, and debating strategy among themselves. For our afternoon attack, all six teams had ended up in a public parking garage, watching while our commanders gestured, shook their heads, and argued on a private line.

Once they'd come up with a vague plan of action it was back into the cars and shuttles. It was a short flight to the target, a decommissioned water treatment plant officially owned by a Naulian investor in the Industrial Sector. Given that he wasn't a known criminal, and given that Internal-Security had refused to believe Xerol... that made this attack all kinds of illegal.

That didn't seem to bother everyone else nearly as much as it bothered me.

In the motivational speech he'd given before we'd lifted off, Xerol had indicated we'd have cover if the intelligence was good. And for it to be good all we really needed was one idiot to take a potshot at us, then we could say we were defending ourselves or something. If there wasn't anyone there, the worst anyone could charge us with was variations of trespassing since the facility was officially decommissioned and unused.

Fucking Alum. A small army wandering around was apparently legal so long as we didn't shoot anyone who didn't shoot at us first.

"You all right in there Kean?" Chen slapped the shoulder of my armor, half shouting to make sure I could hear him over the shuttle's engines. This particular craft had been harder used than the one I'd been in earlier, and it wasn't happy about the weight of my armor.

"I'm fine." I called back, grimacing when the suit leaned to the left as the shuttle banked. I'd been in the damned suit for close to four hours so 'fine' was probably overstating things. I was uncomfortable physically, uncomfortable mentally, and was feeling increasingly trapped by the circumstances I was stuck in.

I hadn't even been able to get out to use a bathroom. Or drink any water.

But by then I was committed. We were airborne, my time to try and find a way to back out had long since passed. The only thing I could do was keep rolling with the punches and pray that this would be the last fight for a while.

"Let's just hope this old can doesn't slam us into the ground. Shit way to go out." I tried to sound glib but it came out more toneless than I wanted.

"Are all Humans as positive as you? Or are you just naturally cheerful?"

I barked out something like a laugh. "Personal failing."

He hit my armor with a chuckle of his own, then turned to the rest of his team. "We're on final approach. Everyone remember our job?"

"Same shit as always boss." One of the seated men patted his scoped rifle, "Find cover, kill everyone shooting at the Lady, then shut up and let her take credit."

That brought laughter from everyone, even the pilot. Several men knocked their forearms together before going back to checking weapons, grenades, or otherwise preparing themselves. Chen let them settle down before speaking, "Damn right. You lowborn idiots remember who buys the last drink too?"

"First man to get shot." A different soldier spoke up before waving at me, "Which means the Savanna is buying us a round tonight."

"Damn right he is. Maybe he'll even leave out the poison."

I snorted, "So long as nobody slips drugs into mine."

To my surprise I seemed to get a vaguely positive reaction. Not quite open laughs but there was a muted rumble of amusement over the whining engines. Again Chen let them settle down before nodding, "Find good fire positions and get set. We prioritize anyone with a gun that can crack Kean's shell. He'll be leading the push on the right flank so I want two of you on that side at all times."

The various men nodded or verbally accepted that, a pair volunteering to stay on my side of the battle. I muttered a quiet prayer to whoever was listening, and after a second I added another prayer to the few Trahcon Aspects I knew. I'd need all of the help I could get if they decided it would be just *tragic* if the Human among them got himself killed while they were busy covering someone else.

...hell, I'd need all the help I could get even if they did help me. This was going to be a far cry from my supporting fire role this morning. Sure, I'd had to take the lead for a minute or two, but that had been temporary.

Today... today I was a battering ram, and I was supposed to support Nynsi's team as far into the facility as I could get. Sure, I was practically immune to normal gunfire which was more than could be said for anyone else. But the moment anyone brought out something that could penetrate the suit's outer armor... I was a fat, slow, easy target.

I didn't have more than a minute to start stressing myself out again before my new boss's voice came strong across our radios. *"This is Xerol. Everything is proceeding as planned, expect the operation to begin in three minutes. I wish that I could join you all in this fight. Know that I have the full confidence in our plan, and full confidence in all of you. We have stood them off for two months now, and have given our foes only defeat when they dared approach."*

"Fucking right." Someone agreed, others grunting or muttering their own approval.

"For all those who go into combat this day, I ask that the Pillar of Power gives you all the strength to strike down our enemy. I ask that the Pillar of Kin reminds you all to stand beside your brothers and sisters, Thondian or no. And I ask that the Pillar of Hearts steel yours against what we must do this day. May they all lift our souls to the heavens to stand with the Paragons."

My companions all made small gestures with their hands and bowed

241

their heads slightly.

"I shall be waiting for you all when you return. Good luck. Control out."

"Right." Chen waved for everyone to rise, "Everyone up, guns at the ready. Final sound off."

My eyes slid over my displays while his people reported their status. Barriers, full strength and holding. Actuators, all blue with no overheating or stress. Gun, linked and cold. All systems online. I hadn't taken much of any damage on the last run, mostly cosmetic chips to my already misshapen appearance. Nothing concerning.

"Kean, ready to go." I called out when it was my turn.

Chen's helmet bobbed in a quick nod. "Lady Shaaryak, this is Chen. My team's ready."

"This is Nynsi Shaaryak. All teams prepare for disembarkation. Team Five will drop first. Team Four will strafe and suppress the target once they have confirmed hostiles. All remaining teams prepare to cover Team Two when we breach the interior."

Our pilot barely waited for her to finish before shouting back "Everyone get ready to hang on back there, and leave the doors open so you can get back in if this falls apart!"

"Good advice." Chen called as he pulled a sniper rifle off of his back, inspecting it and occasionally bouncing against me as the shuttle accelerated.

The next thirty seconds were some of the longest seconds of my life. Just standing there, the armor auto-correcting for the shuttle's movements, waiting for the inevitable to occur. It felt like I had an eternity to worry about everything going on. What I'd already done, what I'd have to do before the end of the day. The tirade that Trenah would undoubtedly give me the moment she woke up.

How much I already regretted saying yes to Xerol instead of trying to find a hole in the ground to hide in.

It was practically a relief when the pilot shouted again. "Landing hard!"

I had to reach up to grab a massive bar in the ceiling to stay upright as the shuttle hurled into an atrociously sharp turn. Chen swore rather impressively and had to grab me to avoid falling, nearly dropping his rifle. The swearing grew worse when the overworked compensators suddenly resumed working, then flicked out when we weren't more than twenty feet from the ground.

Two Thondians bounced off the bulkhead as momentum asserted itself, cursing up a storm while the doors groaned open. The entire shuttle felt like it was about to tip over as I went for the exit. Our pilot managed to get it the final feet down to the ground before anything broke, everyone else gathering themselves and bailing out as quickly as they could.

I lumbered out of the side street we'd landed on, emerging from between a pair of beat up small businesses. There wasn't any foot traffic, or ground vehicles, which made me think the True Son may have been telling the truth after all.

Of course the sniper round that bounced off my left shoulder helped with that thought.

"Fuck!" I leaned forwards, accelerating to my pathetic top speed. "They're ready for us!"

I vaguely heard Chen yelling at his people to move their asses, but I was too preoccupied trying to get to the nearest entrance to really pay attention Two more heavy shots had taken chunks from my shields by the time I made it around the low wall that surrounded the old plant.

Across the cracked parking lot I could see a loading door finish sliding closed, and several windows all filled with the flashes of guns going off. A lot of that fire came heading my way for a few seconds, then swept above me as the other teams began landing.

One of the shuttles in particular came in close enough that I froze up for a second, convinced that the damned thing was going to land on me. The shrieking from the low-shields alarm startled me into moving again, and I managed to get my ass in gear while several dozen heavily armed Thondians began returning fire in earnest.

I managed a few bursts of my own, mostly aimed at a pair of second floor windows that overlooked the door. I don't think I really accomplished much but it made me feel like I was contributing.

"Rehat, move up! Yetherin, the door!" Nynsi's commands came as she sprinted forwards, sliding in behind me to use my bulk as cover. "Maintain suppression!"

The gunfire rose in volume as the rest of her team rushed around us, most pressing their backs to the wall while a single figure began frantically working the control panel. A glance at my rear facing camera view showed Rehat's team running across the open ground and drawing a lot of fire in the process.

Wincing at the sheer amount of sparks flying from their shields, I cut loose on full auto to try and help cover them. The shadowy window I was shooting into seemed to go quiet but that didn't stop someone else from getting a line on one of the charging men. He went down in a boneless tumble, bits of glass from his shattered visor flying everywhere.

"Doors open!" The man at the door snapped out, "We're good to go!"

"Cieran, lead! My team hold here, Team Two advance!"

Swallowing, I let off the trigger and heaved myself backwards while the various Thondians got clear. Keeping my rifle ready I moved past Nynsi and carefully entered the building.

The interior wasn't much to look at. Plain cement floors, tons of piping along the walls. and cheap lights on the ceiling. But that was pretty much secondary to the fact that no one was shooting at us, or seemed to be in sight at all. Just a long, empty hallway terminating in another set of doors, this set cracked open slightly.

"Nothing." I reported, accelerating up to a slow jog. "Moving to the next doors."

"Confirmed." Rehat had moved up right behind me and to my left. A place where he could see around me but was mostly protected. The surviving

244

four members of his personal security team followed single file behind. "Several side doors. We'll need those locked down."

Nynsi's reply must have been on a different channel because I didn't hear her say anything. I did see two figures come in behind us and start quickly attaching devices to door handles or control panels.

"This is Chen. My specialist is picking up Internal-Security screaming their heads off. We've got three different district leads all arguing about who should be going in. Think we've got time but not much of it."

"Confirmed." Nynsi said curtly. *"Team Two, pick up the pace. I want hard evidence to give to Internal-Security."*

I fought down the urge to tell her I was moving as fast as I could. Instead I focused on the heavy doors ahead and tried to see if there was any kind of trap waiting. "Approaching the main interior... still no sign of slaves or defenders."

My radio display flickered as Rehat cut me into his squad's channel. "We're not here to impress anyone, Kean. Slow down and take it cautiously."

I grunted in relief. "Don't have to tell me twice."

We slowed as we got within a yard of the door. The Thondians fanned out into a rough shooting line while I used my long rifle to nudge the heavy sheets of metal open a bit further. After a few seconds where nothing happened, I gave it a harder nudge and sent them swinging a few feet.

"Nothing." A slow step brought across the threshold, enough for me to get a better look at the place.

At first glance it looked like what I'd have expected. Catwalks ran along the walls, most connecting to some kind of office built into the second floor of the far side. In between here and there were wide concrete pits with more walkways above them, likely where water would have pooled back when the facility was actually operational.

"Not seeing anyone." I reported.

Rehat sounded as wary as I felt. "Team Two, scatter and advance on the office. Human, looks like someone added another loading hall to the left. Move to cover it."

I obediently began a slow advance, sweeping my weapon left to right as I tried to spot any movement. The room was apparently sound-proofed; the sound of the chaotic battle outside was only dimly audible. Unfortunately the various squad leaders calling out targets and reporting as their own people were wounded or fell was coming through my radio quite clearly... and was making me even edgier.

"Ah... shit. Rehat?" I called when my movement brought me close to one of the artificial ledges. "Found the slaves."

Right below me was an alien I only vaguely recognized as an Xenthan man. I could tell his gender because they hadn't felt the need to give him clothes. Worse, his snowy white body hair had been shaved down to a rough fuzz, revealing pale gray skin and numerous scars. The alien looked lean, starved, and his already large eyes widened further on spotting me.

Next to him was a small cot, a treadmill like device with straps, and what might have been a portable toilet. All surrounded by a cheap prefabricated wall creating a square cell, one of several dozen that stretched out to my right.

"They've got them in little alcoves." I continued, "Each of the old water pools must be filled with them. Can you understand me down there?"

The Xenthan gave me a quick nod and called back in Caranat, "Yeah. You here to rescue us?"

"Something like that." I replied, "White Storm running this place?"

Another nod. "Some four-armed *kolkat*. Heard him run off with others ten minutes ago."

"Thanks. Keep your head down and try to stay quiet."

It was hard to tell but I was pretty sure the alien snorted before settling down onto his cot, his wide eyes glinting like a cat's when I moved past. Sadly whoever else was down there wasn't as stable as he was. Questions, shouts for help, and outright begging started up almost at once. It got worse when of Rehat's people took a quick glance into of the other pools on his way to the nearest stairwell.

"Hey... hey! Who's up there!? Get us out of here!"

"Help! Please you have to help us!"

"For the love of the paragons, get us out! I'm begging you!"

"I'll do whatever you want, just get me out of here!"

Taking deep breaths to try and stay calm, I shifted farther to my left, getting away from the pit to make sure none of them could see me. There wasn't anything I could do at the moment. Nothing beyond what I already was doing.

Of course knowing that didn't make the pleading any less painful. Nor did it throttle the urge to completely kill my external microphones.

"*No one in the old control room.*" Rehat's voice came across the general channel a few minutes later. "*Looks like it's a mix of a lounge and an office. We're looting it.*"

Nynsi's reply was punctuated with the heavy thuds of her pistol firing. "*Do so quickly. A good portion of the enemy's fire just cut out, they are likely heading for you as we speak.*"

A truly painful burst of feedback cut Rehat off before he could even try to reply. The voice that followed was rough, like a man who'd smoked a pack every day since he was born, and cut with the slight lisp I'd come to associate those few times I'd heard a Naule speak.

"*Well now... how very bold of you, Shaaryak. To cower in your mansion and send your alien loving whore of a niece to lead your army in your stead.*" A mocking laugh broke his words apart, "*What, did your brother take your cock when he stole your lover?*"

A furious chorus of whistles was the initial response, then Nynsi's cold voice answered, "*You must be Yarrath. As uncouth and barbaric as I'd expected. Do all of us a favor and end your own miserable life.*"

"I see that gray bitch you captured talked more than was good for her." The White Storm leader, Yarrath apparently, didn't sound particularly perturbed. *"And I'm afraid I can't fit suicide into my schedule today. There's just no room what with massacring your little band, inserting a slave web into your neck, and maybe sampling you before I give you to your father."*

It was Nynsi's turn to gain a mocking tone, though I could still hear the rage in it. *"You forget that I have no father. He's legally dead as far the Ascendancy is concerned. And you will soon be joining him. Internal Security will be here soon enough... if you think you can capture and rape me before they arrive, best of luck."*

There was a quick snarl of anger, then it abruptly cut out.

"Everyone on alert!" Nynsi snapped, *"Pull back to defensive positions outside the compound!"*

"You heard her!" Rehat thundered, *"Fall back!"*

I threw my metal clad ass into reverse before he even got to the second sentence, glancing rapidly between my front and rear views to make sure I was moving in a straight line. Thirty seconds later Team Two came pounding down the metal stairs, sprinting roughly in my direction. A couple were holding onto tablets they'd picked up but the rest hadn't had time to grab anything.

Of course the sound of their retreat was anything but quiet, and the prisoners reacted as I could have guessed. They'd quieted a little but now their howls and pleading resumed at full volume. They were loud enough that I didn't hear the massive motors start up, and if I hadn't been staring right at them I might have missed the far door slowly opening.

"Doors!" I snapped, rising my gun as I tried to back up more quickly.

"Move it!" Rehat growled before changing direction, heading for me. "Kolshin, lead the teams out. Kean, you and I are rearguard."

I swallowed heavily as everyone else ran for their lives, wishing I wasn't in this death trap so I could have been right among them.

The sight of armored figures nudging through the opening doors pushed that thought aside pretty quickly. It pushed all thought aside except for the focus of aiming and cutting loose as I kept backpedaling. Rehat joined in with his rifle, again settling in behind me, and for a short period of time we actually did it.

With how slowly the heavy loading doors were swinging aside we had a perfect kill zone. There wasn't any cover, and even with their better gear none of the White Storm mercs made it more than a few yards inside before our rifles dropped them. After several tried and died or scrambled back trailing blood, the rest stayed in cover and simply fired blindly around the corners while they waited for the door to finish opening.

As soon as it did they came through in three groups of three. One set came right at us, another sprinted right towards some old purification equipment, while the last headed for the stairs and the upper floor office.

We focused on the three in front of us, by some miracle actually syncing up our fire onto the same enemies. Rehat fired in bursts, keeping his weapon cool, while I simply kept my trigger down. My rounds ripped out their shields while his more precise fire found the weak points in their armor. Two fell with torn apart throats, the third dove into one of the slave cells the moment his shields failed.

"Almost there." I glanced at my ammunition and coolant levels and winced. Fifty percent down on the first, dangerously close to the red line on the latter. "Shit... oh shit. Uh..."

Rehat fired a burst off to the right, getting closer in as shots from the left group tried to hit his legs. "What!?"

"We've got a fucking problem." I managed as my mouth went utterly dry.

Yarrath's gravelly voice echoed back, "Ah, the short fur in his little toy. And one of the twins. I'll be handsomely rewarded for your heads.

Rehat risked a quick glance around me as the gunfire abruptly stopped, letting him see the same thing I had.

A suit of power armor larger but slimmer than mine finished shouldering its way into the room. It was painted a snowy white with bits of blue, the arctic camouflage horrifically out of place in the beat up old facility. Of course the heavy barrelled canon mounted where a right hand should have been fit in far better, and took up most of my attention.

"That," Rehat said quietly, "Is bad. I don't suppose yours can stand up to it?"

I had to fight down a whimper. Or hysterical laugh. Neither would have been appropriate. "That's a joke right?"

"That's what I thought." He grunted. "Right, new plan. Run!"

I didn't bother questioning him. We both turned and bolted for the exit, a torrent of gunfire following us the moment we turned our backs.

II – XI

My shields collapsed in the opening seconds. I expected to hear the familiar hailstorm, but the White Storm were far more disciplined than the True Sons. They did their best to shoot around me rather than through me, leaving that for their boss.

I got lucky in that. For whatever reason, maybe he didn't expect us to simply turn and bolt, he was several beats slow in opening fire. The first heavy round missed wide, while his second hit my left shoulder just as I reached the exit. Its impact sent me stumbling and nearly shattered the armored pauldron, but I was out of his line of sight before he could get a third shot off.

"Fuck!" I slid when I tried to stop, sparks flying up from my flat feet. "The door!"

Rehat was way ahead of me, already working on the controls. Ignoring me entirely, he directed his words to Nynsi, "They've got armor of their own! Kean's can't take it, they have at least two full squads supporting!"

There was a curse before Nynsi spoke, *"You can't outrun them with Cieran's armor. Seal the door then fall back, we'll position to cover you!"*

I took a glance at my rear view yet again and spotted her tall frame at the end of the hall, silhouetted by the far doorway. She was firing wildly at something out of sight, several members of her personal team doing the same near her.

Movement to my front jerked me around to see a merc becoming visible as they came on; they'd already caught up with us.

Cursing in English, I settled my targeting reticle and put a burst into their chest. Their shields held, and the professional asshole swiped a grenade from their belt and threw it in a single motion. The moment it cleared their fingers they were diving out of sight, leaving me to stare at the canister flying towards me.

I had just enough enough time to step forwards and crouch, the closest I could come to ducking. The grenade actually bounced off the huchbacked plating over my head before landing behind me. It detonated in a muffled thump that killed whatever power my shields had recovered... and naturally cut the coolant feed to my gun.

"They're trying to shut the doors!" Yarrath's enhanced voice snapped, "Get in there!"

"The suit's blocking us!" I'm guessing it was the same merc I'd shot who replied. He leaned his head right around the edge of the closing door, then frantically jerked it back when I sent a pair of rounds within an inch of his helmet.

"Any time now dammit!" I snarled.

"Shut up and shoot!" Rehat's fingers kept dancing across the controls, "It's closing, and it's locked up! You're welcome!"

Yellow warning lights started flashing above us as the doors started to slowly swing closed. Slowly being the operative word.

I took a few steps back as he retreated from the control panel, heading towards me. His jog became a frantic dive when two more grenades whipped around the edge, another one bouncing off of my armor.

The twin detonations sent warnings pinging all over my display as I fought to stay upright. Several fragments had gotten into the various joints, cutting artificial muscle strands, and my remaining cable to my gun snapped to leave me without computer assisted aim.

Using that as their cue, two White Storm tried to dart in, both clutching shotguns in their hands. By luck they jostled one another as they tried to fit through the shrinking gap, giving us enough time to recover and open fire.

The Naule in front collapsed quickly, splattering his Thondian partner with black blood as he screamed. I didn't have time to shift my aim before the latter fired a grenade from the under-slung mount on his weapon.

Unlike the others that one exploded on impact. The blast tore the entire left pauldron off and sending me stumbling back. My gyros fought to help keep me upright for a moment, then they gave up and let me crash onto my back. Alarms howled as I shook my head, trying to clear it as Rehat fired over my collapsed form. Someone let out a brief howl of pain, then a final burst ended it.

"You alive in there?"

I groaned and slowly rolled to my right, wincing as something dug into my left arm. "Yeah. Ow. Left wrist is locked up. Armor on that side is fucked."

Rehat let out a curse and backed away as I got my feet under me and began rising. "We don't have long until they get that door open."

"How long?" I asked, mildly surprised he hadn't just left me behind.

The doorway a few yards away pinged once. Then again.

"Seconds." He replied grimly. "Move your metal ass! Cousin! We need to be ready to seal that door!"

"Already primed!" Nynsi shot back, *"We're moving to clear the retreat, move!"*

I dutifully fought to get up speed. Various damaged pieces of the suit groaned in protest, bits of metal shrieking as they ground on another. Ahead I saw Nynsi, her people, and the rest of Rehat's team vanish as they moved out. The gunfire that had been muted in the main chamber rose steadily in volume, making it clear that there was still an all-out battle occurring outside.

Rehat kept pace, "Kolshin, status!"

"Ikshi is dead, Athen is wounded. We're covering the Lady's left flank but we could really use your aim sir!"

"We're moving, stay mobile and get Athen to a car!"

"Working," An explosion punctuated his words and led to a painful cough before he resumed, *"On it!"*

I winced. Rehat had already been down a man before we'd gotten inside. Losing another, then with at least two wounded meant he was at fifty percent casualties already. God alone knew how bad everyone else was doing. People I knew, by sight if not name, were dead or dying even as I forced my broken suit to keep moving.

Christ we'd bitten off way more than we could chew here.

There wasn't time for more conversation before the lights behind us began to flash again, a quiet chime alerting everyone to the fact that the service doors were sliding open again. That the next round in our prize fight was about to start.

Except the service doors weren't the only ones moving. Ahead of us, yellow lights started to flash as our gateway to freedom started to slide shut long before we were close.

"Someone find the override for that exit!" I shouted, putting on as much speed as I could. Rehat shot ahead of me, but it was clear to me that he wouldn't make it before it closed. Which meant I had no chance in hell. And even if the controls weren't overridden completely from somewhere else, by the time he stopped, worked the panel, and got the doors open enough for me to fit through... we'd both be long overrun and killed.

"Yetheren's down!" Nynsi snapped, *"Rehat!"*

"Not close enough!" I shouted.

She swore. *"We'll hold the landing site, find an alternate route!"*

"We need a map!"

Several silent beats passed before Chen let out a pained rasp that was barely intelligible as instructions, *"Take the last left side door."*

Rehat got there when I was about half-way, wasting no time in yanking off the extra locking mechanisms that had been put up on our initial way through. He was just finishing that when the gunfire began to ping off of my back, giving me all the encouragement I needed to keep moving.

I barely made it before Yarrath managed to force his way into the hall behind us. The heavy thuds of his massive weapon drowned out the regular gunfire, but by some miracle I only took one more hit. Of course that was enough to break off one of the armor panels over my engine and nearly sent me falling onto my face, so I wasn't all that lucky.

"Get in here dammit!"

"I'm working on it!" I snarled back, forcing my way into the side hall and wincing at the tight fit. There wasn't more than a foot of clearance on either side, or above me for that matter. Rehat waited for me to get through then slapped the controls, shutting and hopefully locking the thing behind us. Not that the locks behind us had held but maybe it would slow them down.

"Where the hell are we going?" I demanded.

Chen managed to groan out the next set of instructions. *"Ten yards ahead, turn left. There is a cargo elevator on your right almost immediately. Send it up on its own, with luck they'll waste time recalling it. Have Kean keep moving past it, three yards beyond is another doorway that will lead to another service hallway."*

"Will I fit?" I asked, trying to count the distance as we moved.

"On the schematic? Sure. Real life? No clue. You wanna go back?"

That was a stupid fucking rhetorical question. I was mostly worried about how long it would take me to get out if I had to bail. Making sure I could egress in a hurry had been part of my upgrades, but I hadn't really accounted for battle damage. With how fucked up the left shoulder was it would probably take me close to a minute to get out.

God I was getting heartily sick of learning things the hard way.

I kept moving past the elevator while Rehat ducked inside to get it moving. Just ahead I could see the door, and behind I could hear the sounds of

255

movement and shouting. Several more careful steps let me see the next door set into the wall... and it was going to be a tight fit.

An awkward button push with an over large finger got it open. An equally hesitant shuffle carried me inside, my pace only quickening when I realized I wasn't getting stuck.

This hallway was dark, only the faded yellow glow of backup lighting providing any illumination. It was hardly creepy at all really, and it was made worse by the sense of claustrophobia that I picked up as I moved. There might have been a inch or three on both of my sides and above my head, and given the damage I was basically banging my left arm off of the wall with each step.

"Quiet!" Rehat snapped, appearing in the darkness behind me as he closed the hatch. "Keep moving!"

I did so, grinding my teeth a bit. It wasn't like I could help bouncing off the walls given my suit's state.

"Another fifteen yards and you will find yourself in a storage room." Chen continued to give us instructions, *"It has its own cargo entrance back into the main pool room. You can hit those fucks from behind."*

"I thought we were trying to escape and evacuate, not double back." Rehat noted a heartbeat before I could voice the same opinion.

The pain in Chen's voice got worse, *"Big fucker shot down our first car. Everyone is grounded until we can take him out. Most of us are pinned down. Lady's keeping him distracted, can't last long."*

"Fuck." I exhaled.

"Fuck." Rehat agreed, "Forget what I said about quiet."

He didn't need to say it twice, my left side began clattering once again as I sped up. "You have a plan once we actually catch up to them?"

I took his silence as an indicator that he didn't.

Swallowing, I directed my next question to Chen. "How many of them are ahead of us?"

"*Unknown.*" Chen offered helpfully, "*Maybe three, four squads here total.*"

Meaning we'd only outnumbered the enemy by about a third when we'd begun our attack. If I remember my old military adages right, that was way below the three or four to one you were supposed to outnumber someone by when you were attacking. Which meant I'd been wrong.

We hadn't bitten off more than we could chew.

We'd run headlong into a goddamned brick wall.

Reaching the end of the darkened hall, I reached out and slammed a metal hand into the control panel. The door slid open with a quiet hiss of hydraulics, revealing the pool room once again. And, just as before, it was empty except for the muted murmur of slaves talking rapidly, trying to figure out what was going on.

That murmur grew, several shouts making me wince as my feet pounded across the metal floor.

Sure enough, I'd hardly turned towards the doors we'd left through not more than five minutes ago before a helmet-less Thondian strode purposefully into the room.

"Shut up! Now! I will fry the lot of you if you don't-behind us!" He scrambled for his gun, only to jerk back as I put the first burst into his armored chest. My second burst finished his shields off, while Rehat slipped around me to fire at the same time as my third volley. His armor held against my shots, but my companion simply put two bullets into his skull.

"Keep mov-" Was all he had time to say before all fucking hell broke loose.

Our access corridor's exit was parallel to the hall we were moving towards, which meant we had zero warning before a small horde began to emerge. A veritable mob of True Sons of the usual gang variety; no armor, just small arms, maybe cheap shield belts. But there was a lot of them, and

257

they were between us and our escape. Most were Thondian, but I picked out Naule, a few squat Chezzek, and horrifyingly, at least one Human.

I hesitated, then forced my emotions aside and accelerated directly towards them.

It took them a moment and about four of their lives to realize that the two of us were on their right and charging. I fired in short bursts to try and keep my heat and ammunition in good shape, not needing many shots to kill them. Pistol and shotguns began firing wildly in reply even as Rehat quickly picked off the few smart enough to try and keep moving to get around me. Still, their usual shitty accuracy or not, I was a big target, and my half recharged shields started to fall quickly under the barrage.

Even more of them piled out as I closed the distance, and I had a good look as the front group belatedly realized that I didn't intend to slow down. Months, years, later, I could still recall some of their faces... my fucking cameras capturing their moments of fear perfectly as I charged.

"Get back! Surround hi-" A Naule woman not more than a yard from me died messily, my gun tearing her guts open when she tried to provide some kind of guidance.

From there things got blurry. I swept my arms and gun from side to side, slamming bodies away from me as people screamed. Rehat kept shooting in a slow, measured pace, killing anyone who seemed to know what they were doing. Once and a while he would use loose a technical grenade out to burn or electrocute gang members, helping to clear my path as I murdered my way towards the entrance.

The bodies piled up quickly. Some of them even tried to jump on me, as if I was some kind of wild animal that they could simply swarm over. My companion executed most of them, others I simply batted aside with my bulky arms. A few times I stepped on... pieces. Sometimes still living ones that screamed horribly beneath my full ton of weight. But never for very long.

It didn't take long for their morale to break.

These were probably conscripts dragged into this. They weren't trained soldiers. They were given guns and told to go fight or be killed. The sight of an eight foot tall metal monster, probably covered in blood of multiple flavors at this point, was more than they could bear.

I let them run. Maybe a dozen were left to do so, throwing their weapons away as they fled across the pool room. I didn't know how many we'd killed. Two or three times that many, at least.

I wanted to vomit. I wanted to break open my suit and puke my guts out until there wasn't anything left. And once I was done with that, I was going to find a dark hole to hide whatever the hell I was away. Even more than when I'd made my first kill in Trenah's shop... I felt unclean. At least that poor bastard had a chance. Not much of one, but a chance of making it a real fight.

These poor bastards... They hadn't had one. Maybe if I'd been on the far side of the room, and they'd been disciplined enough... but from ten yards away, forced into a bottleneck, my armor, battered or not, had more than held up against their increasingly panicking efforts.

This wasn't fighting. This was simply murder.

Rehat didn't say anything, just stepped over the corpses and moved ahead into the familiar hallway once more.

It was strangely empty. The doors on the opposite end were open, and I could see flashes of gunfire, but there wasn't anyone visibly in sight.

"Moving." Thankfully my companion was still capable of speech. I was pretty sure my throat had swollen shut. "Status?"

"*Not fucking good.*" Chen's voice was hard and a little slurred. "*Move your asses!*"

We did.

The short hallway felt like it stretched on forever as we moved. I couldn't help but notice the now open side doors, the attached locks thrown aside. That probably explained where all the True Sons had come from, though where they had been until now was anyone's guess.

At the exit I trampled over the corpses of three White Storm and two of our people, then emerged into a scene from a war movie. Fires burned randomly as tracers snapped wildly in every direction, sending puffs of dirt up as they struck the soil or leaving pockmarks in walls.

More bodies were everywhere. True Sons. White Storm. Xerol's people. I tried not to look too closely.

To my right, Marn and three of her team members were crouched behind a burning air car, jerking up to snap off rounds before ducking quickly back down as their opposites replied in kind. A few gray forms rose up from a crater, and what the fuck had caused *that*, trying to rush them only to be ruthlessly assassinated by the remains of Chen's sniper team.

But the real fight was to the left.

Yarrath's battle armor wasn't pristine anymore. Cracks riddled the chest and back plates, and his entire left side was badly scorched, the leg limping noticeably as he moved. Despite that, he still spun quickly enough, massive weapon roaring at his direct opponents as he completely ignored a few long range shots sparking off his plating.

Chehat dove behind yet another burning aircar, howling in pain as blood shot out from the leg he wasn't quick enough to pull in. Sensing an easy kill, the Naule tried to shift left to get a clear shot, but flinched back and brought his left arm up to cover his head as when Nynsi tried to put a round through the thin visor.

For her part Nynsi had lost her helmet at some-point, and white bandages were stained red around her left bicep. Acting completely unbothered by either, she slipped into a quick dash, firing her short ranged weapon as rapidly as she could to try and draw the enemy away from her wounded cousin.

"Fuck off bitch!" Yarrath spat through his speakers, contemptuously sending a burst into the ground at Nynsi's feet that sent her tumbling to the ground with a growl of pain. "It would seem that your father has his work cut out for him before he can sell you off!"

Her reply was unladylike in the extreme, and came with several more bullets directly into the suit's head.

Rehat moved right in a quick crouching run, motioning me to move direclty in as he did. I advanced as quietly as I could, which was probably not quietly at all, but considering the continuous gunfire it turned out to be enough.

"Come on you little whore. You can't hurt me. Your grenades are long since spent, and while your pistols are impressive they're still useless." Yarrath managed to sound bored, "You've got no grays here so I'll be polite and let everyone else leave alive."

Nynsi had to have seen us, but to her credit she didn't indicate as much. Instead she actually spat on the ground and kept her focus on her enemy's canon arm. "Do you believe me to be a fool? You would never honor such an agreement."

A grim laugh came out. "No, I'll enjoy gutting your friends and making you watch."

I was about ten yards away when Rehat brought a hand up, his wrist-comp alight as he fed targeting data to his technical launcher. The Discharge disc whipped out to detonate in a flash of blue arcs, Yarrath snarling in surprised anger as his left limbs seemed to seize up. Gritting my teeth, I made my own move, rushing as the mercenary began to spin around.

His left side was where most of the damage was, and I did my best to keep my aim there. My bullets rattled off just as so many had done off of my own armor, but I thought a few found cracks and holes to cause real damage.

Rehat kept running laterally, triggering an incendiary to help cause more damage to that side, then another discharge to slow him down. Between those and my gunshots we managed to blow off an armored panel and break another, and for a few seconds I thought we might actually pull it off.

Then he started replying in kind.

While I was the bigger target, Rehat was the priority one. Yarrath got his right arm across his waist, the gun thundering at full auto as he liberally hosed down the entire area where Rehat was standing. There was a cry of pain as several rounds tracked across his chest, then his shields failed to let a trailing shot blow his left arm off at the elbow.

Xerol's heir collapsed without another sound, his gun falling from limp fingers as he dropped.

"Cousin!" Nynsi's shriek came as she charged in, trying to get onto the damaged left side, and distracting Yarrath for the few moments it took before my charge brought me to him.

To say that two powered suits of battle armor colliding was loud would be understating things.

I'd dropped my gun in my rush, giving me two hands to his one. More than that my construction model suit had more direct strength, which meant when I brought my fists down onto his shoulders the entire frame of his suit groaned at the impact. But where I was the stronger he was far more agile, and he had much more natural range of motion for his limbs.

My follow up punch saw my left hand slam into his weakened left side, letting my fingers tear out some kind of supporting bar. Yarrath still had his speakers enabled so I heard his snarl of rage as he twisted and crouched, dodging the right hook I'd aimed at his head. His own right arm rose, trying to jam his gun right into my chest, but I managed to get my left down to bat it aside before he could pull the trigger.

I tried to grab the weapon, to use my strength to tear at it, only for him to slip out of my grip and fire as he did it. Rounds hammered along me in a diagonal line starting at my foot, trailing across my leg and onto my chest. Alarms were shrieking around my head even as plating sprung free, gyros fluctuating wildly as I tipped backwards from the impacts. My entire left side lit up with pain from my shoulder to my elbow, my tongue throbbing as I bit down on a scream.

Shaking my head once, then twice let me see clouds above which meant I'd fallen somewhere in there.

"This armor cost a small fortune to modify so that I could use it." a coldly furious voice spoke from above me, "And it will cost me another fortune to repair."

My vision cleared slightly as I forced my eyes to focus. I was on my back, most of my display flaring in red as systems failed. Of course that was secondary to Yarrath's battered and smoking form looming over me, gun arm leveled at my head.

"Don't move if you want your short-furred pet to survive." He spat, presumably to wherever Nynsi was.

"Still." His head turned contemplatively as he regarded me, and then to where Rehat had fallen. "Rather impressive actually, even for a pair of aliens. And this armor. I had never contemplated re-purposing construction models such as this, perhaps it is a more affordable alternative."

"Wasn't that bad..." I gasped out, trying to keep him talking as my eyes flickered across my systems, desperate for something that would get me out of this. "...Pretty inexpensive really."

There wasn't much. My suit was dying around me.

It was taking it a while, most of the core systems were still intact within the engine mount on my back, but so much of the control wiring and musculature had been shot to pieces that my scratch built computer systems couldn't handle it. They were trying, and failing, to compensate for the lost paths, and the engine wasn't adjusting the draw properly. Half of what was left was shutting down due to a lack of power, and the other half was shorting out from too much.

"Thank you for the demonstration." Yarrath nudged his gun a bit to the left, "Now, be a good little alien and-"

A grenade slammed into his armor before he could finish. It must have been some kind of armor cracking model because it staggered him, even more bits of armor and suit flying away. I jerked my gaze around to spot the culprit; Chehat Shaaryak had one hand clutching at a wound on his chest, his other was pulling another grenade from the belt of a dead guardsman.

Yarrath twisted, slammed a foot onto my chest to keep me pinned, and cut loose with his cannon.

Rehat's brother died instantly when the gunfire practically bisected him.

But he'd distracted him for long enough to make the bastard fuck up. He hadn't realized that my arms were longer than they should have been, and even with his armored foot pinning me I easily got my right arm up to dig into his left side again. I didn't try anything fancy, I just did my best to grab onto whatever I could and start yanking.

I must have gotten something important because he stumbled off of me, left arm dropping to dangle uselessly at his side. Yarrath he swore violently, suit jerking and stumbling while he fought to get his gun around to finish me off.

Nynsi saved my life by ending his.

She must have grabbed Rehat's technical launcher because an orange disc streaked in from that direction, vanishing into the opened side of Yarrath's armor.

"No! Wai-" There might have been a tiny beep, and then fire flashed out from the gap. He began howling at once, his gun triggering randomly as his one working arm beat against the suit's chest, desperately trying to put out the fire that he couldn't reach. The armor staggered away from me, flailing wildly as the screams continued, fire visible through the seams as the alien burned.

Nynsi slowly approached, her pistol up... only to lower as she simply let it continue.

It took the bastard over a minute to die. Or at least for his screams to trail into wet gurgling sounds that cut out entirely as the suit's electronics burned up.

Somewhere nearby sirens were blaring and the gunfire was fading away. Internal Security must have been finally figured out who should show up. That or everyone capable of fighting was dead or too tired to continue. Either way everything went quiet as Nynsi and I watched Yarrath's armor collapse face first onto the pavement, greasy smoke curling out of the many breaches in the suit.

Neither of us said anything until the swarm of police arrived.

II – XII

An hour later found Nynsi and I sitting against one of the ruined perimeter walls, watching the cops handle the remainder of the battle's aftermath. Well, that was a bit disingenuous, they'd pretty much handled the entirety of it.

They hadn't outright called us prisoners but we all knew what we were.

Not that I'd have been much use anyway. My left arm was in a sling and I'd gotten several pieces of my own armor pulled out of it. One of the various beings I'd prayed to must have actually been listening because none of them had been deep. I'd have a nice collection of thin scars but it hadn't taken the medic long to patch me up.

I was one of the luckier ones in that. Xerol had sent fifty six people into the battle, including the shuttle pilots and drivers. Nine had been lucky enough to not get hit at all, sixteen would never move again, and the rest of us were in various degrees between the two.

Of the squad leaders, I'd seen Chehat die, and Horthan had been hit by a sniper. Rehat had still been alive when they'd airlifted him out, a heavy tourniquet on his arm. Chen had been on the same shuttle. Apparently the stubborn ass had taken two shots to his right leg but had kept fighting prone while one of the shuttle pilots had stitched his wounds closed. Marn was the only one uninjured, sitting with the rest of us while we waited.

"Is your armor repairable?" Nynsi asked, nodding to the slumped over pile of metal.

I glanced at it before shrugging. "Probably. Not sure how comfortable I am with the idea. Stupid thing feels like it's cursed."

She let out a soft huff. "I do not believe in such superstitions... though I cannot blame you for the opinion. Still, without it you wouldn't have been here."

"I didn't do much."

"Untrue." Her head shook sharply. "Without you we would not have been able to kill Yarrath while losing so few."

I snorted. "Few."

"Few. I feel my cousin's loss, and those of my people... but I am a rational being. Even more would have died, and I would likely have followed them." Another shake of her head punctuated her words. "I thank you for being here. And I apologize for it. This was not the battle we expected it to be."

Someone else replied before I could, a voice I wasn't thrilled to hear. "And what did you half-drowned idiots expect?"

We both turned to see Ashul'tasir stalk past a cordon of Internal Security as if they weren't there. They might as well not have been from the way they all avoided so much as looking at her. She wasn't in her usual clothes either, instead she was clad in a blue military uniform. The Imperial triple crescent decorated each shoulder, but apart from those the only decoration was a pin on her lapel.

A cresting wave carved from obsidian.

I'd never seen it before, but from what I knew of her its significance seemed obvious; the icon of Imperial Intelligence.

"Looks to me like you hit three squads of White Storm, a veteran team of True Sons, and half-a-hundred idiots." Tasir continued. "I'm ascribing your survival to Kahsh, only that vain prick of an Aspect would cause shit like this to happen."

I sighed and let my head fall back against the wall. "Hey Tasir. How was Terminus?"

"That slum won't change until the universe freezes." Tarah flexed in and out, "I expected you to be happier to see me. Especially since I'm the reason you all aren't being shipped off to cozy jail cells."

Her tone was arctic enough to shut me up, leaving Nynsi to speak for us. "Then you have our thanks. May I ask as to the specifics?"

The old Trahcon stared her down for a few seconds, taking her sweet time before answering. As per fucking usual. "Since you actually found the poor souls they were shipping in I spun the whole the thing as an authorized Intelligence operation. That's going to choke up a lot of the rich idiots in the Core City, and I'll have to deal with more meetings than I want to even consider. But it keeps all this above the water."

Nynsi let out a slow exhalation. "Then I am corrected, you have our deepest gratitude. The family will naturally provide all aid an assistance we can moving forwards."

"Good. Saves me the trouble of officially conscripting the lot of you."

Dark eyes narrowed at once. "That is officially illegal on Alum."

Tasir's tarah lowered as she gave the taller woman a scathing look. "Don't tell me what's legal and isn't you little brat. I helped write half the fucking treaties that stabilized this place. The only reason I haven't bothered to drag your uncle in before this was because the forms are a pain in the ass to fill out."

Under normal circumstances I was pretty sure Nynsi could have brushed past that. Sadly today was anything but normal, and it was easy to see her temper fraying. I snapped a hand out to grab her wrist before she could say anything that would get us in trouble. She twitched when I touched her, clearly surprised at the contact, but it worked to help keep her temper under control.

It also made Tasir give me an unreadable look, one tarah twitching down before she continued. "If you lot don't have any other stupid comments you can fly your bruised asses back to Koshun Minor. I'll handle the cleanup. Tell Xerol I'll be in his office first thing tomorrow to discuss our next phase."

I couldn't stop myself, "Next phase? Wasn't this the end of it?"

"Would have been if her prick of a father was present." A hand waved at Nynsi, "But he wasn't. This isn't over until that bastard is dead."

My slump grew worse at that statement. I really wanted to argue with her... but I couldn't. What little I knew made me think that Xerol's brother wouldn't just give up, even if it was probably the smart thing to do with today's events. At the very least he might make an effort to get rid of Xerol.

Which would drag me into yet another fight since I still lived in the mansion. Even if I didn't, I hadn't done anything to make myself less of a target. If anything I'd done the fucking opposite.

Sad as it was but I liked the irrational anger that her point brought up. Some part of me knew I was being stupid. That I'd been the one to agree to come with on these raids. That I'd at least had the *option* of leaving, of probably living comfortably and anonymously in another city under Internal Security's protection. Hell, I probably could have gotten Trenah transferred to wherever I was once she was out of the hospital as well.

But I hadn't. Instead I'd decided to stay. Instead I'd ended up risking my life. I'd ended up killing a whole lot of people. Sure, they'd have done the same to me. Maybe that mattered. Maybe it didn't.

What mattered was that my irritation at Tasir allowed me to focus on something else for a few minutes.

While Nynsi got to her feet and began motioning for everyone else to do the same, I stayed in place. "You could have at least told me about Trenah."

That earned me a bewildered expression from my friend, and a strangely interested one from Tasir. "It was for her own protection. I know the little bitch hates me with the passion of a hurricane, but I do like her. She'd have done something stupid if she'd been awake for all of this. Tell me I'm wrong."

I couldn't. Which made me even more irritated. "I really want to punch you right now."

Tasir showed me her teeth. "Feel free. Just remember I'm going to slam you through that wall in reply."

"*Cieran.*" Nynsi's hiss was somewhere between alarmed and furious. "You can do this in private."

Her words didn't really calm me down any. Her hand clapping down on my wounded shoulder did. I bit down on a yelp of pain, giving her more than enough time to haul me up to my feet. I glowered at her, then at Tasir, but kept my mouth shut as Nynsi not-so-gently pushed me towards the remaining cars.

Most of the wounded were already being taken out in the shuttles. The heavy vehicles had stood up better than the lighter models, and one was enough to take everyone but the two of us. We got to get into Nynsi's car since she'd parked it behind a building to keep it safe.

The luxury and the slow-acting painkillers comforted my body, but the loss of a target in Tasir meant my brain started going over everything yet again.

"That anger was unlike you." She said once we were airborne, once it was clear I wasn't about to start talking. "What happened inside the building?"

I told her in short sentences. I also told her about Trenah, though I left out that it had been Rane to give me the information.

"I did not know she was on planet." She said finally. "I promise you that. As for the engagement... it was a battle. A greater one than you, or we, were truly prepared for. What just happened is not something that can be altered."

"You weren't there." I shook my head tiredly, "I was pretty much immune to anything they had. I could have just scared them off. Tossed them aside. I didn't have to do what I did."

Her low voice became gentle, "And would Rehat had survived if you did anything else?"

"I..."

"They would have killed him. Then swarmed you." She continued,

270

"Pretending that anything else would have occurred is unrealistic."

I thought about that for a minute or two before speaking again. "There are some things people shouldn't do. Even in battle. And even if what I did was normal for this time and place... I'm not a soldier. I don't know how much more of this I can take."

She actually turned her head at that, dark eyes finding my right hand. I glanced at it to discover that I was tapping several fingers against the armrest in an unsteady rythym. Feeling more than a little self-conscious I managed to clench the hand into a fist to stop.

Nynsi returned her gaze to the controls. "I can tell. In truth, had we known what we were walking into, I still would have pushed my uncle to attack. In a different manner perhaps, but as a means of forcing the authorities to move at a minimum. But I would not have brought you with in that case. You would have gone home to stand guard with Ghai."

I wasn't sure how I felt about that. A little better maybe, but not much. "...we could have used Ghai's help."

"Yes, we could have. But she was the only one we had left who could reliably command the reserves in our absence. Who could protect my uncle."

Yet another inconvenient truth in a day filled with them. Though I honestly wasn't sure how well Ghai would fit in to a full on battle. I didn't doubt for a second that she was a skilled soldier. She'd easily stood with Trenah at the back of the bar, and from what I'd heard she'd taken down practically all of the other traitors in the mansion by herself. That being said she wasn't exactly good at communicating.

Not her fault but a problem all the same.

But still... if she'd been with inside the plant? If she was half as good at manipulating energy as Trenah she could have easily held off half the mob. Tossed them away without killing them. Pinned them against the floor while we'd run past.

I lost myself in that fantasy until we landed at the mansion. We'd barely left the car before Nynsi was off to meet with Xerol, and I was conscripted to help get the wounded to either the medical wing or their rooms.

Strangely that was the only bright spot of the day. Proof that fighting, killing, and bleeding alongside my alien hosts had done what it was supposed to. I'd upgraded from persona-non-grate to something close to tolerated. I helped a couple limp their ways to their beds and was actually thanked for it, one even calling me by name. A few others gave me little bows of thanks when I shuffled around delivering meds, and I never once heard the words 'short-fur' directed at me.

Mostly they'd upgraded to 'Savanna'. I didn't like that much either since it was the first half of the Caranant word for 'Human', like they were too lazy to add the single syllable to make the full word. Still it seemed like they meant it as an impersonal term more than an openly hostile one, so I supposed that it could have been worse. Maybe a third big fight would cause them to switch to my actual name.

Small victories. Small progress. Large cost.

I managed to get a few extra painkillers from doc Rae before heading to my own rooms. My already long day didn't get any shorter when I got there, I'd barely opened the door before a message from Xerol came in on my wrist-comp. I seriously considered not even looking at it in favor of crawling into my bed and feeling sorry for myself. Sadly I still had some little bit of professional pride left. A few gestures with my right hand brought it up... and I groaned as I read it.

Five minutes later I found myself shuffling into the mansion's command center rather than collapsing into bed. Nynsi, Ghai, and Xerol were all present. Both women looked to be somewhere between angry and apoplectic, and even Xerol's rigid control wasn't quite as in place as usual.

"Thad bad?" I asked.

"Close the door." My host instructed. "And sit."

That bad then.

I did as instructed, settling my tired ass at one of the workstations and spinning the chair so I could face everyone else directly. "Too much to ask that he's wishing us a good rest of our lives and apologizing for trying to murder all of us?"

Ghai's tarah quivered as she let out a raspy huff of laughter, but neither of the Thondians seemed to really appreciate the commentary.

"No." Xerol said flatly. "I thought you restrained your poor sense of humor when not intoxicated."

Between the painkillers I'd just taken and the strange numbness I felt in my brain, I might as well have been. "Today's not a normal day. What did he say?"

I could tell that my host wasn't impressed by the fact that I wasn't offering him the usual polite deference. Something in Nynsi's body language told me that she was similarly displeased, while Ghai... just kept up her quiet chuckling.

Xerol stared at me, then at his Harath'krem, then let out a very soft whistle before speaking. "While you were all in transit I received several messages from my brother. All were routed through several dummy accounts that were deleted shortly after being activated. Internal-Security is attempting to follow them but I have little expectation of success."

He turned and tapped on a console, bringing up several files. "I will warn you all in advance that his sanity has evidently deserted him. They are not pleasant to listen to."

Joy. Grimacing, I settled back as he opened the first message on the main screen behind him.

The Thondian man who appeared looked a bit like Xerol. He had the same chin and hard features, but it was clear that Nynsi must have taken more after her mother. The only thing she'd gotten from dear old dad was her extremely long and elfin ears. He wore White Storm armor sans a helmet, and looked to be standing in a run down hotel room.

"*Brother,*" His snarl was a more accented copy of my host's, "*I have heard of your little counter-attack. That your little army has defeated the guards I left to protect the merchandise. How like you to value the lives of lowborn and alien trash above that of those sworn to you. Know that I am not alone in resisting your pathetic adherence to false doctrine. That your life will end, and the position that should have always been mine will belong to its rightful owner."*

It cut out there.

Nynsi broke the awkward silence, "You were not wrong, uncle. He is not sane and he intends to murder you."

"Yeah." I agreed, "What did he mean by false doctrine?"

"I am a Traditionalist, and supported by that bloc on the Patriarch's Council." Xerol answered. "It is a combination of a religious and cultural movement. The details are not important, we can discuss such matters when we have survived this campaign. More relevant is that in calling me out as such, I believe he has revealed his backers."

Ghai's features scrunched up while her tarah rose in anger. "The Hammer."

I blinked in confusion. Nynsi noticed and elaborated, "The Hammer of Koshun is a radical faction within the Ascendancy. Internally they are rather progressive, they deride the caste system, loathe the governmental structure, and have an increasing well of support among the midcaste and highborn. Diplomatically... they are virulently anti-alien. The only ones they tolerate are non-Imperial Naule."

"Ah." I nodded. "Sounds like your dad would fit right in."

Xerol nodded in agreement, "He likely is an unofficial member. It would be within their usual patterns to infiltrate the White Storm as a means of increasing their direct power. Before we continue, there are two additional messages. One for each of you."

Before I could ask who he meant, he'd already hit play.

"*Brat.*" If Chacksin had been angry before, he'd taken it to another level in this one. His voice was lower, practically biting off each word. "*You have gone beyond being merely disappointing, you have become something anathema to the very essence of what it means to be a Thondian woman of your birth! Not only do you cavort about in battle like some Trahcon whelp, but you have allowed an alien, a Human, to defile you! Any mercy or leniency I might have once shown you now has no chance of occurring. Once I have dealt with your pet and my traitorous brother, I will personally handle your retrieval. You will perform the actions for which you were meant, but only once I have exacted sufficient pain as payment for your transgressions."*

His lips twisted into a smile, his sharp teeth almost gleaming. *"I look forwards to seeing you soon, daughter."*

Nynsi's hands curled into fists and shook in anger, but apart from a long hiss she stayed silent. Xerol moved straight into the third message before any of us could speak.

I didn't need to ask who it was directed to. Chacksin made it clear from the get-go. *"Defiler. Creature. Faithless beast. I lack the words to properly describe you, cretin. I know what you truly are, and from which pit you emerged. That such a beast dared to lay with my wayward spawn... you will suffer as such an animal should. I will tear out your eyes. I will shatter your teeth. I will rip your very tendons from your bones and let her listen to your screams. And when I have shattered whatever excuse for a mind you have, when you have finally lost any sense of yourself and truly become nothing more than a breathing corpse... I will let you live as an example to all of your pathetic kind."*

The video ended.

I opened my mouth but no words came out.

Ghai twitched her head in a tiny shake before whispering. "Your stunt at the dance continues to haunt you both, Nynsi."

A muscle in Nynsi's cheek twitched. "He would have been a priority target given my father's past even without my actions. That being said, you aren't entirely wrong. I owe Cieran beyond the payment he has been given. He will be under our complete protection until my father is dead."

I'd have felt better about that if I hadn't been attacked in this mansion once already. And if I hadn't just gone with on a pair of offensive assaults.

And if I wasn't mentally and physically exhausted.

Still... I supposed it was good that I wasn't going to be alone in this without Trenah.

Speaking of, "Trenah's due to be woken up next week. Will it be safe for her to be transferred here?"

All three of them turned to stare blankly at me.

"What?" I asked defensively. "It's a legitimate question."

"It is," Xerol agreed, "I am more curious as to how you know that. I have no information on her status so I find it difficult to believe that you do."

I shrugged uncomfortably, "I found someone who did."

Nynsi made a disgusted sound. "One of her many conquests no doubt. She likely has at least a few among the staff at the hospital at the rate she goes through them."

Part of me felt a little nettled on Trenah's behalf. The rest of me told me to keep my mouth shut and let her run with the assumption. I wasn't sure *why* I felt the need to keep Rane'li out of this, but some instinct in the back of my head told me it was important to do so.

For his part I didn't think Xerol bought the idea but he nodded slowly and accepted my silence. "In truth I do not believe it will be safe here for her. Not until my security teams are healed and prepared for battle again, which may take several weeks. I do not believe my brother will act against us immediately, he will know Internal-Security will be on alert and watching this home. So for now we should all rest. Tomorrow we will discuss our options and how Tasir and the Empire factor into this complicated situation."

The three of us nodded, rose, and then headed for our beds to get what sleep we could.

Tomorrow, and its problems, came too soon.

III – I

Date (Terran / Imperial)
6/30/2189 || 11/06/2261

"Boss, what in Ashahn's name did you do to my suit?" Illyahn's tarah were tilted down in despair as she gaped at the armor. "You put it in a trash compactor for fun?"

"Good morning to you too." I grumbled. "Thank you for being more concerned about my health than you are about a exoskeleton."

A broad hand flicked in my direction, "You're welcome boss."

My tired glower bounced off of her thick skin. "You're not getting a raise this year."

"I suppose it's a good thing you don't pay my salary then." She replied cheerfully, though her grin faded quickly as she took a step closer. Her bright eyes lingered on the arm I still had in a sling, and then up to where I knew I had deep circles under my eyes. "You look like crap. Guessing you feel worse."

I grunted. "Pretty much."

Illyahn nodded slowly and lowered her voice, "You want to talk about it?"

The offer surprised me. Not that I didn't like my assistant but we didn't exactly know each other all that well. Hell, we'd only met two weeks ago. Then again, she was both a Trahcon and a fairly supportive person from what I could tell. I probably shouldn't have been as taken aback as I was.

"...maybe later." I deflected. "Right now I need a repair time-frame."

She looked me over a second time, then nodded in acceptance before turning back to the armor. "Was any of the core structure compromised?"

"No, thankfully. Lot of damage on the left side, definitely internal damage but nothing to the skeleton." I waved at the other side, "Not as much on the right. Cables got cut again, need a better solution for that."

"Rane's still working on a secure wireless connection." Illyahn pointed out. "But we can't exactly transmit coolant."

I glanced at her, "Rane'li. They hate their names being shortened."

"Oh, right. You have any idea why?"

"Nope." I shrugged, "I've got a meeting where I'm probably going to get yelled at. See what you can do getting started, don't worry about the armor plates. I'll handle those when I get back."

A broad hand came gently down on my good shoulder. I brought my own arm up to bump against hers before turning away and leaving the garage. The meeting with Tasir was occurring in the usual conference room and it didn't take me long to get there. Even though I took my sweet time heading up the stairs to make sure that I wasn't early. One night of sleep hadn't really left me in a better mood, as Illyahn had noticed, so the last thing I wanted was to have to talk to anyone on my own.

As it happened I was the last person to show up. Nynsi and Xerol were seated next to one another at the head of the table. Tasir had taken a confrontational position at the far end, lounging in the same uniform she'd been wearing the day before. All three of them fixed me with rather displeased stares that didn't lessen when I silently took a seat near the middle of the table.

Xerol folded his hands together and nodded once I'd settled, "That is everyone. Regrettably Rehat is in no condition to join us and will be remaining in the medical suite for some time."

I perked up at that, "He's going to make it?"

"By the Pillars' wisdom and the Paragons' blessing, yes." His normally rigid posture loosened for a brief moment in an almost-human slump of relief, "Doctor Rae will fit him for a prosthetic once he is stable. Sadly we did lose three of the wounded last night, and many of the rest are not combat ready. That leaves us in a precarious position unless you can promise support."

That last bit was directed at Tasir, who shook her head as I could have guessed. "I started my day off with a screaming match with the Board. If you get attacked I can make sure Internal-Security is listening and ready to get their asses over here. More than that? Can't. Sorry to say it but you're still just the personal side-show to their main objective."

He'd clearly expected that answer because he simply tipped his head in acceptance. "What were you able to determine in regards to that?"

The briefing that followed provided some bit of vindication. Apparently the theory that Trenah and I had come up with was more or less spot on. No fewer than five separate organizations that contracted to the Crescent had purchased 'indentured servants' from various front groups that the True Sons and White Storm had created. All of them were panicking and waving away any and all debts before Tasir or the Imperial Ambassador showed up at their door.

Strangely the result from the Crescent was far more muted. Kolkris was one of the more powerful warlords in the Far Reaches, controlling a broad swath of worlds and interests beyond Alume. But this was where her headquarters was, her palace, and she had been strangely quiet on the issue. According to Tasir that made no sense at all considering that the woman was certifiably insane.

"Bitch should be apoplectic and foaming at the mouth." She growled, "Instead I'm not hearing anything out of those maniacs. No investigations, no purges, nothing."

I considered that. "Is she so unstable that she doesn't really think it's a problem?"

Tasir's tarah flexed out, "Fuck no. Her personal safety and the defense of her territory is something she never takes lightly."

Nynsi stirred for the first time, "How much does that matter at this point? We are in agreement that my father's interest in us is personal against

279

the White Storm's operation to weaken the Crescent. But with their slave deception removed what path do they have to continue?"

Her words made me nod in agreement, "Especially since you and Internal-Security are openly going after them. Not like they can just restart what they were doing. You think they're going to go after the Crescent directly?"

"No," Xerol shook his head, "My brother is many things but he is not suicidal."

"But he will be desperate." Tasir countered, "His bosses aren't going to be happy with him fucking all this up by getting you involved. He goes back to them now they're likely to execute the bastard and send his head to Kolkris as a peace offering."

A soft whistle came from Nynsi before she spoke, "Then what are his options? There are hundreds of thousands of Crescent soldiers on planet, then millions contracted to them as employees. Harming any of them would merely provoke them."

"Kolkris herself?" I suggested, "She have any packmates he could try and assassinate?"

Tasir flicked a hand, "Iriahn'kolkris is living proof that with great power comes madness. Bitch is one of the strongest wielders of sorcery alive, trained under priests of Mahkahs as a Huntress. And she's got five living children nearly as good as she is."

I blinked at that. "Her own children?"

The old woman made a face, "She's one of the Reachers that acts like one of you aliens. Actually raised her own children, keeps them around as some fucked up facsimile of a pack. Unnatural."

We aliens all gave her unimpressed looks that she ignored.

"I suppose it's possible he might try to turn one of them against her. Can't say any of them really love the madwoman so maybe someone's looking for a promotion." Tasir exhaled as her tarah lowered, "Honestly that's a thin rope. I know most personally or by reputation and it's not their style. They'd break down her door and slug it out, not ally with an enemy to assassinate her."

"Someone else then?" I shrugged my bad shoulder and immediately hissed in pain. "Ow... one of the other warlords? There's, what, a half-dozen or so who might want her gone?"

A gray hand waved in my direction, "Sure. Yulaz and Zaen both would love her dead, but again, they'd do it themselves. Ravt... maybe. That bitch has enough cunning to manipulate an idiot like Chacksin but Alume is a long way from Xentha, and she's got her own problems keeping her little Empire defended."

"Riush?" Nynsi suggested.

This time it was Xerol who shook his head. "She is the one who set the balance of power in the Reaches. Much of her power relies on maintaining that. Killing Kolkris would destabilize things far too much for her liking."

I frowned, "Then we're down to what? Some disgruntled bodyguard or lower ranked person who will help him, or we're completely off track and he's planning something else."

"Welcome to my fucking life." Tasir looked as disgusted as she sounded. "But searching for that data is my job. I don't want you lot involved unless I specifically call you in from here on out. You're not in any shape for another offensive, and my superiors aren't going to want the Ascendancy claiming any credit for this shit."

Xerol seemed to consider that. "It is likely that the Patriarch's Council will do so regardless of the outcome."

"Which can be ignored so long as you don't do anything more than you've already done." She countered. "Stay in your bunker, get your troops fixed up, don't go swimming in deep water, don't run with sharp objects, the usual."

His voice turned dry. "I shall endeavor not to create more paperwork for you by dying accidentally."

That made me blink a little in surprise. I'd have honestly thought he'd be taking Tasir's commanding attitude a lot worse. Especially since she was making it damned clear that he was her subordinate. It had to be rankling him given what I knew of Thondians.

Then again... Xerol was definitely a pragmatist even when it ran counter to his culture. Working with the Imperial spymaster was probably the smart move at the moment. Especially since she'd just saved him from all kinds of legal headaches.

"And you," Tasir turned her attention to Nynsi. "All of that to you too. And make sure there's guards around your cousin every minute of the day."

Nynsi nodded primly. "There are four outside of Rehat's medical room at all times. I already have a rotating schedule set to ensure that remains the case."

The older woman grunted. "Good. I'll keep a few of my people at the hospital watching your people there."

I perked up at that. "And Trenah? Are you going to wake her up and transfer her here?"

"You think that's the best idea?" She challenged. "Chacksin's not smart enough to leave this alone and focus on his actual mission. She's safer where she's at."

"She won't see it that way." I predicted.

Tasir made a sound that wasn't quite a laugh. "No, she won't. Little Laria stays where she is until it's safe to wake her. Then I'll leave it up to her, I'll swear it on any Aspect you want."

It would have been more polite to say that wasn't necessary, but I wasn't sure I trusted her farther than I could throw her. "Ashahn is fine."

Both Xerol and Nynsi gave me warning looks, but Tasir simply nodded. "By the Highest Aspect of Aysh, I promise I'll go along with whatever she wants."

I considered the words. Considered her posture. "All right."

"Good. Now we can move on to other things. You two," Her eyes slid back to Xerol and Nynsi, "Are good. This is for me and him."

Whatever tiny bit of relaxation and relief I'd managed to feel died just as quickly as it had started up. My quick glance to Nynsi gave me nothing except for the tiniest shakes of her head as she stood up. Xerol didn't even give me that much, instead he just rose along with his niece and then headed for the door.

Nynsi gave me a gentle pat on the shoulder much like Illyahn had, then she was gone, and I was alone with the Imperial.

III – II

The door shut on a silent room. I stared at Tasir. She stared back. After about two minutes of that she made a disgusted sound, got up, then walked over to the low cabinets set underneath the windows. After a few moments of rummaging she came back with an unmarked bottle and two glass cups.

I watched as she poured a finger's worth of midnight black liquid out into each, accepting one of the cups when offered.

A single sip made my eyebrows shoot up. It was strong, layered, and completely lacking in the aftertaste I'd come to expect from Trahcon food and drink. "That's very good. What is it?"

"Some unpronounceable combination of chirps and clicks." A shoulder rolled as she sampled her own. "We call it Vekki Dark. Xerol will throw a fit we're drinking it, shit's expensive even by his standards."

"I don't know anything about the Vekki." I admitted while doing my best to ignore the second part of what she'd said. "Aside from the fact that they make good drinks apparently."

Tasir gave me a faint smile, "That's all most people know, and those paranoid carrion like to keep it that way. Pricks. Figured we'd have comforting drinks while having an uncomfortable conversation."

I disguised my unease by taking another measured sip. "You finally going to tell me why you don't like me?"

One of her fingers tapped against the table. "I like you just fine, kid. You're easily the most tolerable non-Imperial member of your species I've ever run into. I just don't trust you."

"Fine," I corrected myself, "You finally going to tell me why you don't trust me?"

There was the slightest of nods. "I'll tell you, but I want something else first. I want a story."

I blinked. "A story?"

A sharp nod, "Your story, to be specific. Not the fogged up version that Laria told me when she was drinking. I want to know everything. Where you're from, who your family was, why you jumped on a cryo ship. I want the ship's name, I want the year you left, I want to know about the Matriarch who saved you."

I took a third pull from my drink to cover up my total confusion. "...I thought you were annoyed that I found out about Trenah."

"Oh I am." Her left tarah quivered in suppressed emotion, "But I already had one of my people back-trace the hacker to that wounded girl here. You going to tell me what I want to know or not?"

Thinking about it, I couldn't come up with a reason not to tell her. It seemed like a fairly simple, if weird, request. Plus it might distract me for an hour or so from all the other crap flying around inside my head.

So I told her. Told her what it had been like growing up in the middle-class suburbs of Phoenix. Talked about the car crash that had taken my family. About the cousin who'd tried to help me stay on my feet. How I'd eventually given up and volunteered to be flung out into space as a frozen statue.

She was mostly a passive listener up until that section. Then she wanted to know every single detail about what had been going on. The name of the ship? Pegasus. Scheduled day of departure? End of March in Twenty-Forty-One. How many colonists? Close to a thousand, plus a crew of four dozen. Our destination? Proxima Centauri, same as the two ships ahead of us.

Tasir nodded slowly when I got to the part. "Themis. It's a miserable ball of rock in that system, was your people's only extra-solar colony before the invasion. Tell me about the Matriarch."

"Uh..." I rubbed at my head with my working hand trying to remember. "Maybe average height for a woman, a good head taller than Trenah. Not as built as you or her. Dressed well, very precise in how she spoke. No tattoos that I could see."

285

"Accent?"

"I didn't speak Caranat then." My good shoulder rose and fell in a helpless shrug, "Translator gave her a pretty neutral accent to my ear."

A displeased look made her tarah quiver as she threw back the rest of her drink. "Bitch thought ahead. Most of those are programmed to assign accents between languages to stop everyone from sounding the same."

That made me blink, "Is she some kind of criminal or something? She told me was technically an Imperial citizen."

"Probably is, for both of those." Tasir filled half her glass before looking to mine. After a moment I pushed it over and let her refill it as well, and she resumed speaking as she did. "Three hundred billion of our species in the Empire makes it easy for certain people to lose themselves. I've heard rumors about some stuck-up bitch calling herself Matriarch for the last century but you and Laria are the first ones I've met who actually ran into her personally."

I frowned, "So you don't trust me because I was saved by a mystery woman?"

"That's one reason." She brought the bottle back and considered it before asking another question, "What do you know about Trenah'laria? About her past?"

It was hard not to squirm. "That something fairly awful happened to her, but that it wasn't any of my business. It still isn't."

For a second her expression came close to being approving. "No, it's not. I don't even know all the details, but I know that this Matriarch helped get her out and helped her stay hidden. Considering what she was leaving, that means whoever the bitch is she has a lot of pull in places I don't like people having influence."

"Ah..." I murmured. "You think I'm some kind of agent? A plant? To do what? Influence Trenah? Get in with Xerol?"

"It was my first thought when you stumbled into my bar." She agreed,

286

"Didn't take me long to decide that was a stupid plan. Xerol may like you but he hates the Ark Fleet, and I doubt he's got any positive emotions for the rebels on your home-world either."

I shook my head, mildly disbelieving that anyone could consider me a spy. "I'd have figured a spy should speak the local language at a minimum. What was your next thought?"

"That you were still probably a rebel from your home-world, but that they'd somehow learned about my group here." Tasir gave me a self-deprecating smile, "A bit ego-maniacal of me but it's all I could really think of since you weren't making any effort to learn about the High Families or Crescent."

A snort came out before I could stop it. "Maybe I'm plotting it out long term. Get close to Xerol then cozy up to his business contacts."

She waved a hand, "Too long term for your people, too risky given that there's practically none of you on this planet. Few Xenthans either, which makes it hard to make contacts and move funds."

I made a noncommittal sound and drank some more. "What was thought number three?"

"Once I got what I could out of Laria about the Matriarch, I started thinking you were one of hers." Tasir said. "Someone to keep on eye on Laria, or me, or just to test inserting an agent onto Alum."

She rolled her eyes when I started to say something, "I know, I know. I was grasping for anything that made sense by that point."

"You ever consider that I'm what I say I am?" I suggested.

"No, because your story doesn't add up. Still doesn't."

"I-"

She interrupted me again, "There was no third ship."

That left me staring blankly for a few seconds. "Uh... what?"

Tasir reached out and picked up the bottle, filling my glass to the rim before settling back. "Fifty years ago I did some time on your home-world, training agents to identify and hunt rebels. I still have contacts there and got in touch. They sent me everything they could pull up from the archives left over from before the invasion."

"And..." I shook my head, "They told you the *Pegasus* didn't exist or something?"

"They found everything I could have asked for on the first two. Building records, recruitment records, launch dates." She rolled her left hand in a throwing away motion, "And yes, both of those ships were taken by pirates in the last decade. But there was no information telling me a third ship existed."

"But-"

She cut me off yet again. "A third one was planned but never got started."

"I remember..." I gaped at her for a few seconds, then fumbled until I got the cup in my hand. A mouthful of the alcohol let me speak somewhat normally, "You're lying. I remember it. Volunteering. Seeing the pictures. Waiting the day before we went into cryo."

"Kean-"

"I *remember* it." It was my turn to interrupt. "You think I'm lying when you admit you don't know what I would even be doing if I was. I'm not lying dammit!"

Both of her hands rose, "I'm just-"

I didn't remember getting up, but the next thing I knew I was upright and slamming my fist onto the table. "I remember it!"

In hindsight the threatening posture and loud noise were a stupid combination. It may have made my inner neanderthal feel strong and powerful, but cave-men didn't have to contend with aliens who toss things around with their minds. An old, powerful, and paranoid alien who'd probably been a lot more on edge than she'd been showing.

Tasir's back tightened up while her tarah twitched, an invisible wave of air lashing out. It hit me, the chairs, and table in equal measure, flinging all of us away from her. There was enough upward direction to lift me clear from my feet and send me a good couple of yards through the air.

I had a lovely view of the ceiling before gravity did its usual thing. My last clear memory before things got blurry was hearing the furniture slamming into the walls, and a flash of pain that ran from my ass to the back of my skull.

When I came back to reality I was face down and stretched out, my head resting on a pillow while someone sprayed cool liquid into my hair. Nearby I could pick out a pair of voices arguing in low tones, though it took me longer than it should have to realize it was Nynsi and Tasir snarling at one another.

"Easy there." Doctor Rae's mellow voice came from somewhere closer to me, "You've got a brand new cut in the middle of your fur. Pretty sure your brain bounced around a bit too."

That sounded just typical.

"Ow." I managed to groan into the pillow.

"Painkillers should kick in any minute now." He assured me, "Try and stay still while I make sure you don't have a crack in your skull. You came down on one of the chairs."

So. Fucking. Typical.

True to his word the pain began to fade very quickly. That made me feel somewhat better, though I could have done without the arguing in the background. Thankfully that didn't last very long. Couple of minutes at most before one set of feet departed and another drew closer.

"How is he?" Nynsi asked. "That ancient creature didn't kill him did she?"

Rae chuckled, "Don't worry, *Kasha*. He may have another little scar under all this fur but he'll recover. He'll need to stay awake for a while. I'll need to order in some specific drugs to make sure he doesn't suffer long term effects from the blow he took to his head. Core City Hospital will have them, they like to be prepared for anything."

"Will he be able to remain unsupervised?" Nynsi asked.

"Best to keep one set of eyes on him," Rae replied. "He might be all right to supervise work, but probably should take it easy for the rest of the day."

"Is he awake?"

"Yeah." I mumbled. "I'm fine now."

To my vague annoyance neither of them took my word for it. Instead they got me around and seated on the floor so that the doctor could run me through a series of questions. Who I was, what had happened yesterday, what had gone on this morning, and a dozen other annoying things to make sure I hadn't suffered any memory loss or confusion.

Only when he was sure I was as stable as I ever was did the doctor help me stand up. The world didn't spin or tilt but Nynsi insisted on escorting me back to my room while Rae wandered off to order the appropriate pills. I made a few protests that I'd told Illyahn I'd be back that went completely ignored, and soon enough I was being pushed into my bed.

"I'm not even clean." I muttered half-heartedly, "Are you seriously going to just sit around in here for the rest of the day?"

Nynsi gave me a droll look. "Of course not. I will stay until lunch and then order either Illyahn or Erana to watch over you."

"I'm reasonably sure I can manage to not die without supervision."

Her voice turned even drier, "Of course you can. Because physically threatening a battle-hardened Imperial officer is the mark of a sane and rational being."

I glared at her because I didn't really have any other comeback.

"Honestly Cieran." She continued talking while she bustled around, grabbing one of my chairs and pulling it alongside the bed. "She told me what happened while the doctor worked. I don't believe her theories any more than you do, but you didn't do yourself any favors by reacting irrationally. I honestly thought better of you."

That made my glower turn into a grimace, and I felt myself deflate a little into the bed. "I know that dammit. I just... ugh. I'm not... used to any of this. I didn't get any sleep last night, every time I closed my eyes I saw... I'm sure you can guess."

She made a sound somewhere between a low growl and a hum. "Ah. I suppose that would explain your unusually poor temper this morning. I will admit to forgetting that combat remains new to you. I have no real excuse beyond the distraction of my father's messages. I apologize for that, I should have pushed to delay Tasir's questioning."

"I... thank you." I closed my eyes and tried to steady my breathing, "I'll be all right, I think. Humans are adaptable. I just... need some time to adjust and process it."

The chair creaked a little as she settled into it, "If you need, Ghai does have some training in psychology. From before her injury, obviously, and it may not be well suited to your species. But it may be better than nothing."

"...maybe." I said after a few moments. "Not today. I don't want to think about it anymore today. Next week if things are calm I'll think about talking to her. Where did she pick that up?"

"She and Iyaht have served my family for nearly a century. They have gained a rather eclectic group of skills over that time."

The name made me stir a little, cracking open one eye. "How is Iyaht? I don't remember hearing much about her."

Nynsi's expression was grim. "Still in a medical coma. There is another complication, her birth pack learned of her wounds and are petitioning for her to be moved to an Imperial world for long term treatment."

I blinked, "I didn't know she was Imperial. Can they do that?"

"Born Imperial, but emigrated after her compulsory military term.

Ghai and Rae are discussing it, as they are her current packmates the decision will be theirs. But I believe they are leaning towards agreeing."

"Are Imperial hospitals that much better?"

"No," Nynsi gave my wounded arm a pointed look, "But she is less likely to be attacked by someone looking for revenge in one of them."

"Fair point." I yawned and shook my head, then did it again when Nynsi leaned over and poked me in the forehead. "What was that for?"

"To ensure you are not falling asleep." She retorted primly. "Yawn again and I will resort to pulling on your fur to see if that actually does hurt you."

I couldn't help but snort. "Pulling on hair is usually seen as childish. Or a particularly girly way of fighting."

Her head tilted a little to the left and forwards in a way I wasn't familiar with. "How fortunate that I am both female and quite secure in my adulthood. Consider that while we discuss your assistants."

We spent most of the next hour talking about how both of them were doing. In terms of her actual job performance in terms of Illyahn, and in terms of her wounds and how well she treating me in regards to Rane'li. Since the answer to all three was 'surprisingly well', we drifted into small talk about anything besides what had happened yesterday.

Somehow we ended up on the subject of our native languages, and were trying to teach the other the extreme basics when we received an unexpected ping from Nynsi's wrist-comp.

"Interesting." Nynsi mused as she closed the message.

"Please tell me it's not bad news." I shook my head slowly, "I don't think I can take more bad news."

"It's a peace offering from Tasir."

I blinked. "A peace offering?"

Nynsi schooling her expression into perfect neutrality told me what it was even before she spoke, "Trenah'laria is being woken up this evening, and will be transferred here tomorrow if she wants to be moved. I am specifically told to inform you as soon as possible."

"Huh." I offered, "Should I be confused or happy?"

I'd meant it as a half-serious joke, but Nynsi visibly contemplated it before speaking. "Ashul'tasir can be Thondian at times. She does little without a reason, without a motive. This is a peace offering for harming you, but it may be something more. I will make a few discreet inquires to see if she is taking any other actions."

"You don't have to do that." I protested.

"I am your host." She retorted, "It is my duty to see to the well-being of my guests, especially when they demonstrate an inability to do so on their own."

"...you're not going to let that go anytime soon, are you?"

She showed me her teeth in reply.

III – III

They brought Trenah in overnight, settling her into the mansion's small medical facility. I decided to visit first thing in the morning and Ghai apparently had the same plan. Not that I minded, it made it a lot easier to carry enough food for everyone with the extra set of hands.

Of course whether we'd be eating the food or wearing it was an open question from the snarling I could hear before we even made it to the door.

"-not happy about any of this!" Trenah's voice was rough but as loud as ever.

"You never are." Xerol's voice remained steady, "We are all committed at this point. There is little else to be done."

"If I wasn't fucking tied down in this fucking bed I'd beat you within an inch of your fucking life!"

"I am glad to see that your injuries have not affected your vocabulary." Despite the early hour, when Xerol appeared in the doorway he was already immaculately dressed. "Your packmates have arrived. I will leave them to your tender mercies."

Ghai gave her boss a droll look while I rolled my eyes and stepped aside so he could pass. Xerol acknowledged us both with a polite little bow before heading off to whatever was next on his to-do list for the day. I followed my... companion? Acquaintance? Friend? I wasn't really sure what Ghai was to me. We got along, but we didn't exactly hang out even if she was one of the few people in the building who seemed to genuinely like me. Fuck, I didn't even know her full *name*.

I followed my friendly coworker into the room to discover that Trenah had been speaking literally.

She really was tied to the bed.

Besides that little fact, she looked even worse than I'd anticipated. She was limp and reclined under a thin sheet, with several lines running from a nearby machine under the covers. Her wounded leg obviously had something entirely wrapped around it under the blanket, and there was a pair of straps around her waist holding her down. About the only part of her that was free were her arms and head, even her tarah had been carefully slotted into her pillow to stop them from moving.

If I hadn't just heard her ranting I would have sworn that she was too beat up to be her usual self.

"Get that stupid expression of your face." Trenah groused, "I've looked worse."

I managed a wan smile, "True. I've seen you naked."

Her bark of laughter was genuine but a bit raspy, and it cut off quickly. "Fuck you too. That food had better be for me."

Ghai got a tray set up on a swing arm and adjusted the bed so that Trenah was upright and had her tarah free. While she did that I separated out the portions we'd gotten for her, and within a couple of minutes we were sitting in chairs and were eating bread and various cold cuts; standard Thondian breakfast fare.

"I'm guessing Xerol told you how bad things are going?" I asked.

Ghai let out a sharp exhalation, "Not bad."

Trenah, showing off her aged wisdom, flicked a bit of bread at her. "I'm strapped to a bed, half of the security detail is dead or crippled, and a maniac wants to gut us all and display our heads on his wall. Shit's bad."

The other woman considered that, then rolled a shoulder and dipped her head in a sheepish shrug. "Could be worse."

"...true." I allowed. "Could be a lot worse. We could all be dead."

"I might still kill you both." Trenah grumbled.

I made an indignant sound, "What the fuck did we do?"

"You're an idiot and she's letting you be an idiot." She sent more of her breakfast in my direction. I proved my superior maturity by simply catching the small bit of bread and popping it into my mouth. "I suppose I shouldn't have expected anything better from a male, but the mute over there should have known better."

"Sexist." I muttered, "Still, what did we do?"

Trenah gave me her best 'are-you-that-fucking-stupid' look. "Besides getting involved in an alien dispute that's turning into a small-scale fucking war?"

I nodded, "Yeah, besides that."

"Besides volunteering to be a literal fucking walking target?"

"I think that goes with the first part doesn't it?"

"No," She growled back. "It doesn't. You could have just stayed in the back or pretended to analyze crap. Instead you wandered around without any actual training with a giant target on your furry head. Don't even try to tell me that you were useful as anything besides a diversion."

Since that was exactly what my my role had been I really couldn't argue with her. Maybe Nynsi was right and I'd done something worthwhile in the endgame of the fight, or maybe that was just her trying to buoy my spirits a bit. Either way I didn't think Trenah would accept that as a valid reason for doing what I'd done.

"It seemed like the best option I had." It was my turn to shrug, "I can't say it wasn't stupid but I didn't like my other options either. At least now we have plenty of money and the locals are tolerating me."

Ghai nodded slightly, "Staff. Cordial."

Trenah frowned at her, visibly translating the two words in a proper sentence before making an unhappy sound in her throat. "They aren't looking like they want to strangle you in your sleep anymore?"

I shook my head, "No, thankfully. All it took was two sleepless nights, a bunch of physical trauma, and a lot of dead True Sons."

"Concussion." Ghai added.

"Plus a concussion." I amended.

Turquoise eyes narrowed from the bed, "Who the fuck hit you hard enough to rattle your thick skull?"

"Tasir." I grimaced, "She's convinced I'm a spy for someone, the Matriarch in particular. She thinks I'm lying about where I came from."

That earned a quiet snort. "Old bitch doesn't know you that well. You're a shit liar."

"I'm not that bad at it." I protested.

"Terrible." Ghai agreed, "Awful."

"And stupid." Trenah continued, "Saying you're a good liar isn't the kind of shit you do when people are accusing you of being a spy."

I set my plate on the floor so that I could rub at both of my temples. "Yeah yeah. Point is I did something stupid, she bounced me off a chair, plus a few other things. I've got a nice new scar on the back of my head and pills to take for the rest of the week. I also learned my lesson about startling old Trahcon."

Neither woman looked like they believed me about the last bit but it was Trenah who spoke again, "Sure you did. You learn your lesson about accepting gifts from Thondians yet, or has that shark not bitten you in the ass yet?"

"I don't remember getting any gifts. Just work and potentially lethal situations."

Ghai smiled a little, "Assistants."

It was my turn to frown, "How are they a gift? Rane'li is just staying busy while she recovers, and Illyahn's practically taken over the work on the exoskeleton. All I really do is learn from her, pilot the thing, and get shot at a lot."

Her smile faded. After a moment she put her own plate down on the floor, then rested her arms on her legs before quietly speaking, "Thondians revere power in all its forms. Authority. Nynsi giving you command of her people is not a small thing. Even just the two of them is a declaration."

I stared at her for several seconds. "...all right, I'm with Trenah. Why didn't you tell me that sooner?"

"...I was busy?" She flinched when Trenah threw more bread at her. "Apologies."

A hand rose so that I could rub at my forehead. God. I'd picked up that Thondians liked to be in control, but like so many other things I'd apparently underestimated the importance of it. I'd also started treating everyone around me as Human again. Strange Humans maybe, but I'd started applying Human motivations because their actions didn't seem all that different.

I'd managed to forget that just because their *actions* were similar didn't mean that the reasons *behind* those actions were.

Fuck but I really needed to stop doing that given how often it was biting me in the ass. I'd thought I was better about that but maybe I'd only really adjusted with Trahcon. Maybe I needed at least one or two slaps upside the head per species or something.

"Xerol said I'd understand what Nynsi was up to when I figured out what his goals were." I looked at the man's bodyguard, "I haven't really had time to think about it, and apparently I'm not as well adjusted to their species as I thought. I don't suppose you could educate me on that as well?"

If it was physically possible for her raspy voice to get any drier, she managed it, "Not hard to see it."

I spent a few more seconds thinking furiously about it, putting together bits of conversations and things I'd heard. "She... wants me as an employee or something?"

"Harath'krem." Ghai corrected, "Alien, exotic, you have potential. Your species would give her notoriety. Infamy and fame equally. Maybe a way to make contracts with enclaves in the Reaches. Your inexperience is, in some way, a boon. Few prejudices, few preconceptions. Easy to direct."

Trenah nodded tiredly, "Xerol's grandfather picked her and Iyaht up for similar reasons. Having them at either side made him more presentable outside the Ascendancy. Plus they're both extremely good at killing people."

"I'm not." I noted.

"She doesn't need a killer. Bitch does that herself." Trenah sighed, "She wants outside viewpoints. Inroads to groups that aren't under her uncle's boot, just like how he created his own little enclave here."

Something in her tone made a flash of inspiration hit me. "Oh. That's why you two hate each other, isn't it? She wanted you originally."

Lips and tarah twitched in disgust. "And she didn't like taking no for an answer."

That certainly explained a lot of their relationship. And why Trenah had been so hell bent on me being careful around her.

Ghai noted my falling expression and spoke again, "She is fond of you. Makes her more determined to bring you in. Her fetish is also a factor."

"Her academic interest you mean." I let my head fall back as I groaned. Not that I wasn't kind of interested in return but this didn't seem like the time or place to consider a cross-species relationship. Especially since I apparently didn't have a good grasp on her culture or her motivations. "I do genuinely like her, but I'm not really interested in becoming part of... whatever all this is. Not long term anyway."

Her rasp grew a bit more pronounced as she kept forcing herself to speak full sentences. "It may be best if you did."

A tired growl came from the direction of the bed. "Ashahn's bloody ass. Don't you even fucking think of suggesting that."

I looked down to see Ghai spread her hands and tarah in supplication. "You're wounded and will need care for at least a year. More. No matter how this ends you will likely still be targets. White Storm does not forget their enemies."

"You're saying we'd be safer staying here even after Tasir deals with Chacksin." I said, "You think they'd really send assassins or put bounties on us? We're not exactly central to what's going on."

Ghai started to reply, then winced and brought a hand to her throat. Trenah muttered a soft curse and spoke for her. "Stop talking if it hurts that much dammit. And yeah, the fuckers would, Cie. It's their style. Even when they lose they try to hurt everyone who helped make that happen. Part of what's helped them build their little confederation."

I rubbed some more at my temples to try and fight back the rising headache. "Great. So you're angry because I'm apparently doing what I should be doing?"

"No you damned idiot." She growled, "I'm fucking angry because you if you had any sense in your fur covered skull you'd have bailed and holed up down south until I could come and find you."

"I wasn't going to leave you behind."

That earned me a tired glower. "...there are times when I really don't understand your human brain. You couldn't defend me if someone came after me, and you know I'd be able to track you down if you left."

My arms crossed my chest. "I wasn't going to leave you behind."

Her glare sharpened before she groaned and let her head fall back. "Stubborn furry bastard. What's your plan at the moment?"

"Keep my head down, do my job, don't leave the mansion, don't play with explosives." I summarized. "Tasir and Nynsi both made it clear that no one is to take any chances at this point."

"Good." She exhaled audibly through her nose, "Keep doing all that. I'll try and think of a way for us to not get dragged too far into the aftermath. If the bitch tries to give you anything else find a way to say no, and by Ashahn whatever you do *don't* sleep with her. That'll fucking complicate shit."

"So keep doing what I'm already doing."

"And find me a new doctor, one that I can actually drool over." Trenah continued as if I hadn't spoken. "This one's too ugly. And if you don't bring me a hard drink with dinner I'm going to kill someone."

"There it is." I sighed, glancing to Ghai. "Here I was hoping that a near-death experience might make her a bit more mature. Stupid of me."

Trenah gave me a rude gesture with both hands while Ghai laughed.

The conversation turned less serious after that, thankfully. I filled Trenah in about the state of the suit, then we chatted about various gossip running around the mansion. After maybe an hour she was visibly struggling to stay awake. Her eyes finally closed in sleep in the middle of a conversation about Erana and how she was doing as Nynsi's secretary.

"She looks worse than I'd thought she would." I said after we'd left the medical suite and were wandering back towards the hangar. "The mood I expected, but..."

"Battered." Ghai agreed. "Care."

I glanced back over my shoulder as if I could see her limp body I the bed. "Yeah but you heard her. She's so damned stubborn."

A rasping bark was her first response to that. "Water calling river wet."

"Yeah yeah," I sighed. "Maybe I can draft Illyahn into playing nurse."

"Good idea." She nodded before glancing at her wrist comp. "Meeting. With Trenah at dinner?"

I nodded once. "See you there."

III – IV

Against my better judgment, I did make an effort to smuggle a tiny amount of alcohol into Trenah's room. Unfortunately for her Doctor Rae had expected someone to try that and made me turn out my pockets before he let me in. He'd berated me, then Ghai, then Trenah, then drank the small bottle in front of her before leaving us to deliver her dinner.

Trenah had grumbled about the lack of alcohol but I could tell that she appreciated the company. She'd apparently spent most of they day managing my money for me since I'd added her as an authorized person. Evidently only one account wasn't quite enough because she'd split Xerol's payments across half a dozen and then invested the rest in a variety of local groups.

Now I had money on Alum, Cathia, and Terminus. I had no interest at all in visiting the last, and when I'd told her as much she'd simply shrugged.

"Better to have some there in case shit really gets fucked."

I pursed my lips, "If you say so. I'm honestly surprised there's banks on Terminus from what I've read about the place."

"Rich pirates have to store their cash somewhere." Trenah twitched a shoulder, "You're not wrong though. I didn't put much there, enough to buy a flight somewhere the fuck else if we end up on that slum."

Thankfully we didn't spend all that much time on the exciting world of finance. Instead we mostly returned to the same topics from breakfast; trying to figure what the hell our next moves were going to be. In the end that mostly amounted to Ghai doing her best to convince the pair of us that we should stay even after Tasir found Chacksin and put a bullet in his head.

She never said it directly but even I could tell that she was really asking us to join her Pack. Well, asking Trenah. I just came along as part of the package. Not that she didn't like me. I was pretty sure she was at least fond of me, but I was equally sure she was completely smitten with Trenah. Which would have been funny as hell in almost any other situation.

From her tired responses Trenah clearly knew what she was after as well. I didn't think she really wanted to sign up, but her injuries and the size of the mess we were in had changed things since our conversation in the garden. After maybe an hour she'd kicked Ghai out so that the pair of us could talk in relative privacy.

"You changing your mind?" I asked after the door had closed.

My friend closed her eyes and sagged back into her bed. "...fuck. I don't know. I don't *want* to but there's a lot of advantages to it. It'd mean a lot less work for you to begin with. She and Rae would help keep my broken ass from falling apart for another. Plus the safety of living here."

"Plus Ghai is over the moon for you."

She blinked, clearly needing a second to process the Human idiom, then to my surprise she actually grimaced. "Yeah, there's that."

I frowned, "Not interested?"

"I like her. Be interested in seeing where that goes." She exhaled, "But my last serious thing... fuck. I don't even like thinking about it. Makes it hard to think about, especially since this isn't exactly the best time. What do you think?"

"About working here or legally joining their pack?" I asked.

"Both."

I grimaced, reaching to rub at my neck. "Ghai's not bad to be around, but I don't even know her full name. Or really anything personal about her. And I don't know Rae at all, or Iyaht if she ever comes back. Plus I don't know about working for Xerol long term."

"Me either." She glanced down at her broken body with a disgusted expression. "I don't know if this gives us many other options."

"Your earlier idea? Going somewhere else?" I asked. "I'm not thrilled at the idea of putting our lives in the hands of Internal-Security but maybe... any other planets? Cathia's supposed to be pretty stable, isn't it?"

Her head shook. "Yeah but I can't go there. Can't go to any of the other mostly safe planets in the Reaches either. Don't ask me why."

I didn't. "The Empire?'

"They'd only let us in for a short stay unless we officially settled." Trenah's lips twisted down. "Then we'd be conscripted to validate our citizenship. That's seven decades of service for me, no idea how long the term is for a Human."

So much for that idea. "So we either stay here and risk our lives, or we go to a planet that's even less safe and risk our lives. But here we'd at least know the terrain and have allies."

"Allies that want us to work *for* them, not *with* them." Turquoise eyes closed tiredly. "We're stuck between a lot of sharp rocks at the moment. Maybe... shit. I might have an idea but it's a bad one. Give me some time to think on it, if you still want to be stuck with me."

"I'd have already left if I didn't." I smiled as I stood up. "You want me to try again with the drinks tomorrow?"

"Is that a serious fucking question?"

We'd both laughed and then I'd left, heading back to my own room to try and get some sleep. Maybe tomorrow I'd corner Ghai and try to actually get to know her. Or maybe I'd bring Illyahn with on a visit to Trenah. She'd definitely like the extra company, and having someone she could harmlessly flirt with for a while.

For once I actually fell asleep quickly, thinking about what I could do to keep Trenah's spirits up rather than on the things I'd done.

Of course the first night I might have slept well in the last month was ruined less than an hour in. Just before midnight the building's alarms and intercoms began a shrieking chorus that scared the hell out of me.

Sadly trying to throw my blankets off, scramble to my feet, and cover my ears all at the same time didn't go well. I managed to get tangled up and slam into the hardwood floor hard enough to lose my breath. Thankfully the blankets cushioned my skull so at least I didn't get another concussion out of the deal.

The alarm cut out while I was freeing myself, Nynsi's voice replacing the klaxon. *"All staff and guests, we have five perimeter alarms tripped! Arm yourselves and report to your defensive positions!"*

Oh great.

It took me a few minutes to throw pants on, hastily buckle on my armor, and then grab my submachine gun before tearing out into the hallway. I caught sight of a few guards ahead of me as they hit the stairs but wasn't surprised to find myself bringing up the rear. This was the security wing after all, they'd probably drilled this a hundred times.

I headed for the garage while most of them seemed to head outside. Probably to secure the grounds and investigate what the fuck was going on. My ego was salved a little when I started to run into the other members of the Reserves, many of whom were still trying to pull armor on as they ran this way and that.

Illyahn and Erana were already in the garage when I got there, the elder sister helping the other with her protection. That she was doing so despite the fact that her own armor remained sitting in a heap next to them earned her several points in my book.

"Boss." Illyahn greeted me when I slid to a stop next to them, "Little help?"

I batted at her hands, "I got hers, get your own on."

She backed off, reluctantly I thought, and picked up her chest plate. I glanced up at Erana to find the young woman biting nervously at her lip while her tarah twitched wildly up and down. Up close she wasn't quite as comely as her sister, though she had the same tattoos bisecting her eyes.

"You're new to this too?" I asked.

"Yes." She said quietly. "Um, we haven't formally met, honored Human. Are you a Guide or a Hunter?"

Something told me that telling her she was a good decade plus older

305

wouldn't go down well. "I'm not really sure what the dividing line for my species would be to be honest. Probably a Hunter. See what I'm doing with your left arm? Do the same to your right while I check your back-plate."

Erana gave me a quick nod and did as instructed. "I'm sorry. I'm... um, I'm not a very good Trahcon, I'm not... suited for this."

"I'm not suited for this either so don't feel bad." Her armor was a lot lower quality than mine from what I could tell. They'd probably bought it themselves before they'd been assigned here. It would probably stop light rounds but she hadn't had time to pull a proper under-armor weave on.

Given her height, that left a lot of her exposed.

"I'm guessing you two are both assigned here?" I asked. "Sit in the back and use your sorcery?"

"Yes. Um, well, yes and no." She took a quick breath before replying, "We're to assist you in preparing your powered armor and ensure no one attacks you from the rear."

My fingers paused, "...Nynsi order that?"

"Yes."

I surprised myself by growling. Illyahn I could maybe understand. Young for her species but from her calm demeanor, and the confident way she was armoring up, she had experience in a fight. I'd rather her not be here, but if the mansion was under attack I'd accept her picking up a gun to defend it.

From the uncontrolled way her tarah were shaking Erana was clearly on the verge of a panic attack. She should have been barricaded in her goddamned room, or helping the doctor prep his medical tools or something.

...fuck.

"Illyahn." I glanced at my assistant, "Soon as you're done, get your sister back to your rooms. Have her lock the door and jam anything you can move in front of it. You can stay and guard her or come back, your choice."

The amazonian Trahcon went still. "...we've got our orders from the

Lady, boss."

"I don't really care." I said flatly. "If you're really my assistant, then do it. I'll take any blame that gets thrown around."

She stared at me for a handful seconds, then grinned. "I think I could really get to like you, Cie. I'll be right back, come on you!"

Her sister managed a squawk of protest when her larger sister hauled her off. I watched them go then got back to my own preparations.

The suit was technically functional if still banged up. We'd fixed the internal problems and I'd gotten most of the armor back on, which was good. The problem was that the armor that was still off was the rear-left protection over the power core... which was insanely bad.

I hesitated for a bit, mulling it over, then started booting it up anyway. So long as I kept my ass to the wall I'd be fine, and it wasn't like I'd be of much use outside of the thing. And the expectant glances from the staff members moving cars into blocking positions made their opinion pretty clear. All of them knew how many losses we'd taken in our last fight. How few security guards remained to run out and serve as the first line of defense.

The Reserves were worried. And they wanted a Human meat-shield.

And they'd be pretty upset if I refused.

Triggering the hydraulics, I watched the torso slide open before starting to climb up the cursed thing. I'd just balanced myself on its shoulders when there was another ping across the intercom system.

"All forces," Nynsi sounded both disgusted and tired, *"Stand down. It was a harassment operation. Evidently my father believes himself to be in the SRT. Team Five will remain on perimeter patrol, all other teams stand down."*

About the only part of that I got was the stand down order. I was about to try and comm her to ask what the hell was going on when she beat me to the punch; my wrist-comp lighting up with an incoming call.

Sitting down on top of my armor, I tapped the accept button. "So what the fuck happened?"

The floating screen flickered once, then updated to show Nynsi's irritated features. *"We can discuss that in a moment. How tired are you?"*

I blinked. "I'm pretty awake but I don't know how long that will last. Why?"

"I need a sparring partner and you're the only one available."

Another blink. "How am I the only one available?"

"Just meet me in the ballroom, please."

Ten minutes later found me doing my best to stretch my tired arms out while Nynsi removed her armor with furious, jerky motions. Underneath she proved to be wearing the form fitting under-suit that... well, fit her very well. Of course that fact that she'd managed to get into that either meant she was a hell of a lot faster at it than me, or she was so paranoid that she slept in it.

Considering the message from dear old dad, I was betting on the latter.

"So..." I drawled as I stretched my legs, using the motions to adjust the fall mats she'd pulled out of a closet.

"No one from outside the family would risk harming me in hand to hand sparring." Nynsi tossed her gauntlets aside before starting to stretch as well. "Rehat is obviously unavailable, and Ghai is occupied standing guard over my uncle. That leaves me with you or one of the sisters."

That reminded me. "Speaking of, what the hell is with Erana being assigned to the reserves? She was on the verge of having a bloody panic attack."

Dark eyes blinked rapidly. "She what?"

I told her what I'd witnessed, and subsequently ordered. She considered that as she carefully settled into a lunge position. "...I see. Speaking honestly I assumed she was as combat capable as any other young

308

Trahcon. Most of them are rather eager to see battle. Was her sister the same way?"

"No, Illyahn seemed like she could handle herself."

"Ah. Very well. I will speak with them in the morning."

I nodded and did my best not to stare. Her stretching routine was far stiffer and more cautious than mine. It must have been something more than just their culture and language that kept them so upright. Maybe all the cartilage plates left them inflexible.

"So what happened tonight?" I asked as I loosened my arms. "What was that about harassment and SRT?"

Her lips twisted. "Special Reconnaissance Teams. The Ascendancy's premier commando force, they specialize in what we call disruptive assaults. I believe your species refers to them as terror attacks."

I winced. "Harassment... those fuckers just wanted to wake everyone up, didn't they?"

"Yes." Nysni growled before eyeing me. "How much training do you have in close combat?"

"I can wrestle, know the basics of boxing. Did a bit of fencing in college." I paused self consciously. "I wasn't very good at the last."

"How fortunate that we won't be using blades. I believe we should avoid causing damage to another. Grappling and slow throws only?"

I nodded, blew out a breath, then settled into a low staggered stance. Nynsi had just begun to draw herself up but paused on seeing me lose most of my height.

"...this will be interesting." Her own stance was, as I could have guessed, far more upright than mine. Hands came up near her breasts, fingers flexing and spreading as she took a cautious step forwards.

I slid a little to my right and did my best to take in all of her at once. We continued that slow dance for a few more steps; her slowly advancing while I retreated and made her keep turning to face me directly. That lasted until she was in grab range, where she made a quick lunge.

Batting aside her right hand with my left, I surged upwards directly into her guard. That seemed to take her by surprise and I managed to get my right hand around the back of her neck before she could block me. Our foreheads banged together as we grappled, one of her hands clamping on my forearm to try and wrench it loose while the other went for my waist.

I let her so that I could get my left hand around her shoulder, grasping my hands into a firm lock before surging upwards at the same time I twisted in place.

Nynsi was a lot heavier than I'd have guessed, which was saying something given I'd expected her to weigh more than me just from her height.

I had to seriously work to actually throw her over my hip and bring her down onto the ground, her breath coming out in an explosive gasp as most of my weight came down on her chest.

"A point for me?" I asked. The same neanderthal part of me that had noticed how well her under-armor fit thought that being half on top of a woman was all kinds of interesting. That the woman was an alien who I really shouldn't be thinking about in that way didn't bother it at all.

Damned hormones.

She blinked a few times before chuckling, some of her anger fading. "That's what I get for underestimating you. Off."

I obliged and we both got back up to our feet. "Can we expect more late night wake up calls?"

"In all probability."

Nynsi's new stance was far more balanced, far more serious than her last. I retreated laterally when she made a quick advance, then made the mistake of buying a feinted attempt to grab at my head.

The moment I straightened and brought my hands up to deflect she surged forwards and dropped her own arms to grab my legs.

I got a nice view of the ceiling as she heaved me up before rather gently driving my back into the mat. Of course the soft fall didn't stop her weight from coming down on me, and it was my turn to gasp as the air was driven out of my lungs. "Ow..."

Hands planted themselves on either side of my head as she smirked down at me, "One to one."

We ended up going to best of nine, which she handily won five to two. My only other win came when I went into an extremely low stance and got an ankle, jerking her leg up and out from under her. Even getting it close to parallel with the floor had unbalanced her enough that I'd managed to take her down.

But mostly I got my ass kicked.

The sad truth was that in a close quarters fight size and strength mattered a lot. I wasn't exactly weak, but Thondians didn't operate on Human scales. She might not have been as strong or brawny as a Thondian man, but she was at least as strong as me and weighed a lot more. Combine that with her definitely superior skill and I didn't have much of a chance.

When we'd finished putting the mats away, we wandered out in the hall to settle on the same bench we'd sat and talked on last time.

"We can expect anywhere from weeks or months of events like this." Nynsi explained quietly. "They'll continue with minor night raids or sabotage infrastructure at first. Maybe engage with local media if they want to be particularly irritating. Then it will progress to sniping, bombs, or other such impersonal attacks."

I let my head fall back against the wall. "I think I get it. They'll wear us down with all the alerts and problems, make us run around until we're sick of it. Then pick us off when we make mistakes. Do that until we're weak enough they can finish us off."

"Essentially. It is The most basic strategy employed by the SRT. Particularly effective against our own race." Her eyes closed as she sighed. "The loss of control, the loss of face... it can and does lead to poor decisions."

"I can see that." I frowned, "But that's a pretty long term strategy for someone being hunted by Imperial Intelligence and Internal-Security. Plus whatever resources your uncle has."

Nynsi gave the tiniest of nods. "Yes, which worries him. And myself. My father is either very confident he can avoid us for the duration of such a plan, or this is simply the first step in another. And I will not be getting any further sleep tonight in case he intends to lull us into a false sense of security before striking."

I considered that. It made a kind of sense in the same way as the long plan, just condensed. Wake everyone up, then fall back and let them relax, then hit them again just when they started to sleep. "...shit. Now I'm going to be up all night as well."

"My apologies. However, I would point out that you are not unintelligent and would have likely considered that sooner rather than later."

"Yeah, wasn't blaming you." I waved a hand vaguely, "Think I'm going to go back to the garage. See if I can't get ahead on fixing the suit tonight."

She nodded and rose alongside me, "If you are capable of multi-tasking, I would like to continue our language lessons as well."

I paused mid-step and glanced back her. "Would you?"

"If we are going to continue to work together for some time, it would be best if you could understand more than merely Caranat." She pointed out reasonably.

"Uh huh. And this has nothing to do with your, ah, academic interest?"

For a split second she seemed to lock in place, then shifted her weight a little in the same embarrassed pose I'd seen only a tiny handful of times. "No."

In spite of everything I felt myself smiling a little, "Liar."

It was amusing to watch how quickly she changed her body language towards one of anger, "That is an exceptionally rude thing to call one's host, Cieran Kean."

Snorting, I turned away and repeated myself in English. "Liar."

"...yout... area... rude."

"You are rude." I corrected as we started walking to the garage, where we would spend the rest of the night waiting for an attack that never came.

After all, Chacksin was too busy murdering cops up north to bother with us.

To my complete lack of surprise, Tasir didn't invite me to the emergency conference the next day. I honestly didn't mind. The meeting was occurring at the local Internal Security District Headquarters, maybe as a power play by Tasir to stop Xerol from hosting. Or maybe just because they'd been the ones actually attacked last night.

Plus I was exhausted from spending all evening working, teaching English, and learning Kho'voik.

I'd shuffled back to bed an hour or so after everyone else had roused themselves, and I didn't wake up again until well after noon. Evidently our all night session had given Nynsi confidence because the first thing I felt was one of her hands playing with my hair. I slowly opened my eyes to find her sitting on the edge of my bed in the same suit she'd left in this morning.

"Enjoying..." I yawned, "...yourself?"

I expected her to pull away but instead she ran all of her fingers across my scalp once again. "It is far softer than I thought it would be. The texture is quite pleasant as well. Is this inappropriate?"

Considering that she was effectively petting me, definitely. On the other hand it was a fairly pleasant way to wake up. "I won't tell anyone if you won't."

"I will take that as a yes." She slowly stood, reluctantly pulling her hand away. "I had lunch delivered for you. If you could please eat and clean yourself?"

I nodded through another yawn, "Sure. Thank you. I'm surprised you didn't just go collapse into bed."

Nynsi stepped back so that I could throw my blankets off. Thanks to a night of paranoia I'd gone to sleep fully dressed with my armor at the foot of the bed. "I've had two energy drinks and will likely need more to make it to this evening. Once you're ready, please come down to the armory for a discussion."

That made me pause before rising. "The armory?"

"Yes. I will explain then. Will you be ready by the next hour?"

A finger-slide over my wrist-comp brought up the time, "Yeah, easily."

She gave me a little bow that I quickly stood up to return, then left. It took me until the door had closed behind her to realize that I'd been staring at her ass again. Dammit. I needed to stop doing that. And I needed to not encourage her anymore than I already had. There were already enough rumors about us, adding fuel to that particular fire could complicate things. *Would* complicate things.

Xerol seemed fine with us being friends but I was fairly certain he wouldn't be thrilled if we became more than that.

Of course that was assuming she was even interested. Yes, she seemed to like me. And my hair. But was she angling for something more than that, or did she just want to encourage me to stick around? And how would anything physical even work? I sort of assumed the parts would kind of line up but I'd drawn the line on doing any, ah, 'research' on that particular subject.

There was also the fact that I wasn't sure if I really liked her or if I was reading way too much into things thanks to the complete lack of Human company.

"Get your head out of the fucking gutter." I told myself firmly. "You can think about that later. If there even is a later."

Fortified by my self-improvement speech I did my best to get ready. Cleaning up after a night of working on the suit was my first priority. Once I was done showering I debated about what I should wear. Well, not what outfit I should wear so much as whether or not I should wear the first layer of armor underneath. That debate lasted just as long as it took me to remember every fucked up thing that had happened to me since I'd woken up on this planet.

The form fitting under-suit went on.

Once I'd gotten a casual outfit over-top I wolfed down both of the small sandwiches that Nynsi had brought up. She'd also delivered a bottle of Demtri, a brand of iced tea with enough alien sugars and uppers to leave me shaking if I did anything more than sip at it. It was probably terrible for me but it got me woken up in a hurry.

I was still a bit early so I took my time wandering downstairs. I paused twice to simply enjoy the sunlight coming through the windows. Frivolous maybe, but it wouldn't be long now before we were stuck inside of several months of darkness. I wanted to bask in the simple pleasures while I could.

Nynsi wasn't in the armory when I arrived, but Chen and Marn both were. Like me they were in casual dress, and under their sleeves I could see the tile patterns of armored cloth. So at least I wasn't alone in my paranoia.

"Hey Kean." The male of the pair glanced at me when I entered. "The lady invited you too huh?"

"Apparently." I gave them both a polite, neutral bow that they returned. "Afternoon Chen, Marn. Any idea what this is about? She didn't say much."

Marn regarded me without much expression. She was a particularly blunt-faced woman with larger than normal armored sections along her throat and jawline. "I presume the conference this morning. We were not allowed into the room."

"Huh. Who all was there?"

She twitched a shoulder, "Internal-Security from three districts, Tasir, some of her people, a representative for the Imperial Ambassador, and two agents of the High Families."

I fought down the urge to whistle. "Big event."

There was a grunt from Chen, "Yeah but it was missing a few people. No one from the Crescent showed up. I'm guessing that's what we need to talk about. Plus tomorrow."

"Tomorrow?" I frowned. "What's going on tomorrow?"

The man's face twisted and his body shifted to show... disgust, I thought. "The Board of High Families summoned Xerol for another hearing. Which is annoying at the best of times, but those smug little bastards are at their damned resort instead of at their normal tower in the Core City."

I waited but he didn't elaborate. "...which means?"

An irritated whistle came from Marn. "It's in the Ocean-Front, and it's a security nightmare because it's so close to the Crescent's headquarters. The parking structure is separated a good half-mile distant to maintain a no-fly zone in the area. Have to ride a monorail the rest of the way. An elevated one."

"Shields?" I asked.

She nodded, "And other measures, but there are a great many things that can go wrong over that distance. It would be much simpler if we could simply fly in and then out."

Ah. I supposed I could see how that would make protecting Xerol a lot harder but I wasn't sure what it had to do with me. I wasn't of much use outside of my armor and I seriously doubted it would fit on a passenger train. Or be appropriate for a meeting with the High Families.

Neither of them seemed in the mood to chat further so we settled into a companionable silence. Chen looked like he was checking Strike-Wave scores on his wrist-comp while Marn simply leaned against a wall and closed her eyes. I elected to follow her example, but had only just relaxed when the door hissed open to reveal Nynsi.

"Everyone is early. Good." She closed the door behind her before pulling a small device from her belt. It was a small black box with a dial and buttons on one side, nothing particularly impressive.

At least until she set it on one of the workbenches and turned it on.

"Gah!" The not-word came when a piercing whine rose and then trailed off into a kind of static buzz, "What the fuck is that?"

317

Marn had also flinched, reaching up to cover her long ears, lowering them when the initial shriek faded. "A jammer. You believe there are listening devices present?"

"Tasir's level of information at the conference was... concerning." Nynsi replied, arms crossing high on her chest as the three of us came to stand near her. "If she could have informants or listening devices then my father certainly could."

"Likely does." Chen flexed his hands into fists before relaxing them. "We don't usually sweep the cars for anything besides explosives, and Ullika had access to all of them."

"Quite." She tipped her head towards him, "I believe this room to be secure but I am taking no chances until we can conduct a full sweep of the building. And all of our vehicles."

The tall man shook his head, "Fuck. Do we even trust the staff we usually use for those checks?"

She exhaled through her teeth, "I did before this morning. Still, that is a discussion for later. First you should know what occurred after the perimeter sensors were tripped"

The short version was that Chacksin was a hell of a lot more skilled than the True Sons. He'd used a series of petty crimes to lure Internal-Security teams from the River District and the Outskirts out into the open. Then he'd hit them with a mixture of snipers and car bombs, vanishing before reinforcements could show up to pin his people down.

Seven cops had died and at least twice that many were wounded. Internal-Security was in a complete and total uproar but most of their dedicated combat types were already going after the True Sons thanks to our discovery of the slave facility. *That* mess had turned into something like an open battle in the northern Industrial Sector. The gangsters were getting their asses kicked but they were dying slowly enough to make things difficult.

From what Nynsi could tell the various district branches were now arguing with each other over what to do. The local cops wanted those in the other districts to show up and help them crush the problems, flush out Chacksin through sheer weight of numbers. Those in the Core City and

Ocean-Front were refusing anything but more investigative types. They wanted to keep their heavy teams to protect the Board, the other wealthy elites, and the city's primary starport.

To make matters even more complicated Tasir and the Imperial Ambassador both wanted to bring in commando teams to hunt down Chacksin on their own. That was the only thing everyone else on Alume refused to even consider, which had left the Imperials in a snit.

"So it's a complete and total mess." I said when she finished. "No one's actually in charge and no one can agree who should be dealing with White Storm."

"Essentially." Nynsi agreed.

Marn stirred, "What about Crescent? Are they still not communicating?"

There was an angry sounding huff before Nynsi tilted her body right and forwards in what she'd told me meant anger. "The White Storm's Captains declared Chacksin rogue this morning. Kolkris evidently believes them."

I frowned. "I thought she was a paranoid lunatic? Why is she buying an obvious lie?"

"That is an excellent question. First, however, we must discuss what is occurring tomorrow." Dark eyes flicked between the other two Thondians present. "The pair of you are the only squad leaders we have left with my cousin still recovering. Chen, as the senior leader you will be accompanying Ghai in protecting the Patriarch."

He didn't look thrilled but nodded, "I'm down to three in my squad and you've got one of them protecting *Tarath* Rehat. I'll need more men."

"You'll have them." Nynsi promised, "Teams One and Three have enough recovered men between them, you'll be taking all ten with you. Marn? You will be commanding the mansion's defense with everyone that's left."

The taciturn woman nodded, "I would be happy to do so, *Kasha* Shaaryak. But it would be more appropriate for you to have command."

"Tasir is holding a second meeting, one that my uncle would prefer to be at rather than listening to the High Families berate him." Anger touched her voice and posture before she smoothed both out, "I will be going in his stead. Cieran will be my bodyguard, if you consent to such a thing. You will be paid per your contract with my uncle."

I blinked a few times before rolling a shoulder in a Trahcon-style shrug. "I can go with but I don't know how useful I'll be."

Nynsi made a dismissive motion, "It will be held at the same building as this morning. We will be surrounded by Internal-Security forces, Imperial Agents, and the Paragons alone know who else will be invited. A bodyguard is more of a formality."

I started to nod, paused, then snorted. "You just want me there to annoy Tasir, don't you?"

The lady of the house somehow managed to look even more superior and stately than usual. "I am certain I do not know what you could be referencing, Cieran Kean."

Chen and I both smothered grins while Marn simply shook her head and focused on more important things. "I understand your reasoning in all three assignments, *Kasha,* but I'm afraid I do not understand why we must discuss this in private. These are hardly confidential matters."

That was a good point and I settled down. "Are we up to something else?"

A tight exhalation went with Nynsi's slight nod. "Tasir has a potential contact, a Crescent officer who is willing to talk. However they refuse to be seen anywhere near Tasir or any member of Internal-Security. Tasir... volunteered Cieran and I to meet with them in her stead."

I noted the hesitation. "This isn't something we can decline, is it?"

"No." She said shortly. "We cannot."

"Well shit. Will we have any kind of backup from her end?"

"She claimed that we would," There was another sharp breath. "We will see if any such aid is provided. That is why I wished to speak with you both on this matter. If things are not what they seem we may need extraction."

Marn nodded seriously. "Where will the meet take place?"

"The Temple of Iriahn in the River District."

The location made me grimace. Meeting an informant wasn't anything like agreeing to open battle, so I didn't really have any practical objections. The location on the other hand... "I've seen it, never been inside. Can't say that the Aspect of Greed and Indulgence is the kind of god I want looking over a clandestine meeting though."

Chen huffed, "Perpetually optimistic *and* superstitious. You really are fun to have around."

"Fuck you too." I shook my head while he chuckled, "That's not a very large temple but it's right on the river. Lot of traffic going both ways if we have to run for it, but also a lot of apartments overlooking it. Your father could setup snipers anywhere."

Marn titled her head a hair to the left, "He is correct, *Kasha.* I do not like the idea of you going there with only one guard and vague promises. Perhaps he should go in without you, if you are willing?"

That last bit was clearly directed at me. "I can't say I like that anymore than both of us going in, but it's probably smarter."

Nynsi waved a single hand. "No, we will go in together. I do not mean to offend, Cieran, but you have no familiarity with the Crescent or their people. Additionally, if we must shoot our way out it would be better to be near one another. Laria would find a way to assassinate me if I sent you in alone and then lost you."

The only female squad leader huffed. "Then at least take additional guards with. I will have the reserves here. Take a half-team in a car."

"And leave Rehat with fewer protectors?" Nynsi shook her head once. "No. He must be defended at any cost, especially with my Patriarch out of the mansion."

Neither squad leader looked happy with that but they didn't argue with her.

"That is everything for now. Prepare your people as best you can but allow them to believe I will be remaining here. Cieran? Please stay in your usual routine. I know you will want to but do not discuss this with Laria."

I grimaced. "She's not going to like that. At all."

A shrug. "In that case simply blame me. She will anyway."

"Fair point."

III – VI

The inside of the Temple of Iriahn was as ostentatious as you could expect given that particular Aspect's nature. Lots of gold and silver reliefs of a male Trahcon, almost all of them showing him lounging amid art or wealth. Plus a few of him indulging in fine foods or, ah, more carnal activities.

A priest wearing only a gold plated kilt offered us wine when we entered. Thankfully he didn't take any offense when we refused, and helpfully pointed us to the stairs leading to the second floor balcony. He also didn't comment on the fact that we weren't really dressed for church being covered necks to feet in armor.

"Are Human temples anything like this?" Nynsi asked we walked across the main area of worship. Couches, throw pillows, and other comfortable seats all surrounded an obsidian statue of Iriahn. Other doorways were all along the walls but none were open.

"Not really." I glanced around. "Some of them can get pretty fancy but most aren't this, ah, over the top. What about Thondian ones?"

Her lips twisted down, "Manifestly not. Honored copies of the Pillars are always built in the open air, and none are anything like this. At least the Temples to Ashahn have *some* sense of good taste."

"I've never been in one of those. Or any of the other Aspects for that matter."

She twitched a shoulder as we reached the stairs, heading up to the second level. "Iriahn and Ashahn are the major gods they worship here. I believe that says quite enough about the priorities of the local Trahcon."

I thought about that as we walked. I didn't really know all that much about the polytheistic faith that most Trahcon followed, save that it sounded vaguely similar to Hinduism. They had a whole lot of Gods or Aspects that may or may not have been part of some greater whole. And, so far as I could tell, all of them had their good and bad sides.

But part of me really couldn't disagree with Nynsi. That the locals worshiped a literal representation of greed and excess probably *did* say quite a bit about them.

The second floor proved to be a circular balcony overlooking the first. More couches and lounge chairs were setup near the railing so everyone could look at the central statue in relative comfort. The main difference was that the doors up here open, showing off private rooms that seemed to be much smaller copies of the main worship area.

Nynsi checked her wrist comp, glanced around once, then set off for the second door on the left. Inside we found that our supposed contact was already present.

A Trahcon man of average height was sitting on a long couch in the center of the room. He wore full armor colored burnt orange with black highlights, the binary sun logo of the Crescent on his chestplate. The most striking thing about him was his facial tattoos, wild bright red patterns covering everything but his Tarah.

"A sandwalker and a savanna walk into a room?" He shook his head when I closed the door behind us, "It's like the start of a bad joke."

Nynsi took a calming breath as she stopped about a yard away. I joined her but turned a bit, trying to make sure I could watch both him and the door we'd come through.

"In the interest of avoiding personal names, what should I call you?" She asked.

A gray finger tapped against his face, "Red will do. I know who you are, Shaaryak. The savanna I don't, and I'll just call him that unless he takes offense."

I shook my head once. "I'll tolerate it. I won't tolerate short-fur."

He nodded agreeably. "Very well. Your Imperial friends want to know why Kolkris and the Crescent aren't acting during the current crisis, yes?"

"The Imperials gave me a very long list of questions." She replied dryly, "But the only ones I intend to ask relate to current events."

"Good because those are the only ones I intend to answer." Red paused, leaning back as he seemed to consider his words. "There are elements within my organization that fear White Storm has subverted key individuals. Particularly those who directly care for our leader. Her instability has grown noticeably worse over the past several years, a reverse of the recovery she had been showing earlier."

Oh boy. "Poison?"

"Perhaps." He looked my way, "We're not sure but it is a likely explanation. She has angered all of her children to the point where none have been on Alume for the past six months. They took a great deal of our elites with them. What I am certain is that someone in the Evening Crescent's communications department has been subverted."

Nynsi let out a soft hiss, "You tried to call for reinforcements?"

"My direct superior attempted to contact Admiral Leska'kolkris but the return made little sense. She then attempted to reach out through other channels, and the next morning was seized and accused of treason." Red rubbed tiredly at his face, tarah drooping. "A great deal of evidence had appeared overnight. Whoever they are they're doing an excellent job of isolating the Queen."

Her dark eyes narrowed. "You believe they intend to assassinate her."

Red shrugged, "From the news you lot fucked over his big plan. If he doesn't do something equally crippling to us his own superiors are going to murder him the second he leaves Alume."

Which we'd already guessed. We'd even thought he might try and knock off Kolkris before dismissing it as impractical at best and impossible at worst. What we'd apparently missed was just how screwed up Crescent was on the inside. Or, apparently, how badly White Storm had subverted them.

"How would they accomplish it?" Nynsi continued. "Kolkris is supposed to be a vicious combatant on her own, and I find it difficult to believe that a large number of her inner circle has been bought or blackmailed into standing against her."

A snort was his initial response to that. "Sure, the Queen is a one woman army when it comes to a fight. But the only people left around her are the ones who can manage her moods without getting killed. Lot of the more competent types are out at Cathia waiting for Leska to commit regicide."

I shook my head once again, "So people around her have motive but that doesn't explain the *how*. If going up against her directly is so stupid then can he get a sniper close to her? Crash a ship into her palace?"

"Any ship that gets close would be engaged by the defenses." Red twitched his left tarah. "She does occasionally leave so a sniper is possible, but those of us still loyal are doing our best to keep her inside the palace. A direct assault is virtually impossible. The reason I reached out to that old Imperial bitch was that an indirect attack may be possible."

It took me a second to realize what he was getting at. "If they've got someone in your communications teams, they can fake an ID and come in that way."

"Exactly."

Nynsi considered him for a moment, then asked, "What are you requesting from us?"

Red spread his hands apart, "White Storm is on a time limit. Before my superior got herself arrested, she and I sent other members of our pack with sealed data drives by courier ships. As soon as they reach Ithiri and Leska they'll know what's happening. Once they learn of what's going on here I expect both to come at once."

"How long?" She pressed.

"The couriers should be arriving late tonight or tomorrow, depending on how behaved the trade-lanes are. I expect them to demand an FTL transmission with the Queen as soon as that happens."

It clicked in my head. "Which will be blocked if you're right about where your traitor is. That'll make both of them come back for sure, but it'll also tip off Chacksin. The traitor will tell him he doesn't have much time."

A gray finger pointed at me. "Precisely, savanna. What I need from the Imperials is to have forces on stand-by to engage him long enough for the garrison to be alerted. If she agrees, tell her to message the same inbox as before. I will send out personnel to mark the best observation spots, though I'm certain they already know them."

"Very well." Nynsi gave him a polite bow, "We will relay your information and your request."

Red nodded and rose in a smooth motion, giving her a slight bow in return. "Good. I've got to get back to the compound before I'm missed. You both seem professional, hope you don't get killed."

"Travel safely and wisely." A motion had me heading to the door. At a nod from her I cautiously opened it, and when I found nothing outside besides the mostly empty temple, I stepped out.

Nynsi followed, then Red. He gave us a final little nod then briskly headed for a different set of stairs compared to the ones we'd used. Nynsi had us wait until he was out of sight before we likewise got moving.

"Seems like we were wrong." I offered once we were on the ground floor. "About Kolkris."

She let out a whistling sigh and nodded, "I did not know that her children were off world. Neither did my uncle. It did not seem that Tasir did either."

Which seemed like the kind of thing a big-shot Imperial spy should have known. I was about to say as much when several figures clad in gray armor entered the central chamber just ahead of us.

Paranoid instinct got me moving the moment I realized they were all openly carrying weapons. Nynsi was a beat faster than me, going for her gun... something I rather ruined by grabbing her and shoving her against the wall.

It turned out to be the right call because a shotgun roared past to obliterate a painting behind where we'd just been.

"*Ghash.*" A Thondian voice snarled as half a dozen tall aliens moved to block us. All of them had heavy shotguns, their barrels aimed right at our heads. He followed up the probable swear word with a torrent of Kho'voik that I was so accented I couldn't get the gist of it.

Nynsi hissed as she looked at all of them, and then at me. We might have been armored up but our helmets were hanging from straps on our belt. Our new friends hadn't made that mistake which rather limited our options. Especially because the only cover available to us was a bunch of stylish but non-bulletproof couches.

I took a closer look at them and tried to think of any options. At second glance the armor wasn't the same high quality stuff we'd seen from the other 'actual' True Sons. It looked more like these were a bunch of the usual fodder who'd managed to find enough pieces to actually make full suits.

Sadly the guns they were holding looked brand new, and with all six of them vaguely pointed at us that didn't give us many options.

My companion evidently agreed. She kept her gun down while replying in the same tongue. I got about one word in four, enough to tell that she was telling them to get lost. Not that they would, and she'd know as much. She was probably trying to stall for time.

All six of them laughed at her. Their leader recovered enough to chortle out something else, shifting his gun in my direction.

"That is quite enough."

I turned, along with everyone else, to see the same kilted priest standing near the central statue. His hands were on his hips, his tarah tilted up and out in anger. "This is not the place for your alien squabbles. Out. All of you."

The True Sons let out another chorus of laughs, the leader keeping his gun on me but nodded towards one of the others. His grunt took steps to the right, aimed, and then put a solid slug right into the priest's bare chest.

It hammered into invisible barrier and did nothing at all to harm the small man.

"Fine then." The Priest spoke in the stunned silence. "I will evict you."

He made a side-arm throwing gesture and a nine-foot long couch abruptly flung itself across the room at speeds I would normally associate with small aircraft. It struck the shooter end-on, driving him off his feet and slamming him into the curved wall hard enough to crack his armor. What was left of the couch fell apart a few seconds before his broken body tipped sideways to clatter onto the ground.

A scream of fury came from the True Son leader, all five remaining gangster turning to open fire. The priest's other hand rose palm-out in the universal sign to stop, and the barrage slammed into a ghostly blue wall of energy. Nynsi began to raise her gun but I quickly reached out and pushed back down, nodding to the entrance.

"No nullifiers. Poor shielding." The Trahcon man chastised the gangsters as the gunfire fell off. "No grenades. Ashul told me to take you seriously but it is difficult to do so. Especially when you don't even bother to conduct proper reconnaissance."

Any reply that the gang leader may have offered went unsaid when another priest took his head off with a sword.

The four True Sons that were left turned and tried to fight.

All of them were dead in under a minute when twice their number of Trahcon priests jumped them from behind.

I just kind of... stared while it happened.

The priests were all wearing the same gold-tiled kilts as the first, but unlike him each was wielding the same kind of kukri-style swords I'd seen Trenah and Ghai carrying.

Of course I'd never seen the cutting edges of theirs glowing with blue-white fire. Or seen little bursts of static electricity arcing from the weapons to anything nearby.

The True Sons hadn't been wearing the best armor but it had still been *armor*, and the priests had cut through it like it wasn't there. All of the wounds had been mostly cauterized meaning there wasn't much blood on the ground. On the other hand the scent of ozone did not go well with the scent of burned Thondian flesh.

Nynsi took a cautious step towards the first priest when the others lowered their weapons, the fire fading from them. "Would you be the backup that Tasir promised?"

"Indeed." He replied, "Friends? Do clean up the mess, and send someone to buy a new couch. Take it out of my expense account."

I shared an uncertain look with Nynsi before she tried again, "Thank you. We will depart, with your permission."

A gray hand waved. "No thanks are required, the aid was purchased fairly. Tell Ashul'tasir that we did our part, and that if she requires our help again she will need to pay accordingly."

We both bowed then cautiously picked our way through the priests and body parts. Neither one of us spoke even when we'd gotten back outside. I breathed deeply, enjoying the clean air, and from her expression Nynsi was doing much the same.

The walk back to her luxury car didn't take long, and even in armor the seats were sinfully comfortable.

"Can we go one day without people trying to kill us?" I asked while she started up the engine. "It's getting old."

"I find myself agreeing." Her eyes closed for a long moment as she simply breathed. "It is beyond tiring. The new from the informant offers some improvement. We now know that this will be over within the next day or the day after. One way or another."

"Yeah." One way or another. "Report in to your uncle, then head back and eat something?"

She let out low hum. "I see no problems with this plan. Could you please open the connection? He should be back at the mansion by now."

I shrugged and tapped at the car's console. She'd set the display to read in Caranat, probably just for me, so it didn't take me long to start the call.

Xerol didn't pick up.

I pursed my lips, changed to the security list, and tried Chen.

He didn't pick up either.

Nynsi's fingers had tightened around the controls by the time I tried Marn.

She didn't pick up.

"Fuck."

Nynsi didn't say anything, she just jammed the throttle against its stop and pointed us towards Koshun Minor.

III – VII

The mansion was on fire when we arrived.

It was entirely surrounded by flashing lights as various emergency vehicles kept a perimeter. Three Internal-Security cars screamed in to try and force us down before we were more than a few blocks away, only backing off after Nynsi had snarled her identity across the radio. Even then they made it clear we were to follow a direct line to the western part of the grounds.

All of the damage seemed concentrated around the over sized garage. The heavy doors had been blown apart, with parts of them littered across the garden. A good portion of the roof had crumbled on that side, giving the entire structure a slumped appearance. Fire flickered inside but the grisly details were mostly being covered up by smoke.

Several heavy firefighting trucks had landed or were hovering nearby, foam and water spraying out to contain the blaze. More Internal-Security vehicles were lingering protectively above and around them but they paled in comparison to the amount parked on the grounds.

Most of those must have been empty because I could see a veritable army of cops who were busy keeping half of Koshun Minor outside of the walls.

"Everyone's out to see what happened." I noted as Nynsi was finally forced to slow down. "Looks like half of Koshun Minor."

"And how many of my father's loyalists are among them?" She snarled.

I winced and kept my mouth shut the rest of the way down.

Nynsi didn't land gently, the expensive vehicle shuddering with the force of the impact, but I don't think she cared. A fist slammed the shut-down button before she was out, leaving me to scramble after her.

She didn't have far to stalk since three people were already headed our way. One was Illyahn, the woman helping Rane'li shuffle along. Dwarfed by the two six foot plus women was the same detective we'd run into at Forever all those weeks ago. His name was... Wear'ahn, right.

"What happened?" Nynsi demanded the moment we were close to enough to hear one another over the chaos around us.

The detective shook his head, "What it looks like Miss Shaaryak. Someone inside lowered the building's shields and disabled your radar suite. If you had any anti-aircraft weapons they went down as well. The moment your uncle's aerial convoy returned they ran at least three cars and an orbital shuttle filled with explosive into the hangar."

Her entire body seemed to quiver with anger. "My uncle?"

Illyahn and Wear'ahn both looked to Rane'li, who swallowed before speaking, "Casualties were heavy, *Tarath* Shaaryak."

Tarath... Lord.

Not Kasha. Lady.

I'd never seen Nynsi completely lose her composure before, but that title, that implication, that managed it.

She jerked as if she'd just been shot, took a half step back, then desperately put a hand on my shoulder to keep herself upright.

"His vehicle had just landed when the first explosion occurred." Rane'li continued in an almost monotone voice, "From what we can tell he was knocked unconscious by the blast. Harath'krem Ghai attempted to get him inside but the second car detonated before she could. It struck the reserve cars near the ceiling and knocked them loose. One of them landed on him."

Nynsi's mouth opened but nothing came out.

Illyahn sighed and took over, "Doctor Rae let Rehat get up to do some exercises, and they were both in there to greet Xerol when he landed. We think the first blast killed them instantly. Someone got to the door controls but the third car hit the east side and locked them up. Shuttle clipped the other side and detonated just past the threshold. It was probably supposed to burrow right into the mansion proper."

I licked my lips and asked, "Survivors? Ghai?"

"She's still alive." The hand not helping Rane'li stay up rose to rub tiredly at her face. "She might have been the one to make it to the controls. Blast pressure nearly killed her, don't know if she'll make it. They also found Chen and Kush still breathing but not in much better shape. They were in the car closest to the mansion. Already airlifted them out."

Nynsi found her voice, "How many others?"

"...none so far." Rane'li murmured. "There were six members of the garage team working, we've found all of their bodies. We still haven't found two of Chen's guard detail but the rest are accounted for."

"Christ. Jesus fucking Christ." I was pretty sure no one else understood the English swearing but they all seemed to agree with the tone. "Who was in the command room?"

Illyahn's expression darkened. "Almi, Mek, and Erana. Bitch sent my sister to get them something to drink then shot Mek in the back. Used his clearance codes to bring the whole security system down. Erana caught her leaving, the traitor tried to shoot her too. She got away and called me, then I caught the bitch when she tried to bail out the northern staff door."

Fingers tightened painfully around my shoulder, "Alive?"

My assistant growled. "She shot at my sister. Bitch is missing some teeth, and I ripped an ear off, but I stopped myself from breaking her fucking neck. She'll be able to answer questions."

Detective Wear'han waved to the right. "We have her in a secure vehicle with senior agents standing guard to ensure no one attempts to silence her."

There was a sharp nod before Nynsi asked another question, "Where is Marn?"

It was Rane'li's turn to wave towards the building, "She's overseeing the search and recovery efforts. Half of the remaining security team are helping, the rest have locked what staff remain in their rooms and are standing guard."

Cold but understandable given what had just happened.

"Trenah?" I asked.

Illyahn snorted. "Drugged. She tried to get out of bed to help, one of the Internal-Security medics put her under before she hurt herself. Erana is in there with her, and she locked everything. I made her swear to call me if anyone even touches the door."

I felt part of me relax a little, even if the situation in general remained a complete and total cluster-fuck. I knew that Nynsi and Xerol had been interrogating and watching the staff after the attack on the mansion. They hadn't been stupid or lazy about it, firing at least three people and turning a fourth over to the cops. Whoever Almi was, I didn't know her personally, she must have been far more paranoid and clever than the others Chacksin had bought.

Fuck, if Erana or Illyahn had been slower or less lucky she might have escaped altogether.

Beside me, Nynsi sucked in several deep breaths before straightening up to her full height once more. "Very well... very well. Rane'li, Illyahn, return to the control center at once. Inform Marn she is to continue coordination. The pair of you are to reset the entire security system and remove every security code. Generate new ones only for the four of us standing here."

When they nodded, she turned to Wear'ahn. "Detective. You have my utmost gratitude for your organization's aid today. I will not forget it. I wish to interrogate the prisoner as soon as possible, if that is convenient to you."

The slim man nodded, tarah rising slightly. "Just remember that she's in our custody, not yours. She'll likely be executed for the deaths she caused but it's going to be done officially. Not out of hand by you."

Nynsi tipped her head in reply. "I will endeavor to restrain myself. Cieran? I need you to contact the Koshun Minor starport and have two heavy shuttles transferred here under escort. As the mansion's security is obviously compromised, we will be transferring to a penthouse in the Core-City."

"All right." I glanced at everyone else before asking, "How many people are we bringing with?"

Her eyes narrowed in thought before she responded, "The four of us, Erana, Laria, Marn, then three combat personnel of my choosing. I will handle that after the interrogation. Everyone else will be transferred to... the Red Moon Hotel should have space. Can your people ensure security?"

The question was clearly directed to Wear'han, the cop rubbing at his chin before nodding. "I'll have to clear it with District Command, but we know they were all in your uncle's pay. Your pay now. We'll keep them under house arrest there until we can clear them. What should we do with your family's remains?"

"Their souls have departed, what remains are merely empty shells." She turned slightly then nodded towards a grove of trees. "Beyond those woods is where my aunt and cousin Chehat lay. Bury them there. I will... conduct the appropriate ceremonies once it is safe to do so."

Wear'ahn gave her a little bow, "It will be handled with respect."

"Good. Then let us begin."

I started to step away before remembering something else. Nynsi paused when I suddenly grabbed her hand when she went to pull it back, turning to me when I stepped closer to whisper, "Do you want me to call Tasir?"

She closed her eyes and shook her head once, her voice just as quiet. "By the Paragon's... yes, you should. Tell her to meet us at my penthouse. I'm assuming she knows quite well where it is."

The next several hours passed in a tired blur.

I made calls. I helped Illyahn haul a comatose Trenah out into the shuttle. Then I went back and helped Rane'li when her still recovering body gave out on her. During that particular walk I saw several police respectfully carrying Xerol's body to its final resting place.

It was... well, he'd been crushed by a falling aircar. He was broken. Badly.

I won't lie, that sight rattled me. I hadn't known him for very long but Xerol had felt like an immovable object from the first time I'd met him. More of a permanent fixture than a living person. Even when he'd had setbacks or been taken by surprise, he'd always brushed it off with a stoic expression and dabs of dry humor.

He'd been our leader. I'd liked him. Respected him. Been mildly terrified of him at times.

And now he was dead.

And with him went the illusion that we were winning this fight.

We'd won a lot of battles, sure. Killed way more True Sons than we'd lost. Maybe even killed more White Storm than we'd lost. But it was blatantly clear that they had more than enough reserves to make up the losses. Our side didn't.

Our best fighters were all crippled. It would be months or years before Trenah could fight, and Ghai was probably in the same boat. Iyaht had been sent to the Empire. Of the six squad leaders Xerol had started this thing with, only Nynsi and Marn were still upright. We were down to six people who were serious threats in a fight, plus whatever Illyahn and I could contribute.

That was a long way from the nearly seventy soldiers and reserves that had been available when I'd first arrived.

Nynsi had ended up sending half of us on ahead in one of the brick like shuttles while she continued to handle the aftermath. She gave us the address and security codes, then Illyahn had handled the actual flight to the edges of Atrix's downtown. There we found the penthouse taking up the top two floors of a ten story building, a structure dwarfed by the titanic skyscrapers less than a mile away.

Inside it had proven to be a smaller version of the mansion. Same desert themed decorative style, same overly expensive furniture, but a lot more dust.

By the time Nynsi, Marn, and the guards arrived in the other shuttle we'd mostly gotten the place cleaned up and everyone settled in. Trenah was still out, and Rane'li had finally broken down and taken painkillers as well. Illyahn and Erana had been similarly exhausted and I'd sent them both to bed, volunteering to stay on guard until someone else showed up.

The second shuttle came down into the small hangar beside ours, stubby wings folding against its sides before everyone tiredly emerged.

"Building seems secure." I reported before they could ask. "Security system is armed and I extended the security arm to block elevator access. Everyone is asleep right now."

Nynsi gave me a tiny bow, "Thank you, Cieran. I do appreciate your diligence. Marn? Please assign your team rooms and get what rest you can. I have additional calls to make. Cieran will handle security and will rouse you at midnight to begin a guard rotation."

The team leader glanced at her boss, then at me, then nodded. "Of course, *Tarath* Shaaryak."

She and three men I didn't know, all looking as exhausted as her, trooped off in a clatter of armor to find beds to collapse in.

For her part Nynsi made a beeline for the kitchen pantry and the alcohol it contained. I followed, watching as she poured herself a shot of something bright blue before downing it in one go. The glass had barely landed on the counter before she was refilling it.

"Nynsi..."

"No, this is not smart." She didn't even glance me. "But it is necessary. I contacted the Patriarch's Council before we departed the mansion. The discussion was unpleasant in every sense of the word."

I winced. "That the Ascendancy's leadership group?"

"Yes. They did not openly accuse me of scheming to eliminate my uncle so that a mere woman could hold one of the eldest family names but it was certainly implied." Her fingers clenched around her glass as she threw back a second shot. "They did openly consider rescinding my father's exile so

338

that a male of the direct line would remain in control."

That made a bit of anger stir in my stomach. "Xerol's hasn't even been dead for a day and they already want to reward the fratricidal bastard who murdered him?"

"Quite. Thankfully the one who proposed it was rebuked. Less thankfully he pointed out that they only have my word, and the word of alien police that my father is involved at all." She poured herself a third glass. "They will be conducting their own investigation that will be heavy on politics and light on actual facts. I expect that I have no more than a week in my current position unless my father is killed before then."

I shook my head, "God that's fucked up."

Shot number three rose and fell, drawing a deep cough before she pushed the glass aside. "I suppose I should be grateful for Tasir's inside information. My father's plan seems straightforwards at this point."

I frowned, thinking about it for a couple of seconds. "...ah shit, it does, doesn't it? His brother is dead, his main operation is ruined, so he can make a showy display of fleeing the planet. Crescent lowers their guard even more than it already is and he takes out Kolkris. He wins everything he could ever want."

Nynsi nodded tiredly. "Tasir contacted me during our flight here. She agrees and is standing by with a strike team to intercede. I told her that so long as my father does not strike tonight, I will have what assets remain ready as well."

"Are you sure?" I asked. "Not really fully staffed here."

"He killed my Patriarch, Cieran." Her voice was quiet and as cold as ice. "He killed Rehat. He betrayed my family. I will go alone if I must, but I will see him dead or die trying."

My hands rose to rub at my face. "...I'd be a shitty friend if I let you go alone."

She gave me a cool smile, "That and my father would assuredly continue to hunt you if he survives."

"That too." I agreed, "I'll be with you. Not sure what help I'll actually be but I won't bail out now."

"By the Paragon's fortune, your armor survived. It is rather scorched but we were able to load it into my shuttle. You can examine it in the morning." Another slow breath rolled out before she turned, waving for me to follow as she kept speaking. "Erana can remain here to supervise Laria and Rane'li. The pair of them will handle coordination. Illyahn will fly the shuttle."

I nodded as I caught up to her. We exited the kitchen, passed through a dining area large enough to hold a dozen people, then entered the main living space. A few commands on her wrist-comp saw armored shutters begin to slide down, blocking the floor to ceiling windows that offered a view of the downtown lights.

She settled on to the largest couch, motioning for me to sit beside her as she resumed speaking. "We will likely spend the next two days entirely prepared to move at a moment's notice. The Crescent's palace is not a long flight but we may not have much time to act."

"All right." I hesitated, "Nynsi... are you all right?"

Dark eyes closed as she took a slow breath. "I believe you already know the answer to that question."

"I do," I agreed, "I just... well, you're alien to me. I've managed to screw myself up by forgetting that before. I don't want to make a mistake here and make things worse than they already are."

Another slow inhalation. "That is... fair. No. I am not all right. I am so angry that it is a fight not to drive my fist through a table. I had to be restrained before I could kill the traitor. I know what my uncle would have done, how he would act, yet I find myself struggling to replicate his success. The weight of the entire Shaaryak dynasty now rests on my shoulders."

"... what can I do? I'm guessing sparring isn't the best idea."

She opened her eyes, lips twitching for a brief moment into a smile. "Likely not. Swear that you will go with me when the time comes, as you would for Laria. That will be enough."

I bowed my head and murmured, "I promise."

"Then that is enough."

I bit my lip and watched her, thinking about it. Then I sighed and carefully turned around. I felt her confused stare as I adjusted myself and then leaned back. She went utterly still when the back of my head settled into her lap.

"Cieran..." She paused, cleared her throat, then spoke again, "This is a very unorthodox position for a man to be in."

"I won't tell anyone if you won't." I repeated what I'd told her that morning.

Nynsi stared back at me... then I felt a hand begin playing with my hair.

We stayed like that until it was time to wake the others.

III – VIII

Dawn came in the late morning, and Chacksin ul Shaaryak made his move when it did.

"I thought he'd delay another day at least." I grunted as I finished jacking in the coolant feed between the suit and its over-sized rifle. "Impatient?"

"*Probably.*" Trenah's voice came from my wrist-comp, the woman herself now stretched out on a recliner in the living room. We'd setup a second one near her for Rane'li, then Illyahn and I had spent most of an hour getting a holographic table installed between them. Once that was done we'd linked it to a pair of tablets, plus the two-dimensional wall projector that served as a television, getting the closest we could to mimicking the mansion's command center.

We'd just finished that and been sitting down for an early lunch when Tasir had called to sound the alarm.

"*If the fucker had been smart he'd have gone with your idea and pretended to leave.*" She continued, "*Maybe the bastard's cocky after killing his brother.*"

"Maybe." A quick glance at the suit's hips confirmed that my submachine gun and technical launcher were both locked into the clasps I'd added there. If I had to bail out I wouldn't be defenseless. I was only wearing very light armor, and had no helmet, but at least I'd get to shoot back before someone killed me. "Maybe we'll get lucky and he'll fuck up and get killed before we get there."

"*I wouldn't bitch considering how stupid of a plan this is. Especially for you.*"

"I'm not doing anything for her that I wouldn't do for you." I told for the third time that morning. "I know you both hate each other but you're the only friends I have. Plus this might be our only chance to really end this before he starts hiring assassins to kill us or something."

Her weak voice turned annoyed, *"I understand the why you idiot. That doesn't change the fact that it's stupid."*

I couldn't really refute that.

Jumping headlong into a commando attack in the palace of one of the wealthiest, most powerful beings in the Far Reaches was pretty stupid. It got even stupider when you added in the fact that we'd be fighting alongside an Imperial commando team who the Crescent wouldn't be happy to see. It was entirely possible that we were about to run headlong into a three way fight.

It was likely that none of us would be coming back.

Fuck, even if we did it might not change anything. Sure, Chacksin would be dead and the immediate threat against us would go with him. But if White Storm was half as vindictive as everyone said we'd still be in trouble. Even if we pulled off this insane mission the only thing we might accomplish was to buy ourselves a little time before the next crisis rolled in.

Starting up the suit, I began the careful process of getting inside the damned thing. "Trenah... if I don't make it back from this-"

She cut me off with a furious sounding hiss. *"Shut the fuck up Cieran. You're surviving this so I can beat your pale ass to the point where you can't sit down for a damned month."*

I found myself smiling in spite of everything, "Love you too."

"...that better be fucking platonic because you couldn't get me drunk enough to spread my legs for your fur covered dick."

"Bitch." I laughed, "Why the hell would I want to fuck a short alcoholic?"

Someone, it sounded like Erana, let out a loud giggle in the background. *"Asshole, I know you didn't just make a crack about my height!"*

"I wouldn't if you weren't so tiny." I said reasonably. "Dropping in and sealing up."

Trenah muttered a few extra swear words before her voice also became serious, *"Confirmed. Transfer to line two once you're in. Illyahn's already warming the shuttle up."*

By the time I'd gotten everything closed and checked my systems, Nynsi was emerging from the penthouse with her scratch team close behind her. As usual she only had a pair of oversized pistols on her belt, but it did look like she'd added quite a few extra grenades. Everyone else looked like they'd gone fully overboard; they all held rifles, what looked like shotguns were strapped to their backs, and all four had technical launchers to go with conventional grenades.

"Cieran." Nynsi greeted, "Is everything functional?"

"So far." I turned so that I could carefully step into the shuttle that was our ride. "Everything still according to plan?"

"So far." She echoed. "Everyone in. Tasir is already on approach, our informant's last message indicated gunfire inside of the palace and problems with their internal network."

I bit my lip while everyone else squeezed in around me, "Any official response?"

"Rane'li?" Nynsi asked in turn.

There was a short pause before the other woman replied over the radio. *"Nothing yet, Tarath Shaaryak. I don't believe any alerts have gone out."*

"Alert us when that changes." Nynsi ordered, "Illyahn, get us airborne and caught up to the Imperials."

"Got it. Hang on back there."

I got a metallic hand around the ceiling bar just as she hit the throttle. That proved to be a bit excessive since Illyahn was evidently a solid pilot. There was little movement as she accelerated off of the pad, seamlessly merging with the traffic heading towards the polar ocean.

The shuttle lapsed into silence, broken only by Nynsi calling Tasir to

344

confirm that we had caught up with them. Given that no one had any idea what to expect once we got near the target, she didn't even bother giving us orders beyond staying up until she identified a place to land. Nynsi wasn't thrilled with the plan and the pair of them transferred to a private line to yell at one another.

Tasir evidently won because we stayed in a holding pattern near the city's spaceport before Rane'li contacted us again.

"Confused alerts are going out on all Crescent frequencies. Some encoded, some not. The ones that aren't are demanding answers as to what's going on at the palace."

That was our cue. Illyahn didn't even wait for the order before banking and accelerating. I did a final check of my systems while the Thondians around me turned over their guns or tapped at their armor plates. We didn't have long to distract ourselves before the first challenge came in.

"Unknown vehicles you've entered Crescent airspace. Either turn back or we will open fire." A man's voice came across the general channel. Despite his words he sounded more nervous than threatening. *"You have ten seconds!"*

"Fuck off little brat!" Tasir snapped back, *"I'm Ashul'tasir, Imperial Intelligence, personal envoy of the Ambassador. Put your commander on!"*

There was a very long moment of silence before a new voice cut in, another Trahcon man but this one sounded far calmer. *"Imperial. I don't suppose you're on your way to the palace?"*

"And if I am?"

"I doubt you're stupid enough to attack her publicly like this. Not without a Void Fleet in orbit." He paused before groaning, *"Ashahn's ass. Word's going around that she's having one of her episodes. That's a lie, isn't it?"*

"The White Storm and their pet fish are probably trying to murder her as we speak." Her voice turned a bit harder, *"I hate the bitch but we can't afford the instability her death would cause. You going to let us land or you going to shoot us down?"*

345

"...shit. Divert to the main hangar and I'll-"

Trenah's voice abruptly cut in, *"Fucking let them land and keep your mouth shut. Code nine-seven-five, eclipse, three five one, black-fin. That enough for you?"*

There was another long pause, just long enough for him to check something, before the man swore again. *"Ashahn's gaping... disabling the anti-air defenses. Garrison will be alerted and emergency comms will go out to the Armada. Transmitting the last known position of the Queen. Sending coordinates for the garden closest."*

I blinked when he cut the line, but Nynsi spoke before I could even think of something to ask. "Laria, what in the Paragon's holy names was that code, and where did you get it?"

"Doesn't fucking matter." Trenah growled back, *"It got you in. Don't waste it."*

"I want-"

Tasir cut her off. *"Drop it girl. I gave it to her in case we got hit before I could transmit, she beat me to saying it. Focus on the mission, we're on approach."*

…right, because Tasir knew the Crescent's emergency codes but she had no idea that Kolkris's children, her pack, were all off world?

I shook my head. No, not the time to think about that. It would never be the time. Whatever secrets Trenah had I wasn't going to ask about. I didn't ask about her medical records. I wasn't going to ask about this.

"We're diving!" Illyahn called back, "I can see gunfire in the windows! And some in the grounds!"

"Confirmed!" Nynsi shouted in reply, "Cieran? You're the first out when we land. Vahat? You're the best shot we have, I want you to remain in the shuttle to provide cover."

One of the men nodded. He opened a small pouch on his armor, pulled out a scope, and got to work attaching it to his weapon.

"Marn, Nekon. You're on my left and right. Farai? You're our only reserve. Stay behind Cieran and ensure nothing attacks us from the rear." When they all nodded as well, she shifted a little, "May the Pillars guide us, and if we fall, may they raise us to stand beside the Paragons above them."

Everyone but me settled their weapon in their laps, then brought their hands together in a solemn gesture.

They'd just gotten their grips back when we hit the ground.

"Left side!" Illyahn shouted as the door in question swung open, "We've got incoming fire!"

My heart began its usual hammering as I lumbered forwards, the first bullet bouncing off my shields as I landed in the dirt.

The word palace may have been accurate but it didn't even begin to encompass the buildings around us. Even in the middle of a life or death firefight I noticed the staggering display of wealth and architecture that stretched out in every direction. The sheer scale would have been enough to make Czars and Pharaohs weep in envy even before they took a closer look.

Not that I had time to really admire it because a squad of White Storm had thrown themselves to the ground at our landing. A few were trying to get up and run for the nearest entrance, while others were simply opening up from their prone positions.

Bringing my rifle up I settled the reticle over a prone Thondian firing his carbine at the shuttle's engines, then squeezed the trigger. The poor bastard couldn't even try to dodge from his place in the dirt. My third burst broke his shields, my fourth struck the armor on his back.

Marn finished him with a double-burst from her own rifle, sweeping left beside Nynsi as the others followed me out.

Changing targets, I swung around and started firing short bursts at everyone else in sight. A Thondian died as messily when Nynsi and Marn both targeted him as well, and that was enough for the rest of them. I got my first kill after someone volleyed out two technicals, the grenades shredding the fleeing men's shields. That left one of them open for me to hit the back of his knees, taking his left leg off in a single burst.

I settled my aim as he fell and thrashed, putting a second volley into his throat.

And for the first time I didn't want to throw up afterwords.

"We've cleared the landing area." Nynsi reported, "Four dead, two retreated inside."

The Imperial's shuttle came down just as Illyahn began to take off again. Eight Trahcon in sky blue armor quickly hit the ground, a variety of weapons up and ready as they headed in our direction. Their pilot waited until the last had cleared before taking off as well, easily avoiding Illyahn's hovering ship to boost away.

"I patched your girl and Laria in to the Crescent's network." Tasir's voice came from her helmet as she approached, the blank visor upping her intimidating nature more than a little bit. "They don't know where Kolkris is but the last report had her personal guard trying to move her from her suite to her personal hangar. Both were under attack."

Nynsi nodded once, "Split up?"

"Yeah. We'll head to the hangar, you hit whoever is attacking her bedroom from behind."

"Cieran?"

I nodded, not that anyone could see it with the fixed helmet, then got moving again. The ostentatious nature of the palace worked in my favor; the doors were big enough to fit through. Inside the hallways proved to be just as over sized which made it easy to begin a cautious advance.

"*Advance to the next intersection,*" Rane'li instructed us over comms, Trenah's voice barely audible in the background as she did the same for Tasir. "*Then turn right. Follow that hall to the next intersection, then turn left and follow that hall for eighty yards. Then there will be a small open space before you enter the Queen's Hall.*"

"Understood." Nynsi responded, "Any updates from the Crescent defenders?"

"*Negative. I believe communications jammers are being activated all over the complex. We may lose contact.*"

"Understood. Transmit a copy of the building's plans in case that occurs."

The mercenaries must not have stuck around because we weren't attacked as our teams advanced. At the intersection ahead we found our first evidence of a prior battle; five dead White Storm, two dead Crescent soldiers, and a trio of Trahcon dressed as serving staff. Probably the work of the group we'd run into outside.

We split up there, us turning right while the Imperials continued straight.

More signs of battle accumulated as we walked. Bullet holes in the walls. Scorch marks where grenades or technicals had gone off. Art or furniture laying wrecked where a Trahcon might have mentally tossed them around. Bodies from both sides laying slumped where they'd fallen.

The sounds of battle picked up when we neared the next intersection. Gunfire and explosions echoing beyond any ability to tell where it was coming from. Even better, Rane'li's words proved to be prophetic because Nynsi's next request for an update was answered by silence.

I didn't like that silence.

I did like it a lot better than the gunfire that greeted us at the next intersection.

Several rounds struck the shields over my head, and I flinched back on reflex. Behind me Farai barely got clear before I stepped on his feet. His muttered swearing was cut short when some kind of rocket screamed past where I'd just been and exploded somewhere farther down the next hall.

Jesus that was lucky.

"How many?" Nynsi demanded.

"No idea!" I called back.

"Marn!"

The woman in question moved around me and risked a quick look. Another barrage promptly opened up but she skittered back before it could break her protection. "Five. Four with rifles, one lurking on the left with a full grenade launcher."

I winced at that. "Plan?"

Nynsi seemed to think for a moment, "Your shields?"

A sinking feeling opened up in my gut. "Full. I'm going to be bait?"

"Trust that I will kill him." She replied. "Full speed across the hall to lure him up. Once he's dead, double back and lead the advance."

I swallowed and flexed my fingers, the suit's mimicking the motion to tighten around my gun. "Got it."

"Go!"

They started hammering me the moment I'd taken my first step into the open. I returned fire without bothering to aim, just trying to suppress the assholes shooting at me from some kind of make-shift barricade. My shields fell slowly but steadily for the few seconds it took before a grenade hit my left shoulder.

The suit's flat feet didn't handle the stumble well, but I recovered just in time for a second impact on my left leg. That particular explosion knocked me into the wall just as I reached the far side. I bounced off, spinning in slow motion as I staggered backwards before the system's gyros managed to stop me from falling on my ass.

"Fuck." I gasped as low-shield alerts flashed all over my display. "Please tell me that you got him."

"He's dead!" Nynsi shouted back, "If you could please continue!"

In that moment, I really regretted promising Nynsi I'd come along. Sadly it was well past the time for regrets. So instead of bitching about it I sucked in a heavy breath and got my metal ass moving once again.

Three men in white and blue opened fire at once. They finished off my shields in a hurry, but my focus was on the fourth guy. He was scrambling over to a limp body that was still holding on to the grenade launcher that was their best shot at killing me.

This time I settled my aim before opening fire. The rest of the team emerged behind me, Nynsi and Farai likewise shooting at the same man. The poor bastard didn't last long, his shields holding up for the first few seconds before failing as he scrambled back into cover.

"Pull back! Now!" Someone was shouting, "We need the others!"

"No! The Commander said no retreating! We kill that human or die tr-" A grenade from Marn bounced elegantly off a wall before exploding in the middle of them, ending the conversation.

Showing distressing amounts of common sense, the two remaining survivors turned and ran like hell. Nekon contributed by sending Discharges down range to catch the slower of the pair. Nynsi and I finished him off while the others focused on his friend.

Who, rather than try to outrun magnetically accelerated bullets, simply threw himself out a window.

"I really don't like fighting people with senses of self-preservation." I muttered.

Someone chuckled at that but Nynsi cut off any clever response, "Cieran, status?"

I glanced at the side displays, "Shields are at eight percent but climbing. Minor strain on the hip and shoulder plates but they're still attached. I'm good."

"Excellent. Resume the advance, prior formation."

We'd just gotten moving when we were interrupted once again. This one came from our radios as someone broadcast on every channel they could access. I had a pretty good idea as to who it was even before the obnoxious voice began speaking.

"Daughter. I see you did not learn from the fate of my fool of a brother. Or are you merely impatient to honor your rightful Patriarch?"

"Chacksin ul Shaaryak." She replied, "I am the Matriarch of House Shaaryak, and I will see your body incinerated without remembrance for your treason."

There a low, malevolent chuckle. *"You remain as adorable as you were as an infant. Full of unrealistic hopes. Perhaps I will take your tongue to make you more palatable to your betrothed."*

"Perhaps I will name my Human companion as my Harath'krem, so that I might order him to kill you as a proper House Leader would. Perhaps I shall caress his fur as he throttles the life from you." Nynsi retaliated, "In fact I believe I shall do so. Nothing would please me more."

He let out an inarticulate scream of rage that cut off when he killed the connection.

I turned to make it clear I was staring at her, something that didn't seem to bother her at all. Everyone else shifted awkwardly around me, but only Marn spoke into the silence that followed, "Well, lady, you definitely made him angry. I trust that was your plan?"

"Of course." Nynsi tapped the back of my armor with one hand, "Now he will be distracted, diverted. It will give the Crescent time... and it will give us the best odds of finding him first. Come. We have a hunt to resume."

III – IX

I stopped being impressed with the luxurious palace once we reached the long hallway.

Sure, it was still stupidly luxurious. Arched windows gave you an incredible view of the gardens and the ocean in the distance. Chandeliers inlaid with gemstones shone multicolored lights in rainbow patterns. Paintings of various Trahcon hung from the wall every couple of yards, along with small alcoves holding physical pieces of art.

The dead bodies and dark red blood rather ruined the aesthetic.

We got our confirmation that the main battle here was Crescent versus Crescent about halfway down. At a T-intersection some kind of heavily armored barricade had risen up from the floor. The half walls were far less interesting than the uniformed Trahcon laying dead where they'd made a last stand behind it.

There were plenty more dead on the far side, a mixture of Trahcon and Naule in the same uniforms, but those had white bands around their arms.

"All of the communications frequencies are filled with chaos." Rane'li reported. She'd managed to do something about the jamming, that or someone else fighting here had managed to disable some of the jammers. Or both. *"Much of the palace staff appears to be engaging the garrison, and I've got limited reports stating that a good portion of Kolkris's personal guard were assassinated."*

"Kolkris herself?"

"No word. Chacksin's transmission definitely came from the Queen's Hall." There was a short pause before she continued, *"There is a private hangar within that building that he could use to evacuate."*

Nynsi made an angry sound in her throat, "We'll accelerate our advance. Illyahn?"

353

The other woman joined in, *"She's right, there's fighting all over the place. Looks like there's a group of loyalists trying to fight there way across the inner courtyard. If you hurry you might be able meet them."*

"Good. Cieran, what can you see ahead of us?"

Freeing my left hand, I made a short gesture to zoom in my main display. "I'm not seeing anymore bodies ahead. Doors look mostly shut but not sealed."

She considered that for a few seconds, "Marn, take Farai and Nikon ahead for recon. Illyahn, linger back but be prepared to cover us."

"Got it."

The three Thondians didn't have any problems moving around me, then accelerated faster than I could hope to. It didn't take them long to reach the far side. It took even less for Marn to stick her head out then immediately yank it back.

"They've barricaded the entrance to the Queen's hall!" She shouted, "There's a heavy gun firing at something to the east, at least a half-squad covering this door! One has a squad weapon!"

I needed a moment to translate that into terms that I recognized. There was... a machine gun shooting at someone else, and five or six enemies waiting for us with a light-machine gun of some kind. Not that many but we'd be crossing open ground without the same kind of cover we'd enjoyed in here.

"Anti-armor weapons?" I called.

Marn turned and risked a second look, "No!"

Well... shit. That was good in that I should theoretically be immune to most of what they had. Bad in that I'd still be stuck out in front.

The thought had barely gone through my head before our leader confirmed it, "Hold and allow Cieran to lead! He'll take out the guns!"

Oh boy. Pressure.

"We can't be cautious." Nynsi continued more quietly, speaking directly to me. "Do not stop or slow down until you reach their position. At melee range they will have a harder time using grenades or technicals to damage your armor."

I blew out a breath, "Got it."

Getting up to my best jog didn't take long. The armor's heavy footfalls made some of the art vibrate as I moved past, and only the increasing volume of the battle outside stopped everyone within a hundred yards from hearing me. I kept up the speed as I approached the doors, fighting against the instinctive urge to slow and open ornate wooden panels like a normal person.

Instead I announced our arrival to the fight by slamming them open as I bull-rushed into the next garden.

I'd kind of hoped to startle them and buy myself a couple of seconds, but the mercenaries didn't oblige me. Tall figures put quick bursts into the suit's chest before cutting off, while a crouching Naule cut loose with a light-machine gun. Sparks filled my vision as he slammed rounds into the shields around my head.

Cursing, I fired back as best I could and kept my legs moving.

About halfway across I realized the riflemen hadn't changed targets to the companions following behind me. Two tossed grenades in overhand motions, the third aimed an arm at me while a launcher on his shoulder spat out a technical disc.

The discharge hit my right side and exploded on contact with my shields, a flash of electrical arcs making me flinch as the suit's shields plummeted. Both of the incoming grenades must have had some kind of contact fuse because both went off the second they struck the armor.

Words can't describe how painfully loud that was. Only the thick plating and equipment around my head saved my ears. At least until the familiar alarms began howling while the display lit up like a Christmas tree.

My run became a stumble as too many things demanded my attention all at once.

Several cameras had been destroyed in the blasts which left me with a broken view of the world. Gunfire was still ringing off my armor and smashing into systems that weren't covered by heavy plating anymore. At least one round hit my right arm and was only stopped by the thin personal armor I was wearing. I twisted right on reflex to protect that side and managed to overbalance myself in the process.

I got one more step before slamming down onto the barricades that the White Storm were using for cover.

The restraints holding me in place dug into my chest and shoulders, robbing me of breath for a long second as I tried to gather my wits. That effort lasted until someone shoved a gun against the flat roof above my head and pulled the trigger. My ears rang as another alarm went off, and I lashed out with my left arm in panicked reflex.

I must have driven whoever it was back because they didn't make a second attempt.

Another explosion rattled the suit, aided by the sound of more bullets impacting me at various points.

"Get up dammit." I snarled, shoving myself off the barricade I'd landed on. I managed to fall onto one knee and get my other foot planted just as the computer systems adjusted for the damage. My main screen flickered then updated to show three dead mercenaries right in front of me, but four more were up and making a fighting retreat into the Queen's Hall.

I went to bring my gun arm up before realizing that I'd lost the weapon somewhere in the chaos.

All I could do was swear impotently as my Thondian allies moved up around me, exchanging fire as the enemy settled in to a new positions deeper inside.

"Cieran!" Nynsi shouted as she used me for cover, "Are you mobile?"

"Maybe!" I replied, finally taking a good look at my damage readouts and promptly wishing that I hadn't.

All of the armor on the inside of my right was damaged to one extent or another, with several small breeches. Somehow all of the joints were still functional but it probably wouldn't take much to change that. The other grenade had apparently hit my waist on the left side. Thankfully the thicker torso armor had held up a lot better even if the various camera systems hadn't.

I had a dented plate right above my head, and at some point something had hit the power core on my back. I had no idea what they'd hit me with but I was leaking coolant and the right-side shield generator had been trashed.

"Move left!" She ordered, "Clear the space, we have reinforcements!"

I blinked and looked around. After a couple of seconds I saw them, a good dozen Trahcon plus a handful of Naule in the orange and black of the Crescent. None had the white armbands so presumably they were loyalists. Then again the fact that they'd shot at the White Storm was a good indicator as to which side they were on. Above them was our shuttle, Vahat sitting in the open doorway with his rifle sweeping the upper floors.

"Cieran!"

Ah, shit. I shook my head and tried to shake off whatever mental state I'd just fallen into. Heaving myself up to both feet, I got out of the way as quickly as my battered suit and brain let me. I'd barely cleared the space before the Crescent troops had taken my place. One put their head next to Nynsi's as both knelt behind a barricade.

I didn't have much time to recover. Within a minute Nynsi was calling out more orders, "Farai, Cieran! Check the hangar and secure it! The rest of us will advance to the queen's chambers!"

They have must have pushed the White Storm back because she hadn't even finished speaking before the Crescent troops began an advance. Dull explosions and echoed gunfire continued as Nynsi and Marn followed them, while Farai limped in my direction.

I frowned, did a a head count, then saw a limp blank armored form not far from where I'd fallen. "Nekon?"

Farai nodded once. "When you went down he was in the open.

Couldn't get behind you in time."

"Shit." I muttered. "See my gun anywhere?"

He stopped and looked around. After a couple of seconds he turned and shoved aside a dead body before stooping down to pick up the weapon. "Looks intact. You all right in there?"

"Maybe." I flexed my right arm but it didn't feel much worse than bruised. "How bad do I look from the outside?"

"Bad." He said bluntly. "We should probably move inside, lower the barricades then hold the door."

That seemed like good advice so I followed him inside. He handed over my over-sized rifle and I got it settled in mechanical hands before we checked the interior of the building.

To the left was a titanic archway with a shut blast door. Labels in four languages, one of them might have Arabic of all things, declared it to be the Queen's private garage. On the right Farai reported finding some kind of conference or ready room. Maybe where the various pilots prepared for missions or waited for their leader's orders.

Directly ahead was a some kind of reception area, complete with too many doors and an ornate set of stairs leading up. Once we were sure that the party ahead of us hadn't missed anything we fell back to the hangar entrance.

Farai had just started messing with the controls when my display pinged to tell me Rane'li had cut someone else into the line.

"*Kean,*" Tasir announced herself, "*We can't raise Shaaryak. Status?*"

"She's moving with a Crescent team to Kolkris' room. Two of us stayed back to check the garage." As I spoke the heavy doors began to slide open. Inside proved to be smaller than Xerol's old hangar while still being fairly large. Enough that four very large air cars could fit comfortably while a large orbital shuttle was secured to the ceiling above them. The far side was closed up which at least made it simple to defend. I hoped.

"Doesn't look like anyone's in here." I reported.

"*Good. We've captured the primary hangar, bastard has no easy out now. I'm leaving a Crescent force to defend it and directing everyone else your way. Hold until we arrive.*"

I waited until she ended the transmission before muttering, "So keep doing what we're already doing. Great advice."

Farai let out a low chuckle as he wandered back to the entrance. "You're really not that bad, are you?"

"Depends on how drunk and stressed out I am." I said honestly.

He laughed again and we settled into guard positions. Farai stayed near the open doors, specifically near the controls. I poked around the garage until I was sure there weren't any other ways in. Once that was done I lumbered my metal ass over so I could cover him.

After a few minutes I nudged my radio back online, "Tasir, how long?"

When she didn't reply I tried again, "Tasir? … Illyahn? Shit. Jammer must be back up."

"*Shit.*" Farai made a sharp gesture to get my attention. "More bad news. Something's going on out there."

I swallowed and settled my rifle in both hands. Apart from the cars there wasn't much cover in here, and since the cars were under the shuttle I wasn't really eager to hide behind them. Even if my suit had been fully intact I didn't think I'd survive the same kind of impact that had killed Xerol.

Before I could ask him to close the door Chacksin ul Shaaryak decided to make his own.

The north side wall of the garage erupted with a muted flash of orange fire. Dust and debris flared out in a cloud and hid the explosion's culprits for several seconds.

Then a towering Thondian strode through the broken wall only to pause on seeing us waiting for him. He was big enough to carry a light-machine gun as easily as someone else might carry a rifle, though that concerned me a lot less than the men coming up behind him. Five of them had technical launchers on either their shoulders or belts, which was bad, but it was merc number six with his missile launcher that really worried me.

"Defiler." Chacksin ul Shaaryak called, and I could feel his grin even if I couldn't see it. Behind him most of his cronies leveled their guns at Farai, while the rocket carrying trooper casually pointed his weapon at me. "It would seem that the Pillars themselves smile upon me."

"Asshole." I muttered before shouting back, "Surprised you didn't already run."

"Run?" He laughed, his cronies doing the same around him. "Why should I run, human? Kolkris is sedated and ready to be hauled away. All that is left is to remove the vermin attempting to interfere."

They'd taken her *alive*? What the actual fuck? No, that didn't matter at the moment. The fact that there was a missile launcher pointed at me was what mattered. I had to keep these idiots talking just like I'd kept that asshole at the treatment plant going.

And hope that someone else showed up yet again.

I shifted my weight, keeping my broad feet apart and leveled. "I suppose there's a point to this conversation?"

Gloved hands caressed his gun. "There is time, defiler, for us to speak. My traitorous bitch of a daughter won't be coming to your rescue with her little bodyguards, my people are seeing to that. Oh don't worry, she won't be harmed by them. Not when I have an important role for her to fulfill."

Little bodyguards? I wouldn't call ten plus angry mercenaries... oh. Oh this fucker didn't know we'd picked up help.

Hope let me keep my voice steady, "So talk then. Honestly I can't think of much I want to say to someone like you."

"Someone like me?" His own voice didn't stay even. "Do not *dare* judge me Human, I am above the pathetic likes of you."

"Really." I drawled. "Fratricide isn't a big deal to Thondians?"

"Legally I no longer had a brother." It was almost hard to hear him with how low and angry he'd gone. "And now I truly don't. He is the reason I was exiled from Koshun, why I will never step foot on my home-world again. Never see the grand estate of my ancestors. His death was far too kind, defiler. I don't intend to make the same mistake with you."

If being crushed to death by a falling car in a burning garage was kind then I really didn't want to see what he considered appropriate.

"So what?" I asked, "You going to do the same thing your minion tried? Hit me with some drugs and drag me off to be tortured?"

"That sounds more ideal than your paltry efforts at stalling." Chacksin began a slow advance, careful to keep his balance among the debris. "Perhaps your memory is as bestial as your appearance. I will repeat myself. You have no hope, short-fur. My daughter will soon be captured. The mad queen is my prisoner. The last moments of your life will be filled with agony and despair."

"Don't make promises you can't deliver." I warned him.

"I don't." His gun waved in my general direction, "Take one of the beast's legs. He won't need it."

In that moment I really wished I'd been outside of the stupid armor. Yes, it had kept me alive up until that point. And yes, I wasn't much use outside of it. But I couldn't exactly throw myself behind a car while confined in its bulk.

Farai bolted for the door at the same time as I made an awkward lunge towards the nearest vehicle.

I had no idea if he made it because the missile toting asshole didn't have any problems tracking my movement.

The rocket hit me left of center in another horrible crash of noise that made the world turn into a blur. I felt more than heard the armor plates shear away, and something wrenched impossibly hard at my left hip. The suit hit the ground behind the car I'd been going for and gave me even bruises on my chest as I bounced around inside.

When I managed to focus again I could hear Chacksin screaming at his subordinate that he'd cheated him.

Shaking my head, I coughed to clear out my lungs and tried to make sense of what the suit was telling me. Against all odds it seemed like most of it was still functional, though from the way the core's heat gauge was flashing I didn't have much time before it simply shut down. The missile had apparently ripped apart most of the chest plating, shredded enough cameras that I only had a broken view on my right side, and my left hip and knee were both solid red.

I started to try and move only to bite down on a scream when something dug into my hip.

"...still twitching!" Someone, probably the fucker who'd just blasted me, shouted. "Deal with him and let's go! The Captains are offering a fortune for that gray bitch, I don't care about some random short-fur who fucked your whore of a daughter!"

Dammit... where the fuck was everyone? Had Farai gotten out?

Keeping my teeth clenched I kept my left leg as straight as possible while grabbing onto the car with my right hand. The extra leverage helped me get up to something close upright just in time for Chacksin to come stalking around the vehicle.

"...it would seem I will not be killing you after all, Hahk." Chacksin turned back, apparently dismissing me as a threat. "Go back and get our other prisoner. We'll-behind you!"

Gunfire erupted somewhere out of sight. Nynsi's father got his weapon set and went to full auto as men and women began shouting nearby. Short screams of pain joined in at the same time as several explosions began to go off. Grenades and technicals were probably being thrown everywhere.

More important was the fact that Chacksin couldn't hear my wrecked armor rattling as I lunged at him.

He must have seen me in his peripheral vision because he jerked back before I could grab his head. But he wasn't fast enough to stop me from wrapping metallic fingers around his right shoulder and squeezing down.

The Thondian man let out a deep throated bellow of pain as armor crunched. Running entirely on pain-fueled anger, I heaved him forwards and slammed him into the car. His heavy gun clattered to the floor as he tried to twist out of my grip. I retaliated by trying to stand so I could get my other hand around him.

That was a mistake. Whatever was in my leg dug in deeper and the pain made my vision go white. My left hand spasmed tightly enough to draw another howl from Chacksin, then relaxed as I fell into a slumped position against the car.

He ducked away before I could even try to recover, one arm hanging limp and useless at his side.

His other worked just fine, a pistol almost flying from his belt and into his hand. Then it was his turn to lunge for me, easily dodging my sluggish attempt to bat him aside.

Then he shoved the weapon through the gaping hole in my suit and pressed it directly against my left ribs.

"Daughter!" His bellow easily cut through the continuing firefight. "Cease unless you wish your pet to die!"

The battle seemed to sputter to a confused stop. A few seconds later Nynsi responded, her voice as loud and furious as her father's. "Get off my Harath'krem and I will consider killing you quickly!"

Oh. So she'd been serious about the title... that was going to really piss him off.

I was entirely right because he pulled the trigger a second later.

III – X

Getting shot was an experience I could have done without.

"Shut up, I know your kind." Chacksin snarled when a scream came out of my throat, "I didn't hit anything vital."

My body disagreed. I could breathe without blood coming up so I didn't think he'd hit my lung, but he'd at least gouged me badly. Maybe broken a rib or three from the fire that came with each breath. I suddenly knew what Yarrath had felt like, trapped inside an exoskeleton and unable to even clutch at the wound.

"If any of you come closer I will kill this creature!"

"Obviously!" Nynsi shouted back, "That is the only reason we haven't killed you!"

A male Trahcon spoke before Chacksin could reply, "Speak for yourself! The only reason I haven't taken the shot is because the Queen will want to flay him alive as soon as she wakes up."

So they'd saved the Crescent's leader. Yay.

"That won't be happening." Chacksin spat. "Daughter, unless you want me to shoot again you will do as I say!"

"And that would be? Skip the theatrics if you would."

There was a growl that I didn't think carried farther than the pair of us. "You and your lowborn cretins will remain there. The short-fur will be removed from his shell. I will shove my pistol into his mouth and we will enter the nearest shuttle. I will allow him to leave once it is airborne."

"Not happening." The Trahcon interrupted. "You're going nowhere."

"And you wouldn't allow him to live." Nynsi agreed.

I missed whatever he said in reply because Illyhan's voice whispered from the speakers in my helmet. *"Boss, twitch your left hand if you're alive."*

It hurt but I managed to tweak them a bit.

"Is it bad?"

I did it again.

"Shit." She breathed heavily onto her mic before continuing, *"We're bluffing out here boss. The last group of traitors all got together and are making a run for this hangar to get out before anyone can get the anti-air defenses back up. Tasir is trying to pin them down but she's having a hard time coordinating."*

So I wasn't likely to live much longer.

The thought terrified me... and it pissed me off. Everything I'd gone through over the past few months, everything I'd done, it had all led to this? To me being trapped inside of a bad idea while helping a friend do something we'd both known wasn't smart? Something we'd known we had to do anyway?

Fuck. This was... no. I wasn't going to just die like this. If I was going to die I was at least going to finish off the complete and total asshole responsible for all of this.

"Can you move?"

Ignoring the throbbing agony in my side and leg was hard, but I managed to sort-of focus on my display. Ironically enough being stuck prone was actually helping the suit stay online since there wasn't much draw on the power core. The shields on what armor I had were trying to come back up as well. So long as I didn't have to move my left leg, and so long as the enemy only shot what armor I had left, I'd be fine.

Gasping, I flexed my hand for a third time.

"We're going to try something. Be ready."

Closing my eyes I forced myself to breath evenly. Chacksin was well within my arm's reach. If someone could distract him long enough to pull his

365

gun away I could grab him again. If I could get both my hands on him that would be enough.

I just had to be ready, and I had to move as fast as the broken armor would let me.

"-giving you a choice *girl*." Chacksin continued on above me, the argument going on. "Me alive is the only thing that will stop White Storm from placing bounties on the lives of every one of your people."

Nynsi scoffed, "And my alternative is to turn on the Crescent? When I am currently surrounded and outnumbered by them?"

"If you are truly a member of our race, you will." He replied. "You will order your people to fight with me. You will leave with me. You will kill this creature to prove yourself, then produce an heir who you will raise while living in luxury on Koshun."

I moved my eyes past my damage readouts to what I could see through my thin visor. My captor had a boot on my right leg, using it as leverage to hold himself steady while he kept his gun pressed against my chest. Unusually for a Thondian he was keeping his head on a swivel; constantly sweeping left to right and then back again.

Strange but smart. Making sure no one was moving around his sides.

My mostly tilted over position also gave me a great view of the shuttle above us... which was why I was the first one to realize what Illyahn had meant.

Unlike the stubby boxes with their four tiny folding wings, Kolkris's was on the scale of a private jet. Like someone had crossed a luxury airliner with an old space shuttle, then made the whole thing even curvier and more ornate than was necessary. It was being held up by heavy clamps on its wings and some kind of bracing along the main airframe.

And someone was opening the clamps on one wing... letting it begin to tip.

Chacksin and Nynsi had enough time for one more pointless back and forth before the creaking and groaning above us drew his attention.

He reacted exactly as anyone would; he tried to get the hell out from under several tons of falling metal. At the same time someone shouted and guns began thundering all around us, whatever White Storm were left resuming the fight. The cacophony got a hell of a lot worse when the heavy hangar doors began to slide open while an alarm blared... letting in even *more* sounds of battle from outside.

I shoved all that aside and lunged for Chacksin as he pulled away.

I missed his arm but got his gun, ripping it from his grip and crushing it in the suit's paw.

"Dammit!" The gasp came as I made a second pain-filled lunge for him, but the tall fucker was deceptively quick. He threw himself to the ground, rolled under my arm, and bounced up in a quick sprint.

Throwing aside the sparking wreckage of his pistol, I used my right leg and arms to shove myself up to my feet.

It hurt. A lot.

To my poorly trained eyes it looked like chaos had erupted everywhere. My rear view showed two of our people defending the original doorway against someone trying to come in from that side. One of them was probably Illyahn from the helmet but I didn't have time to take a closer look.

On the right Nynsi's company was exchanging fire with Chacksin's guards. The former group was pulling back into the side-room for cover, while the White Storm were diving behind cars and nervously looking up at the swinging shuttle. Whoever had been on the controls had managed to partially grab the thing once they'd gotten Chacksin to move, but I doubted it would take to much to drop it.

My eyes swept over the fighting outside, that wasn't important. What was important was that I could see Chacksin waving his good arm and presumably shouting orders from behind a car at least as expensive as Nynsi's.

"Asshole." I snarled, pushing the pain aside. My legs propelled me unsteadily upwards, my hands clenching into fists as each step caused more agony to run through me. "I am so sick of all of this shit."

My external speakers must have been working, and loudly, because the fucker jerked at the sound of my voice. He ducked just as I threw a wild left punch that left a massive dent in the car's door.

It took me a moment to realize that the snarl of frustration had come from me, but at that point it didn't matter. Still showing his unnatural agility despite a broken shoulder, he twisted away as I wildly swung with my other fist. Swing three saw him duck, and the stomp that I followed it up with did nothing but crush a discarded gun as he rolled away.

"A weapon!" He screamed, "I need a weapon!"

"Here!" One of his people shouted, swiping a pistol from his own belt and throwing it in a single motion.

I clipped his bad shoulder with my next effort. The impact drew a scream and made him bobble the catch, the gun tumbling off to one side.

He went for it, and I went right for him. I didn't bother trying to punch or grab onto him so much as I tried to body-check and then trample the fucker beneath my weight.

I hit him directly, chest to chest, but the bastard got a hold of the broken section of the suit with his good hand. His grip kept him from falling while he got his legs back under him, throwing himself aside before I could slam him into the wall.

My own reflexes weren't quite up to the task of stopping in time, so I still ran right into the damned wall.

Chacksin hit the ground in a roll, came to a stop near the fallen pistol, and put three rounds into my back as I staggered.

"Die damn you!"

Round four slammed into my head as I tucked my left arm in to cover up the giant hole in my suit. The pain was starting to come back as I lost my grip on my anger. I had no idea what was going on around me. I knew that I really should have cared more about that but I couldn't bring myself to look away from my target.

I coughed, ground my teeth, and charged him once again.

He let me close, probably wanting to be able to accurately hit me through the gaps. Not daring to risk the wild swings I'd thrown in my fury, I kept my arm tight and punched at him with a quick jab, which he neatly ducked. True to form, he did so to his right and my left, forcing me to shift my massive frame to keep him away.

"You can't keep me at bay forever, *defiler.*" A three-shot burst made my ears ring as he sent it off my armored head-box. "And your companions will be dead soon enough."

"I doubt it." It cost me a lot to get the words out, pain almost making me stumble. Throwing another jab I forced my legs to keep moving, trying to use my bulk to force him where I wanted. If I could keep pressing him back, into the lines of his mercs fighting and dying just a few yards away, maybe someone would shoot him for me.

We kept up that awkward dance for over a minute. He'd put carefully timed shots off of my armor, trying to make me flinch. I'd throw controlled punches and swipes at him, trying to push him where I wanted. All the while it became harder to focus, the pain growing more intense with each movement. Worse, every time I started to get press him in the right direction, he'd duck under my arm and try and make a break for the hanger, forcing me to rapidly backpedal to stop him from getting close.

He nearly got me twice, and the sane part of my brain realized that this wasn't a fight I was going to win.

Not unless I did something stupid.

I watched as he came at me once more, then finally lashed out with my left arm, exposing myself.

Chacksin couldn't resist. He side-stepped my punch and came in, stretching out to get his pistol at the right angle. It barked twice and another lance of raw agony split the left side of my chest.

And my right hand came around to slam my fist into the side of his helmet before he could evade it.

The blow drove him sideways, his armored frame clattering to the floor with a howl of pain.

Everything hurt. But the sight of him rolling, trying to gather his wits, galvanized me.

Staggering forwards, my throat tore from a scream as I bent over. The metal fingers of my right hand wrapped around his helmet. Yanking my arm backwards to rip it free, I hurled the crumpled metal aside.

"You.." I wheezed out, my hand snapping down again to grab his head. His voice was muffled by the metal, and I continued on as if he wasn't shouting or screaming or whatever the fuck he was doing. "I... fucking... hate... you!"

The gunfire around us slowly sputtered and cut out as I hefted him up, his arms and legs starting to kick as he tried to get free.

Not giving him the chance, I turned and slowly lumbered a handful of steps towards the nearest wall. I got my other arm on his good shoulder and crunched down. His entire body seemed to shudder and convulse as he desperately tried anything to shake himself loose.

I didn't say anything when I got close to the wall.

I just slammed the back of his head against the stone with every bit of enhanced strength my power armor had.

What was left of Nynsi's father fell into a limp pile when I let go. I didn't look too closely at what I'd just done... I was too busy falling backwards as the suit's power core overheated.

Things got blurry around then. My next clear image was that of Nynsi kneeling next to me, her wrist-comp alight as she worked. "Cieran! You have to open the chest! Can you hear me? We have to get you out!"

Out of the armor. Right.

Leaning my head forwards, I jabbed my chin into the appropriate button. The hydraulics kind of hissed and groaned a little. The right side shuddered as it tried to open but the left side didn't go anywhere.

Illyahn appeared a few moments later, grabbed onto what bits of the frame were still intact, then hauled it open enough for Nynsi to get a hold of me.

I blacked out again from the pain when she pulled me out.

"Pillar of Heart... medic! I need a medic for a Human at once!" Nynsi shouted as hands touched parts of my body. "Cieran?"

"...how... do I look?" I managed once I was sort-of aware again.

Nynsi had pulled her helmet off, letting me see her swallow. "You've been shot twice, and you're bleeding badly from a long cut in your leg. I may have made that worse when I removed you."

Oh. Yeah, that made sense.

"Cold." And I was. "Blood... loss."

Illyahn appeared again, her broad hands holding the same foam dispensers I'd seen before. "Here, I'll get his leg. Crescent have a savanna medic on the way."

"Good." Nynsi said as she aimed the canister.

I couldn't feel it when she sprayed it into my body, but I felt it when whatever was inside began to numb the pain. It felt absolutely delicious... so did the slow warmth that came when they put some kind of pads over the wounds.

"Sorry." I whispered as my eyes closed. "Know you wanted him."

"In this instance I will forgive you, my Harath'krem." A hand touched my forehead, "The medic is here. We'll take care of you. Don't worry."

I tried to say something in reply... only for darkness to fall once more.

III – XI

I didn't end up bleeding out.

The first bullet had grazed me and cracked a rib but hadn't really been that dangerous. Just painful and debilitating. The second had hit just under those ribs, somehow missing anything vital on its way through. Its exit wound had fucked up my back pretty badly but they'd stuck some kind of machine on me that helped the muscles repair themselves. My leg had its own lovely flesh wound that had bled a lot but hadn't quite gone deep enough to get any arteries.

I'd have a nice set of scars, and I'd probably be limping for a while, but I would live.

Once the Crescent's doctors had patched me up they flew me to a hospital the organization owned in the Ocean Front. I'd expected to be moved again, maybe to the River District, but instead I was put in the medical version of a luxury suite. I had a terrific view of the ocean, two Crescent soldiers outside my door, and food at least as good as anything Xerol's cooks had made.

The day after I arrived they transferred Ghai in and got her settled on a bed next to me. She was even more silent than usual thanks to her injuries, but it was easy to tell that she appreciated the company.

Nynsi finally visited three days after that, walking in while Ghai and I were watching talking heads go on about the big Strike-Wave game in the evening.

"Cieran, Ghai." She greeted, "You both seem in good spirits."

"Hey Nynsi." I gave her a little wave from my bed. "We're not dead, so that's something. Laying here is getting old though. Do I want to know how much all of this is costing you?"

She shook her head as she walked to a nearby chair, pulling it between our beds before sitting. "I am paying for none of this. Leska'kolkris is the one responsible."

I vaguely recognized the name, "That's... the oldest daughter?"

"Yes. She commands the Golden Armada and is considered the heir to the Crescent's throne. She is likewise paying for full repairs to my estate for our actions in saving her mother."

Ghai made a low sound in her throat, somehow managing to make it an audible question mark. After a few days of laying next to her I'd gotten better at understanding her limited communication. Not that Nynsi probably needed a translation, having lived around Ghai most of her life, but I still spoke up anyway. "Kolkris did live then?"

"She did." Nynsi confirmed. "I spoke with her yesterday. You and I both have her regards and a personal favor each, in addition to what her daughter is already doing."

I blinked. "Uh..."

One of her shoulders rose and fell. "You killed the man who orchestrated all of this, and you did it in a fairly spectacular fashion. And as I am your Tarath'shan, she awarded some of the credit to me."

Ghai actually face-palmed and let out a tired groan.

I pursed my own lips, "Tarath'shan?"

Nynsi slid into the embarrassed pose that I rarely saw. "I did declare you my Harath'krem, did I not?"

"I thought that was just to get Chacksin angry at us."

"Well, yes, but news of it spread while you were in recovery." There was another shrug, "I saw no reason not to make it a truth and filed the official paperwork with the Ascendancy yesterday. Congratulations on being the first of your species to be awarded the title and be made a citizen."

"Thank you." I relied dryly, "I didn't get a say in it?"

Ghai snorted and shook her head.

"Seriously?"

My new... Lord-Patron, I thought the word meant, shook her head as well. "It is given at my discretion, no action or acceptance on your part is required. Likely because no one would even think to refuse such an honor."

That made me frown. "I thought Trenah turned you down."

Nynsi's patrician features scrunched in distaste, "Laria... informed me that her first act would be killing me in my sleep. Do I need to worry about such a thing with you, dear Cieran?"

I eyed her for a few seconds, then slumped back further into my bed. "You know you don't. Still would have liked for you to ask me first."

"I will keep that in mind moving forwards. Additionally I would like to point out that I was not alone in acting unilaterally. The day after the battle Laria filed the appropriate forms with the District offices to bring both of you into her pack."

Ghai perked up at that, a hand gesturing between the two of us before making another questioning noise.

"Both of you along with the Donah sisters." Nynsi answered, "Illyahn apparently requested it. Additional congratulations on your new family."

The Trahcon woman smiled while I muttered about not having any choices in my life. That drew a wheezing laugh from Ghai and a gentle pat of my hand from Nynsi. "I am told that alien men get used to it."

I couldn't help but snort. "Cute. So what's going on with everything?"

Things were apparently still a bit of a mess. Leska'kolkris had arrived not long after we'd gone into the palace. She'd brought more than half of the Crescent's main battle fleet with her from Cathia, meaning there were now close to two hundred warships in orbit. That had been enough to cow the remaining traitors into surrendering or fleeing into the city in panic.

The High Families had lost their collective minds only for the Kolkris family to tell them to shut up and stay out of the way. The Board had then gone to the Imperials only for their ambassador to tell them this entire mess was their fault for keeping Internal-Security back defending their corporate interests rather than hunting down Chacksin from the start. Since the Empire and the Crescent working together was akin to hell freezing over, that had sent everyone scurrying to their private homes while they waited this out.

While they covered their asses Crescent soldiers were flooding into the city to back up the cops. True Son holdouts were being exterminated left, right, and center. More ships were arriving and carrying garrison forces from other planets as their army began assembling in advance of the real fight that was coming.

From Nynsi's description the White Storm was a giant mix of pirates, minor warlords, and more legitimate mercenaries all allied for mutual gain. Their lack of a centralized organization made them less unified than the Great Warlords, but it had allowed them to spread out across the entire region.

"This will likely set the Far Reaches aflame from here to the Ascendancy." Nynsi continued, "We were able to retrieve Chacksin's wrist-comp from his body. In addition to telling us the names of every one of his sympathizers remaining in Koshun Minor, he had a wealth of blackmail material on his own superiors."

"Huh." I shook my head, "He was that ambitious?"

She flicked a hand, "Of course he was. But he also needed it to force them to approve this plan. Apparently it was not popular among the others, they viewed it as too likely to backfire. They also did not like his connections to the Hammer of Koshun. It seems that some had begun to realize they were being infiltrated."

I nodded, "You don't command armies of mercs by being stupid. So it's going to be war between them and Kolkris?"

Lips pulled back from ivory teeth. "The blackmail he owned was primarily related to their business dealings. We have proof that several of their Captains are cheating one another, and more importantly, cheating other warlords."

"Doesn't that kind of go with the territory?"

"Only so long as it is more profitable to ignore it." She continued to smile. "Few would have sided with the White Storm against the Crescent to begin with. With their deceptions public? It will instead be a race to seize their territory before Kolkris can take it all herself."

I frowned. "Kolkris is fine with that?"

"She wants her enemies dead. Who does the deed matters less to her than the end result." So she was a practical maniac. And she owed me a favor. "Fortunately I see little reason for us to be involved beyond this point. I intend to make a profit where possible but nothing more."

"That sounds just fine to me." I said through a yawn. "I really like the idea of doing nothing for a long time."

Nynsi touched my hand with hers once more. "Sadly we will be quite busy. Much of it will not be anything you can help with of course, but we will need to replace those security personnel we have lost."

"And you think I can help with that?" I asked, waving my free hand at my battered form. "The only reason this isn't worse is because Chacksin wanted to kill me slowly."

Warm fingers squeezed mine once, "Perhaps. But you have a quick mind, you are not a coward, nor are you a fool. You have learned a great deal already, and with Ghai and Laria's aid you will no doubt continue to progress."

I glanced at Ghai only to find her eyes closed and her breathing even.

"I don't know." I said quietly. "Honestly I don't know if I'm cut out for that kind of thing. Working on equipment is a lot easier."

Nynsi's dark eyes met mine for several seconds before she tipped her head a little to the left, "I will not force you. If you do not wish the position then Marn or Chen will take my place as commander of the guard. I will only ask that you expand your skill-set enough to better defend yourself."

Considering how dangerous a planet this had been for the past months... I couldn't argue with her.

"Sure." I yawned again, "Thank you."

"Of course." She glanced at Ghai's sleeping form before standing. A pair of short steps brought her closer to my bed and let her reach out to stroke my hair. "Thank you as well. I know you did not ask to be named Harath'krem but I had to be seen rewarding you for your actions."

"Money wouldn't have worked?" I tried not to show how good it felt to have her touching me again.

"Money is a resource, it is not fit as a reward for what you did. If you were Thondian it would have been within your rights to demand the title I gave freely."

I thought about what she'd told me about Harath'krem. "I suppose I can see that."

Nynsi nodded once, then with no warning at all, leaned down and kissed me. I twitched and then closed my eyes on reflex when her lips began moving, the half-remembered earthy flavor again making itself known. She pulled back slowly, letting out a deep breath as she did.

Then she gave a light tug on my hair and straightened as if she hadn't just made out with me. "Now, I have other business to conclude. I will be back tomorrow to spend lunch with the both of you."

"I... uh..."

She gave me a very Human smirk, turned, and left without another word.

I kept staring until I felt eyes on me. Turning, I found one of Ghai's blue orbs open and her own mouth curved in a knowing smile.

"You slept with Trenah." I shot at her, "You don't get to judge."

Her wheezing laughter didn't stop until she fell asleep once more.

III – XII

All of Atrix erupted in celebration when the sun finally returned above the horizon, heralding the start of Spring.

The mansion's ballroom was packed with Midcaste Thondian managers, alien business partners from the other districts, and those members of the staff who'd impressed Nynsi enough to earn an invite. Buffet tables littered with food were setup along every wall, and the broad windows gave an excellent view of the aerial displays in the distance.

Trenah and I were both leaning on canes and settled in so we could watch fighters and shuttles engage in mock dogfights over the Core City. Thankfully this was a fairly casual holiday so we hadn't had to dress up, something we both appreciated.

"There'll be fireworks and drone formations in an hour." She told me, "If there wasn't a war on the Crescent would probably have a few warships skim the atmosphere too."

I smiled and shook my head, "All this for a couple hours of real sunlight."

Her tarah quivered, "You're as sick of winter as the rest of us."

"I didn't say I didn't approve." I sipped from my glass of water. I'd have preferred something stronger but Nynsi had instructed all of the servants to ignore me if I asked for alcohol. "You hear from Tasir lately?"

"Unfortunately." The word a sullen mutter, "She sent more of the what her old friends found on your home-world. None of it's good news."

My fingers tightened around both my cane and my cup. "Still nothing about the *Pegasus?*"

Trenah shook her head slightly, "Found a few build orders in some place called Kay.. Kaynahdah? Your fucking language sucks by the way. At least our letters don't change what they sound like all the time."

I rolled my eyes. "Yeah, yeah. All hail the superior species for your ability to make a stupidly literal language. It's pronounced Canada."

"Ashahn's ass that doesn't even... whoever translated this crap needs to be shot. Anyway, they found build orders but all of them were canceled a couple years before you said you got turned into a frozen statue."

Another sip of water didn't do anything to help me relax. "If they can't even get a country's name right, what are the odds they fucked up translating that?"

My friend grimaced. "Possible but we both know that's a thin fucking rope to hold onto Cie."

"Yeah." I let out a slow breath, "Fuck. I remember the name of the ship. I'm not making that up."

"I believe you Cie. Some shit must have been going down on that planet. We'll figure crap out. Have to if we want Tasir to stop harassing us." Her lips and tarah tilted down, "Speaking of, we get to go over to Irrail next week to pay for what she sent. Stake out to try and catch a smuggler running gear out of the Empire."

Yay. A full day sitting around trying not to look obvious. Or looking obvious so that Trenah could linger with less attention. "Is Tris coming with?"

"Who knows." She sighed, sipping from her own glass before glaring at it. "I'm going to go bribe Illyahn to find me something real to drink. You want to go tell your bitchy lover what's going on?"

"Would it really kill you to pretend to get along with her?"

"Why take the risk?" Trenah muttered as she limped away, heading to where Illyahn was piling enough food for an army onto a plate.

I watched her go before setting my glass on the window sill and looking around. I found Nynsi after a minute; my girlfriend, boss, and noble lord was holding court near the far corner. She saw me coming and politely separated herself from the bankers she'd been speaking with. They exchanged quick bows before wandering away, though not before they gave me questioning looks of their own.

Being with Nynsi was proving to be... interesting in a lot of ways. She'd officially been granted her uncle's title after the old bastards in the Ascendancy had finally agreed Chacksin had been the one to murder him. She felt the need for a certain level of decorum in her public life as a result, meaning I was getting the Thondian version of etiquette lessons every day. Thankfully she didn't want to hide our relationship or anything like that. She just wanted it kept low key and proper when we weren't in private.

But when we were in private... well, that was an entirely different circumstance.

"Cieran." Nynsi said warmly, the pair of us bowing as well. She tilted her body to the right and I did the same to the left. Respect given and accepted. "Coming to rescue me?"

"I'm sure you could handle them." I smiled and stepped closer, trying not to openly appreciate how her suit fit her body. "I'm still popular among the business community I see."

"They've never seen a Human with proper manners."

I snorted and spoke in Low Kho'voik. It had taken a few months but I'd finally gotten the hang of speaking it, though I still couldn't really angle my body to provide emphasis. "I think they're more concerned about what we do at night."

She made a low pleased sound in her throat and replied in the same language, "I do wish you didn't keep the Alum accent between tongues. It's too harsh."

"You have it too." I pointed out, "At least in the lower one."

"It is not the place of a Harath'krem to correct his Tarath'shan." She noted while stepping closer, "You will repay me by escorting me to the balcony so I may watch the sunset."

I gave her another little bow before we both headed for the exit. People casually stepped out of our way and allowed us to walk out into the hall, then we turned out onto a small balcony. The air was still cool and crisp, something I enjoyed even as Nynsi pulled her suit coat a little more tightly around her.

A quick glance behind showed no one following, and I so shifted so I could wrap my free arm around her waist. "Damn. Should have brought you a coat."

"As the lack of one inspired you to do this, I do not mind." Her own arm slid around me a little more awkwardly. Thondians weren't nearly as physical in their affections as Humans or Trahcon, but she wasn't opposed to the concept. Just unused to it. "Did Laria have news?"

"She did." I told her about the limited information we'd gotten, along with the price for it. "So I'll be gone for at least a day or two next week. Need anything from Irrail?"

"I'm certain there will be something you can retrieve."

"Good. A bit of legitimate cover is always appreciated." The sun was already half-gone again, dipping below the southern horizon. "How long do we have to put in an appearance for?"

Nynsi gave me side-look without turning her head, "I am the host, Cieran. Are you that eager to return to my bed?"

I felt myself blush furiously despite my best efforts. "It's hardly my fault that your bed is extremely comfortable, and that I've been on my feet for six hours already. The company is just a pleasant bonus."

A quiet laugh preceded her words, "That is certainly a word for it. It will be some time before I can leave without offense, but I will not keep you here if you are in pain."

"Thank you." Turning, I leaned up and kissed the small bit of natural armor on her jawline. She shivered when my short beard scratched at her skin, a movement that made me smile when I pulled back. "Do you plan to eat or should I ask the kitchens to keep a few plates prepared?"

She thought about it as we stepped apart, "Considering how many more managers and investors I must pretend to respect tonight? A private meal sounds most acceptable. Thank you."

"You're welcome." I smiled.

We headed back inside together and exchanged one more set of bows at the entrance to the ballroom.

I lingered for a bit after she went back in. A glance and a few small hand gestures saw Marn nod and step away from where she'd been standing sentry. She casually fell into an escort position behind Nynsi, something the latter noticed. She gave the head of her security teams a polite nod, then looked back my way and gave me a deeper one of appreciation.

Smiling again, I returned it and then watched her glad-hand, smile, and bow as she worked the room. She seemed to do it effortlessly, conversing with Trahcon, Naule, and Thondians alike.

Beyond her I could see Illyahn and Trenah talking, the shortest and tallest Trahcon women I'd ever seen looking as comical as ever next to each other. They both laughed at something one of them said, covertly sharing a drink between them. Of course their fun ended soon enough, Ghai stalking her way across the room with Erana following close behind.

Not far away I saw Chen, Farai, and Rane'li among a half-dozen others near an open window. All of them had wooden pipes in their mouths, white vapor being blown outside by a small fan as they smoked. The former saw me leaving, raising a hand in a muted wave that I returned as I started to limp back to Nynsi's room.

This wasn't the quiet life I'd thought I would have when I left Earth. It wasn't a perfect life. I'd had to fight slavers, mercenaries, and outright psychopaths. I rarely slept well at night, and despite the efforts of alien medicine my body still ached where I'd been shot. My lover had her hands in businesses I didn't care for, and wanted me to become a soldier. My best friend had a past I knew nothing about, and wanted to protect me from everything.

Neither was human. And even then I didn't think I truly understood what that meant.

But they were my friends. They had become the people I cared most about. Despite the occasional argument or misunderstanding, Nynsi and I still spent every evening together. Despite all of her bitching, Trenah and I still laughed and drank when we could sneak away from Ghai.

It wasn't the perfect life, but it was sure as hell mine.

About the Author

Zach Watson is a fairly hopeless nerd who spends too much time painting little miniatures and studying history. He lives in an old house in Wisconsin with an incredible girlfriend, a loyal dog, and a feline who knows she's royalty.

Made in the USA
Coppell, TX
02 December 2022